Literature of the American West
William Kittredge, General Editor

After
Eden

Also by Valerie Miner

Novels

Blood Sisters: An Examination of Conscience
Movement: A Novel in Stories
Murder in the English Department
Winter's Edge
All Good Women
A Walking Fire
Range of Light

Short Fiction

Trespassing and Other Stories
The Night Singers
Abundant Light: Short Fiction

Nonfiction

Rumors from the Cauldron: Essays, Reviews, and Reportage
The Low Road: A Scottish Family Memoir

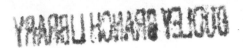

After Eden

A Novel

Valerie Miner

UNIVERSITY OF OKLAHOMA PRESS : NORMAN

This book is a work of fiction. Names, characters, places, and incidents are either the product of the author's imagination or are used ficti- tiously, and any resemblance to actual events, locales, or persons, living or dead, is entirely coincidental.

After Eden: A Novel is Volume 17 in the Literature of the American West series.

Library of Congress Cataloging-in-Publication Data

Miner, Valerie.
After Eden : a novel / Valerie Miner.
p. cm. — (Literature of the American West ; v.17)
ISBN-13: 978-0-8061-3814-5
ISBN-10: 0-8061-3814-9
I. Title.
PS3563.I4647A7 2007
813'.54—dc22   2006024971

The paper in this book meets the guidelines for permanence and dura- bility of the Committee on Production Guidelines for Book Longevity of the Council on Library Resources. ∞

1 2 3 4 5 6 7 8 9 10

In memoriam, dear friends recently gone:

Susan Geiger, Peter Gibson, Susie Innes,
Mary Jane Moffat, and Joan Walsh

The World was all before them, where to choose
Their place of rest and Providence their guide:
They hand in hand, with wandr'ing steps and slow,
Through Eden took their solitary way.
John Milton, *Paradise Lost*

. . . I am the lover and the loved,
home and wanderer, she who splits
firewood and she who knows, a stranger
in the storm . . .
Adrienne Rich, "Transcendental Etude"

I

Near the turn of the twenty-first century

1

She was determined to arrive before dark. Nine hours driving from Somewhere, Nevada, and she certainly wasn't going to stop now. Emily stretched her neck from side to side and took a long breath of warm California evening. Still some green in the land. The ground was a deep golden color, which, she knew, would grow paler and paler throughout the summer until the tall grass itself seemed a mirage.

Phoenix, slumped in the passenger's seat, barked halfheartedly as Emily passed another car. She reached over, scratching the dog's furry blond ears. "Home," she whispered, "you'll be home tonight, girl."

It had been a hectic year in Chicago, and as much as she loved her job she needed to settle into the cabin, prepare it for Salerno's arrival. A refugee racing for the border, Emily stepped on her accelerator, concentrating on the road ahead. If she didn't get stuck behind too many lumber trucks or RVs, she'd make it to Fairburn by six forty-five. And home a little after seven. With an hour of light to spare.

Home. She had said home. Thought home. Felt home. For so many years Beulah Ranch had been Salerno's wacky dream. When Salerno found the land with her three friends Angela, Virginia, and Ruth, Emily had pretended not to think much about it. A good place to camp on spring weekends and maybe five to ten days in the summer. But during the last decade, while building their ever-unfinished cabin, and especially since they moved from the Bay Area to Chicago, Emily had come to regard this rough cottage in the coastal range first as an indulgence, then a sanctuary.

This highway between Lawnston and Jerseydale was the curviest bit of the whole six-day journey and she had to concentrate on steering, although her attention was drawn by discreet exits onto small dirt roads. People cherished privacy here, wanted to be alone with their families and cattle and sheep in their hidden edens. In town, of course, they were quite sociable. Out toward the east, maybe as far as Ukiah, rose feathers of smoke. She hoped this was a controlled burn, not a wildfire. The live oak trees shone brilliantly in the mid-June evening. Prairie-like purple grasses swam in the early evening breeze as schools of tiny daisies floated over the hills.

Here, seasons felt more subtle than in the Midwest, where the world went white for five months, then muddy for weeks before the commencement of summer's terrible used-car green. Her Chicago friends called her a California chauvinist. She assured them that she loved the Illinois autumn—the crisp air, the trees turning somersaults of color around their grand lake.

Now Emily breathed in a sense of well-being. Her body felt more natural in Northern California. Oh, she didn't believe in any sentimental harmony. But she did feel less adversarial where she didn't have to fight for warmth or clean air. Where life pulsed more slowly, as the green hills toasted, new wildflowers emerged and exited, every summer week.

"Welcome to the MacKenzie Valley," a simple wooden sign on the side of the highway.

Her solitude ending, Emily reflected on the peaceful ride with her dog across the country. The drive had been slower than the usual summer pilgrimage with Salerno. She had taken a day off to hike in the Tetons. And she had loved listening to her book tapes, especially to *Paradise Lost* for the last two days. Her job as a city planner was a way to do something and earn a living from it, too. But she would die if she weren't in the middle of a good book. She had always relished Milton's language, the fabulous imagery of the poem, Lucifer's dramatic haughtiness and God's wild rages. During the ride, she had also played a couple of Salerno's solo CDs, but the damn dog whined so mournfully that she had to pack them away.

What a different trip this would have been with Salerno beside her— less predictable, less efficient, more playful. Salerno courted adventure, reaped mishap: a tire blown because of a detour to a beautiful but unsurfaced country road, just for a glimpse of rural beauty. A gas tank gone empty because, while Emily had napped, Salerno had tried to make the extra distance to surprise her partner. After fifteen years, she still believed Emily *liked* surprises.

Now Emily had to prepare for human encounter. For that particular country society where you ran into your doctor at the farmers' market and the haircutter was in your yoga class; where the bookshop doubled as office supply store, fax dispensary, photocopying facility; where you picked up your UPS parcels at Green's Hardware Store. Most cultural events were held in the Valley Community Hall between Montero and Fairburn—everything from Veterans of Foreign Wars dinners to Cinco de Mayo festivities to benefits for the funky community radio station.

Was it better to live in a place where everyone was intimate with everyone else's doings or among city folk who prized anonymity? Odd how she had more privacy in Chicago. People left you alone—gave you space—avoided talking to condo neighbors in the elevator or people seated next to them on the El. Attitudes about courtesy and safety were the reverse here in the country, where it was an affront not to greet, not to chat, not to remember the son had been ill, the horse in foal. Sometimes Chicago felt quieter than the Valley. The noise of buses and drill hammers and car alarms and cellular phones merged into an indistinguishable, if not soothing, blur of sound. Here in the Valley she recognized *particular* voices. Mechanical sounds were unusual enough to be intrusive. The birds were also distinctive, distracting. (Birds in Chicago: of course they saw birds in Chicago—pigeons, gulls, and those small black-brown-dark birds, what was wrong with her?) Here she was alert for kites and ospreys and turkey vultures and blue herons and jays and red-winged blackbirds and egrets and those splendid owls. Here she awoke at sunrise and waited at day's end for sunset. Chicago had the more rigorous climate, but you just bundled up and got through it, especially in winter, trying to ignore the chilled difference between 15 degrees and −5 degrees. In the Valley she always felt the weather, reached after the weather. The soft damp morning fog from the coast. The dry oven heat of August midafternoons. The moist reprieve of evening. These two lives—in the northern city and the western valley— summoned different bodies, different personalities. Was her California self reconstructed yet? Was she ready?

As they passed Fairburn High School and the dump, Phoenix shook herself into a sitting position, wagging her short tail. Emily noticed that the town nursery had expanded and made a note to stop there for pots of sage and coyote bush.

Basket's Grocery: how could that sign have faded even more? Well, everyone knew this was the best place for fruits and vegetables, who needed a sign? Cars were parked every which way in front of the small café cum produce shop. The outside tables were filled with people drinking coffee and tea, chatting animatedly. Ruth was probably still at work inside.

The road from Fairburn to Montero was less curvy, running along the seam of their wide valley. Emily admired the softly folded limbs of land that characterized this section of the coastal range. Hills, really, for the ancient mountains had grown shorter and shorter over the centuries. Sinuous hills taking the shapes of so many sleeping naked women.

Phoenix butted her nose into the window crack. A few quick sneezes and she planted her front paws on the dashboard, Emily's watchful copilot, nodding at Franco's fruit stand, shaking herself portentously as Emily pulled up to the small post office.

Long after hours, she wouldn't run into anyone here, she thought as she fished for her mailbox key. She had been blissfully out of postal reach for six highway limbo days. Who knew how many crises awaited her in priority mail envelopes?

Pushing the heavy glass door, Emily entered a quintessential Montero scene: a tall blond man in a blue work shirt, jeans, and muddy boots was bent down, talking to someone through his postbox.

"So, Phil," he said to the postmaster who was, as usual, working overtime inside the locked office. "Lisa had a bumper crop of garlic and sent this along to you." The blond man wiped his hands on his jeans (he looked familiar, maybe the new owner of the gas station?) and threaded a braid of garlic through the narrow mailbox.

Emily unlocked portal 114 and pulled out large red-white-and-blue envelopes as well as two postcards. Politely, she ignored the men's transaction—a clear violation of the postal code, passing unwrapped produce through a mailbox after hours.

The garlic guy noticed her. "Welcome up," he called.

She nodded, embarrassed that she couldn't precisely place him. She had to get back into the practice of looking into people's eyes.

"Hey, Phil," he called. "Hey, it's one of those girls from Chicago, they're back."

Blushing now, Emily headed for the door, but before she opened it, Phil called out, "Well, good! Is that you, Salerno?"

"No, it's me, Emily. Hi, Phil."

"Oh, yes, the other one. Hi there. And Salerno, is she in the car?"

"No," Emily resisted the odd tension in her voice. "But she'll be back Monday." Everyone remembered Salerno.

"Welcome," Phil called.

"Thanks, nice to be back," Emily returned.

Out in the car she threw the envelopes on the back seat. Planning reports from Vesta. A month late. Of course, they arrived during her vacation. She turned over the postcard with a large, pocked saguaro on the front. "Dearest Em, the gig went well in Tucson. Hope the drive back was safe. Love, S." The second had a photo of Venice Beach. "Dearest Em, Welcome home! Can't wait to see you. Love, S. p.s. Greetings to Dr. Phoenix."

Emily turned on the ignition, allowing herself to feel how much she missed Salerno, how tired she was of driving. But the ranch was only fifteen minutes away and the light would last long enough to take her to their cabin door.

As she pulled off the highway onto their dirt road, Phoenix began yapping wildly. Emily thought of this ebullience as the dog's fox terrier side. She was also part Wheaton terrier and several parts undetermined.

"Who says dogs aren't smart, eh, Nixie? Now you be patient while I secure the gate; this lock is tricky."

Driving in, she noticed the road had been well graded this spring, removing most of the usual February and March rain ruts. The oaks gleamed in the sharp evening light. At the top of the hill, near the corral, blackberry bushes were heavy with fruit. Emily considered stopping at Virginia's house but felt shy. And, unaccountably for someone who had just spent six days in a car with a dog and recorded voices, she yearned for at least another evening of solitude.

The old Dodge crept up the road past Virginia's, Emily holding her breath to make the tires roll more softly.

Birds were gathering at the pond for what Salerno called their evening services—insect collecting, courting, air aerobics, "sex, bugs, and rock 'n' roll." Phoenix barked fiercely, trying to burst through the windshield so she could take a swim. In the distance, over the far hill, Emily could hear Lindsey's dogs and then a whining bark from the west side. This reminded her of coyotes. Were they back this year? Emily hoped so, for she loved their predawn howl-chants. Up, up they drove, farther from the freeway, from the other cabins, high, high up to the ridge and, finally, within sight of their place.

There the cottage stood in all her gawky hospitality. One room plus loft and deck, with weather-darkened redwood siding. "Esmeralda," Salerno called the cabin, Esmeralda perched on the ridge with the rakishness of a dinghy on high seas. It was to this cabin that Emily had driven two thousand miles across the country. It was for this she had made the long trip, for something she would find in the cabin.

Emily hopped out and stretched, revived to the edge of a quiet joy. She admired the wide wingspan and athletic gliding of a turkey vulture and followed her giant shadow sweeping across the western hill. In front of their cabin the purple sage glowed in the late sun. The air felt soft yet invigorating. A light breeze sifted through tall grasses.

2

Phoenix raced madly around the cabin before darting up the hill toward the apple orchard. Emily inhaled the scent of green grass mixed with minty pennyroyal and road dust and wildness—an unclassifiable, intoxicating smell. Their house looked small after weeks of dreaming about it: a short, rain-and-wind-battered brown dress on thick concrete stumps. Out by the back window, two red privy barrels leaned jauntily toward one another, replacements for the current barrel when it filled up with their shit. Country life fostered appreciation of the basics, but she'd always feel squeamish about changing the privy barrel.

Emily circled the cabin before entering, inspecting sources of light and heat. Most of the firewood remained dry beneath a green tarp. Bending down at the side of the house, she turned on the propane that would fuel her stove, heat her dinner. Next she opened the shed door, brushed away spider webs, switched on the solar inverter. As always, when that red light blinked after a long season of disuse, she felt astonished. Emily lingered on the deck, peering at the trees and hills that would soon disappear into darkness.

Curiously resistant to entering, Emily imagined Salerno coming around the corner. Her partner was always the first one in, impatient to determine that winter hadn't seeped through the cracks, that they had indeed pulled down the blind on the west window, and that the old couch hadn't faded beyond color. Then she would fly up the loft stairs, flop on their mattress, releasing clouds of dust to the floor below and exclaiming for all of Mendocino County to hear. "Home. Finally. Home at last!" Emily would grin at her, then go down to shift cases from the car. Today Emily hesitated outside, knowing that even though midsummer was just two weeks away, the empty cabin would be cold.

After a quick omelet, she relaxed on the deck with Phoenix, studying the surrounding hillsides. Blue jays congregated in the oak on the east side of the house; the sun was setting just beyond the Douglas fir. She sipped a glass of wine and wondered at the evening symphony: the popping percussion of the pileated woodpecker; the sassy squabbling of jays; the soft roar of distant highway traffic; the full-throated—almost bovine—moaning of frogs from the pond way below. From the deck she could see across the Valley to the darkness of forested hillsides and the braided landscapes of new vineyards. Closer in, she inspected the coyote bush and the monkey flowers that flourished near the ground beneath the fast-growing sage bushes. Their old windmill whined softly as blades turned in a quiet wind.

Odd, how comfortable she felt here after years of resisting the idea of Salerno's land collective. The first plan had been camping land. Then came the construction of a *modest* cabin and the installation of a *simple* woodstove, then the addition of a *small* deck (to make use of the sun, to get closer to the view). "A shower this summer," Salerno had threatened, promised, before flying from Chicago to her gig in Tucson. For years Emily had repeated the mantra—we don't have time, money, energy—until one night they were lying on the loft mattress sheltered by the timber and plaster of Salerno's happy dream and Emily heard herself suggest that they install a screened front door.

Down below, in the basin of their ranch, a loud generator coughed. Phoenix stood alert, barking against the sound. Soon she returned to her reclining position, fuzzy fair head resting on Emily's toes. No doubt Virginia, or her girlfriend Sally, was finishing a furniture project. Emily had come to admire their woodcraft, even if the noise intruded on early convictions about country tranquility. The ranch was a respite, not so much a place of repose as of unleashed vitality.

Everything was so alive. Look at the stand of four Leland cypresses she and Salerno had planted a few years before. How huge they were, straining against the mesh fence, which had been raised to protect the tender early branches from nibbling deer. Emily grinned, thinking how this tree planting had felt like an arrogance, then became an act of faith.

"How do you expect us to grow trees when we can't even keep herbs alive in our Chicago window box?"

"Trees grow by themselves," Salerno promised. "Look around—trees, grass, wildflowers, all raised without our fretting."

Emily looked dubious.

"Listen," Salerno said. "We just have to plant them carefully. Make sure they're watered early on. Have Virginia check them in the autumn, in case there's low rainfall. Honestly, it'll be fine. Water will drop from the sky. Sun will stimulate photosynthesis. This soil will provide nutrients."

Emily surrendered, as usual, to Salerno's enthusiastic conviction. But neither of them reckoned the trees would grow ten feet in two years. Right now they seemed to be calling out for freedom.

Riddled with restless highway energy, she decided she would do it tonight—release the sturdy trees from their now useless cage. Yes, before the dimming light was gone.

Phoenix cocked her head as Emily untwisted wire hooks and yanked out the first stake. She imagined the cypresses as giraffes while she gingerly negotiated the long, slim branches through the wire, careful not to scratch the bark. Yes, healthy adolescent giraffes. Tall, gangling, gorgeous. She lifted their elegant limbs up and out, where they would catch the sun. The tip of each branch was a pale spring green.

When wire was forced from the last stake, she guided the mesh backward, laying it on the grass, then trying to fold it as if it were a sheet. But this was a sheet still inhabited by the ghost and the wire would not submit. Actually, she should have waited for Salerno; this was a two-person task, like so many chores here. Finally she rolled the mesh into a large cylinder.

Yes! The giants swayed gracefully in the breeze. If she were a romantic like Salerno, she would say they were relishing their freedom, strong dark green arms caressing the air. Sentimentality aside, they did look better without twelve feet of chicken wire around them.

Emily lugged the cumbersome mesh cage to their recycling area. Suddenly she felt exhausted although it was only nine. Maybe she would turn in early. After all, she had just driven halfway across the country to a place as different from Chicago as Venus. She had unpacked the car, opened the house, cooked the supper, freed the cypress trees. Pleased with her modest heroisms, anticipating a well-deserved rest upstairs with the windows open, she was already counting stars through the skylight.

Climbing to the deck, she called, "Come, Phoenix. Here, girl."

Emily turned to find her dog watering the cypresses.

3

Dawn was Emily's favorite time and place: a new, moist, warming world. She started slowly, brewed a pot of mocha java for herself, and then fed Phoenix. From the deck, she picked up a folding chair and drifted out over the swath of freshly mown grass (Ruth always mowed around the cabin to welcome them home) and sat sipping coffee in the sun. A little chilly because morning fog had barely burned away, but this was her cherished moment, a whole day beckoning.

Below, mist still lingered over the pond and her friends' cabins. Among the joys of living on this ridge were the early sunshine and the longer light at night. The sage smelled especially pungent this morning.

Still-wet grass was busy with black beetles. Behind her, Emily heard jays waking one another in the oak trees. Their racket used to annoy her.

Salerno had laughed at her complaint. "Just another one of your WASP cultural limitations."

Emily rolled her eyes, refusing to argue one more time that she was no WASP. She bore the English name of Adams thanks to Dad. But both of Mom's proudly Polish parents were born in Gdansk, and Emily herself was the product of twelve years of Catholic schools.

"The jays, they're like my family," Salerno chuckled, "loud Sardinians. Imagine them as Italian birds who need to yell, 'Ti amo.' Even to say, 'I love you,' they shout, 'Ti amo!'"

Since then, all Emily could hear was *ti amo* when the jays squawked. God, how lucky she had been to meet Salerno. Amazing that this summer would mark their sixteenth anniversary. They had shared so many places and problems and pleasures she could never have imagined when they met at that dumpy lesbian bar on Shattuck Avenue. *Ti amo.* For the barking jays. For the two of them.

The crowded Berkeley tavern was heavy on atmosphere and Emily sat self-consciously at a corner table by the solitary lamp, watching a blond couple swaying languorously to Cris Williamson. Each round barstool was occupied by a lone woman looking determinedly happy in her singleness. How had she let Lucy drag her to Pandemonium? Dyke culture always made Emily queasy—the uniform flannel shirts, the military short haircuts, the gross hiking boots. Maybe all these women were auditioning for roles as Peter Pan's Lost Boys? At thirty-four, she was too old for masquerades. And too sober. Her earnestness had sent her to Mexico as an aid worker for five years, had enlisted her in a Marxist publishing cooperative in Santa Cruz for two more years. Now, a graduate student in a high-powered urban and regional planning program at Berkeley, Emily knew she could be too serious. Impatient.

"Ah, come on, it'll do you wonders to escape your suffocating dutifulness," Lucy had coaxed again and again until she had worn down her friend.

Maybe Emily did feel a little lonely.

What Lucy hadn't told Emily was that she had arranged to meet her girlfriend at the bar. After a drink's worth of polite conversation, Lucy and Ora headed for the dance floor. Lucy called coyly over her shoulder. "Here's the pool. Show us how you swim."

Since Lucy was transportation that night, she was left with two choices—sulk miserably or entertain herself. Okay, she would view this as cultural anthropology. Gulping down the remainder of her beer, she left the security of her dimly lit corner table and ordered another drink at the bar.

"Haven't I seen you before?" asked a woman on the next bench.

"No," Emily said before looking at the speaker. This was her first and last trip to a lesbian bar.

"Could have sworn," the woman's precise voice trailed off.

Emily looked up to find a red-haired woman who unnervingly resembled Sister Mary John, her tenth grade French teacher.

They locked eyes.

Emily stuttered. "Gotta go. I'll be late."

"With a beer in your hand?" asked the woman.

Surely she was too young, too pretty, too colorful to be Sister Mary John.

"Late to what?"

"Pool," she recalled Lucy's injunction. "Pool. My turn at the billiards table." Without further thought, she swiveled toward the dark and even smokier room at the back.

At first Emily was blinded by the glare of an overhead bulb shining onto the extraterrestrially green felt table. Pool. Billiards. Cue. Side pocket. She reviewed her limited vocabulary. Eight ball. Was that right? Eighth ball? She leaned against the wall while her eyes adjusted to the light. "Rack 'em in," she remembered her brother Michael saying when they played pool one summer vacation. Her muscles relaxed. Or was it "Rack 'em up?"

A wiry woman with the blackest hair and pale blue eyes was playing against a gargantuan senior citizen in blue overalls. The small woman was winning—if her smile revealed anything. But that impish grin could express indifference, too. A motley cheerleading squad in flannel shirts (well, one of them was wearing a pretty purple corduroy shirt not unlike her own) were urging her on.

"Go, Sweetie!"

"Atta girl."

Wide eyed, Emily observed as the little woman pointed a cue stick that almost equaled her height and, concentrating fiercely, managed to sink five balls in three pockets.

The tall woman cleared her throat, then achieved a similar feat.

Now only two balls were left on the table. The stuffy room swelled with tension. Sweat dripped from the temples of both players and some of the fans.

With sudden and complete calm, the woman nonchalantly leaned over again, black hair falling into her eyes. Emily wanted to brush it back for her. The player paused for a long time, as if casting a spell with her huge stick.

Emily hiccuped. Oh, no. God, how embarrassing. No. Before she could put a hand to her mouth, she emitted another loud hiccup. Damn beer always upset her stomach. Why had she let Lucy talk her out of wine? As if real lesbians only drank beer. Staring at the floor, she felt everyone's eyes shift from the green table to her red face.

All eyes except those of the dark-haired player, who decisively aimed her stick at the ball, which rolled obediently into the side pocket. The room erupted into applause, whistles, foot stomping.

With dramatic slowness, the small woman raised her head, shifting her glance from the green table to Emily's astonished face. She winked with her left eye, half-smiled, and raised a glass of red wine in salute.

"Lucky hiccup," was the next thing Emily heard, thought she heard.

Then she found herself staring into the wildest smile she had ever seen. And that was the end, or the beginning, of that. A legend they embroidered over time. Every new friend would invariably ask how the bluestocking professional had met ebullient Salerno, who had quit teaching high school math to follow her dream of becoming a jazz saxophonist.

"Ti amo. Ti amo." Emily heard herself say, her head back laughing at the birds, who, at the sound of her alien voice, fell quiet momentarily.

Emily brushed a yellow jacket away from her morning coffee. She stood, stretched her long body, ready to explore the countryside. Sensing her purpose, Phoenix ran around the chair, barking.

"Walk, yes, Phoenix, we'll walk to the gate and back. How's that?"

The wet grass whisked against her trouser cuffs as they trekked east toward the windmill. Phoenix followed as she circled the base of the green metal structure. Emily was still confounded by windmills. Baffling, she would tell Vesta and Ken at the Chicago office. Magical. An elementary engineering feat, she knew, dating back to eighth-century Bohemia. But often, even ten years after erecting the thing, she would turn on the kitchen tap and be amazed that the earth was giving her water for drinking and washing. Fresh water, a simple gift from wind and land. She shook her head, thinking back on that day Salerno had brought the feminist witch to divine water sources. Ludicrous, she had scoffed. Mortifying. Yet sure enough, the lavender lady wearing crystals around her neck found water within half an hour. Emily had come to date her life in two distinct periods—"before Salerno" and "after Salerno." In this second, fertile period, Emily had learned you could believe something you did not understand.

The windmill blades were silent in the still morning. Wind was expected this afternoon. Emily shivered, remembering the fire down on Myles Ranch and how the family would have been wiped out if it hadn't been for water sucked out of the earth by their grandfather's windmill. Today's moist air and wet grass made fire *almost* unthinkable and Emily's mind easily slipped back to gratitude for the beautiful day as she and Phoenix headed down the dirt road.

Salerno had loved this place from the moment they saw it. They were on a long weekend with their Bay Area friends Virginia and Ruth and

Angela. At first, Emily was startled when the discussion turned to land prices. Salerno had planned this all along, had known that Emily would be too practical to look for a country place before they could afford a house in the city, had dragged her up north on false pretenses.

They had been standing somewhere on this hill and, grasping for defenses against the daunting, expensive project, Emily had said, "Well, how would you deal with all this water on the dirt roads? California floods every few years. What would you do if you were stuck in your little cabin on a washed-out road?"

"We'd construct culverts," Salerno had said.

"Yeah," nodded Ruth, "just make some space for the water to run off. Direct the drainage downhill and you have a pond. Voilà!"

Emily frowned at the two of them, as if they had been studying land management on the sly.

They began to laugh, a laugh she now recognized—*sometimes* with good humor—as their "Oh Emily, get off your marble horse" laugh. She knew she would soon be digging culverts.

Later, a year or so on, Emily understood something. Salerno, whose parents had died in a car crash ten years before, saw the land as a new home and the women there as a kind of family. But this was never stated.

Phoenix rooted around in brush twenty yards from the road. "Come on, Nixie, that's a girl." The dog ignored her. Emily swallowed hard, remembering that rabbit Phoenix had proudly brought home last summer. The fuzzy blond creature would never be a fully domestic animal. Emily studied wildflowers—tiny pale purple blossoms defying heavy boots and automobile tires, springing up in the middle of the roadway. Off to the side were daisies. Blossoming pennyroyal.

Reaching the base of the hill, Emily stared at the pond, full from spring rain (and culvert runoff, no doubt). Cattails stood at attention near the far shore. Birds skittered across the surface. Emily loved the pond early in the morning and just before dusk. Here she had sat for a month of mornings after Dad's funeral. He had taught her to swim in Clear Lake all those years ago.

"Hello, stranger."

Emily raised her eyes from the rippling brown water to see Virginia loping across the grass with her grey poodle, Terrence. She liked Virginia but was overwhelmed by her energy—by her skilled carpentry and fancy baking on weekends, by the devotion she showed her high school students. All this and a long-term relationship with Sally, a reserved woman who drove the local UPS truck.

Phoenix and Terrence raced toward one another at full throttle, halted just in time to avoid collision, and began the dance of nose and fanny. Virginia's long arms were wrapped around Emily, pumping in and out as she exclaimed, "Welcome up!"

Emily stepped back, winded and grinning, as ever slightly puzzled by the traditional greeting. Did the *up* refer to hill country? Although Emily's own cabin perched on the ridge, Virginia lived down here in the little valley. Or did *up* mean north from the Bay Area? In this case, shouldn't Virginia say, "Welcome down" to Emily, who came from Chicago? In fact, she was beginning to suspect the *up* had more of a spiritual connotation. Unconsciously, she had taken to using the phrase herself when greeting weekend visitors.

"Just in time for the gala barbecue on Saturday. Sunday is Marianne's fiftieth and she wanted one more party before she grew up," Virginia laughed.

"Marianne?" Emily asked, embarrassed.

"Lindsey's new girlfriend. They've been together six months now. Guess you haven't met."

"No, but I'm glad to greet her in her youth. What should I bring?"

"How about that famous Chicago potato salad? And whatever to drink."

Emily nodded, smiling at the Chicago label, which no doubt derived from the teaspoon of mustard Emily used in this dish. Mustard equals Polish equals Chicago, she reckoned.

Virginia was still grinning fondly. "I'm going to town today. You need anything?"

"No thanks. I thought I'd visit the farmers' market on Saturday. It's still going on?"

"Absolutely. Get there before ten, though, because the great produce disappears early and all that's left are withered beans and Sky's romaine lettuce, crawling with baby slugs."

"Thanks for the tip." Emily was suddenly self-conscious that she had run out of conversation. Salerno was the talker. If she were here, she would be pumping Virginia for local gossip, about her relationship with Sally, about this newish woman Marianne, would be inviting her around to supper that night. Emily still craved a little more solitude, as if she had trouble keeping track of these neighbors she had known for years.

And Virginia did look abashed when Emily said, "Right then, see you Saturday."

Marianne. Marianne. Yes, of course, Lindsey had e-mailed about Marianne. They had been so happy for her because of Lindsey's long grief. Lindsey had nursed their original land partner, Angela, through twelve months of cancer and everyone assumed she would leave once Angela's estate was settled. Emily was very pleased that Lindsey, the youngest of all the ranch women, had stayed on.

Virginia took long strides back to her cabin. Terrence followed Emily and Phoenix uphill toward the old corral but turned back before they reached the burnt oak tree.

When Emily first met Lindsey, she seemed like a kid. A demure twenty-eight-year old, hardly a match for the accomplished and mercurial Angela. Yet she was the ideal companion for her Olympian lover during those last months. Emily would never forget Lindsey's quiet steadiness.

She paused at the broken-down corral in front of the burnt oak. The dripping Spanish moss was transformed into blazing lace by the morning sun. Behind the venerable oak Emily admired several familiar redwoods. Phoenix sniffed at the base of a California bay. Too late, Emily remembered this was where the dog had rolled in poison oak last September.

She walked toward the highway gate, hoping Phoenix would follow her out of the poison oak. Down to her left, she glanced at the ravine, which remained dark and wet in the hottest summers. Each year she planned a hike there. Emily had spotted foxes and bobcats emerging from the ravine on early evenings. This year she would venture down.

4

The next morning was pale pink. Lying on the old mattress, she looked east through the cypress branches at the rosy sunrise. From this angle all she could discern from the front windows were hundreds of green treetops on the Wylies' ranch across the Valley. Thank god Joanna Wylie had said no to Louisiana Pacific. An admirable and unprofitable decision. Rampant clear cutting in recent years made the Valley look as if it were suffering from mange. Through the west window Emily noticed a kite hovering electrically beside the Douglas fir. She stretched awake in the half-warm bed.

Saturday: market morning, cleaning day. She would have the place humming by late afternoon.

Saturday: Marianne's birthday. Someone aged fifty was a little old for Lindsey, she thought. But then Lindsey was one tough kid, telling her Hong Kong-born dad that he could keep his dowry and his nerdy Chinese American fiancé, then shrugging off the noisy disinheritance. Mama was accepting, but also hopeful that her fierce husband and equally fierce daughter would reconcile. Meanwhile, Lindsey seemed satisfied here on the land, living simply like Ruth and Virginia and earning a modest income from apprenticing at the MacKenzie Valley Winery.

Emily pulled up her jeans and threw on a Chicago Bulls sweatshirt.

Maybe Lindsey was going to follow Angela's dream of planting her own vineyard. Was it Angela's dream? Possibly Lindsey had talked *her* into it: she'd been the one who'd studied viticulture and oenology at Davis.

As she drove down to the old wooden gate, her heart expanded at the prospect of a sunny ride through the hills to Fairburn. Morning made this a different country from the one she had driven across two evenings before. Then, in that muted light, the colors of poppies and oaks and sequoias had blended together. Now, the sharp nine A.M. sun distinctly outlined a busy civilization.

Five minutes down the highway, Emily glimpsed a new vineyard. How this land had changed in their own short tenure—from cattle and sheep ranches to hills tightly braided with grapevines. Emily enjoyed the sensation of being attentive, contemplative, observant. Did land shape people or vice versa? Early on, she knew, this place had been a dense redwood forest inhabited by native people. Before the British and Russians arrived in the late 1700s, Pomos hunted for deer and elk, and, depending on the season, fished for salmon and gathered mussels.

Salerno said she was romantic to assume indigenous people found more harmony with the land than European farmers on their small private parcels. If the deer and elk were here before the Pomo, perhaps the animals felt dispossessed.

Okay, so human settlement was never victimless. But there were degrees of encroachment. Worse in many ways than the farmers and ranchers were the damn timber companies. For decades Louisiana Pacific, Masonite, and other firms had been stripping the hillsides raw. At least the Indians and the European farmers lived directly off the land. The timber barons kidnapped whole corners of the environment.

And the vintners? Well, they lived in the Valley and they didn't. They had created a new "here" with satellite services insulating them from family farm culture. To serve them during the last ten years, Fairburn had sprouted an espresso joint, two chi-chi restaurants, a used bookstore, an ATM, and a part-time masseuse (who moonlighted as a cocktail waitress). The vineyards transformed local culture into an odd and sometimes uncomfortable society of nouveau urban epicures and old-fashioned ag families.

Emily enjoyed how her mind sorted and explained when she was alone; in some ways, this was why she became a regional planner. Salerno teased her about how she categorized people rather than seeing them as individuals. This wasn't completely fair, but Salerno did have the greater talent for neighborly gossip.

On either side of the highway to Fairburn vineyards stretched up the hillsides in neat rows. The wine industry drew two very different populations—sybaritic pilgrims on weekend wine-tasting tours and migrant Chicano and Mexican farmworkers who earned subsistence livings. A number of the farmworkers had settled here. The Catholic

Church held most masses in Spanish now; schools were hiring bilingual teachers; Mason's grocery stocked a fine selection of salsas, tortillas, tacos, and Spanish-language videos. Last summer, as Emily was folding her wash at the Ukiah laundromat, a woman walked through selling the best tamales she had ever tasted.

Who were the latest incomers? The cannabis growers? She could deal with a few used hippies cultivating personal euphoria. She felt amused, but okay, with the small hemp industry (eco-friendly, gender neutral—according to the local community radio promo) which produced scratchy socks and dubious face cream and nontoxic firestarter. She supported the "Medical Use of Marijuana" movement. But some of the dope farms were organized crime operations. A state trooper had been killed during an inspection last year. Emily thought now about Virginia's partner Sally, who was growing more and more pot. Salerno had told Emily she'd have to stop drinking zinfandel before she could censor Sally, and Emily supposed she was right.

Of course she and Salerno (and Virginia and Ruth and Lindsey) represented yet another observable social phenomenon—middle-aged professionals who had saved enough money to build a weekend getaway or who had relocated from the fast track to pursue their art and baking and politics and furniture making. You couldn't help being affected by the natural beauty here. As a regional planner she was curious about how each community, each individual, responded to the geography differently and altered the landscape in large or small ways.

Her reverie ended in the parking ritual. Some cars were properly huddled in parallel slots. Several pickups and motorcycles had been left at the edge of the highway, technically in the road. Today every space by the market was claimed, so Emily parked at the post office—aiming for something between decorous and defiant—then walked back to the food stalls set up in the parking lot of the Fairburn Hotel. Clive and Ethel Baxter, now in their late seventies, had placed a small card table at the back of their truck, where they were selling lettuce, red and yellow tomatoes, bristly lemon cucumbers. Oh, good, the flower man was here—with buckets of sunflowers and dahlias and ranunculus. She bought a brilliant spray of sunflowers to greet Salerno.

Arthur, ethereal owner of the used bookstore and the Valley's sole fax machine, nodded shyly, obviously recognizing her as a patron, if not a Valley local. Arthur was perennially distracted. An independent scholar with an almost completed Ph.D. in history, he spent all day behind his counter reading. The Book Box was famous for the best English Civil War collection in California, and the prices were outrageous because Arthur didn't really want to lose his library. But how did he manage to sustain himself on dispatches from the War of the Roses?

Strawberries, peppers, potatoes—the stalls overflowed with basil and arugula and parsley. Garlic, red onions, scallions. Shiitake, portobello, button mushrooms. She bought two eggplants from Christie, a teacher and truck farmer whose three-year-old son sat nearby on the grass examining a small pile of rocks and leaves.

This bounteous carnival of fruit and veg and flowers and healthy people was so pleasurably Californian. Every summer it took Emily a little longer to find her western skin, to relax so her body took up enough space, her speech slowed down, her smile emerged unself-consciously. Despite her love for Chicago's passion and diversity and wackiness, she was always distressed to notice how pasty Chicago people looked—blacks, whites, Latinos—everyone lacked that California radiance and expansiveness. This morning, so early in her annual visit, she must seem foreign.

While the economy of paradise depended on people driving these roads, locals also wanted to make sure that after your visit you kept moving. Emily felt caught in a half-resident, half-visitor limbo. Salerno said not to scrutinize so much. For a planner, she thought, home was the best place to start analyzing.

Oranges. Beaming navel oranges in five-pound green net sacks. She grinned, picturing Salerno's morning ritual—taking an orange and a cup of black coffee out into the gentle sun, then slowly eating the fruit, segment by segment, between greedy swigs of coffee. Each morning was one of the few periods you could count on Salerno's quiet. She had just two speeds—off and rapido. At any other time of day, the girl might throw her arms around Emily or tickle her or start joking or raise some giant emotional dilemma. But early in the A.M., she needed time, coffee, and that big orange. This sack should take her through their next month of mornings.

Just eleven when Emily turned up the gravel road next to the cabin. Good timing, she'd still be able to finish shellacking the trim on the west deck before the afternoon heat. It was going to be a scorcher; already temps had hit the nineties.

Damn, damn bird shit was splattered all around the front door. Vaguely, Emily remembered a mess from yesterday, but their bombardment had hugely escalated. Now she scowled at the mud nest on the door ledge. A fine welcome for Salerno. Of course, Herself would shrug and preach peaceful coexistence, but Emily didn't have the patience. They couldn't spend the whole month dodging guano every time they left the house. Only one solution remained. She set the groceries in the cabin and carried out a chair and broom.

Not completely cold-hearted, she stood on the chair first to make sure their nest was empty. Then she stepped down, aimed the blue broom handle, and whacked the nest from the eave in one blow. Anne Boleyn's head. The solid little mud chamber rolled over—intact—into a knot of manzanita. Emily's brief moment of remorse disappeared in her urgency to hide the nest from Salerno. She tossed the small, well-made thing into the drying creek bed. The swallows would rebuild elsewhere.

Christ, the ice! Distracted by civil defense, she had forgotten the block ice, which was melting in the car.

After Emily placed the ice in their cooler and shelved groceries, she arranged sunflowers in an old milk bottle next to a platter of gleaming oranges. Phoenix began barking. Intruders at the front door. The swallows! She approached but stayed safely behind the window as two small birds circled up and down, frantically searching for their nest. Nests, homes, Emily reassured herself, were portable. The rattled birds sailed back and forth. Well, this was no welcome for Salerno: the cabin under aerial attack. And who was to say they wouldn't just rebuild in the same spot? Emily remembered those dreadful black napkins her partner had nabbed at a garage sale the previous summer. Yes, one of those tacked to either edge of the deck, flapping menacingly, would discourage the swallows.

Line of defense established, she turned her attention to repairing the west siding.

How enjoyable to be working outside—stretching arm and leg muscles as she squatted and measured and sawed and hammered and brushed. So good to be using her whole body after six days of sitting in the car, after ten months of "working" at a computer screen and keyboard and telephone. How odd humans would look if they evolved to perform these tasks. Would they eventually develop large eyes and ears and mouths and fingers on the stems of tiny torsos?

Pleased as she made progress, Emily resolved to complete one chore each day this summer. Yes, physical labor was good for body and spirit.

She could hear her do-it-yourself father announcing this to the whole family on spring renovation afternoons. She had resisted it then (as she resisted so much else he had to say), because sunny Saturdays in May were meant for other things. Now she realized she had inherited this tinkering from her dad and she imagined his curmudgeonly company in the fresh warm air.

Phoenix, meanwhile, snored contentedly on the grass below. This weather was remarkably warm for June. She'd have to quit in a couple of hours when the sunshine hit this side of the cabin.

The swallows continued to swing by—at first every ten minutes, then every half hour, always repelled by the macabre black napkins waving in the wind, like bats from the Inferno. Surely the birds would give up soon, find another site for their nest and their shit. If the black flags failed, she'd tap Ruth's country instincts at the potluck.

As if on cue, Ruth appeared in the road, waving broadly. She called to Emily, "Welcome up!"

Phoenix stood, stared, sniffed, then busily waved her tail as she loped down toward the short, dark woman.

"Great guard dog," Emily laughed. Delighted to see her favorite neighbor, Emily relished Ruth's idiosyncratic blend of New York intensity and go-with-the-flow country pulse. Some people failed to perceive Ruth's determination under all that ironic wit and warmth. She was completely committed to her art and her ten-year-old daughter, Joyce. Both had flourished since she moved to Mendocino in 1989. In her late thirties then, Ruth had left behind a fast-track job as an illustrator in Manhattan advertising. She was determined to concentrate on water-colors. And during these last ten—almost eleven—years, she had three prestigious solo shows in San Francisco and Los Angeles, had branched out into photography. Her New York savings had evaporated, but she earned enough from her organic grocery store and the occasional grant.

For Emily, Ruth was a linotype of herself—she moving back east (although Chicagoans wouldn't call themselves easterners) and Ruth moving here. They were both bicultural in that urban/rural, cross-country way.

Carefully, Emily descended the ladder. Then she jumped off the deck and walked out to the ridge to meet her friend.

Tall, thin Emily embraced short, round Ruth. People saw their *differences*—spinster intellectual and mother artist, ex-Catholic and semi-practicing Jew—but Emily knew Ruth also felt a particular connection to her.

They hugged tightly, Phoenix barking at their heels.

As Ruth bent down to pat the dog, Emily noticed wide streaks of grey in her friend's rich, coal-colored hair. What did strangers see when they met Ruth—a slightly dumpy country matron? Impossible for Emily to imagine brave, volcanic, talented Ruth as a matron.

"I'm here on a mission." Her broad Queens accent was a cheering sound.

Emily saluted.

"A salad mission. Potato salad with no onions."

"Oh, right, Virginia's allergy, good reminder."

Ruth shrugged. "I love Virginia. Truly. But I don't believe it's possible to be allergic to onions. She can't eat garlic, either. I'm sure it's a cultural allergy. In Idaho all her family ate was beef and potatoes three times a day."

Emily laughed. She, too, was bored by Virginia's limited diet. But she'd simply chop some scallions on the side for the others.

"Anyway, you're the salad. Virginia is the dessert. I'm the veg and Lindsey is barbecuing salmon. It's all arranged."

Emily frowned, "Do people remember that our old Berkeley neighbor, Vicky, is picking Salerno up at the airport and driving her here? They should get here around seven. I mean, will there be enough food?"

"Yes, people remember. And there will be tons of food. You don't have to administer here, Emily. That's why this is called a va-ca-tion. Everything is taken care of."

Emily grinned. "You know you can be quite bossy in your own way. For an artist."

"Artists are the worst!" Ruth laughed. "Artistic survival demands aggressive self-determination. We're even more obnoxious, I'm told, than regional planners."

They both turned toward the sound of the windmill purring under a cloudless sky.

"Nice to be up?" Ruth asked.

Emily nodded.

"Great to have you back," Ruth winked. "And in a few days you'll lose that Chicago snow complexion."

"You know, old friend, there's always an edge, even to your welcome. Nothing is ever simple and positive, is it?"

"Boring!" Ruth answered immediately. "That would be too boring. And boring is lethal."

"Lethal?" she smiled.

"A very slow death."

They laughed together.

"See you at the feast." Ruth headed down the hill. "Five thirty for swimming," she called over her shoulder. "Seven thirty for eating."

"See you," Emily called as Ruth disappeared in the tall golden grasses.

Emily's glance lingered in the Valley. Toward the southeast, she noticed a long, dark scar cutting through the sky. The fire was somewhere between Montero and Fairburn. It looked like a large one, judging from the height of those plumes. From the distance she heard sirens. At least it was daylight. Nothing scared her as much as eerie sirens at night, the flashing lights stuttering into the peaceful black sky, making everything uncertain everywhere.

A speeding driver on the highway?

A car crashed into a ravine? Another fire? How large? How close? Every year she argued for a phone, but Salerno said it was extravagant. Salerno, dear Salerno, did she win all the arguments, or did it just feel that way? By late afternoon Emily had completed almost all her chores. The siding trim was repaired and drying in the sun. Now she straightened the cabin.

In the loft she plumped up pillows and straightened the throw rug they had found in Oaxaca twelve—maybe fourteen—years before. Downstairs she stacked her papers and magazines. Salerno complained that she was a newsprint tornado. On the table next to the market sunflowers and bowl of oranges she placed a bag of homemade licorice she had brought from Chicago. Emily nodded contentedly, anticipating Salerno's pleasure.

As she opened the front door, two swallows swooped across her line of vision.

5

The hot late afternoon was perfect pond weather.

"Come on, Phoenix, let's walk down the hill. It's a lovely day and we'll ride back this evening with Salerno and Vicky."

The dog barked and jumped against Emily's thighs, nearly knocking the shopping bag from her hand.

She laughed. "That would be a nice mess—salad, dressing, scallions all over the floor I just swept."

Phoenix continued barking.

"Yes, Salerno, your friend, Salerno . . ."

The barking grew louder, swifter.

"That's right, your favorite musician's coming home. We'll both be happy to see her."

Phoenix stood on the deck, wagging a feathery tail and cocking her large head.

"Come on, girl. Let's get a good start." She gripped the carrier bag. "I'll race you to the windmill." Emily loved running along the ridge, watching the Mendocino hills folding one after another into golden velvet under clear blue sky. In Chicago she jogged sometimes, but the pavement hurt her feet, shins, eyes. Most of her city running was to catch a bus or train, Emily, so conscious of time and destination that she didn't notice the process of moving her arms and legs, never felt part of a larger landscape.

Phoenix raced around and around the water tower until Emily caught up.

"Unfair! You have four legs," she laughed, but there was real annoyance under the joking. Salerno often teased Emily about her perennial expectation of winning.

Downhill toward Ruth's house, Phoenix trotted ahead of Emily, looking back once in a while to see that she was okay.

This year's heavy spring rains had left the hillsides covered with pop-pies and Indian paintbrush. At the curve near the first culvert, Emily inspected lush blackberry bushes, her mouth watering at the thought of Virginia's cobblers and pies. The thistle tops were slipping down their stems, revealing mean little skeletons.

Phoenix darted into a clutch of manzanita.

Fruitlessly Emily called.

She shifted the bag with her salad and swimsuit into her left hand. They used to swim naked, but for two summers now Joyce had been shy in her developing adolescent body, so everyone had adapted to swim-suits at the pond. No doubt they could return to nakedness when Joyce was more comfortable in her new shape. By then, five or six years would have passed. In addition to enjoying the silky water against her bare skin, Emily had appreciated seeing how other women's bodies were aging. Undressing before the mirror at night could be unutterably lonely. Salerno offered no real company because her tight little body remained as buoyant as her spirit.

Phoenix reappeared, so tuckered from her run that she proceeded downhill at a nearly human pace.

As they rounded the curve to Ruth's house, they saw and heard Joyce playing in the pond with her year-old collie, Bobbie. Joyce held onto the plastic raft with her arms and kicked her feet rapidly as Bobbie paddled along side.

"Phoenix! Emily," Joyce called. "Jump in. We're the Coast Guard scouting for sinking boats."

Emily laughed at the memory of that age between girl and woman where one minute you played guilelessly and the next minute you self-consciously auditioned as an adult.

Nodding and waving, Emily ducked behind a broad stone pine to pull on her suit. She left the bag of food in the shade, placing her clothes on top to divert Phoenix.

The pond was still warm from the blistering afternoon. Sweat and anxiety and fatigue washed away as Emily eased herself deeper into delicious water.

Joyce called from the far side near tall grasses, "What about Phoe-nix? Won't she join us?"

"In a minute. First she needs to sniff out her territory. Besides, she might be scared of that ferocious beastie next to you."

Joyce giggled, then turned to quiet conversation with Bobbie.

Here from deep in the bowl of their own valley, Emily looked up at her ridge, the cabin, windmill, water tower. Over to the south, she could make out Virginia's fecund vegetable garden, but not her friend's cabin, which was hidden in the redwoods. And just off the road, further west, Lindsey's chicken coop was the only sign of her settlement. They had come close to their dreams of privacy within community.

Emily felt color coming to her skin. The first week in California she always resisted Salerno's ministrations of sunscreen. Her body was so happy in the clean, warm air that she relinquished herself to the sun gods. A dangerous surrender for someone from such a ghostly pale family, but every year Emily went about uncovered until the sunburn on the bridge of her straight nose peeled.

She stretched her long body on the comforting surface of the water. Floating was a miracle. Although she'd swum competitively in college, she'd always hated lying still in the water until Salerno teased away this superstition. Slowly now, she released her head back into the pond as the water covered her hairline, framing her face in green shimmer. With her ears underwater like this, she could hear little pips from Joyce's conversation with Bobbie. The basso *brrrp* of a frog. Cattails swayed gracefully and she rolled over, stroking into a tangle of seaweed. On broiling afternoons she loved treading in the pond, pulling up clumps of seaweed with her toes. Now she swam back and forth.

Her head up in a breaststroke, she watched the masquerade ball of dragonflies in turquoise and orange ensembles. One black-and-white number would be perfect for opening night at the San Francisco Opera.

Phoenix's fur was curled and darkened by the water. Recruited into the canine Coast Guard, her duty required racing against Bobbie when Joyce skimmed a Frisbee across the water. Time passed—twenty minutes, forty-five, an hour? Emily checked her swimmer's watch and called to Captain Joyce. "It's six thirty, honey, shouldn't we dry off and get ready for dinner?"

With a betrayed frown, Joyce turned to Bobbie and Phoenix for support. Finding none, she began kicking her way, petulantly, to the dock.

"I understand there's a birthday party," Emily cajoled, "and that famous baker, Virginia, is bringing dessert."

Joyce grinned, in spite of her reluctance to leave this perfect pond, and hopped up to the deck with the agility of a stage angel lifted by guy wire.

Emily slowly climbed the ladder to the wooden platform. There she lay out to dry for a few minutes in the early evening sun, which was still surprisingly hot. Would the salad go bad in this heat?

This was her own fiftieth summer. In certain lights, she studied lines webbed around her eyes and the longish crease down each cheek. After a meal, she felt the small pot between her diaphragm and pelvis. Vanity was normal. These signs also invoked anxiety because health was an unpredictable family legacy. Wasn't Baba, who immigrated from starvation in Gdansk in 1920, still an excellent seamstress with a sharp wit? And wasn't this grandmother's daughter Teresa, Emily's own sweet Momma, dead now for thirty-five years? It made no sense, no genetic sense, because Teresa's father had lived to the age of ninety and all her brothers and sisters were still flourishing in Polish Catholic neighborhoods on the east coast. It made no moral sense because if anyone should have died early, it was Emily's arrogant father, Peter. How different life would have been for this exchange. Teresa had been beautiful, smart, musical. If only she hadn't fallen in love with Peter Adams, who locked her away in a Burlingame split-level ranch house. When Emily said such things to her gentle but infuriatingly rational brother Michael, he would shake his head and remind her that they wouldn't exist but for the communion between both their parents. It never occurred to Michael that Emily thought their nonexistence might not be a terrible thing. She'd told Salerno that while she loved Michael and liked herself well enough, she didn't believe that the two of them were a decent trade for Teresa. Salerno insisted that Teresa hadn't died for Emily, for her sins, her future, her happiness. Teresa's death and Emily's life were distinct phenomena. Being confined to the split-level house hadn't killed Teresa, either. But Emily didn't believe this.

Six forty-five. Emily looked up to see Joyce leading the two sopping dogs into the house. Salerno and Vicky would be driving through the old wooden gate any moment now. Combing wet hair with her fingers, she decided she was dry enough to get back into her jeans and shirt.

As Emily approached, the house seemed quiet. Joyce had disappeared. No music. No chatting. No barking. Strange, because everyone's car was parked outside—Lindsey's and Virginia's and Ruth's. And someone's red motorcycle. Did Marianne, the grandmother grad student, commute on a motorcycle from Berkeley?

As she climbed the steps to Ruth's door, Emily heard murmuring. Feeling freakishly formal, she knocked, and when no one answered she shouted, "Yoo-hoo."

The murmuring ceased.

Suddenly a cheerful voice, "Emily?"

"Hi there." She stepped awkwardly into the cabin.

"Come on through," Ruth called, "we're all on the back deck."

The scene felt right and not right. Everyone was there. Ruth's radio babbled news sotto voce in the background. Lindsey, whom she hadn't yet greeted on this trip, jumped up and gave her a long, tight hug. It took Emily a minute to register that her younger friend had trimmed her long satin hair to shoulder length.

"You look great," was all she managed, before Lindsey was dragging a small, round black woman to her feet. This was Marianne, whose face opened into a generous smile as she extended her hand.

Virginia introduced Eva, a Valley neighbor, who, judging from her black pants and shirt, was the owner of that nifty red bike.

Emily remained uneasy. What was with the low-key mood? And where was Joyce, who specialized in being at the epicenter of any event before bedtime? The table was set, the barbecue glowed red through a white beard of coals, but no one had touched the open bottle of zinfandel. They were sitting around cold cups of coffee.

"What's up?" she asked in spite of herself. She didn't want to engage in anything except birthday festivities and gossip.

"Probably nothing." Virginia stood and poured Emily a full glass of wine. "I mean, Salerno's not supposed to get here until seven or so, right?"

Emily, sipping, nodded warily.

"And it's only six fifty now. Besides, with Bay Area traffic, they could be held up till midnight," she stumbled ahead. "She was flying United into San Francisco, right? Vicky is picking her up in the city, right?"

"No, Oakland."

Their strained faces alarmed her.

"Nonstop from Tucson to Oakland. Flight 4105."

She looked from one long face to another until she saw tears streaming down Lindsey's cheeks.

"There's been a crash," Emily spoke steadily.

"Eva just got here," Virginia stammered. "She heard a fragment five minutes ago on the car radio."

"We don't know the whole story," Ruth stood and embraced Emily. "Eva didn't catch where the flight originated. Just that there was a crash at Oakland and they're searching for survivors."

"We phoned and phoned United," Lindsey sniffed, "but couldn't get through."

Coldly calm, Emily stared at the unfortunate messengers. "No other details?" Her voice faded, then she dropped the glass. They all looked at the shattered goblet, at the beautiful red zinfandel dripping between the deck boards. Ruth scurried to mop it up.

Marianne sat Emily down in a chair.

The others, caught in their own stunned silence, watched as Emily stiffly accepted the new woman's caress.

Then she returned to them. "No other details?"

Ruth held Emily's hand tightly.

"The plane was late," Eva deliberately recited the news report. "Some kind of mechanical trouble. They thought they'd fixed it before departure. Then, as they were landing—approaching the bay—a fire erupted, I mean they don't have any idea, and the plane dropped into the water."

"Landing in the water," Ruth leaned forward, taking her hand, "it's better than crashing into the ground. Safer. People—many passengers— survive water landings."

"Besides," Virginia snapped, "we don't even know if it was Salerno's plane. Eva didn't get the flight number or anything."

Emily looked from one to the other of her friends. Abruptly, she dropped Ruth's warm hand and walked over to the railing. She stared out at the pond, where so recently she had been floating with frogs and dogs and dragonflies, where less than fifteen minutes ago she knew that Salerno was driving the beautiful, rippling ribbon of road between Lawnston and Fairburn.

Her reverie was broken by Joyce's voice. "Phone, Mom, it's Vicky."

II

6

It was early August and she sat on the west deck, her back against the warm cabin wall, with Phoenix beside her, waiting for the sun to set over Salerno's tree.

Phoenix lay still, eyes open to nothingness. Emily's attention played between the small tattooed sticks in her hand and the gingering horizon. She fingered the implement cautiously. Was it one object or two? Phoenix looked up. Emily knew the dog craved touch and she tried to be attentive, but right now she had feelings only for the dead. She wanted to crawl into the warmth of Salerno's ashes buried around the base of the stately Douglas fir.

That tree was why they built here.

"Imagine a house," Salerno had it all designed within five minutes of reaching the ridge, "where we could sit every night and watch the sun set."

Emily had nodded indulgently. She hadn't been with Salerno long enough to understand the power of her wishing.

First of all, it had been Salerno who knew they were destined to spend their lives together. Salerno who seduced her that night in the pool room. Salerno who found them an affordable house to rent in Oakland. Salerno who . . . when Emily teased that Salerno ran their lives, she said, "We're a good team—imagination and deliberation, inspiration and implementation."

Fire and . . .

How would she survive without Salerno's fire? During the past two months, Emily had lived underground, had often thought of pulling the warm dirt over the two of them as they drifted together down into the earth. The image was always interrupted by the memory of what she had found there—the tools, fetishes? Now these objects lay limply in her lap. Emily also dreamed of entering the sea. For weeks she drove forty minutes every morning to the Mendocino headlands to hike the coastal trail through grasses and ice plant and fog. At first she prayed, just followed the path reciting comforting childhood prayers, prayers that she and Salerno had learned in different parts of California and had abandoned in their teens. Hail Mary. Our Father. Agnes Dei. Would Salerno find this peculiar supplication betrayal or communion? She couldn't help herself. Phoenix always trudged close behind, her chattering tags barely audible above the ocean roar.

No one knew the cause of the airline crash. Maybe the fuel tanks. Maybe pilot error. Lindsey and Virginia talked endlessly about the FAA investigation, the class action suit. Emily wondered off during these conversations, staring out a window, sometimes seeing what was on the other side, sometimes not. Knowing what caused the crash would not bring back Salerno. Eventually the others stopped discussing the accident in Emily's presence.

If she was preoccupied with anything outside grief, it was with the weathered sticks. She hadn't shown them to anyone, for they came wrapped in secrecy. The wood looked like elderberry. More than half of each stick was split, with the pith removed. Keeping the sticks a secret allowed Emily to wonder, magically, whether they were real or not. In like manner, she imagined that Salerno might reappear any minute. (People made mistakes all the time with dental matching, and god knows Salerno's dental records were minimal.) Salerno could return abruptly, apologizing for missing the plane, for not calling, carrying yellow freesias and ready to play Emily a new piece of music.

The objects were slightly longer than a foot. Emily had considered leaving them in the ground, caressed by Salerno's ashes, but this impulse dimmed in her own urgency to learn more about the people who had previously lived and died on this land. The curator at the county museum could tell her more.

Phoenix barked, drawing Emily's attention to the red gold ball setting on the horizon. Emily stared directly, as she had every night for sixty-one days, willing the sun to burn away her pain. Just as she had sat, in the brightness of each morning, in Salerno's chair, at Salerno's spot, turning red, then peeling, red, then peeling, until her skin, too tired to burn, went brown. Ruth said she was trying to bake away her grief. But Emily did it as much in hope of melanoma. Where was the line between restoration and destruction?

"Hi there, stranger!"

Considerately, Ruth had waited until after sunset. Emily's neighbors had learned that she rarely spoke to anyone until dusk. What a burden she was. The sooner she finished Salerno's papers and found a buyer for the land, the better off they'd all be. Her boss, Ken, had given her ten weeks' compassionate leave: she had accepted it as a prescription—she *would* recover by the end of August. Three more weeks to go.

Emily waved. Smiled wanly. Phoenix provided the real welcome, wagging wildly and barking. Emily knew she should rise, bring out another deck chair, or invite Ruth in for a cup of tea. She was rooted to the spot even as she felt grateful for Ruth's gentle attention. For the concern they had all expressed. Despite her reclusiveness, Ruth and Lindsey and Virginia continued to ask Emily to supper, to Sunday brunch, on whale watching expeditions, even on trips to Ukiah for women's softball games.

Emily managed a nod, slipped the object into an old red flannel shirt, and set it aside. "How's Joyce?"

"In high drama," Ruth laughed. "The first damn spot has appeared on her panties!"

"No, no, she's too *young* for her period."

Ruth smiled wryly.

"Really?" Emily's eyes widened.

"Really."

Emily suddenly longed for the girl's companionship. She missed their walks and talks and games of Scrabble.

Ruth said something.

What, Emily wondered. She'd lost the capacity for paying attention.

Ruth tried again. "We're having a potluck for Joyce's birthday on Saturday night. Can you come?"

Then, before she could decline, Ruth noted, "It would mean a lot to her."

Emily's breath caught. She wasn't ready yet. Besides, her plan to sell the land increased her nervousness around the neighbors.

"Thanks so much for asking," Emily shook her head regretfully. Then, "My brother Michael is coming up this weekend."

Eventually she'd have to tell Ruth and the others that Michael was helping her with the land sale. But she needed everything in place first, so they wouldn't try to talk her out of it. This was the best way. After all, they were just being kind to her in Salerno's memory.

"You know," Ruth was careful, determined. "Michael would be very welcome."

"It's just the Beulah Ranch women, right? He'd feel out of place." Emily spoke more defensively than she intended.

"Well, yes, and Eva. Do you remember her—the forest ranger? She's been taking Joyce on hiking weekends. Bird watching."

"All women," Emily shook her head. "Michael is so shy."

Ruth had another thought. "At least come for cake. For Joyce, the new woman."

"We'll see," Emily answered distractedly, wishing Ruth would leave her with Salerno and the fetish.

The bright streaks of color had dissolved. Emily breathed more easily in the dusk.

She turned to see Ruth ambling down the fire trail. Had they even said goodbye?

"Thanks," Emily called after her, hoping her voice was loud enough.

She peered into the darkening, to the bruised purple clouds out west, the blue-black sky above. She used to get depressed at the end of June, knowing days would shrink shorter and shorter. Now she clocked the minutes lost each day, as if they might bring her closer to that unattainable sleep.

7

Saturday morning, ten thirty, and the sound of a car crunching up the road startled Emily.

Michael, Jesus, Michael was on time. No one arrived on time in the country. Of course you wore a watch, but life didn't tick by. You got slowed down by tractors or sidetracked by neighbors at the post office or detoured by friends' errands. People arrived fifteen to thirty minutes late without thinking to call. (Of course, Emily herself didn't have a phone.) Or folks came twenty minutes early because there hadn't been anyone in line at the propane pump. People attended more to the *idea* of time than to precise movements of the clock. Michael, though, was an urban man, a punctual lawyer.

What she really should have done is washed this week's accumulation of dirty plates. Hopelessly she surveyed the small, cluttered cabin. How did she amass so many dishes? If Salerno had left a day's worth of clutter in the sink, Emily would get very annoyed (Was this current mess a weird invocation of her haphazard lover?). She had to stop courting sentimental madness. Emily washed her hands and walked out to greet her only brother, who had driven three hours to excavate her from a thicket of deed, will, power of attorney, bank account, and insurance papers.

In the doorway, still wiping her hands on the sides of a slightly seedy T-shirt, she watched a light green car pulling under the oak tree. A new—newish—no, probably brand new BMW. Well, he had the money; he traveled a lot for work; he needed a safe car. At least he didn't have a vanity license plate. Michael enjoyed class and quality, not ostentation.

She waved and smiled.

He stared through aviator sunglasses, out the tinted windshield, toward her. It took him a minute to wave back, as if he were trying to reconcile this middle-aged countrywoman with his pretty little crinoline sister. Whenever he saw her these last ten years, he looked momentarily surprised she was no longer a girl.

Michael waved diffidently and unfolded his long body from the sleek automobile.

She smiled at his weekend ensemble of bright yellow Lacoste golf shirt and stone-washed jeans. But the tasseled loafers! She should have told him to wear running shoes.

Verticality energized him. "Em! Em!" he called.

She ran across the deck, down the steps, then broke apart, crying in his arms.

As 1950s children, they had been amiable adversaries, he complaining about how she tagged along and she bristling at his bossiness. He envied the attention she, the baby, received from their parents and she was jealous of the special mother love for a son, the firstborn.

They had reacted in opposite ways to their father's strict perfectionism. Michael attended to Father's proper posture, values, speech patterns, politics, an understudy eager to perform seamlessly when called upon. Emily drew away into church and scholarship and volunteer work. They prized the differences as much as they fought. And when, in their teens, Mother grew sick, sicker, then died, they reached détente. College separated them. Michael's Stanford law school friends were capitalist caricatures to Emily's fuzzy Berkeleyites. And when she disappeared (as he named it) for five years to do community health organizing in Mexico City and then for another two years to edit in a Marxist publishing cooperative in Santa Cruz, Michael had assured their father that she would return.

She did come back, although a lesbian and a graduate student in regional planning wasn't the prodigal incarnation he anticipated. Still, Michael was sophisticated and, as a new real estate lawyer, had clients in all parts of the city, including the Castro. He worked hard at being brotherly. His most disastrous effort was the dinner party he hosted for his sister and her new lover with his "gay friends," Nigel and Walter, who owned a flash apartment house. She had stormed out during the crème brûlée, in the middle of a row about Proposition 102. Salerno had chased after her, demanding why she had started a discussion about property tax with mini realty moguls? Salerno was a better person than she would ever be. So was Michael.

In recent years they saw each other every six months, coming together with the mute good will of siblings separated by a long-ago war, fond of each other without understanding why, ready for connection, unsure how to achieve it. Sometimes they visited Baba together in Pennsylvania; sometimes they found one another during a California summer.

Roles shifted as Emily came to feel protective (at a distance—everything with Michael was at a distance) about his solitary life. Michael was more than the successful lawyer their father had cultivated. He was funny. Clever. Active in city politics and avant garde culture. But his capacity for intimacy had died with their mother. Oh, during the sixties, she had been reassured that he was no virgin when they swapped sexual liberation stories. Still, he never seemed to have a girlfriend for more than a year. Emily had hoped for a while—despite Salerno's certainty to the contrary—that he might be gay. This was before the plague, of course. Now she simply wanted him to be safe and happy, probably a contradiction in terms. Gradually, Emily came to accept that her tall, slim, earnest brother was an old-fashioned bachelor.

Regarding him now, sitting across from her on the shady side of the deck, she imagined Michael as a seventeenth-century Italian monk with a tonsure of blond hair ecclesiastically nipped from the back of his head.

She poured glasses of sun tea. Salerno said it tasted better than iced tea that had been boiled and chilled. Emily couldn't tell the difference, but she had prepared it all summer.

"How are you doing most days?" he asked quietly.

"Okay. Fine." She was distracted by a greyish-white kite hovering twenty yards away.

"You don't look fine," he blurted, "you look exhausted."

She shrugged, but was touched by his concern.

"I remember how hard it was to sleep for months after Mom died." He shook his head. "I think I imagined I was keeping some kind of vigil and if I fell asleep, I might miss her or God or something."

"Oh, Michael." She realized that they hadn't talked at length about their mother in ten years.

He gulped his tea.

They both stared at the kite.

"I'm sorry I couldn't get back, to be here after the crash, to come to the funeral," his voice trailed off uncertainly.

"Well, Australia is pretty far away. You were in the middle of a three-month business. . . . Besides, I didn't reach you on the phone," she reassured him, "couldn't find out where you were until the day before the memorial."

"Where was it?"

She stared at him.

"The memorial," he repeated cautiously. "You had a service or something?"

She thought of the things they didn't do—the rituals Salerno would have gagged on. They did not have a goddess circle. They did not have a mass. It was a small group—the land women—gathered around the Douglas fir at sunset. Each of them spoke. Joyce recalled Salerno teaching her about the stars on summer nights. Virginia played a track from Salerno's last CD.

"That tree," he nodded, "yes, that's a fine place. I can see her liking it there—on the edge."

Emily felt comforted by her brother but also painfully restless. Maybe her heart was too sore for this intimacy.

Respecting her silence, he turned to the jays' conversation.

Emily poured each of them another glass of tea and wondered how she would cope with Michael's solemn company all weekend. She could start by pulling out bankbooks and insurance forms and deeds. Desperately, she wanted these matters settled so she could be driving with Phoenix across country to the Flat World. She ached for busy Chicago—her job, the reading group, plays at the Goodman, jogs around Lake Michigan—a life that might offer forgetfulness. They had prescribed time for her pain. She needed distance, too.

"Lunch?" she asked, surprising them both. "I have lots of salad things and a fresh baguette and . . ."

"Lunch?" He looked embarrassed. "It's—uh—only eleven fifteen. I mean, I ate a big breakfast, but if you're hungry . . ."

She stared at this steady, reliable family clock. Of course he was right, but they couldn't just sit here. She didn't want to be abrupt with the business questions, but she had run out of everyday conversation.

"Have I ever taken you to Big Trees Park?" As soon as she asked, she sensed she was speeding. It would be far more reasonable to talk here a while, enjoying the view.

She spoke again, loudly, precisely. "The giant redwood forest. Lots of first growth."

He tried to look interested.

Emily persisted in a calm, natural voice, "Very shady, as you might imagine, so it's a great place for walking on hot days like this. Don't you want to stretch your legs after that drive?"

He agreed to the expedition, a little too eagerly, she thought, as if he were humoring her.

As they rode down Valley Highway, Phoenix barked excitedly and Michael quizzed her about the vineyards, which had proliferated since his last trip north. "I hear that the timber industry is selling land to vintners now, that they find it more profitable than reforesting once they've harvested the big wood. Is that right?"

"Yes," her voice was vague, "I've heard something like that."

They both grew quiet as they walked into the redwood forest.

At each visit these beautiful behemoths startled her. Some were wide as houses, others taller than apartment buildings. She loved everything about the park, imagined the whole Valley looked like this during Pomo days, before the Russian hunters, before the Anglo farmers hacked out orchards for planting and cleared ranges for grazing, before the lumber companies discovered their organic gold. These woods had been a sacred place.

As they padded deeper into the grove, the ground was softer, damper, layered with needles and branches. The walking was so different from hiking on the headlands, gazing up at the ocean, or wandering around the ranch, observing the vineyards and hilly farms. Here the air held more moisture, more life. Michael had the same hushed reaction, save for the moment when he extended his hand as she stepped over a log. They proceeded together and separately. Well, perhaps not separately so much as silently, for walking with another in the embrace of these ancients was a kind of worship, the experience heightened, deepened, by the sharing.

They approached Emily's favorite tree, a glorious colossus whose trunk fanned out at the bottom like a skirt. A black skirt because the tree had survived a huge fire: the first four feet hollowed, glistening in black metallic scales. A tree that had lived despite or because of the fire in her belly. A tree that transcended suffering as it grew high beyond the shade of others, higher and higher, reaching for the sun. She breathed slowly, savoring the woodstew scent of moist earth and redwood needles and bay leaves.

Emily and Michael continued walking among the titans, stopping here and there to examine a mushroom or a frail green shoot grown from the motherlog of a new tree.

"Strange," he murmured, looking around, then up, up toward the patch of blue surrounded by branch tops, "it's so enclosed here. Not claustrophobic but . . ."

She remembered Michael's irritating habit of pausing midsentence for what felt like a minute, two minutes, while you waited, wondering if he had become completely distracted or was still trying to extricate the exact words. He was unaware that you were in the rowboat with him, stalled until he put his oar back in the water.

"Contained. Safe," he said finally. "My image of Mendocino is wilderness, the fierceness of coastal winds, the waves smashing into those lovely headlands."

For Michael's sake, she was glad she hadn't followed her impulses these last two months to jump into that grey ocean.

They stood side by side in a beautiful grove, trees gathered in a circle. The Forest Service workers had been here recently, clearing away underbrush against threat of fire. Something about this groomed ground, an artificial altar to ascendant trees, disturbed her. An implication that beauty couldn't emerge from chaos?

"Salerno loved this grove," she said suddenly, searching Michael's face for signs of vitality. Had the walk tired him? Was he too hot? After all, Michael was a man in his fifties and you never knew how much time a person had left. (Emily now feared that she herself would go on and on.)

He observed her closely, worried or perhaps simply uncertain, about how to respond.

"She always dreamed of performing a concert here—but she would never have done anything that intrusive. Salerno believed in public land, wouldn't have wanted to claim it with her sound from other people's . . ."

He was looking at her intently again.

"Other people's private musings. But she liked to imagine herself playing the saxophone up toward that window in the sky. Talked about riffing with the birds, the wind." Her tone was high, tense.

He nodded, anxiously trying to follow.

"Oh, god, now I'm making her seem like a crackpot." Talking about the dead to the wrong people constituted betrayal.

"No," he whispered, moving closer. "No, no. You just make me wish I had known her, known both of you, better all these years." He was on the edge of tears.

With this, she jumped into the waves, her body racked with sobs, her voice keening, breaking.

Michael held his sister firmly until her weeping ended with a wail fathoms deeper than she had gone before.

8

Leaving the woods, they gained twenty degrees of heat. She had planned this backward, Emily realized: the whole day was upside down. It would have made more sense to review documents in the cool morning and visit here during the biting hot afternoon. She should have invited Michael for dinner last night so they could have started the paperwork at nine or ten A.M.

Phoenix lingered in the shade. Emily called and finally used a leash to tug the reluctant dog back to their car. She and Michael slid in silently, both of them hotter still inside the stuffy sedan. When was she going to learn that she didn't need to roll up windows and lock her car in the country? She watched sweat trickle down his temples, seized by her first memory of his body odor. She was ten. Michael, almost thirteen, had just returned from track practice. He rushed past her into the shower, but not before she recognized his new mansmell. That was when they began to diverge—from safe, androgynous childhood into wild, hormonal adolescence. After that, the gulf became too wide to cross; even grasping the rope bridge of memory was terrifying.

"Hot," he said, perhaps to cut the tension he didn't understand, to break her stare.

"Yes," she nodded, "August."

August. Two months. Had Salerno been gone two months? When was she coming back? Emily's eyes filled; she hated how she would start weeping at the oddest moments—in line for the gas pump, at the farmers' market, in the middle of that stupid movie Ruth kindly dragged her to last month. Why these times? Was she crying for Salerno or for herself? She had to get a grip. Especially now. It was imposition enough to haul Michael up here in a heat wave for financial advice. Unfair to expose him to mental disintegration.

Now she zipped along Valley Highway, taking the familiar curves with cautious but efficient speed. Just past Franco's fruit stand, they noticed dark grey clouds. She could smell the smoke. Could imagine the flames.

"Where is it?" He was alarmed. "Anywhere near your place, do you think?"

"No." Her certainty was sliced by sirens. She pulled over to the shoulder as a red fire truck sped past. From above, they heard the helicopter. Back on the highway she drove carefully around the bends and suddenly they saw, eighty yards ahead, a green fire truck peeling in from the other direction. At the crest of a hill they caught yellow flames beneath smoke-heavy shadows.

"Maidstone Winery," she explained, "it's a new vineyard." Emily steered around trucks and sedans stopped on the roadside.

Phoenix yapped sharply, loudly.

"No, Phoenix. No, girl, we're not stopping."

"I'll never understand rubberneckers," Michael sighed. "Do they get a kick out of loss? Suffering?"

"Don't you think it's more primal than that?" Emily glanced in the rearview mirror at the cars and fire and smoke and wondered if people could spot them as brother and sister, two scrawny blond people talking intensely.

"Now, Phoenix," she lowered her voice. "Quiet, girl." Clearing her throat of the thick smoke, she returned to him. "Curiosity. Yes, that's what gets us into trouble."

"But curiosity is the root of human progress."

"Progress!" she coughed. Damn smoke was filling the car.

"Better we should all live in caves, is that it?" His blue eyes were skeptical.

She thought about the Pomo painted sticks, wondered again about their purpose. "You think high rise apartments are an improvement over caves?"

"They're usually less drafty."

Emily didn't laugh. She was thinking about their tenth-floor condo in Hyde Park, already feelin_ Salerno's absence.

"Well," he laughed to lift the tension. "I'm glad you're going back to the safety of your high rise."

"The safety of Chicago?"

"At least the danger there is from humans," he declared. "No small thing. You have laws, police, burglar alarms to curb human behavior."

She laughed. Chicago was a great, lively city, but a safe one? Were cities safe?

"You can't fight the elements," he frowned. "Now that I see how far your cabin is from the road here, how far you are from a telephone—which reminds me, I'm leaving you my cell—when I experience, first-hand, this hot, brittle weather, I'm absolutely freaked about your isolation."

She stopped at the gate. He hopped out, unlocked and held it open as she drove through.

Emily flexed her knuckles on the steering wheel.

"I appreciate your concern," she said as he returned, then took a breath, "but I don't want, that is, don't *need*, your phone."

With cool deliberation, she stepped on the gas pedal. Heading up-hill, she puzzled that he meant well, but there was something perverse about his sending her *home* to Chicago.

"Emily, it's craziness here. Not just the phone thing. No hot water!"

She heard herself saying all this in the same flabbergasted tone to Salerno.

"No proper toilet," he threw up his hands.

She concentrated on the landscape. The fading buckeyes on the left, the new gaggle of purple wildflowers racing up the hillside, this rich, diverse world. None of her neighbors had money for mod cons. You got used to boiling water for washing. The composting privy was just a little less comfortable than the white porcelain loo in Chicago. After a while you didn't notice the inconveniences. All Michael saw was lack, in-accessibility, privation.

He mistook her silence for a wave of grief. "You'll feel better when you're back at work. Back in the real world."

"The real world!" She was torn between irony and fury. "Do you know who you sound like?"

"Yes," his long, thin throat tightened. "He was my father, too."

They smiled ruefully at each other.

"Dad would have turned eighty this year, you know."

"I know." Her surprising tears came and receded quickly.

Phoenix was yipping, jumping up against the window. "Yes, girl, home." Emily glanced at her brother and said the word again. "Home."

Their afternoon proceeded languidly. A modest lunch—salad, bread, and cheese under the oak tree—followed by endless cups of coffee sipped over variously incomplete documents. Well, she hadn't fallen in love with Salerno for her accounting skills.

Seated at her desk, Michael seemed to perceive how everything fit together and he brought vigor, even enthusiasm, to a task she dreaded. Most of the business was pretty straightforward, he said. With her parents dead and no siblings, Michael shrugged, it was a simple will. Salerno had left everything to Emily—except for those books and pictures she had marked for friends here and back in Chicago. Not that there was much of an estate—a few hundred dollars in a savings account, the saxophone, her half of the land and cabin. The last was valuable in so many regards. Studying the deed now, she was flooded with sadness for Lindsey, Virginia, and Ruth because, despite their right of first refusal, they couldn't afford the property even if they pooled money. Deeper still, she felt a betrayal to Salerno, as she contrived to sell this cabin on this ridge—the setting of their history, the site of their future.

While Michael studied and took notes, she sat at the kitchen table slipping papers into folders and labeling them. Some of the documents were an ancient yellow, like secrets from a library vault. Salerno was only forty-seven years old.

Here and there, her brother made little noises of annoyance or assent or incredulity. Emily hated to admit this, but the papers filled her with a kind of horror—their legal jargon and financial responsibility, their finality. She had almost failed the documents course in grad school. And her Chicago colleagues always teased her about this blind spot.

"Hey, this is interesting," Michael rolled his shoulders back, sitting straighter.

"Yes?" She stirred from clerical tasks. "What?"

"You're named as artistic executor." He smiled.

"Sorry?"

"Salerno has left you all her scores and tapes. I don't know a lot about copyright law, but I could get my colleague Steve to look at this."

Emily's eyes brimmed with longing for Salerno's mournful saxophone. She was shocked at this inheritance, although Salerno always joked that Emily would make a million after she was gone. Shocked that part of Salerno was still living.

"No," she said fiercely. "I don't think I'll do anything with the music."

"Don't make rash decisions," he began, then seeing her stricken face, he stopped.

Abruptly, she announced, "We're invited to a potluck tonight."

Surprised by the shift of subject and tone, he said matter-of-factly, "Oh, I thought we were going to that gourmet hotel you keep telling me about."

She had made the reservation for eight and couldn't bear the idea of an early evening suffocated by more pages of tax and will and deed forms. They could finish their paperwork more efficiently in the clarity of morning.

"I forgot it was Joyce's birthday when we planned this weekend."

"Joyce?"

"She's eleven today." Emily remembered the elaborately decorated birthday cakes Mom had baked for Michael (strawberry frosting) and for herself (chocolate frosting) each year of their childhood.

"Daughter of a friend?"

"Ruth," she glared, as if accusing him of knowing too little about her life.

"Oh, right, the kid who lives in the pond," he grinned.

Joyce loped across the hillside to greet them, golden grasses sweeping the knees of her crimson overalls. In the background Lindsey was setting the picnic table with appetizers, chips, and salsa. They would eat the big meal inside because the land cooled off immediately after sunset. Ruth shouted hello from her blue-framed kitchen window. It was a perfect August evening; as the color-sucking heat of the day receded, the sky and hills grew brighter.

Emily introduced Joyce to Michael.

"So you're Em's big brother," she spoke coyly, provoking Emily to note that eleven these days seemed more like fourteen when she was a girl.

He responded in a teasing voice and away they walked, laughing together.

Emily paused in the dry grass, pretending to play with Phoenix but paralyzed by discomfort. Watching her friends chatting on the deck, she reminded herself this was a birthday party, jokes and good cheer. Green streamers were braided around the front railing. Celine Dion was singing from the boom box. Lindsey wore a blue silk blouse. Virginia, her white dress. Presents—she could see the pile of gifts dressed in foil, flowered tissue paper, multicolored bows and ribbons. A birthday party for Joyce as the group had held every August for eleven years.

Joyce was getting taller, the women loving her more as she grew from infancy to childhood to girlhood, surprising them with her intellect and theatrical talent. This evening looked so familiar, so predictable. So normal. The lives of Emily's friends had returned to normal this month. One by one after the memorial the others had reverted to familiar patterns of work and gardening and baseball games and grocery shopping and birthday parties. Ordinary lives continuing as if nothing had happened. No, as if Salerno's death had happened but wasn't still continuing for them as it was for her, every day, every hour.

"Emily?" Joyce woke her.

She looked up to find Michael chatting on the deck with Lindsey.

"Emily, I'm so happy you came," Joyce whispered tenderly.

The girl's words almost pierced her numbness.

"Happy Birthday!" Emily's voice surfaced. She handed Joyce the present, a book she had brought from Chicago and had planned to give her shortly after arriving in June.

A strange woman appeared on the deck. Michael was being introduced. "Eva," she heard Virginia's strong Idaho farm voice. "Eva Garcia."

Michael tipped an invisible hat.

Oh, god, how she hated silly social games. But what did she want? For them to sit and wail with her, to screech out their lungs until they had no voices, no mouths, no bodies, until all of them and everything was no more? She remembered her reclusion following Mother's death, how for years after—until she met Salerno, really—she tended to withdraw from social events. Would they miss her if she quietly disappeared up the hill to her cabin? Of course they would. Joyce would be distraught. Yes, she had to stay.

The visitor looked familiar. Emily recognized the dark hair framing her thin face. She remembered her from somewhere, some time.

Clearly they were discussing her because Michael kept glancing back.

As she reached the deck, the women were all asking Michael questions. Typical. It didn't matter if males were gay or straight or bi or celibate or almost dead, the women asked and the men answered.

She decided to take her foul mood inside the big kitchen and get to work. Emily fiddled with the salad and vinaigrette, eavesdropping through an open window. At last Michael was asking a question and not on the topic of *poor Emily.*

"I work for the forest service," Eva said. "It's a bit of everything. Guided talks, collecting entrance fees, monitoring growth of laurels and eucalyptus . . ."

Right, the Girl Scout, Emily thought, adding mustard to the dressing. (How had she skipped mustard? What else had she forgotten? Was she fully dressed?) This Girl Scout was here the night of the crash. Ruth's friend from the tutoring project. Yes, and a pitcher on the softball team. She *had* absorbed some gossip in the last two foggy months.

Michael leaned forward.

They were both sweating in the evening heat.

The woman's brown hair was pulled back into a loose braid. Very pretty, very femme. One of those young lipstick lesbians.

Michael's golf shirt looked a little dorky, but it was more suited to the heat than Emily's long-sleeved top.

He asked another question.

A record—two in a row, Emily thought, then registered his expression. Oh, god, he was falling for a dyke—her poor, innocent brother. No, maybe she was straight. Emily didn't know much about her, didn't exactly remember her name—Evelyn, Eve? Well, maybe this really could turn into something. She never believed people were meant to live alone. It felt good to cut through her own grief enough to feel optimism for her big brother.

Ruth was carrying the salmon inside from the barbecue. Lindsey brought in bottles from her winery—zinfandel, chardonnay, and a special pinot juice for Joyce. Marianne had made greens and fragrant pepper cornbread. Virginia and her tall partner Sally were ladling steaming vegetables from pots on the stove into serving dishes.

Emily selected a chair near the end of the table. The others seemed to choose seats more randomly.

They were all there. It would be sensible to tell them about selling the land tonight; they could deal with the common issue together. This way, too, Emily thought, she was less likely to get individual pleas, manipulation, or acrimony. Her decision wasn't individual or personal. She was simply opting for the withdrawal clause in their business contract. She would wait until Joyce went to bed.

"To Joyce!" Lindsey raised her glass. "To Joyce on her eleventh birthday!"

Emily thought how Lindsey had been the prized daughter in her family, how hard it must have been when Mr. Chung disinherited her.

Joyce blushed as they raised glasses, smiling as if adolescence and adulthood were states to desire, as if Lindsey were welcoming her to a benign adventure.

"Hear! Hear!" declared Michael.

Joyce blushed again.

They all dug into the food with the easy silence of family members who had always been around one another, who would have eternity to communicate when the important business of eating was over. Emily noticed that Virginia avoided Eva's onion peas but seemed happy. Everyone was enjoying the food. She was glad she had postponed details of the sale until after the meal.

"Any news of the fire?" Virginia asked.

Lindsey leaned forward. "I called the winery. No one was hurt, but Georgia said a good part of their west vineyard is gone, that and the delivery warehouse. Years and years of work destroyed!"

"How did it start?"

"Some idiot deciding to light a wood fire in midseason." Sally shook her long hair.

Joyce tugged at her mother's shirt. "Do you remember that man from Boston who left his trash burning in a canister when he went into his trailer for a nap?"

"Yes," Ruth sighed.

"And," declared Virginia, her weighty voice causing everyone to stop eating, "the sheriff said . . ."

"No, Ginny," Sally touched her partner's arm, "don't get on that rag again."

"Well, hiding from arson incidents doesn't make them go away." Virginia's face turned a splotchy red against her orange Irish hair.

"Incidents?" asked Michael, his voice rising.

Emily knew she had just lost the battle over his cell phone.

"What incidents?" he persisted.

They glanced nervously from one to another.

Arson. Such an ugly word, Emily thought. A harsh, yawning sound. But with some abstruse part of her brain, she remembered the Latin source was *ardere*, that the word *ardent* also grew from that root.

Eva spoke for the first time. "*Some* people suspect an arsonist."

The scratched knuckles on Eva's left fist whitened. Emily noticed a silver ring on the third finger.

"Well," Ruth joined the conversation reluctantly, "an orchard—an apple farm past Mistral—burned down in late spring. But it could have been the flaky farmer's carelessness."

"Or thugs from Louisiana Pacific who have angled for that land for over a decade," Sally burst out.

Marianne, as a relative newcomer, was watching and listening closely, much more calmly than Michael, but with a concerned eye on Lindsey.

"We don't *know* that." Ruth was firm.

Emily knew she was worried about her daughter. Joyce listened attentively to each person, neither daunted nor anxious.

"Walter is a kind of hippie apple farmer," Emily said to Michael. "We all love him. But he is a little distracted and I can see him forgetting to damp down one of his smudge pots."

Virginia had no patience for what she called denial. "And the fire at the church?" she challenged.

"That little Catholic church I passed in Montero?" Michael asked, alarm deepening his already chiseled features. "Was it badly damaged? Who would set fire to a church?"

"Well," Ruth began, leaning forward on her elbows.

Virginia interrupted, "It's the farmworkers' church. Most of their masses are in Spanish. Some say it was political."

Lindsey jumped in, "Of course it's political! The padre is an old UFW organizer. The Latinos are ostracized everywhere else. They really needed that church."

"And now this. Maidstone Winery," said Virginia, almost belligerently. "The third big blaze in three months."

"In fact, this *is* fire season." Eva's voice was soothing as she deflected rumors. "A natural phenomenon. The number of blazes this summer hasn't been unusual, given last spring's drought."

"Right," Ruth said. Emboldened by her friend's authority, she continued. "And what on earth could connect these three places—an apple farm, a church, and a winery? Tell us, Ginny, who's your arsonist?"

"I don't know," she sighed heavily, her wide eyes chilling Emily. "I don't have an answer, a suspect, but that doesn't mean we shouldn't be careful."

Ruth shook her head in exasperation.

Joyce broke the silence. "But how can you be careful? I mean, how can you be careful of fire?"

How can you be careful, mused Emily, of age, illness, plane crashes? Why do we expect safety? Did the Pomos expect to be taken care of by the elements? Did they imagine themselves to be among the elements?

She glanced around at Lindsey and Virginia and Ruth, grateful for the haven they had provided. There were limits, of course; none of them had crawled into her bed on those cold, dark nights when sleep spit her into wakefulness. How she had longed for Salerno's body—the smooth little legs, the wet muscularity of her arms, the intimate scent—to pull her out of dark alertness and back into dreaming. No, none of these women had been able to slip into her heart and reset it. Still, she was grateful for their patient kindness. Surely they would understand how she needed release from this land, where every starry night and every misty morning she was reminded of a very specific—almost touchable, almost recoverable—moment with Salerno. She owed them an explanation of her plans tonight. Yes, a little later, when they recovered from this terrifying talk of fire.

"Hey, isn't this someone's birthday party?" asked Eva.

Emily observed the authority of her smile.

"Maybe we could conjure a more festive topic?" Eva persisted. "The Fair, maybe. Who's entering what in the Community Fair?"

Michael chuckled, no doubt assuming a joke. Country fairs were for Soroptomist ladies and fat, grass-chewing bumpkins.

For years, Emily had also dismissed the Fair but learned to guard her tongue because Virginia usually entered (and won) the cake competition. Lindsey's vineyard submitted their best wines each fall. And Ruth had judged the art competition for the last three years.

Michael registered his sister's attentiveness and stuffed his smile with a generous forkful of Marianne's savory greens.

Joyce was grinning widely in front of a secret.

"I understand," Virginia raised a distinguished rusty eyebrow, "that someone is a sure bet in the embroidery contest."

Ruth took a long swallow of zinfandel. Emily imagined her friend was still battling her way out of the fire conversation.

Joyce shrugged. "It's a crowded category. But I'm excited to get something in the show. It's my first time."

"I love this kid," Eva laughed, her grey feather earrings brushing back across her shoulders into dark curly wisps of hair that had escaped from the braid. "I mean, here she is an expert hiker, somebody who can outdistance me on these hills any day. She's a whiz at math. And she sews, *sews!*"

"I hated sewing when I was that age," Lindsey recalled. "And wow, am I hopeless at it now."

Amused, Marianne nodded.

"But see," Virginia explained, "we were forced to do it. As a girl thing. Nowadays, in our school, the boys are taught sewing, too. So it's a skill thing."

"Then we've had some success," Eva took a sip of water. "I mean feminism—it's always about choice. So Joyce, here, represents success."

Ruth winked at Eva. "Success, yes, I guess. A great deal of trouble, of course. Maybe a *little* success."

Emily noticed the warmth between them and wondered if something might be going on. Ruth and this pretty new woman. A little romance would be wonderful for Ruth, who had been without a partner for six or seven years.

The conversation skipped along now toward the merry climax of cake and presents. They chatted about sheep dog trials, a new clerk at the post office (was she a dyke?), Eva's exemplary pitching at last week's softball game, Marianne's dissertation advisor at Berkeley, Sally's tales of strange UPS deliveries she had known.

Emily watched Michael sitting back, taking it all in. How comfortable he was in this new group of people. In this room of women. Well, he'd always been more mellow, more tolerant, than she. Had Michael noticed the spark between Eva and Ruth? Emily imagined his disappointment.

Ruth, ever hospitable, noticed Michael on the periphery and asked, "So exactly what have you and Em been doing this weekend? Financial records, no?"

Emily rushed in, "Yes, Salerno's taxes and bills and so forth. Michael has been an enormous help. You know, he's quite an art buff," she added, anxious to change the topic. "I'm sure he'd like to see your latest project."

Michael looked mildly surprised at her detour.

She continued, almost frantically, "You know, those new acrylics."

Ruth frowned and, sensing something, ignored Emily. "Oh boy, those accounts could be tough going. Most artists, musicians, too, don't do great bookkeeping."

"Actually," Michael smiled, "Salerno's papers are in pretty decent order—the power of attorney, insurance, the deed to . . ."

Emily jumped in, literally jumped, knocking a pepper mill on the table. "Even the rights to her CDs. She consulted an arts lawyer last summer and, I had no idea, named me as executor to her musical estate."

Ruth persisted. "So will you clear it all up this weekend?"

"Oh, yes," he smiled.

And then innocently, yes, she could hear it all coming. Oh, stupid, prevaricating, cowardly Emily, there was nothing to do except listen to Michael telling the truth.

"Everything except the land sale—that will take some time."

Mist filled the room. Thick morning fog. Hard to make out their faces. No one spoke. Nothing here except grey silence.

What seemed like three days later, a voice.

"Oh, Emily, no." Virginia spluttered, her cheeks darkening.

Lindsey studied her, shocked and angry, as if she were glaring down the arsonist.

"I thought something like this might happen," Ruth said quietly.

Joyce glanced from one rigid face to the next, perceiving some amorphous danger, hovering. "What? *What* might happen?" her voice shook. Then she turned to Emily, "What?"

They were all watching her.

"Oh, god," Michael whispered, "I'm sorry. This is my fault."

"No, it's *not* your fault," she spoke so everyone could hear. "I should have mentioned it weeks ago."

"What?" asked Joyce frantically, tears in her eyes. "Mentioned what?"

"Well, sweets," Emily lowered her voice, "my life is going through some big changes. And, well, I'm going to be giving up my share in Beulah Ranch."

The child stared at her, eyes blinking with fear and grief.

"But I think I can work it out," she added quickly to the group, "so that if you all want to split my share, we can do the finances over time." She had decided tonight at the table: there was no other ethical approach. "You don't want a stranger moving in."

Michael let a sigh run through his long, slumped body. He had forcefully argued against this. For her economic safety. Since she had such meager retirement savings, he said, she owed herself a land sale on the open market. It was the only safe route.

The women remained silent.

Joyce blurted, "Salerno would be mad. She'd said she'd never leave Beulah."

Ruth stood and settled her arms around Joyce. "Hush now."

The girl began to cry.

Stung, Emily tried to think of something, anything, to check her own tears. She was conscious of Eva's scrutiny.

"Or," Emily struck out again, "if there were someone you wanted to move in—to take my place—I'd sell it to her on time. You won't lose the parcel."

"It's not an issue of controlling land," Ruth's voice rose, "we don't want to lose *you.*"

"Jesus, yes," said Lindsey, "I mean, you're part of this place, part of us. Think how much we've survived together." She fingered her black hair nervously.

Emily examined her plate, willing herself to be elsewhere, in the car with Phoenix, driving east toward safety, anonymity, forgetfulness.

"Think about all of us building the cabins, digging the culverts, filling the pond," Lindsey continued. "Think about the reforestation project on the east eight acres. About disking the fire roads. About Angela and Salerno." Her voice broke. "We've buried them both here."

People stopped eating, drinking. Everyone watched Lindsey closely. Ruth scooted nearer and reached her short arm as far around Lindsey's shoulders as she could.

"Stop it, stop it," Emily heard her own strained voice. "Stop playing with sentiment." She stood up, waving her long hands. "I need to move on. This is real life. They're dead. *Gone.*" She gripped a chair to steady herself.

Lindsey would hear none of it. "No, Em, Angela and Salerno are here will us. Still here."

Emily rocked back and forth on her feet, weeping now. Sally took her hand.

"That's enough," Ruth whispered to Lindsey, but caution was nothing against the younger woman's determination.

"Angela is in that cedar grove and Salerno up by the sunset tree, watching, listening."

Emily saw Michael stand quietly, walk over to the window, and stare out at the full moon rising over their pond.

Lindsey wept into Ruth's ample neck.

Virginia picked up the thread. "Em, you *are* part of us." She sniffed and set her formidable jaw against further crying. "It's something you've never realized, how much we love you. How you're a part of this place."

Emily thought she was going to die.

The silent weeping went on for days. A week. For years and decades.

Until a small voice at the end of the table said, "Emily, you'll be here for the fair, won't you? You won't leave before the fair?"

III

9

Driving east with Phoenix, Emily watched the dry golden hills—could they be any paler?—fold into one another. This wasn't what she planned to be doing in late October. She had intended to travel home to Chicago the day after the fair. Abruptly, her thoughts were interrupted by a noisy red pickup gaining on her. She stepped on the accelerator.

Michael's favorite part of the fair had clearly been the sheep dog trials, during which he sat between Eva and his sister. Emily became preoccupied by the mutual interest between Eva and Michael. Their new friend accepted every one of Michael's invitations—to join all the land women as his guests at Heritage House, to take a walk with him and Emily in Big Tree Park, to have a picnic before the dog trials.

Michael was taking his vacation week in Mendocino County rather than at his Maui timeshare. He claimed to be curious about country culture and realized, he said, that he'd never been to a fair, county fair, state fair, any fair. Emily imagined he was more curious about Eva than about watercolor exhibits and pickle contests, but she said fine, fine, you're welcome to sleep on my couch. Instead he opted for a deluxe room at Heritage House with a balcony over the Pacific. During the week she discovered a brother who was both familiar and different. The same silly sense of humor. An easy social flexibility. She enjoyed getting to know him again.

Emily had tried to talk Michael out of the Heritage House feast. It was such a long drive from Beulah to the coast and really, the resort hotel was over the top in a way he'd never comprehend. One dinner there was worth a week's groceries to Ruth and Joyce. But everyone accepted with alacrity, dismissing her qualms. Lindsey, Virginia, Ruth, Eva, Joyce, and Emily sat with Michael at a window table as he ordered champagne and oysters and chateaubriand for everyone except vegetarian Ruth. The restaurant's extravagant theatricality distracted her embarrassment. How sweet it was that he liked her friends, that he had a crush on Eva, that he wanted to repay them for their summer hospitality, perhaps also for taking care of his little sister.

She hadn't felt this close to him for years. Clearly Michael had changed his mind about the relative merits of city and country. One evening over supper at her cabin, he tried to persuade her to take an unpaid leave until Christmas—a leave he would happily, and easily, subsidize. She explained that Ken, her boss, had already been generous about compassionate release time. Emily didn't say how much she ached to escape and immerse herself in those urban battles of work and traffic. As grateful as she felt for the summer's loving friendship, she feared she would soon lose her capacity to breathe on her own. She was basically a loner. Salerno had cracked that, but Salerno was gone and she needed to return to the city and feel surrounded by her own skin. Besides, Ken was zipping weekly e-mails about their Cabrini Green project and Vesta sent three big "I Miss You" cards. She also had duties to catch up with at the condo. Thanks anyway, she had said to her brother's generosity.

But things happened that week. Good things. Bad things. Fate.

The best part of the fair had been the textile exhibit and the beaming face of Joyce Levy, who landed a second-place red ribbon for her embroidery. Of course they were all proud that Virginia's cake won best in show, but that happened every year. Altogether, it was a perfect fair.

Bleat, bleat. Ah, the cha-cha-cha pickup that had been tailing her for miles had a voice! Salerno would have pulled over by now. Emily was going at a perfectly decent speed on this beautiful road. What was wrong with these people? Didn't they see the sun shining on the Spanish moss, the serpentine streaks in the sleeping grey boulders? Weren't they watching for red-tailed hawks? And osprey, she had spotted three ospreys on this road since August. Phoenix began to bark. Pull over, she could hear Salerno's stage whisper, pull over and then we can forget this pickup ever happened. As she steered to the earthen shoulder, she wished all forgetting were so easy.

Content and tired, they all strolled from the fairgrounds together, Ruth and Joyce, Lindsey and Marianne, Virginia and Sally, Eva, Michael, and herself. The women were laughing at one of Michael's pathetic puns and Emily was enjoying her brother's pleasure at being included. Luckily Ruth's truck was parked across the road and she offered to cart back all the blankets and picnic baskets and lawn chairs to the ranch. Then they would meet back at Ruth's house for a duplicate of Virginia's prizewinning cake and a couple of bottles of Michael's favorite new champagne.

Marianne's humor was almost as corny as Michael's and they were all standing by the fair gate listening to her latest bad joke as Ruth set off across the street, the part of Valley Highway that ran through Fairburn. Out of the corner of her eye Emily noticed Ruth looking both ways, setting a careful example for Joyce. Then Sally tried to guess Marianne's punchline and . . .

Giggles. Hoots. Groans.

A sickening skid of wheels and a heavy thud severed their laughter.

"Mom, Mom!" Joyce darted into the street and was almost hit herself by Robbie Soames driving his motorcycle in the opposite direction.

Oh, no, god, no, Emily thought. Panicked about Ruth, about Joyce, she rushed into the street as well and furiously shouted for someone to call an ambulance. No, she would not accept another loss. Kneeling on the pavement, she was relieved to find Ruth alert, if in pain. She knew not to move her friend, but brushed hair from Ruth's eyes, murmuring comfortingly.

"Broken leg, fractured collarbone; it could have been worse," Ruth reassured them as she was wheeled out of the hospital. She tried to ease the dazed, distraught driver of the Geo, who had visited too many wineries that afternoon. Where such generosity originated, Emily had no idea, but it went a long way toward calming Joyce. And the rest of them.

Ruth was right; she was lucky she hadn't been killed. Her bones would mend. Her fear would subside. Eventually. Meanwhile, she was immobilized.

Someone had to take care of her. Someone had to drive Joyce to school. Thus Emily accepted Michael's kind offer to fund a longer leave from work. Ken said fine, if Emily needed the time. She told Ruth it helped to have a fag for a boss. She would use her spare time to finish repairs on the cabin, catch up on some reading, and fill in for Ruth as a volunteer tutor.

No, she hadn't expected to be navigating the highway to Ukiah in Indian summer. Warm, arid, serene. She hadn't expected much of what the last five months had brought and she was thinking of giving up on expectation altogether. She certainly didn't anticipate anything particular from this visit to the county offices with the artifacts she had found buried near their Douglas fir. She hadn't told the other women about these hollowed-out sticks. She wanted to keep them not so much for herself as to herself, in the way one honors a confidence.

Ultimately curiosity and conscience won out. It wasn't enough to receive these relics; she needed to understand them. How were they used? Who made them? How long had they been lying in the ground? And if indeed these were Pomo tools, they should be shared—maybe put on display at a public museum.

Emily loved this two-lane highway to Ukiah, its sinuous winding up, up, up through fading California lilac and weeping eucalyptus. On each drive she noticed a different, almost hidden, ranch or farm. The Cisco Kid, the Lone Ranger—as a girl she adored TV westerns. It was easy to hide in these hills and, according to Sally, a lot of dope growers lived profitably covert lives right here. At the summit she looked east toward Cow Mountain. Beyond and slightly to the south was Clear Lake. Ever since childhood, she'd had an aversion to Clear Lake. The water-skiing haven nesting in the yellow hills made her claustrophobic. If you wanted water, little Emily had wondered, why not drive to the ocean? So she had always been an ocean snob.

In Chicago, she smiled, she did enjoy Lake Michigan. But even as she peered at that watery horizon, she knew that not far away, neighbors in Indiana and Michigan were looking toward her. She had nightmares of people stuck in the middle of the country dumbly staring at each other across puddles. Of course, many Chicagoans probably preferred their lake's more discrete size, but Emily pined for the ocean. Here in Mendocino, even if she didn't visit the coast for a week, she was conscious of morning fog rolling in from the Pacific. Aware that once the sun set in the evening over the western ridge it was immediately falling into the ocean, traveling miles and hours before it rose on a new Asian day.

Enjoying the sun on her face, Emily took the sharp curves skillfully, grateful that Salerno's pickup was long gone, almost forgotten. She reached into a side pocket and inserted a CD. Immediately Phoenix roused, looked around, then lay back, her eyes wide, listening to the sweet melody from Salerno's saxophone. Virginia had been urging her to market this music, make a "best of Salerno" CD. As much as Emily yearned for her lover's fuller presence in the world, she doubted there would be an audience. Besides, what did she know about mixing music? Then, during the last months, as news of Salerno's death spread among progressive jazz lovers, she had received letters, cards from all over the country and even a few from Europe and Asia, expressing condolences. (This was one thing about Salerno: she had dedicated all her CDs to Emily, had always said if folks minded a dyke saxophonist, they should have their ears cut off.) The sweet sound of Salerno's solo improvisation mingled with the smell of dry California dirt and the sight of a high, cloudless sky so that now on this gorgeous autumn morning, Emily found herself feeling almost happy.

The harried receptionist at the Mendocino Land Bureau was having a tough day. As Emily walked into the cluttered office gingerly carrying her relics in a soft red flannel shirt, she saw faxes flying out of a noisy machine, a cluster of four people waiting uncomfortably on folding chairs, and a short, dark man rooting through the belly of a photocopier.

"Maybe I can help?" she said.

Even as she spoke, Emily heard Salerno's admonition, "You're not here to solve the world's troubles." But the Chicago office photocopier was the same model; she knew all she had to do was release the front lever and pull up the green plastic flap.

"Thanks," nodded the tired man, grateful but not particularly astonished that she had arrived to save the day. As she fiddled with the copier, he tightened the rubber band on his long black pigtail.

"You're welcome," she smiled. "I have an appointment with Mr. Dodgson."

He pointed to a seat while he answered the phone.

The inner sanctum door opened and a tall blond fellow ushered in a man from the first folding chair. Emily was relieved that the other three followed him in. Perhaps it wouldn't be a long wait.

The receptionist cleared his throat. "Welcome. I'm Judson Sands. And you're—?"

"Adams," she leaned forward. "Emily Adams."

He studied an appointment book, his eyes clouding. Sitting a little straighter, he made a mark by her name.

"The artifact lady."

To deflect the coldness in his voice, Emily smiled and pictured herself as a Homo erectus skeleton.

He smiled back. "Mr. Dodson should be free in about twenty minutes. Maybe thirty. I'm afraid it's been a busy day."

"I can see that," Emily looked into the pleasant brown eyes of this middle-aged man. "And it looks as if the busy-ness has spilled into your lap."

She noted how calm she felt, accustomed now to country time. If such a delay occurred in Chicago—an appointment postponed by half an hour with no notice—she would be aggravated. But here, well, first of all, how could they notify a person with no phone? Besides, country time was more elastic. She had an hour's appointment with Mr. Dodgson, yet if she needed an hour and a half she'd probably get it.

"I wonder," Judson Sands asked tentatively, "I wonder if, while you're waiting, I might glance at the artifacts."

His tone was formal, hushed as if her objects were criminal exhibits.

"Sure," she said, scooting forward, holding out the red flannel bundle, unwrapping it.

He leaned over stiffly, absorbed by the two sticks and their faded tattoos. They sat together for several minutes, her back aching from reaching forward.

"Would you like to pick them up?"

"May I?"

She settled the cloth on his desk.

Tentatively, he lifted the two sticks. Were they really a rattle, Emily wondered? Judson Sands inspected the two parts from different angles, holding them up toward the fluorescent ceiling light, making Emily notice, for the first time, an opaqueness. Wordlessly he set the objects down on the red flannel.

Emily thought of the translucence of last night's moon.

"Ah," he sighed, then disappeared back into his mind.

"Ah?"

He said nothing.

"What did you notice?" Emily persisted.

"Have you been out to the rancheria?" His question was clearly intended to be an answer.

"The Pomo reservation?" She was confused. "No, I found these on my land."

"On your land?"

Of course, this man was Pomo. "Your land"—was he charging imperialism? She answered plainly. "A small place in the hills between Mistral and Montero. I was digging near a Douglas fir."

Judson nodded, as if confirming something he had known all along. She waited.

Silence.

She felt mute, agitated, as he turned to his faxes. Mr. Dodgson was a relief and a disappointment. Cordially, he listened to her story but gave the objects only a perfunctory examination. He poked the split section, picked up the rattle, then shook it, something Emily had not dared to do. She was startled by sharp, clicking noises. Setting it to the side of his big desk, he jotted several notes. Not worth inspection, his uninterested face implied. Still, just to be professional, he'd make an appointment with the state's field archeologist.

Embarrassed and irritated, Emily said thanks. Maybe there was nothing remarkable about these things and she was simply a widow with too much time on her hands. Maybe he was a philistine bureaucrat, eager for his afternoon golf date. Gently, she swathed the painted sticks in the soft red cloth and hurried out to her car.

Judson Sands leaned on her parking meter, smoking. A handsome man, fit, despite his small pot belly.

Emily's impulse was to turn back, walk to the post office or the kitchen store. Both men left her uneasy in different ways. She told herself Judson Sands simply needed a break from that avalanche of county forms and Mr. Dodgson's bad breath. The fact that he was leaning on her parking meter was coincidence, only that.

"Hi," she said casually, her hand shaking as she unlocked the car door.

"Any luck?" his voice was equally noncommittal.

She shrugged. What was luck? In some ways, it suited her perfectly that Dodgson dismissed these pieces. She could return them to her imagination, to the ledge above the window that opened out to Salerno's tree. "He didn't think they were much. But I'm coming back next Tuesday to see the archeologist."

He nodded.

Anxiously—why was she so skittish?—she slid into the car and rolled her window all the way down. The temperature had risen ten or fifteen degrees since she arrived. Phoenix jumped in her lap, stuck her face out, to be patted by the stranger. An odd move for her high-strung dog.

"Good luck with the flying faxes," she attempted an offhand farewell.

He glanced down at her, scratched Phoenix behind the ears. Blowing smoke from the side of his mouth, he said, "You should think about coming to the rancheria. Really, you should."

She waved. There was something in his voice—authoritative, laconic, canny, all of these—which stayed with her as she drove back to Beulah Ranch. The sun was almost directly in her eyes as she took the curve to Fairburn. She hated how the afternoons were getting shorter.

10

Roaming the land at dusk, she grew attentive to a closing and opening in herself. Light diminished as the sun slithered west, colors muting. Red-winged blackbirds curved and swooped across the sky. Salerno always loved their nightly performance over the ponds.

Evening had been Salerno's high time. In Chicago, as Emily faded from a long office day, Salerno was catching her musical breath. During their first year, Emily feared that clashing metabolisms would end the relationship. This past summer and fall, Emily waited for dusk up on the ridge, waited for sky to redden behind the sunset tree, to greet Salerno as if she were rising for another blazing night at the clubs.

Tonight she was drawn down to the pond before dinner at Ruth's—Joyce's special spaghetti—before she and Eva drove to the Community Hall for their weekly tutoring sessions. They had been doing this every Wednesday for a month. Emily enjoyed the company and structure.

Now she spotted two regal brown mallards floating at the far end of the pond, near swaying grey grasses. Had they flown in without her noticing—or had they been there as long as she had, camouflaged by colors and silence? There was so much she didn't observe in this intricate landscape, or couldn't discern or begin to comprehend. A rustle in the bush could mean quail or snake or fox or Bigfoot, for all she knew. She still confused the evening's rising scent of pennyroyal with mint. While Joyce could predict weather from night winds, Emily often didn't hear the winds. In the city she learned to block out so much distraction. Here it was different, alertness to small sights and quiet sounds enhanced the daily pattern.

Suddenly her breath caught as sunlight played in a veil of leaves dangling from a twisted oak limb. The leaves were an olive hue, a green she never saw in Chicago. Now she had grown still enough to examine nearby moss, to hear the sharp tap, tap of a woodpecker. Today, alone, she had seen blue jays, blackbirds, a red-tailed hawk and now, somewhere in this tree, if she watched long enough and the light lasted, she might spot a pileated woodpecker. She looked forward to making her dinner report to Joyce and was amused by how much she sought the girl's approval.

This kid reminded Emily of a former self, of a time when she felt free and open, before her mother died. There was a kind of purity to Joyce's conviction and ambition. And unlike the nervous adolescent Emily, Joyce had a healthy self-confidence, which admitted that eager interest in others.

The ranch was dark by the time she and Eva drove through the gate toward the Valley Community Hall.

"God, I hate this time of year," Emily said, aware of her odd anxiety with Eva. The woman paid such close attention that she imagined Eva saw right through her. She wondered if her jeans looked too new and if she should have taken the shoulder pads out of her sweater.

"Why do you hate it?"

"Oh, the light dwindling every day. This weekend, we go off daylight savings and the dark will crawl in earlier and earlier."

"You don't like the dark?" Eva asked evenly.

"No." Emily felt foolish—immature, really—protesting the elements. "And I don't care for the cold, either. If I had money, I'd head for the Southern Hemisphere every October."

"Hmmm," Eva slowed down behind a lumber truck. She studied her companion. "I love winter. It's my favorite season." Eyes back on the road, she mused, "The stillness and quiet and all those subtle shades of grey and brown."

Emily smiled. "You don't sound like an Angeleno."

Eva thought for a minute. "I'm not—three generations in L.A. to the contrary. I never fit in there. That's why I came to Mendocino."

"You came to Northern California for the winter?" Emily laughed. "If you like winter, let me tell you about Chicago."

Eva smiled. "No, not just for the winter. I came because this felt more like home."

She stopped in what seemed to be midsentence.

Emily glanced at Eva's face, her jaw set determinedly, her large dark

eyes swollen with worry. A beautiful woman, provocative with contradictions—the small, athletic body and the lovely brown curls. The
rugged forest ranger and the Latina *dama*. The rich, caramel-colored
skin and the hazel—almost golden—eyes.

Eva cleared her throat. "I mean, more like a place I could make into
home."

"Do you miss anything about L.A.?" Emily didn't usually pry. "You
don't have to answer that if you don't want to."

"No," Eva turned with a wide, affectionate smile. "That's okay."

"Your family," Emily tried, then knew immediately from Eva's frown
that she *had* intruded.

"No, I wish. I was never close to most of them. Not like you and your
brother Michael." She bit her lip. "You seem to have a more amiable
family."

"You never met my father," Emily rolled her eyes.

"Yes," Eva nodded. "One day we'll talk about fathers!"

Emily's turn to fall silent. Driving at night was so different here. So
much blacker. Fewer car lights, no street lamps. Any houses were set far
back from the road. Like traveling through eternity with just your head-
lights for guidance. It unnerved her to drive country roads alone at
night, something she had never told Salerno.

"But my family, see, they believe I deserted them."

"Don't you go back for holidays? Can't they visit you up here?"
Emily didn't understand her own persistence.

"No, I can't go back; it's too far," Eva said cryptically.

Annoyed with her own bumbling and Eva's evasiveness, Emily
wished she had asked something about the completion school, about
Eva's tutoring students. What was the point of such personal questions?
After she returned to Chicago, she'd never see the woman again. Unless
she married Michael.

"The distance, it's not in miles."

"How do you mean?

"My family and I, we live in different worlds. I emigrated—when I
finished high school. Then I went farther—to college. My brothers and
sisters were more loyal; they're gardeners, motel maids, store clerks.
They stayed in my parents' world. Papa thinks I betrayed them."

"Because you went to college?"

"Well, my youngest sister Lupe got away with it."

"You make college sound like some kind of mortal sin."

"It was, in a sense. Papa wanted us to succeed, within his terms. Oh, he'd never say that college was the problem; he's too proud for that. Lupe didn't fall all the way. She got married, had three kids, teaches kindergarten in Ensena."

"I see," said Emily. "Lupe didn't become a forest ranger wrestling bears or accept a position as starting pitcher for the Fallen Angels."

Eva nodded. "She stuck by the family, stayed in the community."

They were almost at the hall. "So your tutoring here, helping farmworkers get their GEDs, that's a way of staying in your community." Oh, god, she was being presumptuous, maybe even offending Eva.

"A way," Eva agreed quietly.

They turned off the highway into the gravel parking lot of a square brown building of prefab, functional charm. Valley Community Hall: the first time she noticed it, years ago, the Veterans of Foreign Wars was hosting a reunion banquet. This lot had been filled with sedans and pickups releasing little ladies and their stiff, flushed husbands. Emily remembered thinking that the hall was just another place they'd always speed by on the freeway.

The current identity of Valley Hall had less to do with the original mission of propagating agrarian values and more to do with surviving on rent contributed by the area's diverse constituencies. Congeniality, or at least tolerance, reigned among the VFW and the dykes and the sculpture group and the aerobics students. As for her own behavior, she sometimes marveled at her ability to greet Sol Johnson, head of the county Republicans, so warmly—as if he really were her neighbor. Hard to tell if *his* recent friendliness had to do with diminishing homophobia. Originally he had tried to block the sale of Beulah Ranch, "responsibly informing" the realtor what kind of ladies they were. Had he changed? Or did he just glance the other way now that they were locals? Another explanation: Lindsey, Ruth, and Virginia were active at the hospice, on the Valley planning board, at the tiny library, so perhaps he had simply come to see them as Virginia, Lindsey, and Ruth. Thus, by association now, she was just Emily, a neighbor. What an optimistic thought. Was she losing her critical edge?

Parked toward the back of the lot were two police cars. Emily pointed and shrugged toward Eva.

"The fires," Eva answered vaguely. "Cops suspect the pickers."

Emily shook her head, recalling the fire earlier this week at Boucler's. Boucler had refused to hire United Farm Workers pickers.

"They called me last night. Told me they'd be here to talk to people.

Said that the Continuation Program was a place they could reach 're-spectable Mexicans.' "

"They said that to *you?*"

"Yup. And I answered, 'Welcome, we're all very concerned about the fires. We'll be grateful to know what the police are doing to protect our community.' "

Emily smiled. "What did they say to that?"

"See you tomorrow at seven."

Emily gathered her books, thinking about her student Rafael. Rafael, father of four, picker of lettuce and fruit, native of Fresno, had spoken no English until he was seven. Rafael, who always came prepared with assignments neatly printed in a black spiral pad. Rafael, who had lost several lower front teeth and who, although he was a decade younger than Emily, always remind her of Uncle Theo, her mother's pensive brother. Rafael saw the fires as a campaign against the pickers. He worried about protecting his family in their crowded house outside Mistral. Those ramshackle tinderboxes would go up in a flash. He said he dreamed about volcanoes, huge waves of red lava engulfing children in their beds.

Or maybe they suspected Roberta, the twenty-two-year-old widow who worked full time at Mammo's Grocery and three evenings a week at the laundromat to support her kids?

Eva opened the trunk and pulled out her big box of coffee and tea supplies.

Emily gathered Eva's papers with her own. As the two women entered the brightly lit kitchen, Emily suddenly remembered.

"Would you like to come to dinner Saturday night?"

"Thanks," Eva said. "That would be fun."

"Michael's driving up," Emily continued, by way of explanation. "I know he'd like to see you."

Eva regarded her quizzically. "Oh, right. What can I bring?"

11

Leaning back into the couch, her feet on the coffee table, Emily stared at flames curling around redwood and cedar chunks in the cast iron Waterford stove. Cold weather this week. A severe rainstorm from the north. As much as Emily regretted losing the hidden fortune of Indian summer days, she did welcome moisture. Storms canceled serious fire danger and this week was the first time she felt safe using the old wood stove. Maybe Eva was right about consolations in the coming darkness.

Sipping her red wine, she tried to read all the flame colors—white, blue, orange. Was there a violet or was she imagining that? If day were closing earlier and earlier, she might as well have the compensation of this inside sunset. To celebrate the wet season's arrival, she had lit candles on the dinner table. Glancing over now, she saw the two brightnesses reflected, slightly magnified, in the east window and felt reluctant to switch on the electric lamp.

She sniffed her wine and thought about a conversation with Virginia this afternoon at the gate. Virginia was angry and anxious about the creationism protests. The tall woman hung on the gate and shook her head. "I've been teaching biology at Fairburn High School for a dozen years. This is the first term I've ever had parents protesting Darwin. It's a small group—five families. Small, okay. But I'm completely undermined by the principal, who's demanding I add a unit on creationism!"

Emily shook her head.

"I'm not a poet, a theologian, a philosopher. I'm a biology teacher."

"It's terrible. Scary," agreed Emily, reaching a hand to Virginia's shoulder.

"Scary is right. Their whole group—the Crusade for California—is ominous!" She threw up her arms nervously.

Emily watched her with concern. She had never seen tough, straightforward Virginia threatened, had always admired her no-nonsense competence. "Well, if there's something I can do, start a counter-protest, maybe? Let me know."

"Oh, god! That's all we need on the school sidewalk, dueling placards." Virginia straightened to her full height. "Thanks, sweetie. Right now, I just wanted a sympathetic ear."

Emily listened to the evening breeze fingering through the shell wind chimes that Salerno had bought her for their tenth anniversary. Could she also hear that big white owl in the oak tree? She'd step outside later—to visit the stars, to clean her lungs with cold night air. And to search for those solemn eyes in the blackness.

It had been a busy week, full in a different way from Chicago life. There so much of her routine revolved around making plans to do things. Here everything was accomplished more directly, without the mediating layers of e-mail, fax, FedEx, answering machines—those inefficient systems designed to expedite work. She was constantly resending copies of reports she had sent the previous week because urgent somethings had got lost among urgent others on crowded desks across the city.

She hated the temporal caulking in urban life—the time she spent filling out courier forms or standing over the fax machine and readjusting paper for ten minutes in the interest of instant communication, the periods stalled in traffic trying to get an urgent meeting that had been scheduled at a mutually inconvenient space or time for everyone involved.

Different in the country—the interstices were exactly where real life happened. Standing in the hardware store, for instance, where Marv Stoneman would be showing her the tube he was buying to mend his grey water system—or waiting to have her groceries rung up at Mammo's, where she would hear dispatches about "tree huggers" or "lumber barons," the language varying according to the complainant. These in-between times could be more fruitful than the errands themselves.

Emily crouched before the stove installing another log, deliciously dry wood from last year's fallen oak.

Warmth from the newly caught log touched her face. She imagined heat rising up the stainless steel pipe into the loft above, preparing the room where she would sleep. Then she pictured smoke billowing out the chimney, blown away, away, toward Mistral. Clearly it wasn't neat or simple. She, the sophisticated regional planner, was beginning to excavate the top layers of country life. She noticed the wine dwindling in the bowl of her glass.

Emily thought back to that heated dinner argument last week. Virginia was defending Sally's pot garden, saying she could grow opium poppies if she liked.

"But the land is jointly held," Lindsey protested. "We agreed on principles for use—reforestation and no power lines and dirt roads instead of macadam."

Although Emily had never met Lindsey's father, she often imagined she saw Mr. Chung in Lindsey's determined square face.

Virginia caught her friend's eye. "And we each agreed on separate yards. I don't tell you to plant cabbages instead of broccoli."

Lindsey shook her dark hair. "We're not talking vegetables. Pot is an illegal drug."

"Hardly a drug," Virginia parried. "I don't do dope myself, but everyone knows it'll be legalized soon. I drink wine. You grow wine, for Christsake, what's the difference?"

Emily listened silently. All the Crusaders for California needed to learn was that their satanic Darwinist was the lesbian lover of a narcotics cultivator.

"The difference," Lindsey shouted, then lowered her voice, "the difference is that marijuana is *illegal*. I'm not talking morality here—I don't care what she smokes—I'm talking *danger*. You've seen the cop helicopters."

"Lindsey," Virginia interrupted, "you're getting hysterical. The bottom line is that it's our garden."

"Don't give me that 'good fences make good neighbors' shit!"

Emily simply didn't know. On one hand, as long as Sally was growing pot for herself—and not to sell—cultivation was a right of ownership. But they were all listed together as landowners. They owned their separate dwellings (houses or cabins, depending on one's mood) and the land was parceled into equal shares. If Sally's horticulture were detected by a sky spotter, couldn't they all wind up in a cell in Ukiah? In the pot versus wine debate, Emily agreed with Virginia. Still, Lindsey was smart to be cautious. Interesting how the youngest of them was the most conservative, or maybe the most careful.

A high-pitched noise issued from the west side of Emily's cabin. How would you describe a coyote's call—a scream, bark, screech? She thought it had the otherworldly quality of a countertenor.

Another screech. She leaned over to the window, cupping her hands on the glass to block background light, but made out nothing except shiny blackness. Coyotes, like jackals and dingoes, were an ancient species, messengers from another world. She was drawn to the unfathomable wildness of their bark. A wildness more alarming and seductive because it was so primal.

One night this summer, Emily had been lucky enough to spot the coyotes howling together. She was returning from the privy and there, in the nearby grasses, was a pack of five baying at the moon. No, it had been in early October, not summer at all, but while the weather was still hot. October. This was November. She had been here since June. Five months. Where had time gone? Five months without Salerno. She wanted another glass of wine. Instead, she grabbed a shawl and walked out to stargaze.

The storm had blown west. Now this sky was filled with lights. A brilliant Milky Way spilled over the cabin's roof. Salerno loved the pyrotechnics of August shooting stars, but Emily preferred the calm of a wintering sky. She looked out at Cassiopeia reaching from the horizon into eternity and remembered Salerno sleeping out on hot summer evenings. Emily hoped she was warm enough tonight.

She still felt unsettled by her meeting with the state archeologist. The tall, cold man handled the two-sectioned rattle as if it were a dead snake. A second-class artifact, he said, guessing it was two hundred years old at most. But he would take it to his colleagues in the city and let her know. Emily wanted to protest, to pull the objects back and wrap them safely in red flannel. But she had to follow through, even if the guy weren't truly interested. Who had she expected, Leakey or Kroeber? Would she ever see the rattle again?

Eva seemed to know all about the appointment somehow. Eva knew a lot in her quiet, understated way. Emily paced the deck, thinking about her new friend.

What a puzzling woman. Take the dinner with Michael. She had accepted the invitation enthusiastically but didn't seem particularly interested in him that evening.

Emily had covered the table with a pretty embroidered Polish cloth her mother had loved. She had placed fresh freesias in the middle. A wood fire and flickering candles softened the room.

Before Eva arrived that night, Michael confessed his already obvious interest. He was tired of being a trendy San Francisco bachelor. Was

Eva attached to anyone? Emily said she didn't know if her ring was from anyone special. Somehow she thought his chances were good. She hoped so; he'd been alone for so long.

Emily registered Michael's appearance and behavior. He had just had his hair cut, no, *styled*. He had done copious homework about local parks, asking Eva serious questions about first growth and reforestation.

At the table, she watched him leaning toward Eva, smiling constantly, even blushing a couple of times. Emily loved her awkward, vulnerable brother. At one point she closed her eyes and saw a sixteen-year-old boy spooning soup into the mouth of their frail mother.

Eva, for her part, had been friendly but hardly flirtatious. She had answered questions with quiet civility and seemed as interested in Michael as she would be in anyone. She was polite, attentive, lively. But the greatest enthusiasm she revealed all evening was for the tablecloth. She also praised dinner. Emily *was* proud of her mushroom risotto. One of those easy-looking dishes that required a lot of preparation, Salerno used to say. Emily had remembered that Eva liked Italian food.

Out on the front deck, Emily scanned the sky for Andromeda, but what caught her attention was the fattening, cheerful moon. Despite her thick sweater, the shawl, and the red wine, she shivered. Quietly she walked to the back deck and stood very still, peering into the blackness. For five minutes she waited for the owl's impassive golden irises. Eventually she gave up. Inside, she glanced out the west window, although she hadn't expected the coyotes, either.

The house felt toasty after the crisp, night air. She unplugged the computer—which she hadn't used all day—and turned off the solar inverter. Before extinguishing the candles, she watched flames play over the remaining logs.

Upstairs, the loft was half lit by moon. Emily hung her jeans and turtleneck on a hook and folded her wool sweater. Content and warm, she stood, examining the changes and constants in her fifty-year-old body. Legs were still in good nick, muscular without being skinny. Breasts were firm, sexy if you liked big bosoms, but personally she had always wanted boobs half this size. The stomach, however, was still pudgy. She had imagined, mistakenly, that active country life would make her trim.

Emily peered out at the sunset tree, its branches reaching toward the canopy of stars.

From under the pillow on the right side of her bed, she pulled out her stripped flannel nightshirt. Why did she still sleep on the right side when she could have the whole mattress? Before Salerno, she had always preferred the left. Yet every night, every morning, for the past five solitary months, she had remained at her station on the right. Although the house was still comfortable from the fire, her duvet felt good, its weight and bulk anchoring her to the bed. Downstairs, the wood stove cracked and popped. Then a skittering. Was she sharing the cabin with a mouse? A lizard? What else?

Phoenix barked once.

Outside the wind rose. No, a distant noise from the highway. A roaring sea.

12

Fog rose like hearth smoke from the belly of the land. Early December peaceful. Nothing dramatically sad about the short days. Just quiet. Not even a sense of resignation. More like a sleeping. As Emily sat at her desk, watching out over the Valley, she understood she had been thinking too much about death.

Now sun emerged through wisps of fog: a different country. Bright yellow beamed from the northern hills. Hello. Are you ready? The cypresses were laced with frost, perfect Christmas trees, nature excavating artifice from the trunk of cultural memory. Steam rose from her cabin, from tiny dwellings on a distant ridge.

The hill by their sunset tree was pale beige, a subdued winter color, threaded with ghostly green. Some hills had already turned that dreamy silver-brown, as if grass were so much nesting material. Eventually spring birds would lift the blades one by one, awakening the land from its long spell.

Meanwhile, winter sun warmed her hands as she wrote, casting precise shadows on the page. She was writing to Georgia about returning to Chicago. Georgia was the ideal city neighbor: friendly, reliable, there for an emergency or even for a favor. They had duplicates of each other's door keys in case one of them got locked out. She had kept an eye on the condo these last six months, sent along the occasional stray letter. And she would be happy to turn up Emily's thermostat the day before she and Phoenix got home.

Restlessly, Emily checked the wood stove, although she could hear it crackling, could feel the warmth. She slid in another small log and recycled yesterday's paper. Washing her single breakfast dish, she noticed she had finished half the cereal this morning. An improvement. So was her housekeeping. She cringed when she recalled the cabin's havoc that morning Michael arrived. She *was* pulling herself together. Had even borrowed his cell phone to facilitate the return to Chicago. Real life would recommence in one month: Work from nine to six, commuting back and forth through ice. Planned Parenthood counseling on Tuesday nights; the Atheists' Choir on Thursdays. She had to change her car oil to winter weight before she left California. It would be frigid by the time they reached Colorado.

Soon she would be shoveling snow off her jalopy, getting the washing machine repaired, buying a new microwave, finding someone to walk Phoenix in the afternoons as Salerno used to do. Did Phoenix still think about Salerno? Dream about her? She still seemed to notice when Emily played her discs. The thought of reentering their untouched life made her want to scream with rage, made her want to die.

As she paced the rough wooden floor, Phoenix watched closely. During their first years, Emily perceived herself as the anchor, the practical one, earning a better living, with a clear career trajectory and a busy daily schedule. As time passed, she perceived her own frailties and Salerno's solid patience. Salerno cut back on her concert schedule to spend time together. Meanwhile, sometimes Emily took too much for granted, forgetting to mention when she had to work on a weekend. Yes, their relationship had been left incomplete. Like Salerno's life.

Phoenix's ears were cocked. Cautious monitor of madness, Emily thought, a perfect Edgar Allen Poe hound.

"Coast, girl?" The words surprised her as much as Phoenix. "Want to go to the coast? You need fresh air. I need fresh air. We'll go soporific if we stay here."

Phoenix continued to stare from her comfortable position on the couch.

"Car!" Emily called, rousing herself. "Go in the car?"

Phoenix jumped up, barking.

Emily checked her watch. "Come on, girl, we'll just make it down to Lindsey's before she takes off."

Driving carefully over the mud ruts, she thought how much she did miss Lake Michigan. There was majesty to that wild water claiming such vast space in the midst of their urban puzzle. Occasionally she could block out all the city-ness, studying the grey, blue, green waves and inhaling the raw wetness of the magnificent water. Now which road did she and Salerno take to the shore? (*Used to take.* Past tense. Past-past tense.) Her internal atlas traced the Ashby exit from 580 to Berkeley; the Valencia exit to the Old Wives Tales bookstore in San Francisco.

The Greenwood exit to Elk; the turnoff from Highway 1 to Ukiah. But what bloody road to Lake Michigan did she and Salerno take every Sunday morning for their jog? Damn. Damn. Each Salerno memory carried new grief.

Noticing them, Lindsey hopped down from her pickup and waved.

"Invitation still open?"

Lindsey grinned. "The invitation is always open, but especially when I'm going to the dentist. Company takes my mind off those shiny steel weapons."

"Instruments," laughed Emily. "Think repair, healing." She ushered Phoenix into the pocket behind the front seat. "You're such a cowgirl, Linz. How can you be scared of Dr. Sara I'll-give-you-enough-gas-and-novocaine-to-make-this-seem-like-a-trip-to-the-movies, D.D.S.?"

"We each have a right to one phobia," Lindsey smirked. "Maybe Mom was chased by a set of runaway false teeth when I was in the womb."

"Okay—one phobia. I'm counting," Emily laughed, surprised how her spirits had lifted.

Lindsey steered cautiously down the dirt road, which needed a serious grading. They would have to fix the culvert by the corral before the next wave of rains.

At the bend a flock of crows pecked at the road. Panicked by the car, the birds exploded upward, shaving the air at a 45-degree angle.

Emily noticed the twin buckeye trees, which had been resplendently pink when she arrived in June. Shorn of leaves by winter, they looked awkwardly naked, their seedpods shriveled into a hundred testicles descending to the wet, cold earth.

All of a sudden, as they approached the gate, Lindsey remembered, "Oh, since I thought you weren't coming, I invited Eva on a post-dentist cheer-up walk."

Emily blanched.

"Hope you'll join us. We'll just do the headlands for an hour."

"That's fine," she said neutrally.

"Or I guess you could hang out over a coffee and wait for us."

Emily nodded. What was wrong with her? Why was she making Lindsey feel embarrassed about a friendly invitation? As she climbed down from the truck to open the gate, she thought of walking Phoenix back up to the ridge. What *was* the problem? So what if she had to change her expectations—a ride with Lindsey, an hour to poke around the shops, pick up the *New York Times* and then a return trip to the land, possibly driving if Lindsey was in nitrous never-never land—what was the big deal?

Relax, she told herself as Lindsey slipped onto the highway. A bracing hike would be good for Phoenix. She tried not to think how she had avoided the headlands trail since her long summer mourning pilgrimages along the coast.

The entire countryside had gone quiet. Roads were less crowded now that summer RVs and station wagons were safely parked in Seattle and Pocatello. Passing the Mistral store, she saw a single car in the parking lot. The shacks lining the highway unnerved her—frail, patched-together structures with plaid blankets for curtains and treacherous stovepipes popping through battered roofs. Rafael and his family lived here. With two other families, they occupied one small bungalow.

"Rafael—my friend, my student, I mean, one of the guys at the Continuation School—lives there," she began awkwardly.

"Oh, yeah?" Lindsey frowned.

Emily noticed thick plastic sheeting over the windows of one house where the makeshift chimney puffed smoke into the already grey sky. "I've never really looked at those places before," she continued distractedly.

Lindsey sighed. "I went there once, when I was working the census. Really crowded and dilapidated. One of the few times I felt the census was worthwhile. At least the county had to acknowledge all those people lived in one house. There were three other 'dwellings' just as packed on this same road."

Emily looked out the window, nodded.

"Of course, afterward, I had to admit the census becomes another piece of lost testimony. Temporary respite from a guilty conscience."

"Well, hold on. You can use the census to lobby for bigger schools, even public housing." Emily tried.

"You know the politicians around here. Lobbying for steeper farm subsidies, better roads. Rafael and his family are invisible."

"There are new people moving into the Valley. All those environmental activists. And the two native teachers at the grade school. Political allegiances are shifting."

"Dreamer," Lindsey shook her head sadly.

Dreamer, Emily mused. No, Salerno had been the dreamer. She set their destinations. Fueled their engine. Emily was simply the driver.

Now they were surrounded by trees—giant redwoods and sequoias blocking out light. The forest primeval. Of course, Longfellow had conjured eastern woods of pine and beech and maple. Pretty enough, but hardly primeval. There was too much sunshine shifting through delicate leaves and between the skinny trunks of those tame forests. Here, as in Big Trees Park, you knew you were a small part of a huge world, a world that literally grew more complicated the deeper you moved. Emily loved this section of the drive—imagined sailing through a long, shadowed nave to the oceanic altar.

Lindsey interrupted her reverie. "How would you like to be a god-mother?"

"I don't believe in god," Emily tried to read her friend's face.

"Well, a *fairy* godmother, then?"

Emily blinked. "Linz, are you, are you pregnant? Are you having a baby?"

"Maybe." Lindsey's eyes held the road, her jaw tightening slightly.

"Truly?" Emily who had always felt too impatient, perhaps too self-ish, to be a mother, marveled at maternal instincts appearing among so many friends. "I mean, this isn't just fantasy to distract you from dental doom?"

Lindsey looked hurt.

She always said the wrong thing around this friend.

"No," Lindsey said. "Marianne and I have been talking about it for several months."

"Sorry," Emily touched Lindsey's shoulder. "I didn't mean to make fun. I was surprised." She took a breath. "Wow! What does Mari-anne say?"

Lindsey shrugged back tears. "She makes a joke of it."

"How?"

"She says if we were co-mothers, her grandchildren would be baby-sitting her children in a few years."

"Co-mothers?"

"Well, if I were the biological mother, then she'd adopt the baby as co-mother."

To Emily, this was a big step for a couple who had been together only eight months. "So would you give up the vineyard?"

"No, I have to earn a living. This new development isn't likely to make Father reinherit me!" She tried to laugh. "But there's a co-op crèche in Fairburn, very informal, among friends. You work one day a week there, pay a small sum, and your kid gets care Monday to Friday."

"You've really got this figured out." She didn't know how else to respond.

"You didn't answer my question." Lindsey turned on the blinker as they reached the highway exit to Mendocino.

"Question?"

"The fairy godmother invitation."

"Oh, yes," she raised her eyebrows, staring straight ahead. Lindsey and the others didn't believe she was departing in January. Or maybe, for fairy godmothers, geography was insignificant. No time for that long discussion. Here they were on Main Street, five minutes late for Lindsey's appointment.

"Yes, yes," she nodded vigorously. "I'd be honored."

Emily waited for Lindsey and Eva near the site of the July music festival. Salerno loved to arrive hours ahead of the performance and picnic at one of the tables overlooking the ocean. She got usher tickets and attended everything—opera, chamber music, and, of course, the jazz. This past summer she had been scheduled to play on July 20 with the Naughty Ladies, three other soloists who joined together for several performances each year. Emily shook herself and looked around for Eva and Lindsey.

Instead, her attention was captured by a strange man. He strutted across a makeshift stage, his back to the beating ocean. Megaphone in a dark-gloved hand, he exhorted people to repent, to accept the love of Jesus, to aim for goodness before it was too late.

Emily had never really *listened* to an evangelist, had always raced by that tall, thin black woman who sang and preached on Michigan Avenue. Godstatic, she thought. She found these pious caricatures scary, as their fierce warnings mingled words of love and hate.

The man's sandy grey hair was close cut, but tiny curls rose in the wind, recalling a beautiful child. He was small and wiry, with an educated voice, vaguely eastern seaboard. But his clothes—Thinsulate parka and chinos and boots—were classic California. At first glance, she reckoned his age as mid-sixties. But he could be in his fifties, a tired fifties.

A few winter tourists took in the spectacle: several snapped photos of the flushed man railing dramatically. Local people continued their conversations, maybe walking a bit faster than usual—in the way Chicagoans ignored construction noise.

"During this month of the blessed birth, let us light a candle each week for the Infant Jesus." His voice gained strength, ardor. "Think of those little flames as sources of heat and purification. Let us purge our unhealthy desires as we prepare our hearts for the Sacred Child."

Emily heard her name, swiveled to find Lindsey and Eva thirty yards along. She felt oddly reluctant to abandon the frenzied prophet. Lindsey looked agitated, though, waving her forward. Eva had turned toward the groaning sea.

"Okay, Phoenix," she tugged the dog. Both she and Phoenix hated leashes, but this was the only way to walk animals on the headlands trail. Salerno used to release the dog once they were far from town, declaring, "What do they think, that dogs are as stupid as those human tourists who topple over the cliffs?" Salerno had a point, but some of these paths did cut close to the edge, especially after the erosion of autumn rains. She nudged the dog forward.

"Boy, you two just missed some weird performance art."

Eva struck out ahead.

Lindsey explained. "Eva knows the guy." Her usually precise voice slurred slightly from the Novocain. "He works with her."

"*He*'s a park ranger?"

"Not only that," Lindsey declared as they rushed to catch up with Eva. "He's her boss."

"Really, Eva?" Emily recalled his cultivated voice, his elaborate Advent analogy.

Eva smiled ruefully. The sun moved from behind a cloud and lit the reds in her long, curly hair. "Yes, this is one of Hayden's 'mission days.' He devotes his free time to preaching for the Crusade."

"The Crusade." Lindsey nodded, jittery.

"The Crusade for California. Apparently the Mendocino branch is one of the most active in the state."

"Oh, right, Virginia's nemesis?" Emily paused to untangle Phoenix from the old leather leash. "I mean the ones persecuting her with this creationism nonsense?"

Eva lowered her voice. "Yeah, that'd be on Hayden's agenda, redeeming schools."

"There should be laws against rabid born-agains threatening teachers," declared Lindsey.

"Instead, there are laws against people like us," Eva said flatly.

Emily's mind raced. "So who's funding them? Are they a national organization?"

Phoenix tugged.

"I'm with Phoenix," laughed Eva. "It's a beautiful day. For the next twenty minutes, at least. Let's not waste it yakking about Hayden." Again she struck out in the lead.

Under the new—and likely brief—appearance of sun, the ocean expanded to a bright blue. Salt water sprayed the women's faces as they meandered north along the sheer and slippery headlands. Emily loved looking down at the small laps of uninhabited beach where water crashed in from the west. This part of coast always reminded her of Scotland and today she recalled a solitary holiday in Kirkubright-shire, then a wonderfully terrifying hike several years later with Salerno at Herma Ness on the northernmost Shetland Island. They had been less frightened by the steepness of the cliffs than by the giant skuas, who divebombed them as they innocently walked across the grasses where the birds had cunningly hidden their eggs. They also met a lot of puffins, far more friendly and charming birds. Salerno had always dreamed of going to Herma Ness. That was Salerno—any extreme (highest, deepest, farthest) of geography or emotion or wardrobe or politics fascinated her.

The Mendocino headlands were grand in windy, sunny weather like this. Although it was early for whales, Emily continued to peer down in case one or two grey behemoths were heading from Alaska to Mexico. Such a blustery day, she could feel the sea air sweeping cobwebs from her brain, the wind so strong at times she thought she might be blown off the cliffs.

"So how was Ruth's visit to the doctor?" Eva asked. "She went last Thursday, yes?"

"Right," Lindsey jumped in, "I can't believe I forgot to ask."

"She's mending right on schedule," smiled Emily.

"That's our responsible Ruth," Lindsey laughed.

"She should be out of the cast in two weeks. Back at work in a month."

"Great!" exclaimed Eva, furrowing her brow.

"Phoenix and I take off New Year's Day. Maybe day after, pending festivities."

"January," Eva worried. "Tough time to drive east. The weather. The short days."

Numbly, Emily stared beyond the horizon. "I've got to get back to work."

In contrast to summer's lively chorus of Indian paintbrush and yellow verbena and bluish lupine, winter settled a quiet dignity on the headlands. Suddenly her attention veered off the trail to a madrone bending backward, sun warming the red flesh like passion lighting up the skin of a lover whose arms are flung back in bed. Emily's eyes filled. Oh, sweet, silly Salerno. Infuriating, generous, tender, hilarious lover. Emily was filled with Salerno's absence and presence. Perhaps it had been too soon to return to these headlands where she had said goodbye after Salerno's crash. Yes, *crash*. That word was better than *death*. On this very path she had wept and raged and muttered and, for the first time in twenty years, prayed. How often in those early days of grief had she been tempted to leap into the grey, watery forever?

How often? Every five minutes, every half-hour, then one day, not at all. Sun ditched behind fast-moving clouds.

The three women approached a cypress grove at the north end where huge Quasimodo-like trees hunched and twisted among themselves. Walking beneath and around the gnarled branches felt like navigating through a fairytale. She loved the suffering beauty of these ancients, enjoyed their summer shade and blessed shelter during rains.

The return walk to town was faster under the grey sky, at the edge of a grey sea, through a light mist. They had to move briskly to keep warm. Emily forced herself to chat with Lindsey and Eva, to leave Salerno momentarily.

Lindsey was hilariously recounting her dental drama, mouth drooping on one side of her pretty face as she talked.

So strange, the things we fear, thought Emily. There was Linz, who had all the courage to stand up to her father, shrug off his inheritance, break into the male field of enology, climb Mount Whitney, and she couldn't face a dentist without all the drugs known to humankind.

Ever-patient Eva listened attentively to each traumatic detail. Nodding. Laughing. Guiding Lindsey back to earth.

Light rain as they approached town. Emily pulled out a windbreaker, but the other two seemed unfazed by the weather.

Lindsey stared at a figure in the distance, laughing, "Hey, there's old Hayden still rolling. Now he's in front of the coffeeshop. Let's go a little closer, shall we? He won't notice. Might be fun to listen."

Eva flushed. "No." She was uncharacteristically abrupt, almost fearful. "No, let's not. Let's go to the Bluebird for their sour apple muffins."

Emily followed the other two as they headed to Salerno's favorite café.

13

Sun appeared late this December afternoon, surrounding Emily with small surprises like the cheerful reddish brown mud on the side of the highway. The grass higher up along the road to Ukiah was that silver beige nesting color. But already, she noticed, patches of bright gosling green, early promises of distant spring. In a couple of months she'd be enjoying those brilliant Chicago winter days, the sun illuminating snowy lawns, the semifrozen lake. Yes, she'd be there soon enough. That's why she had to decide about the Pomo rattle, why she was driving to the Tan Oak Rancheria, to Judson Sands's home for dinner.

She glanced uncertainly at the bouquet of roses on the adjacent seat. Hard to decide what to bring country people, who grew everything. She had considered a bag of Nyland apples, delicious at this time of year, but for all she knew Judson Sands owned an orchard. Clearly he was a Renaissance man, with his civil service job in Ukiah, his Vietnam vet activism, his almost-finished Ph.D. in Native American Studies at Berkeley, his community organizing at the rancheria, to say nothing about his commitments as husband and father. Emily wasn't surprised to discover all this on the rancheria's web page.

Ruth would have understood what to bring. For some reason, though, she didn't want any of the land women to know where she was going. The soft late light reminded her of a voile skirt her mother wore on fancy evenings. Emily had always made her twirl once more by the floor lamp, the warmth of the red and yellow stripes drifting together. Now at the highway summit, orange light pulsed off undulating hills. Ten more miles to Ukiah, then she'd turn on Highway 101 toward the rancheria.

His phone call had been very matter of fact. "Judson Sands," he began, not bothering to remind her who he was (he knew she'd remember the parking lot encounter). She tried not to hear this as a summons.

"How about next Tuesday evening, come meet Marie and the kids over dinner? Then I can show you the rez. Take you to the new community culture hall where . . ."

Where, she thought, *you want to display the rattle I found near Salerno's tree.*

"Where," he continued, low key, "my brother Baxter will be doing some traditional storytelling."

Emily paused to compose an appropriate excuse. The report deadline. Packing. She glanced at the disarray of papers, clothes, dishes, boxes, suitcases. She desperately needed to start cleaning and sorting if she were going to hit the road next month.

"Tuesday night." Emily heard herself. She was looking into the mirror with the embossed silver frame Salerno had bought in Oaxaca. "Sure, I can find you. Thanks. I'd enjoy that."

As she drove now, waiting for Cow Mountain to become visible over the next hill, she wondered if anyone *owned* the rattle. It didn't feel like hers. Did this mean the land wasn't hers, either? She had no desire to be torn between the state archeologist and an Indian activist. She was still enough of an academic to be persuaded by the anthropologist's request for the museum. Judson's claim tugged at her political instincts. Yet how did she know his community was the right one among the local Pomo settlements? And was that itself an excessively academic question? As the sun set, the sky turned a sweet greyish blue.

Maybe she should have left the rattle in the ground. But the sticks with their carefully painted stripes were so appealing. There was still so much she didn't know about the artifact. At first sight, she feared it was a snake, yet even as she backed away she knew it wasn't. Inside a protective casing, the two-part rattle—of course she didn't know that's what it was then—was completely intact, very near the surface where she had been digging to settle Salerno's ashes. Eventually she decided Salerno belonged on the other side of the fir, facing southwest, into her sunset. By the time Emily returned to the object, it had become consolation for her lover's relics. Emily could not rebury the strong, whole *live* thing. Tenderly, she carried it into the cabin.

Curiosity. Salerno often teased Emily about her curiosity. Said she was so deferential, timid almost with people, but not with ideas, facts, evidence. "You can't control your curiosity. It comes from some kind of intellectual entitlement."

Emily had been hurt until Salerno explained, "No, I admire your questioning. I'm a lazy thinker."

Emily could picture her now in those cutoff jeans and coral Hawaiian shirt with sleeves rolled up to her small, firm biceps.

"You lazy? You have more energy than my whole family put together.

"Yeah, for activity. For going places. Finding things. But you like to think. You believe you have a right to know."

"That's not bad," Emily had bristled.

"Absolutely not! It's one reason I love you."

Emily smiled now, remembering her conscientious research since Judson's phone call. At the Ukiah library and the historical society she had found ethnographic monographs, had printed out web pages.

All week she had immersed herself in traditional Pomo economic life and family structure and rituals. Learned there were actually seven or eight distinct Pomo groups in the region with separate languages and distinct customs. Some practiced individual ownership. Some were seasonally nomadic, others more settled. Traditionally, women wore skirts—tule in the lake region; shredded willow bark on the Russian River; shredded redwood bark on the coast. In winter, rabbit skins were used for warmth. The diet was nuts, berries, seeds, bulbs, and roots, but especially acorns. Emily began to regard the oaks around her cabin in a new way. People made all sorts of food from acorns, including white bread and black bread. They baked buckeye in underground ovens.

Of course, Marie Sands wasn't going to appear in a tule skirt offering pinole, but Emily wondered what they would eat. Most of all, she wondered what they'd talk about.

Driving through busy Ukiah this evening, she imagined the white people taking this beautiful grassland, this "Deep Valley," as the natives then called it, and turning the place into a dreary county seat.

These days, the first things you saw were the signs to Walmart and Staples where you could purchase the same towels, swimsuits, and paper clips that people bought in Kansas City and New Orleans. Then you passed the dilapidated motel-apartments, dating back to the 1950s and sixties. Emily wondered if they had ever been pleasant respites, if guests enjoyed meditating on those quiet mountains after long drives up from the Bay Area.

Initially, Mexicans had taken the land, kidnapped the Indians, tried to convert them, used them as slaves. Then came the Russians. Then the English. But it was really the "Americans" who remade Ukiah, gathering local tribes, signing a treaty that clarified who could live on this land, which up to then had simply been earth. Driving along State Street, she passed the Mutt Hutt, where she and Salerno had eaten many a vegetarian Reuben, and the now abandoned Ron Dey Voo, which they had never patronized.

Some of the Ukiah Indians banded together and bought back their land in the 1870s, following the white custom of purchased ownership. They had only enough money for a down payment. With the help of a white financial advisor, they paid installments from the slim wages they earned picking hops. The advisor lost much of their money, but eventually the mortgage was paid. In 1924, all Pomos were granted U.S. citizenship.

The auto wrecking yard was Judson's first landmark, and as Emily passed it she speculated about how much of the cars would be salvaged, how much would simply disintegrate. The county had zoned the rancheria as industrial land, something Judson was fighting—and on the way to Madrone Street, she passed a lumberyard and a timber mill. Outside the faded Foster's Freeze, three heavy-set women sipped coffee and chatted at a picnic table. The one restaurant on Main Street—a taqueria—was empty, although a group of middle-aged men leaned against the front window, laughing. As she turned on Madrone, she saw lights in each of the modest houses. She guessed Judson's place before she spotted the clearly lit number: a wooden bungalow, painted medium blue, surrounded by a cheerful garden.

"Welcome," he called from the steps as she parked.

Taken aback—she hadn't had time to pick up her flowers, let alone collect her thoughts—she blurted from the window, "How did you know it was me?"

"You're an on-time kind of person," he shrugged.

She tried not to hear "city person." Emily fantasized that the women at Foster's Freeze and the taqueria men had simply reached down for their cell phones and warned Judson that a stranger was approaching from the south. How different California history would have been if those nineteenth-century natives had carried cell phones.

"Besides, I recognized your car."

A boy—the twelve-year-old, she guessed, tall and lanky, unlike his solidly built self-contained father—ran out to join them.

Judson introduced Lee.

"Did you bring it? Can I see the rattle you found?"

Judson shook his head as that charming, quiet smile took over his full dark lips. "No, Lee, I told you, the lady brought it to the state archeologist to study."

Lee's face fell.

Judson patted his son's shoulder, then looking straight at Emily said, "The archeologist is just taking care of it for the moment."

His younger children were shyer, a ten-year-old girl named Jennifer and a seven-year-old miniature of his father named Sean.

Emily had expected traditional Indian names, though she had no idea what they'd be.

Marie was graciously delighted by the roses. The pretty, small woman in her early forties apologized for wearing jeans, but, as she explained, she shed her teacher clothes the minute she got home.

She served a delicious lake trout with rice and broccoli—no acorns in sight. The children described school projects. Exhausted, Marie listened happily. She'd done enough talking today, directing a sixth grade play rehearsal.

Judson politely, if impatiently, answered Emily's questions about the cultural center that he and his brother Baxter had started five years before. "You'll understand more when I show you around. Tell us about yourself. You're a regional planner, right?"

The kids were excused to play until it was time for Uncle Baxter's story hour.

"Yes, I work in Chicago. I've taken a few months off to do consulting, to clear up some personal business." She wondered why she was being so coy.

"What kind of projects do you do?" Marie asked.

"Community housing, mostly. Some work liaising between schools and residential projects. I'll resume in January, once I drive back to Chicago."

"You're driving in winter," Marie said pensively.

"Why don't you stay?" Judson cocked his head. "Get a job here? You're a Californian, aren't you, born here, I mean down in the Bay Area?"

"Yes," she answered carefully, wondering when she had told him that. Lately all sorts of people had made it clear they didn't want her to go. Yes, she was a Californian, yes, she belonged here more than anywhere. But at this table, she felt shy, unsettled.

"May I help with the dishes?"

She must have spoken abruptly, because Judson's face fell. "Oh, no, we invited you here to see the cultural center."

"Of course," she smiled tightly.

"And we never let guests wash dishes until their second visit."

His charm was unnerving. Emily held onto her suspicions. She noticed his lively, open face—clearly he felt relaxed around her. But then he hadn't spent the last week reading about bloody struggles between their not-so-distant ancestors. He'd known that whole story for a long time.

The Tan Oak Cultural Center was a long cinderblock building at the end of Madrone Street. They walked swiftly through the blue-black night. Emily studied the stars, recognizing the constellations she saw yesterday evening from her deck.

Judson greeted four women weaving baskets in a brightly lit room. Chatting as they worked, they nodded courteously to the "visitor," as Emily was coming to name herself. A blast of warmth from the wood stove made her appreciate how cold night had grown.

Next, they stepped into a room lined with glass display cases. Judson flicked on the lamp, revealing half-full and empty cases.

"We're proudest of the baskets," he said, pointing to a shelf of large and tiny pieces, finely patterned in brown and beige, and a little black.

What were the original colors, Emily wondered? How had weather, age, and storage transformed them?

"And these, below, are burden baskets."

Emily admired the fine long noses of the baskets women used to carry fruits and grains and acorns back to camp.

"The middle one was woven by my grandmother, my mother's mother."

"Did you know her?"

"Oh, yes, she taught me our history. 'You're the bookish child,' she used to say, 'there's power in your brain. Use it good.' " He laughed up at the fluorescent light.

Reluctant to interrupt his private moment with Grandmother, Emily waited. Then she couldn't help herself. "What's so funny?"

"Bax," he was still chortling. "My brother Bax, it used to make him so mad."

"Why?" Emily noticed how different Judson looked from the stolid man she left in the city parking lot. He was perfectly easy, alive in this newly painted room with its sparkling display cases. She bet the glass had been polished by his eager daughter, Jennifer.

"Oh, the way Grandmother assigned our lives. I'd go to college. Baxter, he would build things."

"But she was right," Emily marveled, wondering how her life would have been different if she'd been close to either of her grandmothers. Language had always been the problem with Baba. And Grandmother

Adams didn't acknowledge the marriage of her impetuous son Harold to Teresa Belefski, let alone meet their mongrel offspring.

"You went to college and Baxter became a contractor, right? Didn't you say he built these?" She opened her arms.

"Well, it wasn't all that direct," he frowned. "Eventually that's what happened."

Embarrassed by his serious tone, she returned to Grandmother's baskets. "What pretty, intricate work."

"Oh, her best stuff isn't here," he shrugged. "If you want to see intricate, you should check out her baskets at the Grace Hudson Museum in Ukiah."

"What are these?" She admired jewelry in the adjacent case.

"A necklace of halitotis shell and disk beads. See the woven twine band? They took ages to make."

"I guess so."

A few more steps.

"Our musical instruments. Lee takes lessons on them from two elders —which is why he was in such a rush, excuse me, to see your rattle."

Your rattle. She detected no irony.

"Here's our prize—a flute of elderberry wood. It's cracked near the base, but there's a perfect one in the Carnegie Museum."

"Really?" she asked stupidly.

"Yeah." He nodded, watching kids filing down the hall to a back room. "They loved our stuff. Them and the museum at Berkeley, which is where I learned so much about Pomo music. Them and the Brooklyn Museum."

"The *Brooklyn* Museum?" Her eyes widened. "Well, at least they're still in the country," she shrugged, immediately regretting her gaffe.

"Whose country?" he raised a heavy eyebrow.

"Touché," she swallowed. "Aren't museums returning artifacts to native communities now?"

"It's a process. A slow process."

He grinned at the kids rushing in.

"Where are they headed?"

"Bax's story hour," Judson closed the light just a beat too quickly for another glance at the elderberry flute.

They walked along the corridor toward the babble of high-pitched voices and squeals.

Judson's brother—this had to be Baxter, a shorter, thicker version of Judson—sat next to the wood stove. He could be older than Judson—no gray on his balding pate, but more lines in his forehead, and a stoop to his shoulders. From the stories of her Indian friends in Chicago, she wondered about those "eventualities" between their childhood and their current vocations. Vietnam, alcoholism, unemployment, maybe prison.

Baxter welcomed the guest with an opening of palms and a smile. Judson winked at his children, tousled the hair of several neighbor boys, and ushered her to an old plaid couch against the wall. The kids were all arranged on blankets near Baxter's chair.

"I don't mind sitting on the floor," she protested.

"I do," he said. "Old leg injury. I have to hold it out straight."

"I'm sorry."

"Khe Sanh was a long time ago."

Baxter had commenced in a soft voice.

She sat forward, to catch his words.

"Deep Winter is coming," he made eye contact with each child. "You've watched the night sky. You've felt the frost."

Sean inched toward his big brother Lee. Lee grew rigid and Jennifer circled her arms around her little brother.

"So fire stories tonight. First, a Karok tale. Where do we find the Karok people?"

A thin girl raised her hand. "They are neighbors, upriver of the Yurok. Near Shasta."

"Yes, good, Olivia. And this is a Coyote tale."

The children cheered.

"About how Coyote helped the Karok get fire from two old women who were hoarding it from others."

The kids grew quiet in anticipation. None of the audience, including Emily, could imagine how to survive a fireless winter. The stove crackled and she saw that it was a larger version of the Waterford that heated her cabin. Could this be a tale about how the Karok sailed to Ireland so Coyote might negotiate a good price on a wood stove?

"Coyote explained he would pay a social call on the old women. Once he was inside, the warriors should knock on the door, distracting them."

The children leaned forward with a collective intake of air.

"When Coyote was safely inside, a brother arrived, raising his bow, hooting and hollering, 'Wup, whoop, whoop!' "

Giggles from the children.

"And while the old women were defending their house from savage, Coyote hopped out the back door carrying a brand of flame from their hearth."

Baxter sipped water. "The old women noticed sparks and ran after Coyote, faster and faster. But when he grew tired, he passed the torch to the mountain lion, who carried it to the ground squirrel, who popped it in the mouth of the frog, who swam across the pond, holding his breath to the other side, where he spat it into a chunk of wood."

The kids clapped and stomped and cheered.

Emily imagined Salerno leaning forward with the kids, loving the whole evening.

"Which is why," Baxter held up a big west coast map, "We have a Tolowa story. Olivia's Auntie Abigail married a Tolowa man. Show us where the Tolowa live, Olivia?"

The wee girl held tight to her right braid as she approached the huge map. Puzzled, she stood for a moment, then pointed a tiny finger to the California-Oregon border.

"Yes, yes," Baxter patted Olivia's head. "Auntie Abigail and her Tolowa kin live even north of the Yurok and Karok."

Olivia sat down, grinning.

"Well," Baxter drew his hands apart, "a long, long time ago, there was a flood in Tolowa land. Water rose higher and higher in valleys, up ridges of great hills. Eventually the rain did stop. But they had lost fire. Each night people stared enviously up at the Moon Indians, whose homes were warm and bright. So the Snake Indians and the Spider Indians schemed to capture some of that good moon fire." Baxter dropped his voice. Emily glanced at Judson's rapt face.

"And that's how the magic started. The Spiders spun a light gossamer balloon. One by one, they boarded. A silky rope fastened it to the earth and secured their safe return."

The children fidgeted in suspense.

Judson whispered to Emily. "Now if this were an educational TV program, the screen would flash with a message, 'Don't try this without parental permission.'"

Emily covered her mouth so laughter wouldn't break Baxter's spell. Was Judson jealous of Baxter's spotlight? More likely, they both specialized in irreverence. She remembered Judson telling her not to take herself too seriously. At the time she thought he'd been fishing for the rattle.

Baxter's voice lowered conspiratorially. "The Moon Indians were suspicious of the visitors, but the Spiders told them they'd come for games of chance. And the Moon Indians were notorious gamblers. Look at what they still do with our tides each morning and evening."

Jennifer listened earnestly.

"While they sat around the fire playing games, a Snake climbed the rope from Earth, slithered through the Moon Village, stole fire, and slid back home on the gossamer line."

Baxter nodded his shiny face triumphantly.

The kids broke into applause.

"Back on Earth, the Snake stored fire in rocks and trees; the people were happy."

"But the poor Spider Indians were put to death as a peace offering to avoid revenge from the powerful Moon Indians."

The room expanded with hallowed silence.

"The End."

Several children raised their hands with questions. Emily and Judson listened for a while before sneaking out the back door of the cinderblock building.

Immediately, her attention was caught by a half-full moon. "Forceful guys, those Moon Indians, if they can make you sacrifice your best friends."

As Emily's eyes adjusted to the starlit landscape, she could just make out the small bungalows and their front gardens, none of them as fecund as Marie's.

"Who are friends?" he asked.

Emily paused. Took a long breath of the cool night. "That's a big question."

She thought she had walked straight into something, that he would ask her there and then for the rattle. She had almost made up her mind that this was the right place for it.

Instead, he changed the topic. "I guess we're kind of opposites, academically."

"What do you mean?" It was getting chilly and she walked a little faster.

"Well, you're in the future and I'm in the past. Regional planning," he nodded with satisfaction, "cultural history."

"I don't see it that way—as mirror images, I mean. More like parts of a continuum. How about a more friendly, interconnected sense: you can't have past without future?"

He shrugged, lit a cigarette and took a long draw. "Past and present, yes. But future? I'm not sure I believe in future."

She felt disappeared like those Spider Indians. Yet she sensed no hostility from him. Neither that nor comradeship. She hadn't come tonight to be liked, but rather to satisfy her curiosity. And because she'd been invited. She certainly didn't come to make friends with Judson Sands. Perhaps they both got what they expected. Visit. Acknowledgment. Exchange of information.

He stomped out his cigarette on the back step.

"I'll just grab my coat and say thanks to Marie."

His eyes followed her.

Her coat was hung neatly in the hall closet. As she peeked into the living room, she saw Marie asleep on the couch, next to a stack of sixth grade math quizzes.

Outside again, Emily smiled. "She works hard."

"Too hard," he shook his head, hiding something.

As she climbed into the car, she said, "Thanks for the evening."

"Glad you could make it."

She thought of Baxter's expression during a particularly suspenseful scene. Here it was on Judson's face.

"We enjoyed your visit."

She tried to contain her pleasure at this remark.

Judson leaned in the window. "You know how to find the highway?"

"Yup," she winked. "I just follow the gossamer thread."

"Well," he waved, "it's a bright enough evening."

Back among the highway hills, she realized she was getting comfortable with night driving. This familiar road took her on so many routines —laundry, photocopying, delivering late FedEx packages to the Ukiah airport. Automatically, she glanced in the back seat before she remembered she'd left the dog at home.

Dreadful Dvorak bleated from station KYYY. She switched off the radio and felt surrounded by pleasant silence. Safely alone in the hill shadows on the thread of tarmac.

"Who are friends?" She still wanted Judson's answer. Could you be friends only with members of your own tribe? Was that why Mom looked so sad whenever she talked about Gdansk? What if you didn't have a tribe? If you weren't a Spider *or* a Snake?

Taking a curve too fast, Emily found herself abruptly facing a four-foot wooden cross. Regaining control, she stared at this car crash memorial to a local high school girl. Her family decorated the cross seasonally—now a snowman, a Santa, and a sleigh. For months, Emily found the memorial's summer and fall plastic flowers garish, sentimental, even an invitation to further disaster, for mourners could easily get hit as they decorated on this dangerous curve. Now she understood that once you started tending a memorial, it was hard to stop. Almost as if doing so would be a final letting go.

IV

14

Ruth's coffee table was crowded with leftovers of Lindsey's damson plum dumplings, Sally's shortbread, Joyce's kugel, and another chilled bottle of Michael's champagne. Ruth had banned talk about the fires. No fear—for at least one evening.

Emily sat sidewise in the old grey chair, her back against one arm, legs plopped over the other. Half-listening to a conversation among Eva, Michael, and Ruth about the latest clear-cutting atrocity by Louisiana Pacific, she also monitored the Monopoly squabbles among Virginia, Sally, Joyce, and Lindsey. Emily stared out the big west window at pinkening sky.

Emily had been looking forward to their solstice dinner. Christmas presents, Chanukah songs, and Virginia's annual stories of her grandmother jumping over the solstice fire in Marmo.

She was feeling good—not so much tranquil as engaged. Angry for Virginia, who was still being harassed by the Crusade for California's abusive letters, phone calls, and, last week, their silent "spirit of Christmas" picket on the public sidewalk across from her classroom. Although the wimpy principal defended her Darwin unit, he refused to solicit school board support. In a democracy, he instructed Virginia, people voiced their views. And this was a very mixed community. Virginia urged him to distinguish between free speech and intrusion. He said a few unpleasant letters and quiet picketers were bearable if they kept the peace. The peace! Virginia was now consulting a lawyer in Ukiah.

The B&O Railroad and the utilities seemed to be going to Virginia, who was brilliantly venting her capitalist instincts against Lindsey, Sally, and Joyce.

Emily had been worried when Marianne said she couldn't join the festivities. She knew how much it would have meant to Lindsey, given their recent squabbles about artificial insemination. Lindsey told everyone Marianne had her own family obligations. This made sense, but Emily wondered about the rest of the story between them.

"How many for coffee?" Ruth's voice sang over the assembly.

She counted hands, then turned toward the kitchen with hardly a limp.

Grateful her friend had mended so well, Emily also felt wistful about no longer being needed to run errands or to drive Joyce to school. Ruth still couldn't do heavy chores.

"Uh oh, that's my signal!" Virginia reluctantly withdrew from the Monopoly game. "Now, Joycie, I entrust my estate to you: don't let sidewinder Sally snatch my winnings."

"Where are you going?" asked Lindsey, scrutinizing the board.

"Christmas pudding!" Joyce declared. "It's time for Christmas pudding."

"*Another* dessert?" asked Michael helplessly.

"No," Eva grinned over the steaming coffee. "Not just another dessert. Christmas pudding, seasonal extravaganza created by Virginia, baker to their Majesties, the Queens of Beulah."

"Come again?" Michael poured himself another glass of champagne. Emily wondered if he still planned on driving back to the Bay Area tonight or whether he and Eva had some kind of plan. She'd noticed their glances, laughter, Eva's blushing.

She turned to her brother, "Virginia lived in England for a year. And since then she's made this dessert every Christmas."

Ruth placed mugs and plates around the dinner table, then lit the menorah candles.

Everyone—except for Michael—watched with pleasurable expectation as Virginia carried the plain brown mound on Ruth's antique gold plate.

Emily glanced at these neighbors who had become so dear in recent months. She also felt happier to be closer to her idiosyncratic brother. Strange, sad, how the loss of Salerno had brought her nearer to each of these people.

She had come to see beyond Virginia's wry stoicism to an extraordinary pluck as she resisted the Crusaders. Emily also enjoyed her sybaritic playfulness when she lavished them with cakes and pies and puddings.

For years, Lindsey had seemed a remote figure, maybe because she hadn't been among the original four members of the ranch collective.

She had simply been the young girlfriend—who knew for how long?—of their beloved land partner Angela. Emphasis on young, a youth exaggerated by her wealthy background. But this summer and fall, Emily had really come to understand Lindsey's painful rift from her father, which effectively cut her off from her mother and two brothers. Was that why she ached for motherhood? Clearly there was a lot left to learn about Lindsey.

Ruth poured coffee, carefully remembering who'd ordered leaded and unleaded. What a stunning contradiction was their Ruth, earth mother to Joyce and—in a real sense—advisor to all of them. Yet at the same time she was an ambitious, increasingly successful artist who invented time for political activism with the Forest Guardians and tutoring migrant workers. Despite her fancy Smith education, Ruth had no qualms about earning her living as just another clerk at Basket's.

Joyce presented the dessert plates to Virginia, winking puckishly. Joyce was emerging into an independent, kind person. Bright, confident, loving like her mother, yet not *too* good, she was always on the alert for risk, adventure. Emily had learned much from Joyce, who had grown up knowing the names and stories of the nonhuman inhabitants of Beulah Ranch. The bucks' antlers, Joyce had explained, drop off in winter and are eaten by rodents. Although the fawns are weaned in fall, they stay with their mothers all winter. The deer didn't nibble from her hands, but they didn't run away from her, either. Emily would never forget walking down the road one evening to find Joyce sitting on the dock while a doe and two fawns drank from the pond five feet away.

As Sally washed forks for dessert, Emily noticed the seamlessness of tonight's collective labor. Sally had been the hardest person to know. She remained somewhat opaque. Emily still worried about her marijuana garden. Yet she admired (envied, in a way) how Sally accepted people's disapproval while maintaining their friendship. What she appreciated most about Sally was her generosity in sharing her carpentry skills. Emily, like everyone else on the land, had benefited from Sally's advice and help in fitting windows, fixing drawers. Once this fall she spent a whole Saturday helping Emily reframe the cabin's front door. In return, Emily invited her to dinner. Sally was delighted to accept, but only if they went Dutch. The door framing had been fun, simple neighborliness, a concept Emily had lost touch with.

At the head of the table Virginia stood ceremoniously, awaiting silence. Joyce turned out the lamp. Their eyes adjusted to candlelight. Sally handed her partner the pot of warmed brandy. An intense smell of hot liquor seared across the table. Slowly she poured a generous amount over the sticky brown orb of Christmas pudding.

Michael leaned forward, curious.

"A lesbian form of mass," Emily teased.

Eva giggled.

"Shhh," said Joyce, thrilled by Virginia's theatricality.

Virginia struck a match, set the flame at pudding's edge, and the gold plate shimmered in blue light.

"Wow!" exclaimed Michael.

Now everyone, including Joyce, laughed at his astonishment.

"Let's make a wish," Eva said abruptly. "A wish to carry us through winter dark."

"It's not a birthday cake," Lindsey looked dubious, ever on guard against sentimentality.

"Well, it is, in a way," Joyce noted seriously. "If you're Christian."

"Atta girl," cheered Ruth. "You teach them their traditions."

"Oh, god," Lindsey blushed.

"Precisely," laughed Virginia.

"Forget birthdays," Sally declared. "Forget Christ. Let's just say this is the first year of our new tradition of wishing over the pud!"

"I wish I had more room to eat it," Michael shifted uncomfortably.

"I wish I could stay here at Beulah with all of you." This slipped from Emily.

"Well, why can't you?" Eva asked intently.

"My job, for one thing," Emily blushed, "it's hard to do midwestern regional planning from a remote hill station in the MacKenzie Valley."

"Take a sabbatical," suggested Virginia.

"You've had too much brandy butter," laughed Emily, eager to derail the familiar discussion. Tonight she'd allowed herself the full fondness she felt for these people in this place. How could she sell the land, leave forever? Yet how could she stay without a job? Without Salerno.

"No, really," Virginia persisted. "Last year's sabbatical is the only reason I have energy and nerve to hold out against the Crusaders this year."

"Nice idea," Emily nodded. "But nobody funds city planners to take sabbaticals."

"I'll fund you," Michael was eating his second helping of Christmas pudding.

"Yes. Yes!" declared Joyce.

"Thanks, Michael, but you've done enough, I couldn't . . ."

"Well," Lindsey leaned forward, her malachite beads beaming green-ish gold from the candlelight, "what about the consultant stuff?"

"Yes, what consultant stuff?" Ruth's brown eyes hinted at betrayal. "No one's mentioned this to me."

Emily patted her friend's arm. "Oh, an invitation from the Urban Education Agency to do a comparative study of housing project costs, but it came a month ago. I never answered. It's probably lost now."

"So, look for it," Ruth insisted, raising a stern brow over smil-ing eyes.

"No, really, it's very nice you want me to stay, but . . ."

Ruth interrupted, "Very nice? What kind of nonsense? Of course we want you to stay. How could you not know that?"

"Well," Emily tried, "I've always thought Salerno was your, I mean . . ." She spoke faster to outdistance her confusion. "Still, my boss might not extend the leave. It's a competitive job. He might say, 'Sure, take off the rest of your life.' "

"Just ask." Virginia grinned.

Emily stared at the menorah and thought of Eva's injunction, "A wish to carry us through the winter dark."

"It wouldn't hurt to *ask*," urged Joyce.

Sometimes Emily wished Joyce behaved more like a child.

15

The dream this February morning had been so vivid. She was tracing her right hand over Salerno's smooth, warm flesh. Oh, let's not get out of bed. She asked Salerno to lie still for ten more minutes—ten more years—so they could bask in the scents of sweat and sleep and last night's shampoo—just ten more minutes to prepare for the winter morning chill. Then she awoke, found herself stroking her own outstretched left arm, alone in their half-filled bed.

Mornings were a slap of cold reality after nights of dozing, waking, semiconsciousness. She'd question the point of getting up. She measured hours until evening, when it was civilized to pour a glass of wine, gradually enter that zone of forgetfulness, occasional numbness, and then, if she were lucky, enjoy three or four hours of sleep, of nothingness. Twice this winter she had slept through till dawn. All the other nights she wrestled with the early hours, waiting for light. And dreading, hating, resenting the cold of a cabin before fire.

Yes, mornings were the hardest, and if she were in Chicago she couldn't indulge her resistance to rising; she'd have no time to think about temperature, fatigue. The alarm would ring. She'd put on the kettle, step in the shower, dry off while she poured boiled water through the coffee filter. Gulp her cereal as she scanned headlines of melodramatic city politics, throw on clothes, and race for the train. She'd be halfway to work before she felt anything.

Recalling this routine, she nimbly slipped from the duvet and pulled on socks and jeans before placing her feet on the chilly wooden floor. At least she had learned to drape clothes over a nearby chair. On especially cold nights, she kept her underwear and turtleneck warming under the pillow.

Of course, the world felt friendlier from a standing position. She watched fog rising from the hills and listened to the jays and could almost smell the dewy grass.

It was so tranquil here. She needed time to recoup. Yes, it had been right to accept Michael's generous sabbatical offer and supplement it with a few freelance jobs.

Climbing down the ladder, she carefully laid paper, kindling, and logs over yesterday's ashes in the wood stove. As the timber clicked and sparked, she straightened out last night's mess of newspapers and books. As soon as one of the larger logs caught, she shut the door, letting draft feed the fire. Next: the soothing rhythm of running water. National Public Radio informed and amused and annoyed her as the water boiled. Then that luscious moment—pouring half the kettle water over the coffee filter and half into the dish basin. Simultaneously, she smelled the bitter mocha java and the lemony soap rising over her hands in the basin. At the same time, the blessed fire would be feeding hungrily, warming the cabin—occasionally she could actually feel the heat on her back—scenting the atmosphere with the pungent assurance of roasting wood.

Dishes finished and a second coffee in hand, she sat at her desk, checking the sky for signs of the day ahead.

This sabbatical was a gift in so many ways. She had never truly slowed down—doing community work in her twenties, zipping through graduate school and into a profession in her thirties, earning promotions and a better job in her forties, building the cabin. Yes, even building their so-called respite had been part frenzy. Since returning here last summer, she recognized that she was physically exhausted, intellectually numb, and spiritually, well, if not dead, at least nearly comatose.

After a second cup of strong coffee, she pulled out the notebooks and files she'd need today. Her second project, comparing after-school enrichment programs in Chicago and San Francisco, was almost finished. It would have been finished last week in Chicago. But here, project by project, she always found or made a little extra time. This was the problem and pleasure and conundrum of freelance work. She could set the schedule and the standards. On Monday she'd begin the assignment about the spread of bedroom communities north of Silicon Valley. This weekend she and Eva were driving down to the Bay Area. The coffee zipped through her bloodstream—no need for the third cup she'd drink in Chicago.

The mist was lifting in the far side of the Valley, revealing patches of blackish-greyish-greenish silhouettes, the ghosts of trees capturing fog.

16

Emily buttoned her heavy parka as she walked down muddy hills to the highway gate. She'd insisted that Eva wait there, safe from the storm-wracked ranch roads. Cool, moist air prickling her skin, pack on her back, dog at her side: if this was fifty years old, it felt all right. She was energetic, comfortable in her bones and muscles (with the exception of that slight bursitis in her left hip), and she hardly noticed the pack's weight.

Colder than yesterday at 45 degrees, but not cold compared to Chicago in early March. Despite recently harsh weather, determined signs of spring appeared everywhere. New birds this week. Grass edging from brownish grey to green. Phoenix seemed to be sensing the change as she nosed ahead, sniffing curiously in the bushes

They really should be taking daily walks. It wasn't enough to open the back door and tell Phoenix to run the land. Dogs liked company, too. She felt guilty about leaving her with Ruth this weekend. Phoenix had barked excitedly when Emily pulled out the rucksack, perhaps recalling their long hikes with Salerno. But she would have a fine time with Joyce and her dog Bobbie.

Whoosh! Hard to tell whether she saw or heard the wild turkeys first. Clearly they had spotted her, for as Emily made the turning by the blackberry bushes, a gaggle of five or six landed heavily on the roof of an abandoned shed. Emily imagined the struggles of these relatively flight-less creatures to escape this haven, flailing upward as if air were as alien as water. Phoenix barked, and the birds huddled closer on the roof.

"Shh, Nixie, enough bullying. We know you're bigger and badder than those birds."

Down the hill toward the pond they continued, Emily intermittently sliding in the mud. Near the dock, last year's cattails bent forward and backward in a silvery water ballet.

Ruth had warned that the storm would worsen today, but Emily knew she was wrong. So far this morning, just a light mist. Soon it would clear up. She and Eva would glide into the Bay Area under sunny skies.

Morning in the country was full of smells and sounds: crickets, crows, coots, hawks, woodpeckers, altogether more buoyant than the world she encountered on afternoon walks. Moisture plumped the air as fog dissipated and the eastern hills came into sharper relief. Spider webs glistened. The manzanita's white, sticky flowers hung pregnant between delicate branches. Now sun caught the supple green growing through the red arms of a small madrone. The young tree looked almost tropical amid the dark, venerable sequoias and redwoods.

At the gate, Eva waited in her red truck.

"Hi there!" Emily hopped into the cab.

Eva smiled, "Off we go."

Normally Emily hugged friends in greeting, but she felt shy around Eva.

"No storm so far," Eva said nervously.

"Oh, I predict full sun by Santa Rosa," Emily deposited her baggage in the back pocket of the cab and buckled herself into the front seat. Ten in the morning. This was a good time to head out, after the traffic jam of locals driving from the Valley to Mendocino or Ukiah for work and before the weaving procession of wine tasters. Once they passed the Mesa Café, she felt truly on the way.

She did know Eva well enough to feel comfortable with silent companionship. Her friend was brave to be going to the Bay Area office to report Hayden's weird harassment. It would be hard to prove because he hadn't touched her and only made his creepy sexual comments, his veiled threats, when they were alone. Mentally, Eva was probably already there, making her complaint. Emily's own reasons for traveling were more benign: consultant research at the University of California library, then some museum hopping with Michael.

They drove south, past Big Trees Park, into Montero. From overhead came the menacing sound of mechanical bumblebees. Emily watched a helicopter swoop into the Fairburn airport. Strange enough to imagine an airport in Ukiah, although it was handy for expressing documents to Chicago. When she first saw the Fairburn airport, she thought it was a joke, an amusing piece of conceptual art, like London Bridge spanning Lake Havasu. Her urban chauvinism vanished as she watched planes landing to pick up paramedics and fire brigades.

"Mrs. Milofsky," Eva explained

"Pardon?" Then Emily remembered the ninety-year-old woman who had opened the hardware store during what Virginia called the Valley's Paleolithic era.

"She had a stroke or heart attack or something."

"Oh, how sad." Emily recalled chatting with Gerald Milofsky the previous week about his energetic mother, about how grateful he was for stalwart Polish genes. Sweet to share Polish solidarity in Fairburn, and once more Emily had wished for a name like Dansky or Wachtel, which would introduce her to the world as who she was. Adams: she hated its Waspishness. Salerno had once reassured Emily her melancholy soul was pure Polish.

They pulled into the graveled post office parking lot. As Eva sent a money order to her brother in Los Angeles, Emily emptied her mailbox. The one interesting piece was a hand-addressed manila envelope. She turned it over several times before tearing the back flap.

Eva unlocked her own small glass mailbox, then sifted through bulk post. Emily longed for the privacy of her condo living room, where letters and documents were discreetly slipped through the door slot. Getting mail at the Montero P.O. reminded her of confession in her childhood parish. By the time she was twelve, Father Dolan knew precisely who was across the screen reciting venial sins of anger and impatience. Sins of despair several years later, after her mother died. Neither he, nor anyone else, could absolve her of that. She stopped attending church, stopped seeking divine love or human love, and decided to spend her life helping groups of people rather than getting close to individuals. Salerno had broken that resolution and then left Emily just as Teresa Adams had done. Ruth still tried to tease her out of her hunger for privacy, her tendency to retreat. Her dear friend simply didn't understand.

Eva sighed at her stack of mail, then walked out abruptly.

Hurrying, while she had a minute alone, Emily pulled out a folder of papers—skimming a contract, a letter from Big Horn Records requesting rights to a performance tape of Salerno's last gig at the Detroit Club and some other music. Big Horn Records! Would Salerno be embarrassed by the silly name or appreciate the self-irony of this Western jazz company specializing in wind instruments? She'd never heard of them, but what did she know? Puzzled, excited, she reminded herself not to delay Eva.

The small woman sat sternly at the wheel, eyes ahead, hand firmly on the gearshift.

"Sorry for the holdup," Emily blanched. "I got distracted."

Eva, clearly weighted down by bad news, tried to look curious. "Interesting mail?"

Emily found the woman's quiet containment intimidating. Odd, because Salerno used to say that about her, that she imagined Emily harboring "big thoughts" all the time. "It's a request for rights to Salerno's music."

Saying this aloud, she blistered at the idea of Salerno's jazz being appropriated by someone else. The music was all she had left of her lover.

Eva smiled thinly, then steered on to the highway. "Great. How wonderful to make her music more available. I'll get in line for a CD."

Astonished, Emily asked, "You know Salerno's music?"

"Sure, I went to her local concerts. And one she did with the Naughty Ladies at La Peña in Berkeley."

"Three years ago!" Emily was disappointed she hadn't met Eva until last summer.

"Yes," Eva nodded. "Salerno was astonishing, so playful and graceful."

Emily listened, on the verge of tears. Cold silence blew across the front seat.

Eva checked her watch. "Mind if I try the news? Might catch a headwaters report."

"Fine," Emily sighed.

Oleander Walters was reading the weather, predicting more storms.

Emily needed a benevolent weekend, and from the tension in her friend's thick brown fingers, Eva could use one, too.

Rain. More rain. Heavier rain. Flooding along the coast. Nothing about the Bay Area. It *might* be fine there. This highway was a little foggy, easy enough for driving.

Eyes on the road, Eva maintained a steady speed.

Obviously her mind had departed Mendocino County. Hesitantly, Emily began, "The letter . . . trouble with your brother?"

"Claro! Trouble. A family specialty. With Jorge, with my father. Whose trouble? One of them wound up in the wrong family, that's all."

"Like the Adamses," Emily leaned toward Eva. "Dad and me. Michael says our parents took the wrong baby girl home from the hospital."

Eva studied her.

Emily wanted to know more about tensions between Jorge and Mr. Garcia. Wanted to share her own anguished arguments with Peter Adams, Esq., but she doubted Eva's interest. Already she had said too much for a friendship that existed in more neutral territory—tutoring, the headwaters campaign, and Beulah Ranch dinner parties. And more recently, in outings with Michael. But there Emily always sensed a strain, as if she didn't belong between the two of them. Eva had many friends all over the Valley because of her activism and neighborliness and tenderness. Where would she find time for a new friend? The trip was a journey of mutual convenience. They both had errands in the Bay Area and they would share driving and gas bills. Simple.

The skies parted as they drove past Valley Hall toward Fairburn. Windy rain pounded so heavily that Emily wondered about the next grape harvest. If Eva's truck was having trouble gripping the highway, what was holding those little vines in the ground? Lindsey said bad weather could wipe out a whole crop. Now Emily kept silence, careful not to register doubt in her friend's driving. Were the white knuckles keeping her truck on the road or her mind out of Los Angeles?

Fairburn was quieter than usual for a weekday morning. Eva parked directly in front of Basket's—behind Ruth's purple pickup.

Ruth stuck her head over the deli case as her friends entered. Hand on the glass counter, she slowly straightened her back. Ruth's increasing agility was gratifying. Last September it would have been hard to imagine nimbleness from that mangled body on the highway.

"Hey," her lips slid into that charmingly suspicious New York grin, "you remembered to stop for my portfolio. I thought you'd fly right by in this storm."

"Even storms stop for great art," Emily replied absurdly. She'd learned that locals regarded any car heading toward San Francisco as a communal stagecoach. How else would they manage doctors' appointments and furniture purchases, keep Lindsey's special no-salt pretzels in stock?

"It's out of your way to take the portfolio over to Stockton Street." Since no one else was in the store, she handed each wayfarer a cappuccino on the house.

"Ah, the stagecoach navigates many perilous routes," Emily winked.

"After last night," sighed Eva, "maybe we need someone to ride shotgun." She swallowed her coffee in two gulps.

Ruth nodded solemnly.

"Last night?" Emily asked.

"Perfect timing," Eva shook her head, "middle of a monsoon. Captive audience. Captive mattresses." She sidled over to the organic produce, fingering snap peas.

"Captive mattresses?" Emily demanded.

"Oh, Em," exclaimed Ruth, "your broken radio! Time to invest in a new one. Joycie is working on the tuner, but she's no magician."

"Captive mattresses?" she pleaded.

"Yeah, it happens every two, three years," Ruth began, "depending on state, county politics, and the boredom level of your friendly local Immigration and Naturalization team. Remember that fire over at Findley's orchard last week?"

Emily nodded. "Our little eclipse of the sun."

"Got reported to INS. Blamed on the apple pickers next door. So they decided to conduct one of their midnight raids."

"At the end of apple season?" Emily asked. "Isn't that a little late?"

"Oh, right on time!" Eva's voice rose.

"The crop is harvested," Ruth explained. "Their salaries are all safely tucked under mattresses—what they haven't already sent home in money orders."

Emily listened numbly.

Ruth continued, "And the feds haul in men plus loot, making a profit and a moral lesson. Very neat."

"Jesus!" exclaimed Emily.

Ruth shook her head angrily.

Eva seemed to have bonded with the peas.

"What possessed those INS guys?"

"Their jobs," Ruth said. "They said they were doing their jobs."

"So were the Findleys," Eva said.

"Pardon?"

"Doing their jobs. It was a controlled burn. They had a permit and all."

Emily felt dimwitted. "So why did people accuse the farmworkers? Why didn't the sheriff tell the INS to lay off?"

Eva shrugged. "Probably gets a cut of the mattress money."

Emily couldn't help herself. "Sheriff Frazier?"

Ruth grimaced sympathetically.

Eva was now studying the broccoli flowers.

Emily shook her head. In Chicago she expected corruption: a big city, good for hiding out. But Sheriff Frazier, whose ebullient wife sold potatoes at the farmers' market?

Rain ran thicker and faster as they approached Jerseydale, where the highway began to writhe into curves. Soon they'd be on the roller coaster to Lawnston. (Salerno used to tease Emily about carsickness.

"Just close your eyes and we'll be done in an hour," she'd say, entering the labyrinth. Emily glared back. "Just close my eyes and I'll puke all over the car!" Salerno scolded in a high-pitched voice, "Language!" Phoenix barked at the soprano and soon they were laughing their way around the last dreadful set of curves.)

"I'm glad you're driving," she told Eva. "I hate this stretch."

"Yeah, I know."

Maybe Eva was still burning from the INS roust. Or her brother's letter. Emily listened to herself rattle on. "Jerseydale. I don't know much about the place."

"Nice houses here," Eva said. "Back off the road."

"Now that's a curious difference between here and Chicago. People there flaunt their fancy homes. Mendocino people hide in the hills. You think it's some outlaw tradition?"

Eva laughed. "No, I think Californians would rather look at the land-scape than at each other. I'd guess there are fewer trees in Chicago."

Emily agreed. "Doesn't Joyce's boyfriend Juan live down this way?"

"Yeah, his father's caretaker at the estate of some lumber baron. The rich guy only visits a couple of weeks each summer."

"She can't stop talking about Juan. Hope we're not looking at a June wedding!"

"Doubt it," Eva peered through the driving rain. "One thing Pablo Torres promised Adelaida was that the boys would graduate college. And I don't think our Ruthie is a fan of early grandmotherhood."

"No, of course. It's just that Joyce is, well, so precocious. Yet she does have street smarts. In spite of those reactionary wackos assaulting Virginia at the high school, the junior high is doing a solid job on sex education—about contraception, AIDS."

"Yeah, Joyce'll be okay," Eva continued. "She's tough like her mother."

Emily grinned. "Last week Ruth was dragging heavy camera equipment miles along the Navarro River. What an amazing recovery."

"With a lot of help from you." Eva lifted her large dark eyes from the road momentarily, assessing Emily.

"I did a little cooking."

"And driving Joyce to school. Taking Ruthie back and forth to the Ukiah hospital."

"It was nothing."

"No! It was *something*," Eva declared, her cheeks reddening, hands grasping the wheel again. "Ruth was grateful. A lot of us were grateful to have you around."

Emily wiped the fog from their breath off the window.

Eva continued. "Rafael, for instance. With the tutoring, you've taken him so far, especially in math. Ruth would be the first to tell you math is not her subject."

"Well, Ruth is Rafael's tutor," Emily said more stiffly than she intended. For the first time this morning, she wished she were driving. "And as soon as she's completely recovered, he'll be working with her again."

"We'll find you a new student," Eva nodded firmly. "There's no shortage."

"I don't know," Emily ran sweaty palms over her jeans, "how much time I have before I return to Chicago."

"I thought you were on sabbatical," Eva protested.

"Sabbaticals end."

"When?"

"At some point." Finally, they had reached the bottom of the winding road and the entrance to Highway 101. "I'd be happy to drive, now that we've reached land."

Eva sighed. "No, I'm fine. Maybe after Santa Rosa?"

Silently they rode past Healdsburg. Eva seemed disappointed—irritated even—that Emily was returning to Chicago.

"You've heard Lindsey's news?" Emily shifted the focus.

"The baby?" Eva nodded.

"A boy!"

"Really? She had an amnio? I'm not surprised it's a boy," said Eva. "A grandson for Mr. Chung. Just the thing to bring him visiting."

"You think Mr. Chung is going to accept his lesbian daughter and her middle-aged black girlfriend just because Lindsey's having a boy?"

"An heir!" proclaimed Eva.

"Really?"

"I say Mr. Chung has been looking for an excuse to reunite with his hot-headed daughter for years."

"That's not the way she tells it."

"Of course not."

How much, after all, did Emily know about her close friends?

"How about a latte here in Santa Rosa—and let me drive? You must be exhausted. It's hard to concentrate in pissy weather like this."

Eva took the next exit and they stopped at Sofrino's. She ordered a doppio espresso; Emily felt like a lady with her decaf latte. Voices low, they discussed the Crusade for California. The Crusade for Virginia, as Sally called it. Rain started to peter out.

Emily cleared her throat. She didn't know why it took her so long to ask—she had promised Michael last week she'd invite Eva for supper.

"Do you have dinner plans tonight?"

Eva stared at the dregs in her white espresso cup.

Taking a long sip of water, Emily waited. Why was she so nervous? If she couldn't come over tonight, Saturday would work. Michael had said either evening.

"You have something in mind?"

"Uh, yes," Emily sat taller. "My brother is a great cook and he said, 'Ask Eva if she'd like to join us for cioppino.' That's his specialty. He remembered you like fish."

"You're staying with Michael both nights?" Eva asked evenly.

"Yes, so if you're busy this evening, tomorrow would be fine."

She consulted the coffee grounds again. "I better not. I'm visiting my cousin and I haven't seen her for a year. But, hey, thanks."

"I see," Emily sat straighter. "Michael will be disappointed."

It took Emily a minute to master the gearshift on Eva's truck, so they made a rocky exit from Santa Rosa.

"Mind if I turn on the news?" Eva asked.

"No," Emily sighed, stuffing down her own surprising sadness at Eva's weekend plans. It had been presumptuous of her to wait for so long. She should have asked Eva days ago, when Michael first suggested it.

The news program gradually faded out as they drove into a pocket of zero reception between NPR transmitters. Eva impatiently flipped off the radio.

Provoked by the muteness between them, Emily said, "The letter from your brother—it seemed to unsettle you. Do you mind if I ask if things are okay?"

Eva stared ahead at the Marin County hills.

Now that the torrents had ceased, Emily imagined the stage curtains raised. Here they were, together in the Bay Area. No, this felt all wrong. She wanted Salerno and Phoenix beside her. Eva, who was Eva? A stranger Salerno had never met. The windows were still cloudy from their mingled breath. Hot, restless, she imagined racing to the airport, flying to Chicago and beginning last summer's journey again. At the end of the trip she'd be greeting Salerno with oranges and sunflowers and kisses.

Eva was still talking. She spoke rapidly, passionately, about her parents, her seven brothers and sisters. About how she had always been closest to Jorge, about the edge between father and son. She had tried to persuade Jorge to come north. Her cabin was large enough to share for a while, until he found a place. But he wanted to stay in the neighborhood, with his family. Jorge was so much braver than she was.

They were approaching the bridge, that elaborate orange sculpture of the Golden Gate that usually opened Emily's heart fast and wide. But Emily wasn't fully in the car. She was picnicking with Salerno over on the grass at nearby Fort Cronkhite, listening to this small, wired woman talk about Miles Davis and Art Pepper and the magic of jamming with a new woman's group she had organized.

"So Jorge finished high school, which was good. Papa gave grudging approval. He was even more amazed when Jorge entered community college."

Emily glanced at Eva's intent face. The woman was staring across the bridge, through Golden Gate Park, all the way down to East Los Angeles.

Neither of them was in the car with the other.

"But last month, Jorge dropped out of college, did what he'd always wanted—enrolled in Vidal Sassoon School. Then, simple as that, Papa kicked him out of the house."

Emily's jaw dropped.

Eva shook her head. "Loosely translated, Papa said he wasn't going to have no prancing fairy haircutter for a son."

"How hard," Emily murmured, exiting the bridge into San Francisco. The Presidio's brick houses were hidden in low clouds. Maybe the storm would find them here.

"He's lucky you're there," she declared, "a sister who understands him so well."

Eva laughed. "We made up a name for ourselves—Hermanoas."

"Pardon?"

"As the gay ones, we were always close. Some people took a while to figure out why."

Emily swallowed hard and hoped her own shock wasn't perceptible as she veered carefully through the dizzying San Francisco traffic.

17

Once again, Emily was alone before the woodstove, watching the cedar and redwood logs catch and glow, sometimes briefly blazing together in flames of yellow or blueish orange. As wood popped and sizzled, releasing scents of wilderness, Emily wondered vaguely if television served a similar purpose in the city, where she used to turn on the flickering electronic light and zone out.

Her mind still raced about the recording offer, which all her friends urged her to accept. What did she know about the music industry? Then she worried about the INS roust and its effect on Rafael's friends. As an American, he was safe, but he'd lost relatives in the raid. The Valley was becoming an unfriendly place, he'd told Emily, Alma wanted to move the family north to Oregon or Washington. Emily could hardly protest since she'd be returning to Chicago in August. Sometimes she yearned to go back sooner, put this painful period behind her, but she'd promised Michael to stay until summer. She owed her brother this much. They had a way to go in their reacquaintance.

Wind whistled through seams of her small house. March brought the promise and betrayal of early spring. Delicate plum and almond and apple blossom appeared; then rains violently scoured their delicate petals to the ground. Grass was no longer golden or platinum or that wonderful silver brown but had turned a pale green. It would be weeks until sunny spring appeared. And before that, more rains to test human endurance. The sad, grim skies barely permitted light, obliterating any memory of summer blue. One benefit of steely weather, of course, was that it inhibited fires; no arson had been reported in two weeks.

Eva and Virginia believed one person, as yet unidentified, was setting the terrifying blazes. Ruth and Lindsey insisted the fires were random. Scared to dwell on the conflagrations, Emily let her temporary status absolve her of opinion.

She patted the couch for Phoenix to join her, but lately the dog had preferred evening solitude on Salerno's rocker. Emily knew she was keeping the fire too hot—probably against the frigidity of a Chicago March. The main question about the music deal was, what would Salerno have wanted? She recalled the first time she heard Salerno play, a stunning metamorphosis. The sax was almost as tall as the girl herself. But once she put her sweet mouth to the reed and started moving her wily fingers up and down those pads, it was like watching her make love to someone else. Soon enough, Emily realized that's exactly what was happening: Salerno made love to the notes, to the audience, to herself. Emily watched that soprano horn tipped up at the end into the most seductive flower.

Salerno introduced her to a whole new world and together they spent intense evenings listening to recordings of John Coltrane, Carlos Ward, Eric Dolphy, Hank Mobley, Cannonball Adderly, Coleman Hawkins, and, of course, Charlie Parker. Eventually Emily could hear their different styles, could distinguish the tenor sax, soprano sax, alto sax. Salerno never referred to her models as Bird or Trane, but always used their full names. After all, she said, Emily would never say Doris or Margaret or Toni for Lessing, Atwood, or Morrison.

Reverence was one of Salerno's unexpected charms. This fey, mischievous girlfriend remained profoundly respectful of the musicians she considered teachers. Teachers she had never met, never heard in live performance.

They also taught her about living, or dying. Charlie Parker, dead at fifty-three of a heart attack and cirrhosis of the liver. Art Pepper gone at fifty-six. John Coltrane killed by a drug overdose at forty. Salerno had no intention of self-destructing. She used to joke that she'd be pushing ancient Emily in a wheelchair along the Mendocino headlands when they were in their eighties. Salerno was full of life and her music was full of her. This was why Emily had agreed to talk to the record company rep the following week.

The next seven days were packed. She would return to Ukiah to consult with the archeologist about the rattle. Her conference paper on mosaic communities had to be mailed Wednesday. Thursday Eva was hosting a big school party for five students who'd passed their high school equivalency exams. She hadn't seen Eva in two weeks, not since that strained trip to San Francisco. She'd have to attend the party, couldn't miss another session with Rafael. Then the weekend brought Joyce's debut as Peter Pan at the junior high school auditorium.

She stood, stretched, switched on an old CD. Suddenly she was watching her lover's sweet face puffed out, cheeks full of air, a chipmunk storing nuts for winter. She studied Salerno's nimble fingers, rippling, tapping down those tender pads. When the girl closed her eyes and sucked on the reed, Emily saw her sipping from a cold stream. Oh—oh, Emily closed her own eyes now, hearing Salerno's voice calling, laughing, whispering. Ah, she tried to breathe out the pain. She was tempted to stop the CD. Her CD. One of five. She could hoard them. She could destroy them.

Would the girl be surprised that Emily had spent almost an entire year here, in this home Salerno had dreamed for them both? Had that imagining come from the same sweet well of possibility as her music? Was Salerno looking down at Emily and Phoenix now? Phoenix had also been Salerno's idea, when the dog followed her home one day in Chicago, full of mange and god knew what else? Emily and the dog listened to Salerno play "Tall Grasses Dancing." Emily wept. Distributing the music would be yet another stage of letting go. But she also knew that the clever elf, who had already designed so much of Emily's life, would never let go.

Emily walked over to her desk and opened the folder containing her very rough conference paper. This year she had become interested in—no, obsessed by—questions she had never really considered before, issues of home and ownership and trespassing in the Valley. She had learned that the Pomos had held onto their territory longer than many coastal Indians because the Spanish had trouble making landfall on this resistant shore. She had read about conflicts between Russian and British settlers. Maybe she was writing this conference paper from the same impulse that inspired Salerno's Mendocino suites, a need to understand place, to claim home.

The paper taught her that ownership grew more and more complicated with time. As vintners nudged out the ranchers. As the Latino grape pickers settled in for the long term, sending their kids to Valley schools. Then there were those who the old timers called "hippies," people of her generation, well-educated sixties folk who had divided into environmentalists fighting the timber industry, dopesters growing cannabis and the "lifestyle professionals," who had moved north to breathe cleaner air, try new vocations, work with their modems at a slower pace. At Beulah Ranch, incomers were variously represented. Lindsey, the incipient vintner; Virginia, the activist-educator; Ruth, the artist raising her daughter in a wholesome environment. Emily had to admit that since Michael prevailed in the telephone battle she was the one with the modem.

The next evening Emily joined in the cheery toast of Lindsey's good amnio news. A healthy fetus, soon to be a son. At dinner, they volleyed names. Lindsey eventually stopped them, said you needed to meet someone before you knew his name. So they moved on to gossip about friends and Valley events. And a mysterious new fire in Mistral.

Finally, over coffee, Ruth gently raised the all too familiar question.

Would they ever finish this conversation, Emily wondered.

She glanced at Joyce, worrying that they shouldn't be discussing pot in her presence, but then the girl had grown up with Sally's garden.

"No one else is growing something dangerous to the rest of us," Ruth persisted.

"What about Linz?" Sally asked. "Those innocent little grapes will be stomped into demon drink at the end of the season." She sat tall in her chair under the framed needlepoint of California poppies she had given Ruth for her last birthday.

Emily liked Sally's contradictions—the dyke truck driver and the homey seamstress-carpenter.

Ruth groaned impatiently.

Emily knew she should talk more but was used to Salerno taking that role. Salerno's absence taught Emily how absent she herself had been in social situations, where she retired to the quiet watchfulness she had developed after her mother's death.

"She doesn't grow on community land." Marianne spoke for the first time, her hand on Lindsey's thigh as she leaned forward. Apparently she had overcome her objections to becoming a mother again. Sally had never been Marianne's favorite neighbor.

Virginia stood up to check the apple pie heating in Ruth's oven.

Lindsey paced the room, pausing at a far window to watch the sunset.

"Couldn't you," Ruth started to shout, then moderated her voice, "just grow a few plants inside, under those special lights? Wouldn't that be enough?"

Enough to satisfy her appetite, her rebelliousness, entitlement, to supplement her income as a UPS driver? Everyone knew that with the company cutbacks Sally had begun discreetly peddling pretty green packets at the finer bars in Mendocino.

They weren't going to settle this tonight. Suddenly the United Nations Peacekeepers landed.

"Pie's ready," Virginia called triumphantly.

"Look, I thought tonight was a party for my son," Lindsey turned determinedly from the window. "Let's lighten up a bit."

"She's right," agreed Ruth, almost apologetically. "We have a property meeting next week. Let's discuss it then. First agenda item."

They were happy to let go for the moment. One by one, they took a plate from the table and approached the stove where Virginia served her deep dish pie, fragrant with Gravenstein apples, cinnamon, sugar, and some secret Virginia ingredient.

Everyone except Sally, who slipped off to the window seat, absorbed in a new needlepoint.

Back at the cabin, Emily filled her cup from the red coffeepot. A bad habit, but it might help her kick the wine drinking. Before meeting Salerno, she drank gallons of coffee. Her lover protested—how could they become two rocking chair crones if Emily corroded her arteries with caffeine before middle age? She was well into middle age now and alone.

She sat at the table, her mind drifting. She had to get back into the conference paper. Why was she procrastinating? Because it was hard to whip up career ambition in these quiet hills? No, it was more than that. *Settled*—did that word describe her? Had she relocated? If so, whom had she dispossessed? How responsible was she for the Pomos' removal? For rifts between the Russians and the English? For the Mexican-American War? We all live in history, she knew this, in the then and in the now.

Lately Michael had been talking about buying land west of Mistral—a bed and breakfast gone bust on the road to Ukiah. He'd fix it up. Just for himself, at first. His announcement touched and terrified her. How long did he expect her to stay? A year. That's all. She had accepted his generous sabbatical, but then she was going home to Chicago. He hoped she'd have a steady consultancy in place here in Mendocino County by August. He kept saying the area needed a first-rate regional planner.

Clearly Michael was lonely, grateful for his sister's company. And what a surprise that the tassel-loafered lawyer fit in so well with these country dykes. Emily thought what he really needed was a girlfriend, a partner, a wife. And she didn't know how to help him find her now that Eva was out of bounds.

"Home to Chicago, eh, Phoenix?" She scratched the dog's neck and was rewarded by a soft purr. Salerno swore their pooch purred, one of the many unlikely claims Emily now accepted. Phoenix returned to the rocking chair.

Sipping coffee, staring at the fire, she thought that while she loved her brother, she still hadn't developed Salerno's tolerance for his profession. And now he was thinking of expanding up here! Maybe real estate development was the contemporary invasion of the frontier. But was Michael's purchase any worse than her own? What were the differences among staking a claim, making an investment, and stealing a home? If land were a commodity, it could be owned. Yet only after it had been appropriated. She wrote down this dilemma and peered into the stove, inhaling the simmering cedar, the powerful staleness of her cold coffee. She didn't want to work any more tonight. No sooner had she thought this but the floor lamp went dark, then the sink light.

Phoenix hopped off the rocking chair, leaving it to creak, creak into semisilence near the corner. The dog raced around the cabin barking, jumping up on Emily.

"Cool it, hey, cool it. No poltergeists tonight, Nixie."

Emily's loud laughter further provoked the dog, who began to yowl.

"It's just the solar inverter. Kaput. All the sun energy gone. Don't you remember the overcast day, Nixie, one of those grim March meanies?"

The dog continued to yelp, so Emily reached for her parka. "Come on, then, let's go count stars."

Daytime clouds had lifted like spider webs in a strong wind. The sky glowed with planets and constellations and a descending moon. Furtively, Phoenix sniffed around the grass for gophers. Thank god, Emily thought, she never caught any.

Looking up, Emily recalled Joyce's lessons about Orion and Scorpio —they were easy to spot. Tonight she believed she could make out Pisces in the distance. Most stunning was the sight of the Milky Way's stellar soup tipped over her roof—a thousand billion lights. The moon was beaming on Salerno's tree. Emily looked closely because the previous night she had sighted an owl flapping its giant wings, sweeping over the grasses between the Douglas fir and a large stand of live oak. "Let Dame Owl snatch the gophers," she said to Phoenix, to herself, to Salerno.

She peered but found no owl tonight.

No deer eyes. No coyote song. The bats had long since flurried from eaves not to return until dawn. She listened for frog horns rising from the ponds and heard nothing. No wind. No traffic.

But the stars shone.

Finished hunting, Phoenix waited at the door while her mad human stood silently absorbing the celestial light.

18

The sirens woke her. Then barking. Emily hopped to her feet before a cold rush of air could glue her bones to the damp mattress. On her toes, she stared out the east window, tracking sound. She saw nothing unusual, only oak trees, their moss pulsing in mild wind, like the wings of frantic birds.

Was it an ambulance? A fire truck?

Phoenix barked until Emily appeared downstairs. She opened the door, and as the dog romped outside she was surprised by mild air, not warm exactly, but less wintry.

Sun blotched through a cloudy sky. As Emily rooted around the woodpile under the bay tree, she noticed reddish brown fungi, the color and sheen of seaweed, clinging to several logs.

Once the wood stove was humming, she carried breakfast to the desk and returned to her conference paper. On principle, she believed in meeting deadlines so papers would be distributed before a meeting. This way people could read articles in advance and come with questions and new arguments.

Two, perhaps three, hours passed before she realized she and Phoenix hadn't taken their walk.

The late morning was moist. Moments of brightness, but not the sunny brilliance she ached for. Often spring felt as long as adolescence. They'd had one beautiful afternoon last week and she would savor that. She'd been driving Joyce back from school when they saw mustard shining cheerily in the fields over on Nyland's farm and the hot bark of madrone pulsing from red brick soil further along the road. You had to store away such pictures.

Phoenix ran ahead as Emily meandered. Salerno always maintained a brisk pace, amused when Emily's trailing mind slowed her feet. Did Phoenix miss Salerno's swiftness, was this why the dog hung back at the beginning of each trip, staring at the door? Emily must be imagining this. It was possible to go bonkers from too much solitude. She used to warn Salerno about that when they were building the cabin. She was a city girl, she'd cautioned. Who would she talk to here? The trees?

Emily dreaded the meeting with that recording guy in Mendocino. Ruth guessed he'd probably be more intimidated by Emily's thousand and one professional business questions.

"Believe me," she had said, "he'll turn out to be some kind of free spirit techno artist who'll cave into anything you ask."

Emily hoped so. She simply wanted to do right by Salerno and she knew nothing about print runs or distribution patterns. Damn, damn Salerno—abandoning her with dog, land, cabin, and now a music contract.

Just then something shifted her attention, a breeze through the mist. Ten feet away she spotted four young bucks munching uphill toward the ridge. How long had they been there? Had they observed her? Good thing Phoenix had already run down to the pond. Animals seemed less timid in overcast weather, perhaps because they could hear better, smell more acutely. At this moment she didn't exist for the deer. She was close enough to make out their emerging antlers, see wind riffling through molting winter coats. Each took a turn as guard. Always one of them was vigilant, ears trumpet taut as the others grazed. There was something exquisitely precise about their relation to landscape and weather.

A quiet, grey day—good for burning—and as she tiptoed down the trail, away from the bucks, she saw smoke rising toward Fairburn, small dark clouds lifting above distant pruning fires. She remembered the morning sirens. Through the mist, one blaze assumed strange life, like inflamed skin around a wound.

Emily mailed her imperfect conference paper before picking up Joyce from rehearsal. The wind grew wicked between Montero and Fairburn. Occasionally, when solar electricity extinguished early at night, she fantasized about tapping into all this wind power. But that would involve expensive equipment and she'd be leaving in summer.

Driving hesitantly into the incipient storm, Emily tried to think of more pleasant things. The sabbatical had worked well. Her land partners were saving enough to buy her parcel, at least to put down a deposit. Ruth mused about using Emily's cabin as a studio. They all talked about putting weekend guests there. Marianne volunteered that she'd be happy to retreat to the cabin when Lindsey's baby was crying too much. Now the solution seemed easy, but it had taken months of faithful waiting. She wanted the cabin to remain in the group.

Joyce ran out to the car, her small arms crowded with books and binders; a green costume spilling out from several brown paper shopping bags.

Emily expected the girl to be bursting with rehearsal tales. Lately Tinkerbelle had been temperamental and last week one of the boys had been felled by chicken pox. Instead Joyce began burbling something Emily couldn't grasp.

"They caught him—Joshua Nyland—apparently he went right to school like nothing had happened."

"Who? What?" Emily steered onto the highway, nervously because the tasting rooms had just shut.

Joyce demanded, "Didn't you hear the sirens this morning?"

"Sirens," Emily's pulse raced. "Yeah, they woke me up! That's right. Was it a fire? I wondered if it were an ambulance or a fire engine."

"Fire," Joyce nodded knowingly, settling her books and bags around her feet. "Joshua Nyland. They arrested him right out of history class at the high school."

"The student grapevine is speedier than my modem."

Joyce pursed her lips. She didn't like being teased, which was what adults sometimes did, she'd explained once to Emily, when children knew more than they.

"Okay, okay, Peter P., give me the scoop. What fire, what motive? Joshua Nyland?" she shook her head incredulously, "That weedy kid with the Vespa?"

"They said it was a revenge arson," Joyce glanced coolly out the window. "Johnny Sandler's farm."

"The guy who grows organic Fuji apples and marijuana?"

"Yeah, Josh's been working in his apple cellar and he wanted a tip in addition to his regular salary. But Mr. Sandler said he was too young to smoke dope."

"Quel surprise," Emily shrugged. "Still, I didn't know the guy had scruples."

"What's scruples?"

"Well, I'm glad that as an eleven-year-old there's *something* you don't know. But I wish the mystery wasn't the definition of scruples."

"Kids grow up fast in the country," Joyce grinned.

Scruples. Emily was still fretting as she sat at her desk with a plate of pasta and Rafael's geometry lesson plan. She should have explained the word to Joyce, told her that she'd been writing all week about ethics, morals, scruples. Light was lasting longer in the evenings. Still, Emily switched on the green lamp. She didn't need the extra electric brightness, but it cheered her, like another brace of warmth. Across the Valley mountains were silhouettes now—shadowlands where you might imagine anything happening—even a sixteen-year-old boy setting fires out of spite. Had Josh committed the other arsons? Emily hoped not. She'd only met him twice—at the Valley talent show, where he sold raffle tickets to support a public skate board ramp. And then, well, at Basket's or Mammo's. The more she pictured him, the more she doubted he was an arsonist.

Yet if he weren't responsible, then everything became vague again. And scarier.

Her pasta was cold and Rafael's lesson page remained blank. Rafael loved geometry. Much more sensible, more useful than algebra, he'd told her. They were doing congruent angles tonight. Guilty about missing last week's session, she forced herself to concentrate. Too many foggy days had numbed her brain, she decided, rising to make a cup of strong coffee. The chilly dimmed landscape shut down your imagination.

Nothing cold or dreary about Valley Hall tonight. Someone had built a crackling blaze in the flagstone fireplace. Red and yellow and black crepe paper skipped along the rafters. At the far end, arranging chairs on stage, was Eva, a transformed Eva. An embroidered ribbon held dark hair away from her beaming face. The long curls fell down the back of a black turtleneck sweater. And she was wearing a full red skirt. Emily had never seen Eva in a skirt. Of course, this was a celebratory night. You were supposed to dress up out of respect, and here Emily was in her usual jeans and purple sweatshirt—what Ruth called her uniform. What a dope. She hoped she wasn't offending the graduates, who, she now recognized, were gathered around the coffee urn in white shirts and blouses and highly shined shoes.

Eva tested the microphone with her ringed fingers. Silver hoops jingled on her arms.

"Might as well say, while I'm testing the mike," her voice rose and her large eyes were excited, "that we'll be cutting tutoring sessions by fifteen minutes to make time for the presentation of the certificates. And a little fiesta!"

Applause rippled across the large room, then people settled in studious pairs at long tables.

Emily looked for Rafael. Ah, there he was, rushing through the door, a thick blue notebook under his right arm. Emily waved him to a back table, hoping to reduce her visibility to others in her mortifying outfit.

Rafael accepted her apology about missing the previous week. Proudly, he showed her the exercises he completed with Mrs. Nyland and her student Rosa. Mrs. Nyland wasn't here tonight, they both noted; clearly she had family obligations.

Because of the shortened lesson, they skipped their usual chat about Rafael's family. Lately, Emily had begun to tell Rafael more about her own life. He was fascinated by Salerno's CDs. He loved music of all kinds and had played with a marimba band in the Valley talent show.

Did he understand the nature of her relationship with Salerno? Well, how could he? She'd spoken of her lover as "a friend, a dear friend, who died recently." This was wrong. But she didn't want to threaten the tentative communication (she wouldn't call it a friendship yet) with Rafael. Perhaps, as an older woman, a teacher, he thought of her as asexual. Was her silence patronizing? And why did Rafael matter so much? His presence, acquaintance, filled a gap in her loneliness. Yes, that, and occasionally in this room she felt she was being useful.

Rafael got the point about congruent and incongruent angles right away.

People bustled toward the ceremony; an air of excitement filled the room. Rafael urged Emily to join him up front, where she could see everything. No thanks, she whispered, but you go ahead.

Ruth brought Emily a plastic glass of pinkish punch. She'd dropped by for the ceremony and Emily was delighted at how completely naturally she moved around.

"Don't sit way back here," Ruth scolded. "I've saved us places in the second row."

"Pretty skirt," Emily admired Ruth's long blue and red tartan.

"Oh, it's something I nabbed in the thrift shop the first winter I was here. I was so cold and poor; it was a great price. Now I love it, but I wish it didn't fit so snugly."

"Looks fine," observed Emily truthfully. "And so do you. You'll lose those five pounds—or whatever's bothering you—as soon as it gets warmer and we're walking the hills again. You could hardly exercise this winter bound up in a cast."

"I guess you're right."

"Friends. Amigos. Hermanas," Eva caught people's attention.

"Come on," Ruth grabbed Emily's arm.

"No, I look terrible," she protested. She nodded again at Ruth's festive skirt. "Everyone is all dressed up."

"You have to talk to her sometime." Ruth raised a dark eyebrow, restrained a grin.

Alarmed, she answered under her breath, "I don't know what you're talking about."

"Your attention, please." Eva was speaking directly to them.

"Sit in your reserved seat," she nudged Ruth's shoulder with her palm. "I'm fine back here."

Even at this distance, Emily could admire the elegant calligraphy Eva had used to inscribe each Certificate of Celebration.

One by one, they climbed to the stage, shy, happy, proud. Solemnly accepting their certificates, Orlando and Esperanza and Isabella and Ricardo and Manuel stepped down from the stage and hugged their families.

The big hall was cozy tonight, with the fire roaring, the happy applause, the relieved smiles. Emily felt nostalgic for her five frenetic, purposeful, youthful years in Mexico City, where she learned, among many other things, how to really speak the language, which had been her second major at Berkeley. Tonight's spring chill was forgotten in this room of good people. The aroma of cypress and bay logs rose above laughter and conversation. They were all urging one another out of hibernation.

Closing her eyes, Emily recognized a different warmth. Someone had spiked the punch. She sat back in her chair, dizzy.

"Glad you could make it."

Emily blinked dreamily, aware of a dazzling Eva leaning on the adjacent chair.

"Uh, yes." she stood clumsily, spilling her punch on the floor. She swooped down to wipe it up with a party napkin. Not quickly enough, because she found herself looking into Eva's brown eyes as the other woman blotted away the mess.

"How about some fresh air?" laughed Eva. "Nobody warned you about the tequila?"

"Guess not. I mean, I guess so—about the air. And maybe a little coffee?" All Emily wanted was to ingest caffeine, clear her head, and drive slowly back to her quiet, empty cabin.

Eva carried two cups of coffee outside. They stood under a live oak in the peaceful evening. Emily sipped sour, tepid coffee from the Styrofoam cup, listening to the crickets and frogs and the occasional swoosh of a car on the highway. She noticed Eva was wearing a light, lemony perfume. Above them, dark clouds almost hid a silver moon.

"I meant to call . . ."

"I'm sorry I didn't . . ."

"And thank you . . ."

"Had to tutor last week . . ."

". . . for sharing the ride down to the Bay Area."

"I hope Ruth explained."

They burst out laughing at their colliding apologies.

"Excellent evening," Emily said. "Those certificates took a lot of work. And the decorations!"

"Oh, it was nothing. I enjoyed it. Sneaked off work early—it was one of Hayden's preaching days."

"Well, next time, call me," Emily said. "I'd be glad to help."

"It's a date, next April," Eva teased, "during the second year of your sabbatical."

Emily shrugged, embarrassed, and drained the coffee cup.

"Have mine," Eva offered. "Once I saw Orlando near the punch, I steered clear."

"Thanks," Emily gulped the rest of Eva's bitter, cold coffee.

They talked for a while about damage at Johnny Sandler's farm. Eva knew some of the firefighters who came from the California Department of Forestry.

"I don't think it was Josh Nyland," Eva said, her face somber for the first time that night.

"You've got other suspicions?"

Eva lowered her voice. "You know the Smiths?"

"That new young couple who bought Silas's place up on Brinkley Road?"

"Yeah," Eva looked around. "There's something about them, about the way they spend money, buying whole cases from the vineyards, dinners several nights a week at the hotel, with slick out-of-towners."

"That Porsche is pretty nifty," Emily caught on. "And the way Bonnie Smith dresses. I mean, those aren't hippie jeans. More like the two hundred dollar designer variety."

"You're joking!" Eva giggled.

"No, I've seen ads, 'to compliment maturing figures. Sartorial body sculpting.' You think they grow weed on some massive scale up there?"

"I think they're watchers. Watching who in the Valley cuts into the market."

"You think they set the fire at the Sandlers'?"

"I think they might have told someone to set it."

"That's pretty frightening."

"The CDF found a metal timing device. No way little Josh had professional tools."

"That's a relief. I kind of like the kid, although he could clean up his act with that Vespa."

"And not a relief when you think about organized crime setting light to the Valley."

"You think they hit the vineyard last month?"

"Don't know." Eva grew distracted.

Emily's mind was on Sally. "Would the Smiths know about the other local plots? How small does their interest go?"

"If you're asking about Sally," Eva sighed, "I'd say it's worth being concerned."

Emily found herself walking to the car.

Cocking her head, she could hear those early morning sirens again. She only wanted to get home, make sure the cabin was okay, check on Salerno's tree, listen to Phoenix purr. She wasn't cold or tired anymore and was hardly conscious of Eva walking beside her until the other woman draped a country arm across her shoulders.

"But really," Eva said seriously, "thanks for sharing the ride last week. I know I was quiet—maybe rudely so—on the way back. I was obsessing about what I said to the board about Hayden and what I was going to write to my father about Jorge."

"How *is* your brother?"

"Let's save him for another time. Maybe during that hike out Lake Powell way that we've been talking about?"

"I'd like that." As Emily climbed into the car, she caught the lemony perfume again.

"Hey," she rolled down the window, "I've been meaning to say—that's a gorgeous skirt." Before she thought better of it, she added, "You looked beautiful tonight, radiant."

Eva smiled. "Reflected glory. Those people studied so hard and they're so happy."

Emily waved. "See you soon."

"Yes, soon!" Eva called.

Slowly she followed the winding road back to the ranch, still feeling slightly high, although she expected the coffee and the cold air had sobered her enough. During midweek in the spring, the highway was pretty clear. No adolescents in their souped-up pickups. It would be a while before the Nyland boy was zipping his Vespa around these curves. Even if he didn't set the fire, Mrs. Katrina Nyland, daughter of a Norwegian Lutheran preacher, wouldn't be happy about Josh trying to score pot.

As she passed Rupert's apple stand, clapboarded shut for the evening, she peered up Old Mineshaft Road and saw a light in what she thought was the Nyland house. Hard to identify people's spreads during the day as the hills folded on themselves and the forests—those areas that hadn't been clear-cut—sheltered their homesteads. Hundreds of lives were tucked within this ancient coastal range. Eva lived up there, not far from the Nylands. Hundreds of lives past and present that she'd never know. Had the Indians found this land secretive, or did they know how to see across and through it? Ever since discovering the rattle, she felt the quiet company of people who'd lived here before.

Lived here before. She paused at the implication that she truly lived here now. Well, yes, even if it was just a year until her consulting projects and Salerno's music contracts and the dispensation of the rattle were settled. For a short time, she did live here.

As Emily drove up the first hill of their property, past the buckeye that had wrapped itself around a laurel, past the cluster of dignified stone pines, she wondered if their highway gate was simply a talisman. Although it barred strange vehicles, anyone could walk around the gate.

"It's mainly to discourage hunters," Lindsey had explained once. "Those drunken guys who zoom onto any property that isn't marked in search of rightful prey. Don't worry, they wouldn't harm you, not intentionally. They just want antlers. You really think someone's going to attack you? Here? In the country?"

Emily had shrugged and she shrugged again now, morning sirens echoing in her mind. Phoenix barked eagerly as she approached the cabin. Some guard dog. Emily's car was the only one she barked at. Emily did enjoy the welcome. Long ago she learned she was meant to protect Phoenix, not vice versa.

As Phoenix jumped all over her, she gentled her dog to the grass. Then Emily glanced toward the Douglas fir, took a long breath, and bid good night to Salerno.

19

Through the front window, Emily waved briskly to Ruth, then gathered the last of Salerno's messy document files.

Ruth remained in her car with a determined expression; she'd told Emily last night they would definitely make this appointment. Emily had explained she'd spaced out on the contract negotiations two weeks before. They'd agreed to leave at nine sharp in case spring rains caused road delays.

Emily stared at her resolute friend and held up two fingers, certain she could pull everything together in a couple of minutes. She'd finish her coffee in the car.

Phoenix yelped, jumping against her knees. "Okay, girl, Ruth says you're welcome. Maybe she'll take you walking while I deal with Mr. Music Man. Or maybe I'll take you walking while she's reading contracts."

Still negotiating, dog and woman raced down the cabin steps.

Ruth shook her head and pointed to her watch.

"Sorry, Ruthie," she pecked her friend's cheek. "I got a little distracted."

Ruth laughed, settled Phoenix in back and turned to Emily, "I'm supposed to be the distracted artist."

As the old truck crunched along the muddy red road, Emily was struck by the sight of new buds on the berry vines. Those tall, daisy-like flowers shooting up from the grass. Schools of violety buttercups. The purpling tips of sagebrush. "Not sure I'm ready for all this spring," Emily whispered.

Ruth drove on with the competent calm of someone who had been awake for hours and quite aware of spring for days if not a week.

"Distracted artist! That's a myth," Emily chattered to deflect her nervousness about the contracts. "Artists have to be superorganized to earn a living, plan time like you do—four days a week at the store, three days for painting and photography—to make art, to exhibit, perform it."

As Ruth pulled on the freeway, she checked her watch again.

"But there's a difference between being competent and being obsessive," Emily teased. "We'll make it to town by ten easily."

"Guess you're right."

"And speaking of savvy artists, what's happening with the book? Weren't you supposed to hear this week?"

Ruth shrugged. "I was going to tell you today. That Santa Rosa publisher . . ." She paused, staring openmouthed at land being plowed next to Dryman's ranch.

"Look!"

Emily glanced over.

"Another damn vineyard."

Emily examined the dark, torn earth and the yellow farm machines gathered by the fence like so many techno dinosaurs.

"Bloody vintners are ruining the Valley," spat Ruth.

Ruth and Virginia complained about this endlessly. Emily sympathized from an ecological standpoint: vineyards drained water from creeks and rivers, fatigued the land, and added pesticides to the aquifers. Still, she didn't believe in putting quotas on types of agriculture.

Ruth's eyes returned to the road.

They passed the shack where Rafael lived and Emily thought about how the vineyards supported his family.

"What about Lindsey, the budding enologist?" she asked Ruth. "You don't object to her dreams of opening a vineyard after her training."

"Well, Linz is budding all over. I'm hoping motherhood will sidetrack plans for her own label. Although I agree with her that Chung's Chardonnay has a certain ring."

"How would she feed herself and the baby? On Marianne's not-so-lavish Ph.D. fellowship?"

She'd always enjoyed arguing with Ruth. So many women evaded argument, as if it were impolite or hurtful rather than interesting. Once when she and Salerno were having a difficult patch, Emily had romantic fantasies about Ruth. Nothing came of it; probably they were too much alike.

"Okay. Okay. I admit what Lindsey's doing is different," Ruth said. "She's not going to exploit her workers. It's a small, specialized organic business. Her dream. I'll drink to that—and from it—if she succeeds."

"Speaking of dreams, what happened with the Santa Rosa press?"

"Well, yes, it's the most amazing news," Ruth flushed. "They're doing a series, very small print runs, of regional photography. It's connected with some grant—and an exhibition. So next September we can all drive down to the exhibition. I'll meet the other five artists. And they'll launch the books together."

"That's terrific!" Emily leaned over and kissed her friend's cheek.

An excited Phoenix, paws on the back of their seat, looked keenly from one woman to the other.

"Yes, yes, you, too, Nixie," Ruth patted the dog, "you can drive down with us and if they don't let you in the gallery, Joycie will be thrilled to escape the chattering adults, walking you and Bobbie around town."

Emily wanted to concentrate on her friend's good fortune. This was a real break. Instead, she stared at the road shaded by giant redwoods. By August she'd be in Chicago. Why did everyone keep forgetting the sabbatical ended in July? Ruth's chat with Phoenix reminded her that she should leave the little dog in the Valley. Phoenix would be happier here. Blinking back tears, she grasped for a change of subject. "How's Sally?"

Ruth sighed at the upcoming curve. "Just about here that Sally got in that wreck."

"God, she was lucky." Emily recalled that eerily lit cross she saw on the highway when she was driving home from the rancheria months before. "Lucky to be walking around. Lucky the other guy wasn't hurt. Lucky she wasn't driving the UPS truck."

"She doesn't do dope on UPS time," Ruth said protectively.

"Smart."

"She didn't look too smart—or lucky—all smashed up in that hospital bed."

Emily fell silent. She should have visited Sally in the hospital, but she was so angry with her—what was it?—stupidity, carelessness, self-destructiveness? Sally was a professional driver. She knew enough not to toke up before taking this paved labyrinth. But habitually smoking too much dope was probably like being alcoholic. Emily wished she could let herself go, get high enough that she didn't care, didn't remember. But marijuana made her cough. Too much wine made her throw up. She had inherited the infuriating sobriety monitor, no doubt, from ever-upright Dad. Odd to think that the two largest crops in this Eden were addictive substances.

Aware of her long silence, Emily said, "But she's doing fine, now, right? Didn't she go back to work last week?"

"Physically fine," Ruth mumbled.

"What else is going on?"

"Virginia's pretty upset."

"I bet." When she'd brought Sally a bouquet at the cabin, Emily remembered, Virginia had sat mute in the corner.

"It's not just the accident," Ruth explained. "Apparently Sally comes home, eats dinner, gets high every night now. Virginia says they never talk."

"That's tough."

"I said, give it time: maybe she's in shock. God, she was so lucky she knew the cop and he didn't do a drug test after the accident."

They shared the shady road with few cars this morning. Emily imagined a time when redwood forests extended for miles. Some of these first growth trees were a thousand years old.

"On a lighter note, I hear you had dinner with Eva at the Cantina last night?"

Emily laughed. "Who are you? Ms. Communications Central?"

"Oh," Ruth smiled, "Eva called about the school. She's found someone new to do child care. And she happened to mention . . ."

"Did she say what I ordered?" Emily recoiled in mock horror.

"Chicken enchiladas, rice, and beans. I asked, of course. Half a flan for dessert."

"You're incorrigible."

"So how'd it go?"

"Eva's a lot of fun. She's been friendlier since I stopped setting her up with Michael!"

"Duh."

Emily laughed. "Poor Michael."

"He'll recover."

"But god," Emily shook her head, "Eva has big grief with this mad zealot at work."

"Yeah, and the board didn't take her complaints very seriously."

"It's all so hard to prove. He makes these comments when they're alone. And the work assignments she contested, the board decided they were arbitrary, not punitive."

"Still, she *is* enjoying having her brother up?"

"Yeah, Sweet guy, Jorge, he met us for dessert. Hip hop L.A. boy. I'm not sure how he's going to fare in the Valley."

"Oh, we can fix him up. Ask Rafael if he knows any cute Latino guys."

"Rafael? Archangel Rafael, who reads the epistles at Mass?"

They both grinned.

This section of the road was Emily's favorite, just edging from the forest, the highway opening to a view of the Navarro River as it widened to meet the Pacific. She could almost smell the salt air. She'd argued with Salerno that they should build their cabin on a golden cliff between here and Mendocino. They both loved the ocean. How divine to have a window on the Pacific, to watch the sun set directly into the water each night.

Nice dream, chickie, Salerno teased, *"but inland is all we can afford."*

Emily countered, "We can't really afford that."

"Sure we can, sharing land with friends on a good, long mortgage?"

"Isn't that the ultimate contradiction in terms—a good *mortgage?"*

"We'll pay it off, just you wait. And then, when we're old and rich, when I'm writing music for major movies, we'll build a second home here. You'll get to pick your golden cliff."

"You're quiet," Ruth squeezed Emily's hand. "You okay?"

Surprised by grief, she said, "Fine." One more word would release the flood. This was the strangeness of loss, the way it hit you at odd moments—when you were washing dishes, listening to the news, driving through a beautiful world with an old friend.

She identified Theodore Curtis as soon as they entered the warm cinnamon bakery. A young man wearing a turquoise turtleneck, black bolo tie, and jeans was seated at a large corner table, sipping a triple latte and studying spreadsheets.

Emily and Ruth exchanged grins, then approached him.

Theodore stood and extended his hand to stiff Emily.

Ruth was more relaxed.

As he sat, he bumped the table with his astonishingly long legs and they all watched the beige foam from his coffee glass slop over the papers.

Ruth raced to the counter for a wad of napkins and quickly rescued the documents.

"Thanks, thanks?" he said in that rapid youthspeak; Emily was disappointed to recognize he was in his mid-twenties at most. This was going to be a waste of time.

She raised her eyebrows at Ruth. Ruth ignored her and smiled at the young man.

"Afraid I'm not making much of a professional impression," Theodore ran his long tapered fingers through curly, shoulder-length black hair.

Oddly, Emily saw a resemblance to the fresh-faced Salerno of fifteen years earlier. But he did have a moustache. She told herself not to get carried away.

"What can I get you?" he offered. "Au lait, Latte, Mocha? And how about a muffin? Their low-fat poppy seed muffins are to die for."

Emily couldn't stop grinning. She didn't know why—was it the arch California lingo? The hippie entrepreneur outfit? The grownup-before-his-time hospitality? The clumsy, anxious introduction? Salerno would love this guy, would invite him home to dinner. He returned with two cappuccinos and three muffins.

Emily stared, trying to remember what had frightened her about their transaction. Salerno would trust him. Theodore Curtis didn't know it, but they had already signed the contract in his translucent blue plastic briefcase.

Over muffins and coffee, he answered all Emily's questions. Then Ruth quizzed him about the size of his company and the marketability of his other artists. He planned to send Salerno's CDs to jazz stations around the country, community radio stations, music stores, women's bookstores, feminist conferences.

Emily watched three gold studs in his left ear glint in the sun. Her resistance had been silly, selfish. The man understood Salerno's audience. Had done copious research, showed clever initiative. (And patience—driving up here twice from the Bay Area. He didn't complain about her missing the first meeting. Could he imagine the terror that trapped her in the cabin two weeks before—fear that by signing away Salerno's music rights, she was making her lover more dead? When he phoned the second time, he simply asked if she'd like to make another appointment.)

Ruth finished her poppy seed muffin and half of Emily's while scrutinizing spreadsheets and contracts.

"Big Horn Records," mused Emily. Yes, Salerno would love the name.

"This all looks fair, clear, appropriate for each side," Ruth pronounced.

Emily watched with admiration, taken aback once again that even though Ruth was three years younger, she had always seemed like an older sister. Did her competence come from motherhood, or from being a New Yorker? Ruth would laugh at both speculations. They might even embarrass her, because she had a surprising reserved side. Emily sat back, watching her friend dickering with the young cultural impresario.

"But I still want Emily to run the contract by Penelope, a lawyer we know in town."

"Absolutely," Theodore nodded his whole body. "You need to be perfectly comfortable. This is like a marriage; we're making a serious commitment."

Emily took a long drink of coffee.

Theodore sighed. "I'm sorry, my partner, Mary, says I get carried away," his voice lifted, "that I put people off with my enthusiastic language?"

Emily couldn't tell if this was a question or more interrogative youthspeak.

Cautiously, she said, "Theodore, it's charming. No, more than that, it's inspiring. Not enough people truly take their work seriously." She could feel Ruth waiting for irony. She made it clear there was none. "You're a wonderful example."

Perhaps she had become too effusive herself because he now launched into an elaborate description of the release party they could have at a shop on Main Street during the Coastal Jazz Festival. They'd invite the media, disk jockeys.

Ruth leaned forward, "Oh, Joyce will love it. Yes, it's a perfect venue. We can take out an ad in the festival program."

"But the Jazz Festival is in August," Emily protested.

They didn't seem to hear.

In August she'd be riding the El to work, watching weekend waves on Lake Michigan.

Theodore blinked at his watch and exclaimed, "Oh, no, I have to get back to the city for another meeting."

"Funny guy," Emily said as she and Ruth walked toward the headlands. "If he's Tomorrowland's CEO, the human race is making progress."

Ruth smirked at her friend's unexpected endorsement.

They'd decided to hike first because while errands could wait, the fickle coastal sun might not. In a buoyant mood, Emily struck out toward a colorful patch of ice plant. She still considered ice plant, with its succulent tubers and overbrilliant colors, an intergalactic species.

Ruth stopped to gaze at giant waves spitting against the huge caves to the south. "Look at that," she said meditatively. "The powerful grey swell rising in an endlessly grey ocean, racing in a frenzy toward shore, as if seeking harbor. Instead of resting in the caves, the waves rush out again, succeeding only in chipping away the coast to which they've been so magnetically drawn. If only I could capture that raw drama in a photograph."

"Reminds me of some relationships," whispered Emily.

"You mean how Sally seems to be destroying Virginia?"

"Yeah, and herself."

"I wish I could do something," Ruth sighed.

"You take care of quite enough people as it is."

"Maybe that's why I don't have a lover?" Ruth asked provocatively, then walked ahead.

"What?" Emily caught up with her.

"I don't know. I was just feeling sorry for myself. And I wonder if I put people off by seeming competent."

"More likely, the right person hasn't appeared." Emily knew this wasn't enough. She often wondered why Ruth remained single. Wondered if that was what she wanted.

Emily waited for a response, but clearly Ruth didn't want to pursue the topic.

They ambled silently among the purple, blue, orange, red, yellow, and lavender flowers springing up in the high grasses along the sheer rock face.

They saw him at the same time on the path ahead: a thick white man with masses of white hair and a loud white voice.

"Hayden," Emily whispered.

Behind him on the small platform four young men played guitars. Each was meticulously groomed: short hair, clean shaven, wearing matching pale blue sweaters and ironed cotton Dockers.

"Today I'm introducing the Good News," Hayden's microphone voice reached out to the people shopping on the far side of Main Street. Children munching fudge, women carrying elaborate shopping bags from gourmet clothing shops, men with giant cameras hanging down to their bellies. No one looked at him. People hiking along the trail averted their eyes.

The young disciples strummed and sang, "I put my hand in the hand of the man who built the ocean."

Emily felt sorry for them and moved along.

Alas, Ruth appeared eager to engage Hayden. Maybe their earlier success with generational barriers had gone to her head.

Ruth leaned comfortably against a wooden fence.

Hayden approached her with a handful of leaflets.

Emily noticed his hands were red and sore.

"Welcome, sister, let me share the Word. Are you receptive to the Good News?"

Emily tugged Ruth's green sweater, avoiding eye contact with the older man.

"I'm always receptive to truth," Ruth said firmly.

Emily felt sorry for Hayden. His eyes were wild, unnerving.

"May the truth of the Lord be with you," Hayden placed his hand on her head.

Ruth stepped back. "So your team supports truth and dialogue."

The boys had segued into "Amazing Grace."

Emily tried to catch Ruth's eye.

By this time, a small crowd was gathering—a honeymoon-looking couple holding hands, a mother with a little girl, three teenaged boys and two old men.

"Good," Ruth sighed heavily. "I was confusing you with that group supporting censorship."

"Censorship?" Hayden's precise voice grew quieter; his eyes narrowed. "No, no, the Lord made us to talk with one another."

"I mean with those people harassing teachers at Fairburn High for discussing evolution. I can't remember the name of their organization."

"The Crusade for California," said the young mother helpfully, "this is them, all right. See their signs?"

"Oh," Ruth nodded neutrally, waiting for Hayden's response.

"God gave us the truth about Creation in Genesis. No need to be confusing children with monkey stories."

"What's wrong with monkeys?"

The honeymooners giggled.

"They have no souls," Hayden pronounced. "Humans have souls. We can be saved."

"Saved from what?" demanded Ruth.

Emily pulled her sleeve again. What a waste. Eva would be so upset. But Ruth was relishing this exercise of free speech.

Hayden studied Ruth's face, angry certitude in his eyes.

"From the blistering flames of eternal fire," he summoned an authoritative voice.

The little girl started to cry and her mother ushered her toward the headlands. She tapped Ruth's shoulder lightly, "Good luck."

"Our Lord saves us all," he proclaimed loudly, as if recalling an old sermon.

"The lord?"

"Our Lord Jesus Christ." His face reddened as he struggled for control.

Emily winced as he fell into the trap. There was something sad about the guy, pitiful.

"But what if you have a different god?" Ruth's voice rose in agitation. "Can you still be saved by Krishna? Allah? Yahweh? Higher Power?"

He squinted. "There's a perfect organization for people like you. 'Jews for Jesus.' " He whispered to her now, "They're some of the happiest people I know."

Ruth shook her head. "I bet they're downright delirious."

One of the old men spoke hoarsely, "This lady is right about censorship. You bar Darwin from schools; Jews and Buddhists from Heaven. Sounds pretty mean spirited for a religion based on love."

Emily took Ruth's left wrist and pointed to the time.

Ruth raised a stubborn eyebrow.

Emily raised two eyebrows and Ruth, who looked convinced that Hayden's new interlocutor could handle the debate, followed her old friend to Penelope's law office.

It was three by the time their truck reached the redwood grove.

Ruth was still fuming. "What arrogance, coldness, inconsistency. Amazing Eva hasn't murdered him."

"Thanks for taking one of your art days to accompany me to Mr. Big Horn and the lawyer."

"It's nothing." Ruth was still preoccupied.

"How's your new project?" Emily tried again, "The ranch animals, day and night?"

"Yup." Nervous, she switched on the radio.

A holistic health program they both hated. Ruth clicked it off.

Emily tried once more to banish Hayden from the car. "What shots do you have?"

"Last count, let's see: ruby-throated hummers, geckos, rabbits, skunk, frogs, blue heron, pileated woodpeckers, turkeys, turkey vultures, gophers, gopher snakes . . ."

"Did you get a rattler?"

"Yes," Ruth said cryptically.

"Good. Keep it a secret. I don't want to know where you killed it."

"You know I wouldn't kill it."

"Yes," Emily laughed. "And I'm sure you photographed blackbirds, kites, owls, hawk, deer, coyotes."

Ruth nodded, her mood improving.

"It's amazing all these critters live on the land with us."

"That's not all—yellow jackets, bumblers, dragonflies, moths, feral pigs."

"The pigs?" Emily held her breath, "you saw them? How close did you get?"

"They're never out much during the day," Ruth's voice trailed off evasively.

"So where?"

"A couple of weeks ago—when Joyce went to that Girl Scout night at Lake Mendocino—I got out my camping gear and . . ."

"You didn't," Emily anticipated the details. "That's too dangerous."

"Not really. I camped down the ravine. "Sure enough, about two A.M., I heard them snortling along."

"Ruth!"

"They didn't notice me. I used very slow film under a full moon," she grinned broadly. "Got some fine shots."

"Yeah, but you might have wound up as a postprandial treat for Mr. and Mrs. Oink."

"Not really. They would have just roughed me up."

Emily exhaled in relief, exasperation.

"Besides, I had Lindsey's shotgun."

"Pardon me?" Emily didn't know what upset her most—Ruth being alone in the ravine; the idea that Lindsey was told and she wasn't; the knowledge that Lindsey owned a gun; the realization that both she and Ruth knew how to shoot.

"Where did you learn about guns?"

"When I moved to California, I took lessons. I thought city slickers should be prepared for the Wild West."

"Come again?"

Ruth shrugged. "Self-defense."

"Self-defense on solo midnight forays into the jungle?"

Ruth nodded, "Yeah, with those giants pigs I did get a little scared."

"Good!"

They drove silently under the dark redwood canopy for several miles until Ruth asked, "What did you decide to do about the Pomo rattle?"

Emily was relieved that she had told the other women about her discovery. She expected judgment, possessiveness, anxiety, but each had simply expressed curiosity. She inhaled. "Funny you should mention it. Judson Sands called last night. They're having a big powwow next month and he wants to borrow the rattle."

"It's quite modest looking," Ruth shrugged, "for something that means so much to so many different people."

"Well, the California archeologists want to make sure the Smithsonian doesn't get it."

"You've heard from the Smithsonian?"

"Yes, and the Brooklyn Museum."

"They'd all pay pretty decently, I guess."

"It's dizzying. I don't want money. The academic in me wants it in a sound institution."

"The rancheria, are *they* offering you anything?"

"A clear conscience," Emily laughed.

"You could always keep it," tried Ruth. "You found it. On your land."

"That's what Judson said."

"And . . ."

"I told him I can't keep something that's not mine. He nodded and said, 'Then give it to us.'"

They went quiet again until they approached the boarded-up Mistral store.

"Judson said if the state archeologist accepts it, he'll insist on digging more around the tree. Of course I shuddered, told him I didn't want anyone disturbing Salerno's ashes. You know what he said?"

Ruth shook her head, frowning.

"He said, 'Now you know how we feel.'"

"He has a point."

"A good point."

"So?"

"Why did I suddenly get to be caretaker?" Emily blurted anxiously. "Of the cabin, Phoenix, Salerno's musical legacy, the Pomo rattle. Why me?"

Ruth grinned. "Maybe it's because you do *take care*. You're attentive, thoughtful, more than most people."

Embarrassed, Emily stared at her lap.

"Look what you did for Joyce and me last winter. Caretaking is in your nature."

No, no, she wanted to scream. I'm a quiet loner and not very competent at that.

Suddenly they were enveloped by a hugely amplified whining. Ruth wrenched the car to the shoulder and a large, loud CFD truck shrieked by. They both stared after the fierce vehicle.

Emily spotted a plume. "There—on the far left. It's not Beulah?"

Ruth peered. 'No, definitely further than our ranch. Brinkley Road, I'm sure."

Emily noticed Ruth's hands shaking.

"Sorry, fire does this to me sometimes. I was raised on Dad's tales of conflagration. Some Holocaust survivors have to keep telling their stories in order to survive. They think the stories protect their children."

Emily rubbed Ruth's neck. "Maybe some vintner brush burning got out of control?"

"I wish," Ruth rolled her eyes knowingly.

"What do you mean?" Emily heard, then tried to resist, her own panic. "How do you know it's not an accident?"

"It's a 'No Burn Day'—didn't you hear the radio announcement this morning? Vineyards don't risk their business licenses on something trivial like that."

"Ruthie, you never think any of the Valley fires are accidental."

"Not lately," she said coldly. "I agree with Eva. They're done by someone or ones who know about arson. They found gasoline sprayed all over the last site."

Emily barely heard her friend over the whir of firecopters and another sirened truck, then a high-speed police sedan. She thought back to the rapt faces of the children listening to Baxter talk about Coyote stealing fire from the women's hearth. Then about the Spider and Snake Indians taking flames from the Moon Indians. She loved the image of that gossamer balloon. But she also remembered how the Snakes murdered the Spiders to forestall retribution from the Moon Indians.

That night on the deck, she was startled by the challenging eyes of a large owl perched on a snag of the live oak. Momentarily, they exchanged stares. Emily resolved not to be scared. *Who. Who.* She felt grateful Phoenix was asleep on the couch for this territorial standoff. She wanted to nod in respect, to retreat inside, to acknowledge this was the bird's land. But was it? Emily had no intention of leaving until summer. So they watched over the evening together.

Oddly, she thought back to those butterfly trays her father collected in what he called the "Far East." The exquisite rows of iridescent, wildly colored wings. As a small child she had loved the trays, coveted them more than any grownup thing in the house—more than the silver bowls from Spain or the Czechoslovakian cut glass vases. Then, at thirteen, she noticed that the corners of some wings—even those of Matilda, the brilliant blue butterfly with the yellow dots—had begun to disintegrate in their airless mausoleum. She felt humiliated for the butterflies, ashamed of her father's acquisitiveness. So she hid the butterflies at the back of the serving table. By this time family favor had turned to the bright plastic trays her parents brought from Hawaii.

The owl leaned her great head slightly forward.

Emily did likewise.

Then she was shocked by a powerful lifting and loud flapping as the bird soared over the moonlit grasses, past Salerno's tree. Emily watched until the owl was out of sight. She felt lonelier than she had in months.

20

The baseball diamond in Ukiah took Emily back forty years—watching Michael slug homers for Widener's Wheelers, named by local Chevrolet dealer Mr. Widener, whose son was the shortstop on Michael's Little League team. She enjoyed a certain cachet as the star batter's sister. Jimmy Widener had a crush on her, which felt creepy because she didn't feel that way about him. Still, she loved studying Michael from the stands as he warmed up his swings, rolled his neck, and waited for the ball he would wham over the park fence. Emily had never wanted to play, but she had fun watching, cheering, jeering, as she was doing tonight.

Many years between then and now, and several immediate differences: Michael was sitting next to her. Eva stood on the mound.

"Women's softball," Michael had mused over the phone. "Don't think I've ever seen a game. Mind if I join you?"

Michael invited himself along often now that he was spending more time at his new weekend place in the valley. "Weekend palace," according to Virginia, who had blanched when she heard he had bought the old Bickerts parcel. "Great taste." Yes, that was something Michael always possessed: an eye for material quality and the wherewithal to acquire it. Emily felt alternately delighted and disturbed by his bed and breakfast project. She knew that country life would force him to slow down. Still, she wondered how much he would enjoy his respite once she returned to Chicago. Most of his local friends were lesbians from the ranch. Dykes and Eva's flaming gay brother Jorge. Well, maybe he'd be fine. Once he had recovered from his profound disappointment about Eva, he said wistfully. "Okay, there have to be *some* straight women in the valley. Maybe I'll meet a young widow." Emily was doubtful. She knew only four widows, all over eighty.

As they set off for the game, Emily said warily, "Of course you're welcome to come with us, but I'm not sure you should be traveling at this stage."

Lindsey, now eight months pregnant, was wedged in the front passenger seat. "Who are you, American Airlines? Damned if I'm going to be housebound in this June heat. Besides, Ukiah has a good hospital; doesn't that reassure you?"

Emily conceded that she was merely the driver.

Michael and Jorge sat in the back seat talking computer games.

At the game they spread themselves across the rickety bleachers. She and Lindsey sat on the second tier. Jorge and Michael and Joyce perched on the top end, cheering loudly for the Fallen Angels.

The Fallen Angels had been recruited from all over the valley—young, middle aged, fat, thin, lesbian, straight, coordinated, not. Teachers and waitresses and farmers. They had a celebratory dinner after each game even though they were 0–4 for the season.

Tonight the Willits Bullets seemed to have uniformly enormous hips and great power swings. At the bottom of the fifth inning, Virginia hit a high ball to left field. As the Bullet ran for it, Emily heard herself shouting, "Drop it, drop it." Appalled by her aggressiveness, she stopped. Lindsey laughed and laughed, her large belly shaking.

"Hey, good, Em," Michael called down, "Just like Dad at a Giants game."

The three well-behaved fans on the Willits bleacher ignored her and clapped warmly as their outfielder performed a balletic catch.

Virginia, who had already made it to second, threw up her hands good-naturedly and sashayed back to the dugout. Virginia's homer would have made the score 1–5, but no one expected to defeat the Bullets tonight.

"Fifth inning stretch," said Lindsey as she stood, rubbing the small of her back.

"Time for neck and shoulder massage," declared Jorge, scuttling down the bleachers.

As he ministered from the seat behind her, Lindsey moaned, "Ah, divine!"

Emily loved the way pregnancy had softened Lindsey's face. She was always a pretty woman; now she looked quite beautiful.

They almost missed the first hit of the sixth inning.

In center field, Ruth valiantly attempted to catch the Bullet ball, but missed. Everyone knew Ruth was assigned the outfield because they usually expected the least action there. Emily felt vaguely reassured to discover one area in which Ruth didn't naturally excel.

"So Sally has moved out?" Jorge asked Lindsey.

"Yeah," Lindsey nodded. "On Thursday. Jorge, this massage is *terrific*. Maybe a little more to the left? That's it, and a skooch harder. Ahhh, yes. I never knew pregnancy could create more kinks; I had enough before!"

"The baby will make you a cream puff," grinned Jorge. "I've seen it happen with my sister, Maria, 'the witch from Manzanita Street,' before little Pepe and now she's . . .'"

"You think I'm witchy?" Lindsey sniffed humorously so as not to interrupt the massage. "Language can be mortally wounding."

"Impossible," he declared, "that's the whole deal about being a supernatural witch. And by the way, you're not really a witch." He leaned closer, whispering, "But supernatural, that's another story, a goddess, perhaps."

"Jorge, you're a first-class flirt," laughed Lindsey. "Shameless. It's hard to believe you're related to that serious, considerate sister of yours."

"Ah, Evita! She has her moments."

Emily leaned into the conversation.

A loud "Shhh" from the top of the bleachers. Joyce's voice, "Mom's at bat. Everyone pay attention. Go, Mom. Go, *Mom!*"

Ruth turned to smile at her fan and the first strike whizzed by.

Despite determined attention, she missed the next two balls. The inning closed.

"Next time!" Joyce called. "Next time, Mom!"

Emily returned to the village gossips.

"So how's Virginia feeling?" asked Jorge. "What is it anyway, separation or divorce?"

Lindsey shrugged. "Right there . . . must be a pressure point nearby, ah, yes, mmm. Separation for now. Sally left the furniture. Ginny feels relieved . . . and scared."

"It's hard to lose someone after all that time," Emily sighed. Sally and Virginia had been together when she met Salerno. "Right decision or wrong, she's bound to be sad."

They both nodded respectfully.

"And the tough thing is, Virginia loves Sally," Emily continued. "She's just gone over the top with this dope. Virginia never got any clear time with her."

"I had a friend like that in L.A.," Jorge said.

Emily loved the way he and Eva said "L.A.," as if *L* were an article and *A* a noun. *L AAA,* she tried silently.

"He was doing crack. Had a mind before that, but once he got into that stuff, man, his brain evacuated to another planet."

Emily glanced at Eva, concentrating on her first pitch of the eighth inning.

"Well, Ginny needs a rest," declared Lindsey. "It's been a hellish year with those Mafia thugs threatening Sally, then Sally zoning out on the highway. And on top of that, Ginny's Christian Crusaders are still escalating their attack. In the summer."

Emily nodded. "Virginia told me this was the perfect day: nothing to worry about except the blackberry crumble she made this afternoon. She said she could actually smell the crumble baking—now that she's aired out the house from Sally's smoke. The crumble turned out perfectly. And if the game didn't, she'd have a good time anyway."

"Funny," Lindsey closed her eyes, "How you discover friends are strong."

"Like you?" Emily ventured. She never knew when she was intruding with Lindsey. They were both such formal people, maintaining different invisible barriers.

"Me?"

"How about this?" she gently patted Lindsey's belly, then drew away shyly.

Lindsey took Emily's palm and replaced it firmly on her ballooning stomach.

Emily was shocked by the baby's kick. Instinctively, she pulled back again.

They both giggled.

"Go Eva," Jorge shouted. "Brava hermana. Atta girl." Proudly, he watched Eva strike out the first batter.

Emily and Lindsey were drawn into the game. If the Fallen Angels had any hope for salvation, it was through Eva, who learned hardball on the streets of *L AAAA.* She was always arguing Dodgers versus Giants with Michael and Marianne and anyone else who grew up in Northern California. Emily herself had lost interest in baseball after

Little League. She was bored by the slowness. Basketball she could understand: the beauty of those lithe, nimble, speeding bodies. One of the delights of Chicago was being associated with Michael Jordon, even twenty-five times removed.

Eva had listened to her complaints about the pokiness of baseball, when was it? Over dinner at the taqueria, during their hike along the Navarro River . . . she must have seen Eva three or four times this month. Her friend just laughed. Laughed and laughed because, she said, slowness was the best part of the game. It allowed you to reflect, to study other people's strategies, to intuit their moves. On the mound, you weren't brain-dead. You were using a special kind of intelligence.

Emily suggested that maybe it was this kind of patience that had drawn Eva to environmental work. In the forest, you had to be alert for different players, possibilities.

Eva laughed again, not unkindly.

Emily decided to leave well-enough—or worse enough—alone.

"Top of the ninth." A reminder from a man in the Willits bleachers.

The next batter, their best, looked all the more threatening in the oversized black Willits Bullets jersey.

Eva, by contrast, appeared almost elegant in her Fallen Angels T-shirt—their uniform designed by Ruth, of course—a long, light green cotton shirt painted with blue, yellow, lavender, and pink wings. Yet there was a toughness to her, the way her thick black ponytail slipped through the back flap of her red cap.

Eva had yanked down the visor to keep sun out of her large, dark eyes, also to keep her opponent from analyzing her calculating gaze.

The agitated batter readjusted her grip and stomped her feet. A man in the Bullets bleacher was heckling Eva. "What's the matter, pitch, lost your nerve?"

She did seem to be taking a long time, thought Emily.

"I wish that guy would shut up," Lindsey growled, loud enough for him to hear.

Jorge looked confident about Eva's concentration. And when she was ready, she delivered a swingless strike, precisely midzone. Two more and the Bullet tossed her hat in the dust, shaking her head all the way to their dugout.

Eva stared down at the dry blown grass and punched her mitt twice.

Out there on the mound, she looked stronger than the woman Emily had come to know this year. Although she was short, those legs were all muscle and her slim brown arms had definition to rival those of the kids who worked out at the Michigan Avenue Gym. The more she learned or observed or guessed about Eva, the less she understood.

Eva struck out the next batter. And the next.

Now it was up to her teammates. Bottom of the ninth. How could they turn around a 1-5 score in half an inning?

Virginia started them off with great hope: a three-base hit. Next came Ruth, who managed to knock a ball past the shortstop, who was so surprised by Ruth's first hit of the season, that she dropped it. Ruth made it to first and Virginia slid home.

"Go, Angels! Go, Angels," they all called. Joyce and Michael moved down to the bottom row to solidify the cheering section.

The Fallen Angels were, as always, graceful losers. Two to five was hardly their most humiliating score. And humiliation wasn't on the palette of the Inland County Women's Softball League. At game's end, the teams filed past one another, each woman from the Angels slapping a high five to each member of the Bullets. Emily smiled at this closing ritual, wondering what the black kids in her Chicago neighborhood would think about these Californian countrywomen using their salute.

21

The team gathered at Lolo's, home of the county's largest calzones and pizzas. They pulled three tables into a triangle so that all the Angels and their fans could sit together.

"Too bad Horace wasn't here tonight," Virginia beamed. "Two runs, a three-point loss! This was our best game in two years." She leaned back laughing, her long red hair touching the bottom of her shoulder blades.

Good to see Virginia so happy. Glancing around the candle-lit table, Emily noticed Eva closely inspecting a scar on the pitcher's mitt, Lindsey and Michael talking about a new vineyard, Jorge and Ruth studying the menu. She felt like laughing, too.

Virginia was determined to get a predictable response: "Well, I think we should send him a postcard at that polluted lake in Oregon. I bet he'd have a helluva better time cheering us on than floating in some scummy pond, fishing for imaginary trout."

Ruth shook her head. "Poor Horace. He tried nobly to coach us for three years, but half the team—whose names will be protected, even the redheaded nostalgic sitting across from me—only showed up to practice once a month."

Eva smiled broadly. "He *is* eighty-five. Said he needed to make the most of the summers he had left."

"Old Horace," Virginia took another gulp of beer, "will go on and on. People with that spunk live into their hundreds."

Spunk. There it was, another shot of grief, right in Emily's solar plexus this time. Unfair that Horace was enjoying his eighty-sixth year and Salerno had vanished at forty-seven. Emily closed her eyes, swallowed, sat very still, until she felt a hand reaching out.

Lindsey put Emily's palm on her stomach.

"What do you think? The rumba or the mambo?"

"Tango," Emily smiled, her eyes still closed.

"Tell us more about the Healdsburg exhibit, Ruth," asked Eva. "When is it?"

"July. Just two weeks now. The photos are mounted, ready for hanging. I hope you'll all come." Her excitement quelled as she looked anxiously at Lindsey.

Ruth turned to Emily, "You'll be back, right?"

"Yeah, I'll be home from the conference two days beforehand."

"Conference?" Virginia asked. "What kind of conference?"

"Oh, just a regional planning meeting." She was vaguely ashamed she hadn't told any of them, not even Ruth, about her paper on rural communities. She worried they'd think she'd been spying on them. And perhaps she had, although not consciously at first. This paper became one way to justify the work leave to her boss—research for a major article. California was fieldwork. Of course the paper wasn't really about them and their baseball games and tutoring and crusades for free speech. It was about the rattle, about location, dislocation, trespassing, home. You couldn't think about the rattle without accounting for the Spaniards and Russians and nineteenth-century Americans. You had to include nouveau invaders—vintners, dope growers, environmentalists, even Beulah Ranchers, for it was on their land that the rattle had been discovered or recovered.

"What's the conference topic?" persisted Virginia.

"No topic. Just an annual conference." She played nervously with the melting candle wax. "In Minneapolis. Should be hot as hell. And humid."

Ruth and Eva regarded her skeptically.

Then Ruth granted reprieve by turning to Lindsey. "You'll make it to the exhibit?"

"If I'm mobile," she grinned.

Emily wondered if Jorge were right, if having a baby would slow Lindsey down. She'd never seen her so mellow, never felt as close to her as she had this evening.

Their waiter carried a heavy tray of pastas and pizzas and salads. Emily noticed Jorge trying to catch his eye. There was a fifty-fifty chance the guy was gay. He looked Latino. How lonely Jorge must feel in their quiet Valley after the buzz of downtown Los Angeles.

Joyce talked over the clattering dinner service. "Juan is coming to the exhibit. Mom and I are going to pick him up on the way. Juan wants to be a painter."

"Juan?" Michael asked before biting into his calzone.

"Man!" Jorge laughed. "You gotta get in the loop, man. Juan and Joyce, they're an item. He's the novio of our girlfren'."

Eva rolled her eyes and explained to Michael. "Juan is Joyce's classmate. He played the leading Lost Boy to her Peter Pan. They're very good friends now."

She fluttered her long eyelashes at Joyce, who giggled excitedly.

Emily shook her head.

"Tell us, Em," Virginia urged, "what's happening with the new Salerno CDs?"

She drew a long breath. "Your expectations will be reduced by the name of this entertainment giant: Big Horn Records."

Ruth interrupted. "Theodore is a professional. Penelope said the contracts are pristine and more than fair regarding subsidiary rights and royalties. The name's a little funky; the style a tad casual, but it's the perfect label for Salerno."

"So when's the launch?" Michael's face grew distracted.

"August," Emily said distantly. The whole thing would be a fiasco and she'd waste another month here. One more extension and she'd lose her job.

"What part of August?" he asked urgently. "I've got to be in D.C. that month, but I could rearrange."

Emily was touched by her brother's interest. Of course, he had always enjoyed Salerno's music, had loved talking to her about Pepper and Coltrane and Cindy Dufur.

"Ferragosto," said Ruth. "August fifteenth. Salerno has a piece called that."

"Perfecto," Jorge waved his palms over their heads. "The Assumption of la Virgin. My favorite holy day. I'll be there with bells on."

Eva watched closely from across the table.

"Bells, yes," Emily was swept into his high spirits, "lots of bells. And maybe a veil and a blue dress? Salerno would adore that!"

Evening was still bright as they walked out to Lolo's parking lot. They had carpooled from here to Ukiah but now were separating. Michael left in his BMW as Eva and Jorge drove off together, talking rapidly. Emily envied their relationship, wished she weren't so stiff with her own brother. Virginia was driving Ruth and Joyce home.

"First car there, leave the gate open!" Lindsey climbed in the seat beside Emily.

Phoenix barked huffily until Emily put her leftover lasagna in the dog's bowl.

"Now keep it in your dish, girl, and don't slop all over the back seat." Phoenix sniffed happily, then tucked into her treat.

"I love this soft light," Lindsey said as they rode through the hills. "I hope my son is born on a night like this—soft, warm, breezy."

"Sounds right," Emily answered feebly. The baby was one more example of Lindsey's daring. Pregnancy and birth sounded hard enough, but rearing a child! Emily had a tough enough time taking care of Phoenix. She glanced back to check on the dog's meal.

"I've been thinking of naming him after this place, this home where I've felt I could be myself for the first time."

"Yes?" asked Emily, who wasn't partial to naming kids after trees and storms.

"I was thinking, I don't know, River. River Chung, that sounds kind of cool. Or Hawk. I love those red-tailed hawks, but . . ."

"But?"

"Well, Marianne says she'll divorce me if I ruin his life like that." Emily maintained a straight face, focusing on the road.

"Then I considered traditional names, like Kin or Yuen after my favorite uncles."

"Both sound good to me," Emily nodded. God, even naming a child was a responsibility. But fun, too.

"Still, I've always loved Malcolm and Keith."

"Yes, those are distinctive. Very nice."

"Presbyterian," Lindsey shrugged.

"Pardon?"

"Malcolm was the name of our youth minister in Seattle. Malcolm MacFarlane. And I had a high school boyfriend named Keith."

"I didn't know you were raised Presbyterian," Emily said.

"Yes, those Scots were big missionaries in Mom's section of Guangzhou. It's funny, I've never been able to tell which part of me is Presbyterian and which part is Chinese."

"What do you mean?"

"Hard-working. Self-critical. Guilty. Reserved."

"Yeah, well, you do express each of those traits at times," smiled Emily.

"Then I go back to the Chinese names because I want everyone to know who he is. I mean, Valley people are always assuming I'm Indian or Latina if they don't know my last name. 'Lindsey,' I could be anything."

"That's unsettling," Emily stumbled. "Blond hair, blue eyes, they protect me from some kinds of mistaken identity."

"There aren't many Chinese up here anymore."

"Anymore?"

"Yeah, there used to be lots in Northern California. They came to work on roads and railways. Took part in the Gold Rush—in the tailings, sites abandoned by white guys."

"Right, and I remember they actually deported the Chinese from some northern cities down to San Francisco," Emily reflected.

"Eureka got rid of all their Chinks by 1937."

Emily winced. "The U.S. stopped immigration then with the Chinese Exclusion Act. Was it the late 1800s?"

"Very good, Em. 1882."

"I did study California planning history. Although this chapter was more like ethnic cleansing."

Lindsey sniffed. "They couldn't keep us out for long. Witness Angus Chung, successful Hong Kong entrepreneur, who immigrated to Seattle in 1960."

"Your mom came then, too?"

"Yeah, why?"

"Well, you're thirty-three, born in 1967. You're the oldest?"

"Good planners, my parents. Old Angus wasn't going to start reproducing until he had his children's college tuition in the bank!"

"Truly?" asked Emily. They had only ten minutes before they reached the gate and there was so much she didn't know about Lindsey. There would be other conversations, of course, but she suspected that the logistics of the car journey, the fact that two self-contained people didn't have to make eye contact, fostered this special intimacy.

"He's a careful man, my father."

"Like my dad," said Emily, "but in different ways. I inherited caution from him."

"Anyway, I think a Chinese name might be best. Not that there's anything wrong with being identified as Latino or Indian. It's just that he's Chinese."

"Quite Chinese," Emily nodded, thinking how Lindsey resembled Angus Chung—responsible, ambitious, precise. She wondered once again about the identity of this baby's father, but Lindsey never talked about that—either the source or the method of obtaining sperm.

"Kin." Lindsey rolled the name around on her tongue.

Abruptly Emily asked, "Your mom is coming down for the birth?"

"Mom will arrive after he's born. She could never handle a home birth with a funky California midwife. She'd be terrified."

"Oh, that's a disappointment."

"Yes, yes," Lindsey muttered, then carefully added, "I'm glad you mentioned it."

They were driving under an arcade of moonlit oaks.

Emily waited.

Lindsey persisted. "The midwife suggests two attendants. Marianne will be there, of course. And now that Mom can't come, I was hoping you'd be willing."

"Thank you. I'm flattered," Emily stared at the vineyards under silver light. "But I, well, I have no medical training. How about Ruth? She's had a baby." Emily was talking faster and faster. "I bet she and Marianne, both of the mothers, would be perfect."

Silence.

"But," Emily asked desperately, "What would I *do?* And why me?"

"Your job would be to be there. To boil water if you insist on practical activity. And why? Because you knew he was doing the tango!"

They had reached the gate. Emily hopped out in the fresh night air to unlock it. She inhaled the sweet scent of damp grass, which reminded her of corn Mom grew in the back garden each summer against Dad's objections. Vegetable garden, she said. Flower garden, he insisted. Vegetable garden/flower garden, they would fight over and over each spring. Come summer, Mom won out with her corn and tomatoes and amazing (grotesque, Dad called them) zucchinis.

Slipping back behind the wheel, she looked into Lindsey's watchful eyes. "Yes, I'll be there. I'd be honored."

The cabin was cold. She should have lifted the west blind to let in the late afternoon sun. Emily watched Phoenix pining by the wood stove. "Too dry for a fire, Nixie, sorry." She switched on the radio for more company: a folk music program.

Wind called up the hillside, deep and hollow, like men shouting from a distance.

Strangely, she thought about the two snakes she had seen earlier in the day. Up by the blackberry bushes—a small black one wearing a brilliant coral band around its neck. Later, a huge, ominous-looking reptile sunning on the path to her car. Five feet long with brown splotches on a yellow background. Rattler! She had panicked, then recognized markings of the helpful gopher snake. Snakes. Bats. Spiders. Cohabitants.

At the end of the song, a bubbly announcer—was this Michele, who owned the gas station? Almost everyone in the Valley seemed to have a show on KYYY—recited the next day's weather report, ending with the familiar, "Tomorrow is a *no burn* day."

"Forget the stove, Nixie. Come on, we'll be toasty snuggling in the loft."

The wind pursued its low whistle.

Upstairs was flooded with light from the fat moon. From the east window, she watched the cypress dancing in this cold, clean air. Phoenix was already asleep. Their bed was warming.

Emily closed her eyes, grateful for the day. For Lindsey. It was almost a miracle. When she returned from Minneapolis, she was going to help a baby be born.

22

The off-white hotel room was larger than the ground floor of her cabin. A Kelly green rug almost sang as she entered. She double-locked the heavy door and immediately bounced on each of the two queen-sized beds, then lay quietly to determine which was firmer. The one by the window would be best—farther from shuffling feet and ringing voices and clacketing housekeeping carts. A nap! She closed her eyes.

It had been a long flight, surrounded by those cheerful Minnesota seniors returning home from Hawaii. She had told herself to relax and enjoy their good spirits, but she had stiffened into a familiar creature, "Emily the Crank, a woman in rigor mortis before her time." Even Salerno's nickname didn't prevent her from annoyance at the junior exec in the row behind, who used her tray table to catch up on years of e-mail, so that Emily felt as if Morse code were being transmitted directly through her spine. What had happened to her? She routinely flew three or four times a month.

She turned on her side. In fact, it had been a year since that routine. Country living had put her out of practice. Odd that when Salerno was alive she thought nothing of these business trips. How much time she had wasted—time they might have spent talking in front of the fire, or taking long walks or snuggling in bed. But Salerno's music had taken her away, too—all those nights when she was performing until long after Emily's bedtime. That's how their life had been. Who could have imagined death might steal in so abruptly? Who could imagine Emily staying in the cabin for a year, mourning Salerno, talking to a tree every night?

Wide awake. Her eyes wandered the room: a huge TV with remote control. Three telephones. One between the beds. One on the desk attached to a fax machine. One reflecting in the mirror, was attached to the bathroom wall. Apparently people in Minneapolis didn't miss calls.

At the far end of the bureau stood the mini bar. Everything a visitor could want or need or think she needed.

What Emily needed was rest. Again she tried to doze. But she was alert, irritable, feeling oddly unsafe. And surrounded by noises—the distant ping of elevators, an electronic drone seeping in from the room on the right. Human voices from the floor below. She sat up, looked out at the buildings along Nicolett Mall, listened to buses wheezing, horns barking. Wake up, Emily, this is the city. You've stayed in a hundred hotels. You're not Sacajawea wandering in from the prairie.

Reluctantly she sat up, snapped open her briefcase and scanned the conference program. Forget napping. There were two important panels this afternoon.

In the blue and white tiled bathroom, she turned on the perfect shower, set out a thick towel, and undressed. Yes, she was here to learn more about her profession, make contacts for the final consulting she'd do before leaving California, catch up with old friends—not just Chicago colleagues, but people from almost two decades ago. This was her favorite conference because every year her graduate school pals organized a reunion dinner. She was excited about the paper she had labored over all spring. She'd feel better once she got into the conference swing.

Emily sat at a long table with another panelist and two respondents. The large room was only one-quarter filled. Not because of the hour: one-thirty was prime time in convention land. It couldn't be the competition, three other rather dreary panels. Maybe people would file in late.

Madeline, her assistant from Chicago, waved warmly from the front row. Emily smiled back. Just as the session started, Vesta, Ken, and Douglas slipped in the back row.

Maybe the problem was their title, "Home and Trespass in the Evolving Western Community." "Trespass" might sound moralistic. "Home" could be read as sentimental.

Most people stayed for both papers.

Lots of questions about San Diego gang boundaries for her copanelist, Maria.

No one seemed interested in Emily's paper until Madeline asked brightly, "Most of us know your writing on immigrant communities in Chicago and New York. How will this excursion into California regional history impact the larger work?"

Emily was unreasonably annoyed. Madeline meant well, but what peculiar words, *excursion* and *larger work*.

She took a breath. "Frankly, I'm dealing with completely different spheres here. The MacKenzie Valley is a rural community where lines of residence, culture, and claim overlap more than they do in cities."

Madeline was nodding rapidly, blushing, taking notes.

Emily glanced to the back row for one of her colleagues to pick up the obvious thread, but each seemed distracted. She heard her voice winding down into a silent room.

A hand shot up in the third row: a young woman whose black linen suit was accented by a red scarf. "In your paper at Albany last year, you were anti-assimilationist. Are you now more interested in interacting populations than in cultural autonomy?"

Emily nodded. Finally someone was willing to address basic contradictions. "It's not a question of dismissing cultural autonomy, but rather an issue of seeing cultural identity within the historical moment."

She felt pleased with her answer, although, as the other panelist talked, she thought of a dozen additional points. When the session ended, she stood, stretching, expecting Vesta and the others to come up and confirm dinner plans. Instead, they waved from the back row. They were in fast-track mode, of course. Ken held his thumb up; Vesta mouthed, "Great paper!" Doug blew a kiss as they headed to the next session.

Before she had time to feel hurt, Emily found herself facing Madeline, who delivered further condolences about Salerno and, after a quick hug, brought out photos of her twins. Behind Madeline, the young woman in the black suit examined her fingernails. Finally Madeline left and the woman moved forward to thank Emily and describe her thesis at Northwestern. They exchanged cards.

Chilled by the air conditioning, dulled by the buzzing voices and the blur of faces, she headed outside for oxygen and caffeine. The July afternoon was hot and humid. She'd almost forgotten the wet midwestern heat. Nylons stuck to her damp legs; her suit felt like a heavy masquerade costume.

Walking through the city crowds, she told herself the paper had gone well. Surely Vesta, Douglas, and Ken would say this over dinner. The other panelist had been enthusiastic about her work, suggested they stay in touch. What more could she want—a chance to air her views, a couple of new contacts?

She took in the pleasant pedestrian mall with a stone church, boutiques, a television station, a fountain. Further along, she could see department stores. Several restaurants had set out chairs on the sidewalk, but Emily was drawn to the inside cafés. Which was worse, air conditioning or humidity? Well, she better get used to this because she would only have a few more dry California weeks.

Ambling along the wide, clean sidewalk, Emily remembered how Salerno would say, summer or winter, midwestern weather was equally foul. Not suited for human habitation, she liked to tease Vesta, a Chicagoan, suggesting that European settlement around the Great Lakes must have been an elaborate form of cultural penance. Vesta parried that the natives had done quite well in this area for hundreds of years before the self-flagellating white people arrived. Emily did miss Vesta's humor and passionate political arguments. Maybe Vesta was hurt that she hadn't written more this year. Emily hadn't known how to respond to the sympathy notes her colleagues sent. She did remember everyone with Christmas/Chanukah/holiday cards, but Emily knew she should have been in closer touch. Maybe she should have consulted Vesta before asking Ken for the leave of absence. So much, so much she had left undone or postponed or forgotten. She would apologize over dinner tonight, tomorrow night, whenever.

Emily stopped at a postcard stand, selecting a photo of the skyway for Joyce. And one of the Metrodome for Eva, who was, unaccountably for a Dodger stalwart, also a Twins fan. Further along, she found Caribou Coffee and ordered a double latte.

At a corner table by the window Emily groped for words. "Hi Joyce, look at the clever way these people navigate the city in winter." She was stalled, translating one world into another. Is this how Rafael felt during their American history tutorials? She could start with something familiar, "Hi Joyce, I'm at a coffeeshop, like Brad's in Fairburn." Not at all like Brad's—in sterile urban cafés people expressed consideration by ignoring you rather than by greeting you. And the window looked out on Nicolett Mall, not the Valley Highway. She imagined the dusty Fairburn pickups and battered compacts parked every which way outside Brad's. She would glance over toward the hardware store and the post office to see if she recognized anyone going in or out. She thought about Marianne stopping in Brad's on her way up from Berkeley for the weekend and how the two of them fell into a long talk about Lindsey's family, Marianne's grandchildren, and Emily's mixed feelings about Michael moving up to the country.

She sat straighter and took a long gulp of latte. No point in romanticizing country life. You could have the same conversation in your Chicago neighborhood—well, maybe people wouldn't know quite so much about you. But the distinction was more than the degree of intimacy; it was the quality of time. Urban people were usually somewhere for a purpose—at a café, for instance, to catch up on laptop work or to meet a particular person. An interruption that might be rude in Chicago would be the opposite in Fairburn, a required courtesy. Gertrude Stein had dismissed Oakland with "There is no there there." Sometimes in Chicago Emily felt there was no "now now." The present was never allowed to intrude (except in an electrical blackout or a stickup) on the planned meeting or conversation or task. But maybe this was changing with the influx of cell phones.

"Do you mind if I join you?"

Emily looked up to see the graduate student in the uncreased black linen suit. A thousand city excuses collided, but Fairburn cordiality triumphed.

"Not at all," she heard herself say. "I'm just having postcard writer's block."

"I'm Pauline," the young woman reminded her, smiling as she perched on the adjacent chair. "I was blown away by your paper. I'm getting more and more interested in these distinctions between rural and urban planning."

Emily blinked, returning to this familiar universe. She was flattered that the student would seek her out. She liked teaching but had only done adjunct classes here and there.

Pauline continued avidly, "And the way the profession is going nowadays, you really have to choose."

"Choose?" Emily asked blankly. The concept of choice had evaded her this year. She did remember Berkeley, plagued by the privilege of all those options—architecture, government work, consulting, so many more possibilities than her mother had had.

Pauline regarded her closely, as if to determine whether Emily were the same smart person whose paper she had attended. She nibbled on a chocolate wafer. Then, very respectfully, and a little more loudly, in case the aging mentor were going deaf, she said, "Choose between rural and city planning. Yet they really are related, especially in the intermountain states and further west."

"Choose," Emily rolled her eyes. "Between rural and urban—no. Certainly they're intertwined. The part I'd omit is the planning."

The wafer slipped from Pauline's hand into her cappuccino.

"I'm not being sarcastic," Emily assured her. "I do think our profession could use fewer strategy papers and more community-involved analysis and history."

Pauline pulled out a small yellow notebook. "So we do more intervention and less blueprinting."

"Intervention? I don't know," Emily shifted uncomfortably on her tiny seat. "More like facilitation—but before that, a lot of watching, listening."

"You know, in class last week, I talked about needing to do more observing and the professor laughed gently. He asked the other students who was going to pay me to observe."

"Sounds like a wise guy," Emily shook her head. "Still, from a practical perspective, he's right, unless you go into a more academic field like cultural geography or anthro."

"No," Pauline interrupted, leaning forward. "Those separations are so artificial. How can you write policy if you haven't strategically immersed yourself in a community the way, well, the way you've done in Mendocino County."

Stop, Emily wanted to say. Wanted to explain she had stayed at the ranch because of Salerno, that she hadn't done a single thing strategically. As she groped for words to explain to this stranger, Pauline whizzed in again. "I'm organizing the colloquium series next year. And you said you'd be back in Chicago next fall. Would you be willing to drive up to Evanston one Thursday afternoon and talk with us?"

"Yes, of course." Emily was pleased. She'd attended several lectures in that series. Vesta would be thrilled that someone from the office had been invited to present. She could feel her own rush of career adrenaline.

Pauline thanked her profusely, stood up, brushed off her still-unwrinkled suit, and promised to e-mail Emily with possible dates.

Emily waited for Pauline's departure before setting out toward the hotel. Vesta had probably left a voice mail about dinner. They had so much catching up to do. Her legs felt heavy in the humidity and she found herself walking slowly.

Pauline's enthusiasm buoyed her but also left her at odds with the reference to Mendocino research. Why did she need people to approve her time off as a professional project, as if "observing the MacKenzie Valley" were more consequential than meditating on Salerno and helping Ruth recover from an accident and tutoring Rafael and reuniting with her brother and joining protests against obscene clear cutting and being a birth attendant for Lindsey. Had that visit to the Tan Oak Rancheria been observation? She recalled Judson's proud tour of the cultural center, seeing Marie sprawled on their couch exhausted from teaching.

Had she deceived Pauline? No. While she was living her life in Mendocino, she had also asked questions. That was second nature. She'd studied indigenous customs and judicial history out of simple curiosity. Had she also been using these people all along?

No, no, no. Salerno would identify this Catholic guilt in a second. How familiar was this insecurity about her own integrity. The nervousness that when she finally achieved something (as she had with this modest conference paper), she didn't really deserve it.

She resolved to go back to Chicago with renewed commitment. The conversation with Pauline, the conference stimulation, the chat she'd have with Vesta and Company, all this would rev her up again for the real world.

She walked faster, matching steps with fellow pedestrians, people with places to go. Looking up, she saw several conference badges. One of them on her fellow panelist, who nodded hello.

Returning to Chicago entailed leaving California. She'd have to get the car tuned up—if there still was an automobile under all that country dust. People had stopped remarking on her Illinois plates, which were dirty to the point of being unreadable. Packing wouldn't be much bother, she reckoned, and the land transfer would go smoothly.

Emily felt herself tearing up. She would have to leave Phoenix, who was so much happier, thinner, healthier in California. She couldn't rip the dog away from Beulah for her own solace. The apartment was too cramped for Phoenix, even if it was her first home. Sniffing, she devised different ways of asking Ruth to take the dog.

"Ms. Adams?" The man was touching her elbow, speaking in a southern accent.

Emily turned, smiled, discreetly glanced at his nametag. Charming the way conferencegoers wandered into city streets wearing these tags, like kids running out to play in bibs. (Emily always left her tag in the hotel room. Salerno had warned her that wearing a conference badge advertised you as a good target for pickpockets.) She read the friendly large script, "Jesse Fairfax, Atlanta Community Research Institute."

As they shook hands, he said, "I've been thinking about your paper, your responses all afternoon. Very stimulating."

"Thank you," Emily fought back her blush.

"We're organizing a regional symposium for December and I believe you'd be a great addition if you're free."

"December," Emily nodded happily, "yes, my calendar is quite open in December." She smiled to herself, thinking how no one had asked her about her calendar in months, not since she accepted the most recent consulting project.

"I'll get back to you once I've firmed up plans in Atlanta. May we exchange cards?"

Emily reached in her purse for the grey plastic wallet of business cards.

"Chicago, eh?" he asked. "You commute between Chicago and Mendocino, then?"

"No, no. Chicago is my base. This year in California has been special."

"Well, you've produced some fine work there, fine work. We'll be in touch."

"Yes," Emily grinned. "I'll look forward to that."

A blast of cold air socked her as she entered the hotel. Salerno used to say that walking into Chicago buildings in summer was like jumping into a glass of ice cubes. Odd, how present Salerno had been all day. Maybe it was the constant talk about Chicago. The imp would always be with her. Emily didn't need to keep vigil by a tree.

She noticed a rush of people leaving the Minnetonka Room. Checking her watch she realized, damn, that she had missed the session on distance consulting. No, that didn't matter. She was returning to Chicago. People expected her—Vesta, Pauline, Jesse Fairfax—she'd better get to her room and make those dinner plans now.

The tenth floor corridor was eerily quiet during this in-between time—before people returned from afternoon sessions. She was completely out of sync with the conference, but she'd recover the pace. Two fall invitations already. In her office colleagues gauged success partially by how often you were invited to take your show to someone else's camp. Distracted, she walked straight into the housekeeper's cart. A row of tiny shampoo bottles shot to the ground, reminding her of Michael's boyhood torpedoes.

"Oh, sorry." She started to apologize to the maid, who rushed out of a room she'd been cleaning.

"Perdon, Señora," the dark young woman blinked. "Señora is hurt? My fault."

"No," Emily reassured the woman, whose nametag said, "Hi, I'm Juanita." She bit her lip. "It's my fault. I was daydreaming."

The woman looked blank, frightened.

Then in Spanish, Emily repeated. "My fault, excuse me. Let me help with the shampoo bottles."

Juanita brightened momentarily, then regained professional reserve. "No, gracias. No hay problema," she spoke rapidly, collecting bottles, looking around. "Hasta la vista!"

"Hasta la vista!" Emily went on her way as instructed.

She sneezed at the gardenia disinfectant in her room. Checking the phone, she felt a pang that the light wasn't blinking. She rang Vesta's room and left a message. Then did the same for Douglas and Ken.

Suddenly she felt exhausted. Not relaxed enough for a nap, she indulged in channel surfing. Oprah, a Cary Grant movie. The Weather Channel reported 80 degrees in Northern California, clear skies. Lindsey, she recalled, loved the Weather Channel. The other ranch women teased Lindsey about her small satellite dish, but the girl said she'd die without weekly doses of *The Simpsons,* and *NYPD Blue.* Too early for those shows. Maybe she could sleep after all.

The phone rang three or four times before she picked it up.

A woman's voice. "Emily?"

She struggled to surface from humidity and gardenias and conference buzz. "Yes, this is Emily." Puzzled by the caller's voice, it finally came to her. "Vesta!" She sat up.

"Is this Emily Adams?"

Ruth. For half a second, she wondered if she were still dreaming, then she came to. Ruth was phoning midafternoon in California time.

"Ruth, are you all right? Joyce—is there something wrong with Joyce?"

"We're fine, hon." She was clearly relieved to relocate Emily. "But there's been a fire."

The cabin. Phoenix. Salerno's tree. All her papers.

"On Mineshaft Road."

"Eva!" Emily's heart pumped faster. "Is she okay?"

"Eva's fine. They burned down the house next door. And no one was really hurt."

Emily took a breath, leaned against the backboard.

"It's Jorge. They've arrested him. Charged him with arson."

"Jorge?"

"The cops think they've finally nabbed the Valley arsonist. They're tying it to some L.A. gang conspiracy."

"But Jorge has only been in the Valley a few months."

"They're claiming he's part of a Latino network. Some of the young pickers are from South Central, too."

"I'll be there tomorrow—afternoon, or supper time, depending on the flights."

"No, no," Ruth objected. "I just wanted you to *know*, I didn't want you to hear about it on the TV or anything. The evening news always features fires, even when they're not local. Nothing you can do here. Finish the conference. You've been looking forward to it for months."

"This is idiotic!" Emily ignored her friend. "Jorge is the gentlest soul in the country. The idea that he was a gang member!"

"Apparently he was, Em."

"What?"

"Eva told me last night—after they'd put out the fire, after they'd arrested him. He was in a gang for a while. She thinks he was proving something to Papa. Papa got wind of it, and a few broken bones later Jorge turned in his uniform. That was ages ago. His second year of high school."

"How is Eva taking it?"

"You know Eva."

"What's that supposed to mean?" As they talked, Emily grabbed the airline timetable.

"Tell me. How was your paper?"

"Oh, fine." She jotted down likely departures.

"Emily, you spent weeks on it, you can't simply say, 'Oh, fine.' "

Sometimes Ruth was annoyingly maternal.

"You didn't answer me. How's Eva?"

"You know. She took care of what she could. Found a good pro bono lawyer for Jorge. And she's back at work. Thank god, creepy Hayden is on vacation this week."

"But how is she *feeling*?"

"Terrible," Ruth blurted. "Frightened. Enraged. Stoic. You know Eva."

Why did Ruth keep saying that?

"You could call her," she added.

Emily's stomach clenched. She began reading timetables to Ruth. "It looks as if I'll be there by early evening. Will you tell Eva?"

"Honestly, Emily, there's not much to do right now. You might as well finish the last few days at the convention. I know it means a lot to you."

"Ruth, I'll see you tomorrow. I'm coming home."

V

23

The traffic between San Rafael and Novato was moving intermittently and Emily fidgeted to the dissonant music seeping from cars and vans and trucks. Next to her, a woman in a silver Lexus talked animatedly on a cell phone. Sitting in the Volvo station wagon ahead, a husband-and-wife-looking couple argued vehemently. The man in the bright green Mustang bobbed his head to music, eyes closed, mouth puckered. Was she the only driver among thousands who had not prepared some diversion for the Highway 101 bottleneck? Any thinking person would expect congestion in Marin on a weekday afternoon. Still, she'd hardly been a thinking person since Ruth's call.

In her dreams, flames licking the belly of her woodstove tumbled into different colors. From the window she saw smoke plumes rising to the ridge. Small, controlled Valley brush burns billowing. She watched fire devouring grassy hillsides. The conflagration was growing on itself in the way of Salerno's music—higher, wider, zigzagging toward complete centeredness, as if it filled the world and there was nothing besides that bright, hot, enveloping whine.

Traffic inched along, although she couldn't remember stepping on her accelerator. Here the freeway was lined with beige and white storage locker facilities. Emily always wondered about those storage rooms of affluent Marin County—what treasures and stories they held. They did, however, look fireproof.

In the dream, flames had stopped at the cabin steps. Phoenix was barking and Emily dragged the dog inside to prevent smoke inhalation. Salerno remained in bed, oblivious.

Now Emily could tell they had reached Sonoma because of the car lots. Used cars. New cars. White. Blue. Green. Otherworldly grey. Every make, size. Even the new Volkswagens. She loved the perversity of these new Bugs, how you couldn't tell if they were coming or going.

The drive north had never felt this long.

Now they were moving a little faster past Santa Rosa's discount stores. Vans and trucks darted quickly on and off the highway. Salerno had always made Emily do the driving here. She'd close her eyes, don earphones, and say, "Wake me when it's over."

Reaching Windsor, Emily took a long breath at the semblance of countryside. Too many new vineyards, true. This land would crumble in a few years from monoculture. From here she could see the hills ranging north. More contour in Healdsburg and finally, the winding road from Lawnston to Jerseydale. The further north she drove, the hotter it got. Ruth had said that the Riveras' house went up in a flash.

The route from Jerseydale to Eva's place in Fairburn seemed endless despite the blessed lack of lumber trucks. It took forever to navigate the curves. Finally she was gazing gratefully at that old sign, "The Mac-Kenzie Valley Welcomes You." Did people paint the sign to keep it fresh? she speculated numbly. Summers and winters were harsh, to say nothing of the relentless spring rains, so someone must be tending it.

Happy to be back, she felt unnerved by how foreign Minneapolis had seemed. Coffee everywhere. Loud, mechanical noises and gigantic construction cranes. The organized economy of conversation. Still, toward the end, she was getting the pace. Yes, she remained a functioning professional. She reminded herself about the conversations with Pauline in the coffeeshop and Jesse on the mall. Her paper had gone splendidly. And Vesta had left a voice message, suggesting dinner.

Emily would have returned the call if she hadn't been racing to the airport. She'd ring from here, explaining . . . what? That she needed to return to the Valley because a friend had almost burned to death? The hills were noticeably paler than they'd been just a few days before. Would they fade so much one day that they disappeared?

She drove straight to Old Mineshaft Road, where smoke greyed the early evening light. Next to Eva's was the black shell of her neighbors' house, glistening from the fire retardant and water used to "save" it. Almost paralyzed by self-consciousness, Emily forced herself to knock on Eva's door. As she waited, a neighbor parted her purple flowered curtains and peered out. Emily waved to Mrs. Ruiz, who smiled anxiously before disappearing into her kitchen. As Emily waited for Eva to answer, she noticed the heavy bootprints in each mangled yard.

Otherwise the neighborhood looked recognizable, in that discomfiting way your mouth feels after a tooth extraction—familiar, but sore and uncertain. Arid heat enveloped her as she stood on the creaking deck and she had to lean against the railing; it was at least 85 degrees in the early evening. Must have been a scorcher today. She drank a lungful of the dry, hot air—tonic for midwestern mildew. Her tired legs reminded her it was two hours later in Minneapolis and she hadn't eaten lunch or dinner. Sighing, she conceded to herself that Eva was out. Best thing was to go home, make a quick omelet, and call her from there.

Driving up dusty Beulah Ranch road, Emily heard squeals and laughter from the pond. Joyce and her dog Bobbie and . . . Emily peered out, but couldn't quite identify the other child-otter. She waved, pulled over, and jumped from the car.

"Emily! Emily, come join us," Joyce sang as she treaded water and splashed Juan—of course that's who this was. He'd grown inches since *Peter Pan* two months before.

Emily grinned. "Maybe I'll stick my toes in the water."

"Boring, boring," teased Joyce. "Come in. Come play with us!"

The little girl had grown more beautiful through the summer, her brown hair lightening, her olive skin darkening. Bright eyes glinted with high excitement.

Approaching the pond, Emily observed half a dozen frogs peep and leap from the muddy bank into the water. No matter how softly you walked, animals sensed you, then skittered or ran or flew away. At the dock she realized she was still wearing her conference suit, so instead of sitting down she held a bench for support, dangling one foot, then the other.

"Ya hear about the fire?" asked Juan. "A big one on Old Mineshaft Road."

Joyce, sunk into a large black inner tube scoffed, "Of course she wouldn't hear about it way off in Minneapolis."

Juan shrugged, then yanked Joyce's left foot, almost capsizing the tube.

"Actually, Juan, I did learn about it at the conference. Joyce's mom called me. I just drove by Eva's place, but she wasn't home."

"That's 'cause she's in the house with all the adults," said Joyce, "making dinner."

"Dinner, hmmm. Maybe I'll join them."

"Don't go," cried Joyce. "Stay and play with us."

Emily watched Juan's face fall. Joyce was a little tease.

"Maybe tomorrow," she winked, "you look like you're doing fine without me."

A relieved Juan waved broadly.

She hobbled over the grass stubble and pennyroyal in her pumps. Obviously she'd ruin the nylons before reaching Ruth's. But the lovely scent of pennyroyal flowers seemed to open fully on the hottest days.

Climbing the wooden stairs to Ruth's cabin, she recalled an evening almost this hot a year ago, when she walked into Ruth's house to find her friends gathered around disaster. Holding back tears, she wanted to retreat to the pond, reel back the entire year, warn Salerno that she shouldn't fly, that she had to drive up from Arizona.

Emily stood unnoticed in the doorway as people buzzed around the oven and table. Astonishingly, everyone was there—Ruth, Lindsey, Marianne, Virginia, Eva, Jorge, even Michael. What was he doing here midweek? Ah, the bail money. Well, good for him. One day she'd apologize for calling him a capitalist louse back in the old days.

Virginia was the first to detect her, and before Emily knew what was happening the tall, bony woman was hugging her. Then they all gathered around for more hugs and kisses—Ruth, Lindsey, Marianne, Jorge. Michael demonstrated his Adams heritage by waving self-consciously from the corner. Eva, loaded down with dishes, beamed.

Undone by the attention, Emily pulled a face. "I can't leave the Valley for more than three days and chaos ensues!" Then in a more serious voice, "Tell me, someone, how are the Riveras? Who do they think set the fire?"

"This is practical Ruth speaking. Let's sit down to supper, then we can talk. I think we each got different reports today. Excuse me while I rouse the kids first." On her way out the door, she placed a gentle hand on Emily's neck. "Nice to have you with us, friend."

Ruth called to Joyce and Juan. Then called again.

Eva deposited the dishes and hugged Emily. Stepping back, she looked her up and down, "Whoa-ho, hijole, look at this lady's blue skirt and blouse, the pumps, the hose. Nice legs. I've never seen you in legs."

Emily blushed, remembering Eva wearing that red skirt at the tutoring graduation. "Yeah, well, I bought them in Minneapolis. Women are expected to have legs at a professional conference."

"So how did it go, your paper?" asked Marianne.

She held the chair for Lindsey, who sat tentatively at the table, tenderly cradling one side of her belly.

"Okay," Emily said.

Marianne continued, "My thesis advisor gave a paper in Minneapolis last month. She said it was a great city. Tell us about the conference, the panel."

"Thanks for asking, but maybe later. I need to eat something. I need to hear what's going on with this fire."

"Of course," Marianne said.

Ruth returned from the deck, hands in the air. "Adolescent Sudden Deafness Syndrome—they both suffer severely." She sighed, "No doubt when they're exploding with hunger, they'll join us in swimming regalia. Prepare for an invasion of the wet and soggy."

Emily discharged her nervousness by folding napkins. She couldn't believe how long it took to get basic news. Of course they'd been living with this for a day and a half. She was speeding on city time.

Grinning widely, Jorge sat across from her. The police must have pretty vivid imaginations to peg this guy as an arsonist.

As if reading her mind, Ruth said, "See how perfectly he fits the criminal profile—Latino, young, male, new to the Valley."

Emily shook her head in disgust.

"Hey, you're leaving out 'gay' and my diabolical three-month record as a fifteen-year-old gang member."

"I always think it's a mirror image vision problem with local cops," Virginia hypothesized, carrying a rye wheat baguette to the table. "Difference is deviance."

As people broke off chunks of warm bread, she persisted, "Personally, I bet it's the vintners."

"What do you mean?" asked Michael.

"Well, what do we all know about Jaime Rivera?" Virginia waved her fork.

"That he has gorgeous eyes," Jorge grinned.

"Also," Emily joined in, "he's been organizing the pickers."

"Don't be facile, Ginny," Lindsey argued. "You see 'vintner,' 'logger,' and think 'evil.' "

"Relax," Virginia sighed. "I'm not talking about small organic vineyards like Melody Vines. I mean corpmonsters like Kendall Jackson and Fetzer."

Ruth took a long drink of water and added, "No, Lindsey's right. There would be far less messy ways for the vintners to get rid of Jaime. The INS, for instance."

"Let's put all the suspects on the table," Marianne leaned forward. "Virginia says the vintners. The cops accuse angelic Jorge."

Lindsey grumbled, "Does anyone think this is related to the Nylands' fire?"

"Cops *still* suspect those pickers," said Virginia. "Because the Nylands laid off two dozen people after the berry harvest."

Ruth demanded, "Why would they hurt the Nylands? They're about the fairest, most reliable gig in the Valley."

"Yeah," agreed Eva. "People know that Nylands is only going to be a short-term job. They didn't sack the pickers."

"So who do you think is responsible?" asked Michael, taking a drink.

"Could be the drugsters," Lindsey spoke urgently. "Jaime was known for more than organizing. He grew his own stash and then some. Personally, I think the dope mob is the scariest thing in the community."

Virginia looked down at her plate.

Emily wondered if she'd heard from Sally lately. She felt sad about Virginia's loss, but also relieved by Sally's absence.

"So," Ruth challenged. "We're all thinking of different motives for different fires."

"Sure," shrugged Marianne, "Think about that tent settlement of Big Tree defenders. When they got torched, everyone knew it was the lumber consortium."

"Except that," Eva's voice was soft and the rest of her sentence slow in coming. "Except the small details didn't make the newspaper. I heard about this guy's technique from my friends in the CFD. There's a pattern. Well-placed cotton rags, usually soaked in gasoline or kerosene. Some explosives."

"This guy!" said Ruth. "Do they have a suspect?" She looked at Jorge. "A legitimate suspect?"

"No, by 'guy,' I just mean your average psycho-sociopath who plays games with other people's lives."

"I hope your CFD friends are wrong," said Emily quickly. "I prefer accident or random animosity." She took a gulp of wine, glanced around at the nodding heads. Her flight and traffic jam were almost forgotten and she was glad to be back on this glorious land with her friends despite the horrible topic of conversation.

"Yeah," Lindsey sat back, "the way you're talking about this psycho-socio guy, he could set the whole Valley ablaze."

"Man, this talk is getting too eerie for me," Jorge got up for another bottle of wine. After filling glasses, he raised a toast, "To my benefactor!"

Michael grimaced and lowered his head.

"Yes, to Michael," joined Ruth.

All glasses were raised.

Eva wore a tense, grateful smile, but Emily sensed her anxious distraction.

"How about a few charades to celebrate?" cajoled Jorge. "I guarantee that will lure those mermaids inside."

After requisite groans and half-hearted excuses, people cleared the table, leaving plates for the sopping wet Joyce and Juan, who must have heard the word *charades* telepathically because they now appeared at the door. The children ate quickly as adults gathered in the living room for fierce competition.

Everyone, that is, except Eva and Emily, who slipped out the side door. They sauntered silently toward the lower pond where the cattails grew tall and tensile and the red-winged blackbirds were beginning evening commerce. Emily loved this period, half an hour before sunset. A benevolent time in the softly lit landscape.

She had missed this evening ritual in Minneapolis, where she had seen neither sunset nor stars. Of course, she could have found both on the wider prairie, but there was nowhere outside the Valley where she felt such a part of this vast eternity.

Suddenly aware of the silence, she said, "Did you know that most migratory birds fly at night? They get better distances in the colder, stiller air, navigating by the stars." She felt pleased with this ecological detail, which she heard on the radio driving north.

Eva smiled, "And today you chose to migrate during a rush hour heat wave!"

Emily laughed.

"You left the conference early," Eva observed in her neutral voice.

"I was worried," Emily declared swiftly. Then more cautiously, "About you."

They both faced the pond. A mallard landed on the brackish surface, casting circles of light behind him. Emily turned and saw Eva's face was taut as blown glass.

"I was so scared," Eva confessed. "First the fire. That huge, threatening light ripping through darkness. And the heat, when we went outside. The dense smoke. All so strange, so violent, in the middle of a peaceful mountain night."

Emily knew. She had pictured it all the way across country, on the drive up Highway 101, around the breathless curves from Lawnston.

"We were all right, of course. Jorge and I knew that in minutes. We phoned 911. We helped Jaime and Rosa carry out los niños. I don't know. I was petrified and perfectly competent at the same moment."

Emily put her arm on Eva's shoulder and felt her trembling.

"The worst part was afterward. Lying on Ruthie's couch, I got more and more frightened—we came here while the firefighters were mopping up—thinking about what might've happened, not just to Jorge and me, but to the Riveras and the Martinez family on the other side. It's been hot as hell this week and everything is tinder."

Emily nodded.

"Then!" Eva pulled away in anger. "Then when they came for Jorge, well, I knew I was being punished."

"Punished?"

"Why, why did I have the hubris to believe I could take care of Jorge, rescue him from L.A. in my magical Valley?"

"*He* says he's happier here. This stupid arrest is a racist stunt. He's got a great lawyer." Emily knew she was babbling, pretending to be in control. "And they'll find the real arsonist or arsonists, or whoever. They're a threat to too many people. I mean, we're talking the local economy, people's jobs. Lives."

"That's what happens to perfect lives. They get destroyed."

"What?"

"I don't know." She swiveled toward Emily, holding tears behind a rueful smile. "I think I love this place too much. I've been too happy here."

"Too much. Too happy. For what?"

"Maybe I don't deserve it." Eva's eyes lowered in embarrassment.

"That, as Salerno would tell me, is Catholic hogwash guilt!" Invoking her lover's name, she found herself taking a step back.

Eva sniffed. "A wise woman. I wish I'd known Salerno. Meanwhile, I'm glad I know you." She reached for Emily's hand. "I'm glad you came home—even if it was a little early in the day for optimum aviary migration."

Emily swallowed and grinned. Squeezing Eva's hand, she turned toward the pond. Several other ducks had landed and the darkening water around them was utterly quiet.

Crickets played from a cedar branch.

Then—from behind them—a siren of sorts.

Loud, heavy footfalls.

Joyce's voice. "Emily, Emily. The baby. Lindsey is having her baby!"

24

The alarm rang painfully loud. Turning it off, Emily closed her eyes, then realized, shit, this was the morning of Virginia's logging protest. That's why she had to get up in the dark. Why she'd set the alarm for the first time since she'd been in the country. She stumbled down the stairs and fired the kettle.

Emily stared out the dark window, thinking she hadn't been up at this hour for a month—since the night/morning of Malcolm's birth. She wondered now if the owl were still hunting, and she walked out to the back porch. Driving from Lindsey's cabin after a night of birthing, Emily had felt otherworldly. And just as she had stepped from the car, the giant bird had swooped into the deep branches of a venerable oak.

This morning, wobbly but hopeful, she scoured the branches of the giant tree. Suddenly those eyes appeared—haunting or manic or be-jeweled—staring straight through Emily. As her own inferior retinas adjusted in shades of darkness, she could make out the shape of the huge animal rotating her head to the east, the west. The bird peered again at Emily as if to demand, "Are you *still* there?" and receiving no answer from the awed spectator, she lifted herself in a windy rush of feathers.

Someday Emily would tell Malcolm about meeting the owl on his birthday. It might be an omen that he'd grow up to be a wise man or a pilot or an ornithologist.

She had raced back to Lindsey's cabin to find her brave friend lying on the bed, gripping Marianne's hand. Three weeks premature; no one had expected this. The midwife could arrive in ten or fifteen minutes, Lindsey reassured Emily. And when Lauren, a weathered, middle-aged woman, did appear, she got right down to business, kicking out Eva,

Joyce, and Ruth, reminding Emily and Marianne of their assigned tasks. She was so efficient that Emily believed the baby would arrive momentarily. But it was a long, tedious, agonizing, sometimes hilarious (as they composed dreadful limericks to distract Lindsey between contractions), surprising night.

Emily had felt like she was at a play, occasionally listening for offstage coaching. A little divine intervention seemed more desirable. During the force of contractions, Lindsey was characteristically brave. Emily recalled physical assaults she herself had weathered—terrible weeks of back spasm, a month of pneumonia, bouts of cystitis—yet none of it compared. She knew this from the ravaged distortion of Lindsey's sweet face and the deep growling screams that seemed to emerge from the center of the earth. Marianne stayed focused. Lauren was eerily silent, efficient. Emily tried to imitate their alert confidence.

Then, suddenly, or finally (time had turned to taffy and so had her exhausted legs from the long day of flying and driving), something happened. A head. Black hair crowning a blustering red face. Tiny shoulders, arms, belly, legs, feet. All this from Lindsey's torn and bloody vagina. Mama was crying, holding baby. Malcolm was crying. Emily was crying.

That night she had been so tired, she might have imagined the owl.

Now a month had passed, an eternity from July to August. Lindsey's mother had come and gone. Lindsey had returned to the vineyard, baby strapped to her stomach or in a basket beside her as she worked. And Malcolm was becoming a more and more distinctive person. Part Lindsey—those dark brows, the strong jaw—and part, well, Emily had no identity for Dad, but part owl, she reckoned. Without telling Lindsey, she'd begun searching the Web for good graduate schools in philosophy. A harmless, idiosyncratic pursuit, the sort of thing she imagined godmothers did.

The kettle whistled in her still-dark cabin. Emily paused a moment, bare feet soaking up heavy dew from the deck's wooden planks. She was happy here, outside, alone, in the blue-black morning. She wondered whether Malcolm had felt similar reluctance about leaving his mother's dark for busy, bright civilization.

Unaccountably hesitant to switch on a light, she tuned into KYYY and listened to Virginia's voice as she drank coffee.

"I'll repeat details for anyone who has tuned in late."

Late, Emily smiled to herself, Virginia thought five thirty in the morning was late. Sometimes she doubted her committed friend's capacity for understanding average human frailty. Still, Virginia had won that big teaching/mentoring award, so she must know something about people.

"Forest Guardians and supporters are gathering at the turnoff to Eucalyptus Road to stop lumber trucks carrying illegal clear-cut down Knolls Hill. We urge everyone to wear white—a hat, scarf, shirt—and if you can't join the solidarity blockade today, please honk to show us your support. We expect most protestors by seven."

Emily stared at the scarred table, sipping coffee, listening to a friend who sounded slightly more brittle on the radio than in person. But who was she to talk? Her own activism had completely evaporated this last year.

When a person turned fifty-one, life was more than half-finished. But how? Had it truly been thirty years since she worked in Mexico? Twenty-five years since she returned? Seventeen since she met Salerno in that smoky poolroom? All that had happened. All that was over. What was left? Going back to a still-foreign city to live in a comfortable high rise condo? Alone. Returning to her satisfying job with her excellent colleagues Vesta and Douglas and Ken. Growing older, old. With so much undone. Unattempted. Unimagined.

Lately she'd tried to take a different view. Maybe this was corny, but it had something to do with Malcolm's birth. The fight that he and Lindsey put up for his life had changed her. Then, too, she drew spirit from Virginia's angry optimism, from her own, unexpected reconnection with Michael, from Eva's vivacious dedication to tutoring, her job, Jorge. How could she be dying amid all this life? So maybe Mexico and graduate school and Salerno weren't over. They remained part of her, shaping her still. Of course she had practical reminders of the inextricability of past and present—all those nervous phone calls from Theo the Impresario as he planned Salerno's damn disc party.

Virginia was still going strong on the radio. Just one more cup of coffee and she'd go fetch Eva and Jorge for the blockade. Sun was rising and today would be a scorcher.

Driving through the Valley as the morning heated up, Emily marveled that the land survived the harshness of August each year, when temperatures usually reached the nineties and often went over a hundred. The unpaved roads were ground to beige-brown powder, which coated the bottom branches of trees. Bloom gone from the buckeye. Grasses brittle. Wildflowers long disappeared. The landscape bore an almost lunar barrenness except for the hills of neatly braided grape vines bordered by stalwart coastal redwoods.

Since childhood she had resisted California's August. A month of tomatoes and peaches, yes, but also a month of short tempers and too much iced tea. The whole family would be eager for summer heat to subside while lamenting lost possibilities: trips not taken to the lake, irises unplanted. Maybe the worst part of August was dreading school in the equally intense September heat, when she would sit in class wearing back-to-school mix-and-match outfits she and her mother had carefully selected, clothes designed for children in the colder heart of the country. Knowing that she'd have three, maybe four more weeks of summer before autumn allowed her to be comfortable in her clothes, her skin.

Emily mused as she drove. About late summer pleasures—people sitting on their decks at night talking to neighbors. The sensation of sliding between cool sheets, because temperatures always dropped off by bedtime. And there were those August scents—the brilliant citrus of Meyer lemons, pungent eucalyptus oils, hamburgers sizzling on the grill, the good, clean perspiration of a friend moving through chores, the swelling evening aromas of mock orange and jasmine. Memories from deep in her body made Emily realize she would always be a Californian.

Lots of traffic on the route to Eva's. Tourists, delivery trucks, local folks running errands before the heat of the day. Some honked and waved at her, now that she was a Valley regular.

Californian wasn't a simple identity, a point illustrated by the fight between Virginia and Michael at Lolo's the previous week. Emily had tried to ignore them, concentrating on how much she loved Lolo's old grain storehouse transformed, with minimal adjustments, into café, art gallery, and Friday night dance hall. Lolo pleased almost everyone with her eclectic menu—a cross between nouveau bistro and hot dog heaven.

Emily had warned Michael not to provoke Virginia on this issue. But Michael was passionate about free speech and—as he put it—he enjoyed a reasonable, if heated, exchange. Emily savored Lolo's spicy enchiladas and found herself gazing at the sparkled ceiling. Was she praying or waiting for the plaster to drop? Michael, like Vesta and a lot of her Chicago friends, was incredulous about passionate (or wacko) California environmentalists. After all, the West was a boundless frontier, where everything was ripe for picking and replaceable tomorrow, if not before.

Michael babbled away, weighing the merits of corporate property ownership against Virginia's land rights argument. "The company bought the acreage," he said coolly. "It's their call."

"Trees are communal heritage."

"For that matter," argued Michael, in his best Stanford debating team posture, "so is your land. If it belongs to anyone, it belongs to the Indians."

"Actually," Virginia flew back, "we have a lot of native support on this action. Representatives from the Tan Oak Rancheria are joining us in the barricade."

Emily looked down from the ceiling and took a long breath. No way to skip the demonstration, she had promised Virginia a month ago. But she wasn't ready to face Judson or Baxter Sands. Maybe someone else would come from the rancheria. Yes, yes, she had to decide about the rattle soon, but with Lindsey's baby, Jorge's arrest, and three more fires in the last week, she had allowed herself to postpone the decision. As she turned up Mineshaft Road, she checked herself in the rearview mirror: the white scarf and white T-shirt showed off what little tan she had. Virginia would be pleased that she'd remembered the uniform. Sweat dripped down her spine.

Someone waved. Jaime Rivera, working on the south frame of his new house. He'd have it enclosed before the November rains. Meanwhile, he and Rosa and the kids were sleeping at neighbors' homes. The oldest boys stayed with Eva and Jorge. Emily carefully parked in a spot she hoped would be shady by the time the protest was over. Virginia had promised they'd all be free by lunch. Before she pulled the emergency brake, Jorge hopped out to greet friends.

Eva, hunched in the front seat. "I'm not sure he should be here." She smiled, in spite of herself. "He was parading around the house this morning like Paul Revere or Nathan Hale. 'I'm a citizen. With a right to voice my beliefs!' he was going on in this deep TV anchor voice. Jaime's kids were rolling on the floor in hysterics."

Emily studied her face. "Well, he's right."

Eva opened the door, then turned back, "Nothing we can do about it."

The two women ambled toward the small clutch of protestors. Even on edge of the highway, they could hear Virginia's voice through the bullhorn.

"Jorge may be a little reckless," Emily tried, "but it's his ebullience, friendliness, that's made his makeshift salon such a quick success here."

"I hope he's that charming with the judge."

"The hearing's at the end of the month?"

"Yeah, August 28. Feast of St. Augustine. Believe me, I'm lighting candles."

"It's wonderful, your devotion to Jorge."

"Ah, look at you and Michael. You practically married him off to me."

Emily blushed, stumbled on a twig and when she looked up, was struck by Eva's challenging grin. Her stomach turned as she recalled Ruth's light-hearted interrogation about their recent dates. Had Eva considered them dates? What did this beautiful, accomplished woman think of her?

"Look," she interrupted her uncomfortable thoughts, "Isn't that Joyce and Juan holding the 'Guardians of the Next Generation' banner?"

"Santa Dio!" exclaimed Eva. "That girl is growing up."

"Hey, guys," a voice from the left, behind a table piled with armbands and petitions. It was Ruth—wearing a long wedding veil.

Emily broke into laughter. "Where did you get that?"

"Second-hand shop in Fort Bragg." She draped the lace over her shoulders. "Do you think it will stop gossip about Joyce having no father?"

"Not really," Emily was still giggling.

"I love it," grinned Eva. "A little guerrilla theatre."

"Yes, Virginia approved. Said I represented the Virgin Forest!"

The smile vanished from Eva's face.

Alarmed, Emily glanced around for Jorge, then spotted him joking with waiters from Lolo's Café. "You okay?" she asked Eva.

"Yeah." She inhaled. "But check out the oak behind Jorge."

Emily waited until her glance would seem natural. A turkey vulture flew low above the crowd, casting a long shadow on the yellow dirt road. Then she saw the man.

"I should have expected him," Eva continued in a subdued voice. "He's the ranger in charge of this region."

At first Emily didn't recognize Hayden in his dapper park uniform. He looked younger, more normal. She wished she comprehended the depth of Eva's fear. Oh, he'd been a jerk, all right, but Eva acted ter-rified. She worked too hard and too successfully with the youth programs for her job to be threatened. Hayden was just a puny, aging bureaucrat, you could see that even from this distance.

By seven thirty, the sun was full and hot on the hills and even here in the shady redwood grove people were pulling off their sweatshirts. Thirty or forty people, not the hundreds Virginia had anticipated, but a sturdy bloc, a good mix of locals.

Virginia stood on a stump and called everyone to attention with a yellow bullhorn, her words interrupted several times by the friendly honks, raised fists of passing motorists.

"Good morning and welcome!"

A little too loud. She coughed and modulated her voice.

"We're here to save what's left of Knoll's Hill forest. To end threats to the Valley's ecosystem."

Cheers. Clapping. Emily watched Joyce and Juan raising their banner up and down, up and down. Juan made a mean whistle between his thumb and forefinger. Did she notice a shadow of moustache above his upper lip?

"We're tackling four main issues here," Virginia declared. Deliberately, the experienced teacher explained, "Clear cutting. Unbridled use of pesticides. Wiping out endangered species. And chopping down the one last bit of Valley first growth."

Walking in from the highway were Judson and Baxter Sands with five rancheria kids.

She wondered if Baxter would speak today, felt calmed by the idea of sitting on a blanket, listening to his moon stories.

Virginia plugged on. "Clear cutting is just plain ugly."

A loud whoop of agreement, applause.

"Worse, it erodes land, fouls MacKenzie Creek, the Navarro and Albion Rivers."

Hayden shifted from foot to foot, making notes in a grey steno pad.

Odd behavior, thought Emily, for none of this could be news to a park ranger.

"When the trucks from Lumber Corps arrive—they usually start at eight A.M.—most of us think they'll turn around. If they don't, some protestors will practice civil disobedience, linking arms across the road. This is for people who have taken nonviolent training. Let me repeat— only for people who have passed the course. We strongly advise other adults, and require anyone under eighteen, to step aside. You'll be valued witnesses."

Groans from Joyce and Juan and the Indian kids, who had walked over and introduced themselves to other representatives of the "new generation."

Emily felt a surge of enormous hope watching the ad hoc camaraderie among the children. Too sentimental? Eva was also smiling at the kids.

Virginia's overamplified voice again. "Of course they don't call this clear cutting. Their double speak is *group selection, variable retention, alternative prescription.*"

Next, a member of Responsible Loggers described his group's reforestation efforts and the precariousness of maintaining both their livelihood and the environment.

Baxter stepped forward, not to tell a story, but to bless the gathering with a chant. Then four waiters from Lolo's led them in protest songs.

Emily and Eva were holding hands with dozens of others in a large circle, singing, "We are a gentle, angry people." Emily was so filled with political nostalgia, the pleasure of Eva's proximity, optimism about today's events that she didn't notice the man approaching.

"So I'll see you at Salerno's CD party."

Emily turned. Judson stood with his hand extended. She linked Eva with the person on her left and stepped back from the circle. Smiling, she shook his hand, wishing she hadn't been so namby-pamby about the rattle. She should have decided months before, but she still felt torn. Emily shook herself. How did Judson know about the CD party?

"I played clarinet in college," he answered without being asked. "Still fool around with Bax on his trumpet. Been a fan of Salerno and the Naughty Ladies for years. I didn't know until I saw Theo at a concert last month that you were related to Salerno."

Related. She nodded.

"That she was your partner."

"Yes," Emily smiled. "I'm glad you'll be at the party. Hope Marie will come, too."

The gnawing whirr of truck engines invaded like hostile aircraft.

Quickly, urgently, Virginia joined arms with her civil disobedience class. Emily was surprised to watch Judson join them. Not Baxter. Someone would have to drive the kids home if there were arrests. Emily didn't believe it would get that far, though.

Across the road, she saw Ruth, bridal veil askew, holding tightly to Juan and Joyce, who were desperate to represent the next generation on the line.

Lolo's boys linked elbows with other protestors, singing, "We Shall Overcome."

Eva gripped Jorge's right arm.

Emily walked up and clutched the left arm. "The sheriff wouldn't be amused by your channeling of Paul Revere—in fact, it would be a sure infraction of bail."

"Oh, mannn," Jorge circled his curly head. "What kind of fucked-up country is this where you get arrested for protecting trees?"

"Pretty fucked up," Eva answered under her breath.

Emily nodded toward the skinny photographer. "Look, they won't do anything violent with the media here."

"*The Valley Voice* is hardly CNN," sniffed Eva.

The trucks inched forward. Protestors sank to their knees, then sat down, arms still linked and voices raised in righteous song. Supporters stepped back, singing from the sidelines.

Hot now. Sweltering. Emily wiped sweat from her neck. Eva looked flushed. Why hadn't she brought water? With each breath, she felt she were drawing fire into her lungs.

Time passed tediously. Demonstrators chanted. Truck drivers sat menacingly in their cabs, engines growling. Forty-five minutes after the trucks arrived a cell phone rang in one of the rigs.

Half an hour later, the green trucks inched forward again.

The protestors' voices grew shaky. Everyone was exhausted. Emily noted Joyce's intent, intelligent focus.

Second by second, another half-hour passed.

Piercing the still-blistering air: a police siren. Emily went rigid with the high, mean whine. Jorge squeezed her hand. Closing her eyes, she saw flame, orange light, eating through the trees, sucking along the tinder grass toward her cabin.

She looked up to see Sheriff Roberts pull his shiny new white van in front of the trucks, which were now just a few yards from the protestors. Grabbing Virginia's bullhorn, he broke into the sweaty morning, "Back, back, all of you."

Was he addressing the truck drivers? The people on the ground? The supporters?

"All of you."

Emily moved into the shade with Eva and Jorge. She spotted a reporter with Hayden.

Virginia and her comrades refused to budge.

The trucks remained stationary, engines spewing noise and exhaust.

One by one, Roberts read Miranda rights to protestors, then guided each to the van.

Another hour passed. Six protestors still sat on the road, singing.

The heat and truck fumes made it harder and harder to concentrate.

Roberts ordered the drivers to cut their ignitions.

Finally, the van was filled. No one was left on the ground.

Emily watched dumbly as logging trucks backed away to allow Sheriff Roberts to cart off his criminals. The other protestors began farewells, headed for their cars.

Suddenly a familiar voice blared through the bullhorn. Emily turned to see Joyce standing on her mother's information table shouting, "Post-protest meeting at Lolo's. We'll meet there in half an hour to talk about bail and plan the next action."

Silence in the hot grove. Then a whoop from Jorge and tempered applause from the clutch of tired demonstrators.

Emily followed Eva to the car. She wanted to believe they had accomplished something.

Those huge, hissing trucks alarmed her.

Her circle of friends had looked so small and vulnerable on the dusty ground.

25

On Lansing Street, Emily slid from her car and immediately felt the chill. Reaching into the back for her parka, she reckoned the coast was thirty degrees colder than the Valley. Phoenix would have loved the Big Horn celebration. She always recognized Salerno's music and knew a lot of the partygoers. Still, Emily had wanted to drive alone. She'd declined rides from Lindsey, from Eva. A whole crew were coming from the ranch in Marianne's secondhand SUV (apparently the combination of grandmotherhood and comotherhood had been enough to make her trade in the Harley for a more inclusive vehicle). Emily wanted to travel alone tonight, to split when she needed to, not to come at all. For a week she had fantasized about taking off for Chicago while they were partying, leaving Phoenix in Ruth's kitchen, a farewell note on the oak table.

As she walked along Main Street lined with tourist cars, past the shops, she worried once again if it wouldn't have been more in Salerno's spirit to hold the party at Lolo's. Ruth had argued half a dozen times that an off night during the new Coast Jazz Festival was the best possible way to publicize the new CD. A perfect gig.

Salerno had never believed in perfection, said something had to go wrong to break her spell of anxiety. Now that she was a ghost, she'd have a perfect gig. A safe enough time, perhaps.

Five doors away from Rhythm Riley's and Emily was startled by the blaring lights. The Big Horn van stood in front and she watched Theo's long hair swaying as he unloaded crates of CDs. Country time: she wasn't surprised the music was just arriving, although Theo had promised the CDs would dominate the shop window during the entire festival week. Emily had agreed to arrive early tonight to greet people, but now something drew her across the street. She was wandering directly into the sunset.

Salerno always strolled the headlands before a festival performance.

Emily was allowed to accompany her if she remained silent and promised not to fret that Salerno's outfit was getting damp from fog or worry that they'd be late for a gig (which they were—by two minutes—twice). Emily had learned a lot about silence from Salerno. Silence as a companion. Silence as a respite. But she felt so alone now, and without Salerno's stillness her head rattled with decisions about packing clothes, shipping papers, and safe driving routes to Chicago.

She remembered standing here with Salerno in the high grasses, enjoying the wind as she studied the ripening sky. Tonight's sunset would hide behind those grey, white, silver, and black clouds darting across the west. Salerno used to muse about Japan, just beyond the horizon. She talked dreamily of Tokyo's great music scene, hiking with Emily in the Japanese mountains. She had finally gotten an invitation to play Tokyo and Yokohama this coming fall. The letter arrived before everything happened. Everything.

Death. Emily watched the sky darken. Tears coursed down her cheeks. A fine mist shrouded her body and she recalled Baxter's gossamer balloon sailing to the moon.

Something pulled her back along the broken pavement toward the lights, the voices, the stream of Salerno's music. How long had she stared out toward Yokohama? Long enough to avoid greeting early arrivals because she could see Jorge and Eva at the rear of the store chatting with Mr. Big Horn. Inside, she identified several other Valley faces—a Lolo waiter and a vintner pal of Lindsey's—but she was startled by the number of folks she didn't know, people who were buying Salerno's CDs, discussing her music, standing at the wine and cheese and mineral water table.

Poor Jorge looked like he was trying to hit on Theodore. Surely he'd been in Mendocino long enough to know that long hair and three gold earrings did not a gay man make. She still felt grateful, astonished, that Jorge's charges had been dropped. The prosecutor could present no evidence to warrant a trial, of course, but some Ukiah magistrates were pretty racist. Oddly, the detectives never went after anyone else. Next week her friends would be trooping back to the courthouse for the Eucalyptus Road hearing: Virginia, Judson, Lolo's boys, and the others. Emily worried how the arrest would affect Virginia's job. Her friend brushed off this concern, declaring free speech a civil right, a bloody educational example. Emily didn't press, but she doubted the school principal regarded criminal conviction as a pedagogical contribution.

"Take off your parka and make yourself comfortable."

A deep voice. Tune in, Emily. Michael.

She kissed his cologned cheek.

Michael tried to conceal the concern that he knew annoyed her. "Glad to see you."

She was not, she'd insisted often enough, not the little girl in blond pigtails Mom made him walk to school. Suddenly she realized how wet she'd gotten in the fog. Touching the nest of sodden curls, she smiled ruefully at her brother. Then she noticed someone observing them—a middle-aged woman, pretty, with weathered country skin, greyish black curls under a red-ribboned straw hat. The stranger wore a cheerily embroidered blouse and flowered skirt. Emily must have been staring because Michael turned and noticed her, too.

At this, the woman offered a small grin.

He nodded politely.

"Do you know her?" Emily whispered.

"No," he shrugged, reddening.

"Mendoline" was playing now, one of the first pieces Salerno had written after they bought the land. Vital yet elusive, unlike the work of others who took Coltrane as a guru and modeled their music on his. Salerno's sax was her own—deeply melancholy, especially in this piece. Listening, Emily could see the landscape fading from gold to beige to a faint grey silhouette in the dusk. Now she waited for the next part, yes, here, where Salerno made the sax sound like an educated wasp, zipping and zinging them straight into the hot dawn of a new morning.

The ranch crowd caused a loud, bright commotion as they swooped in the front door, waving to Emily and Michael, to Eva at the back of the room. Lindsey wore a brilliant green blouse and culottes, Malcolm strapped to her front in a yellow baby sack. They were followed by Marianne in a flowing magenta dress. Joyce wore her junior high graduation outfit. How festive they were, perfectly decked out for Salerno's perfect gig.

Virginia and Ruth arrived, gingerly carrying one of Virginia's masterpieces in a huge white box. Theodore bumbled forward, flapping his hands to clear space on the table.

"Sorry we're late," Lindsey buzzed Emily's cheek. "We had to wait for the pièce de résistance to emerge from Ginny's temperamental oven," she wrinkled her nose. "The propane crashed halfway through and I thought we were in for a major artistic tantrum."

Emily laughed.

"I brought a case of our dessert wine. It will be super with lemon poppy seed cake."

"Lemon poppy seed?" Emily was curious. "Ruth's idea?"

"Yeah," Lindsey frowned. "You like lemon poppy seed, right?"

She nodded, grinning.

A huge wave of sadness buckled Emily's knees. Tonight was harder than the memorial. Everyone dressed up, celebrating. She'd overheard a guy at the cash register declare that the essence of a musician was the music. Some vintner friend of Lindsey's. What could he possibly know? The sax was one of Salerno's joys, perhaps the clearest expression of spirit, but it wasn't Salerno. It wasn't their long hikes in the Cascades. It wasn't their sloppy popcorn and soda video marathons when they'd watch three Woody Allen movies to escape a frozen Chicago weekend. It wasn't the sweet scent of Salerno's neck—something between apricots and almonds—when she awoke in the morning, all warm and gorgeously vague. The music was something she made, something she pulled from the air. Something she gleefully shared with whoever listened. But music wasn't the woman herself. Nothing was left of Emily's lover. Nothing. She had been extinguished when that fiery ball dropped into San Francisco Bay.

"Hey, Em, are you okay? Did I say something?" Lindsey handed her a glass of red wine. "You're shivering and your hair's all damp. This'll warm you up."

She didn't want to warm up. She wanted to race back to the ranch and lie on the ground beside Salerno, sink with her into the earth.

Cautiously, Lindsey put her arms around Emily and there they stood, Malcolm gurgling between them. "Hey," she whispered. "I know. I remember what it was like after Angie died. The bottomless sorrow, the immobility."

Emily regarded her younger friend, who had bravely reconstructed her life—staying after Angie's death with the land women whom she didn't know all that well. And now refusing her father's recent summons to a comfortable Seattle life with Malcolm, persisting with her vineyard dreams. Emily gulped the air and hugged Lindsey back, making a couple of idiotic baby noises to ever-cheerful Malcolm. She sipped the wine.

Theodore teetered on a makeshift podium. Emily imagined him slipping straight onto Virginia's exquisite cake, which she had crowned with fresh lemon curd frosting. Lindsey was right about the wine's warming effects. She refilled her glass.

"Attention, friends. May I have your attention!"

Voices lowered. Conversations stilled. Salerno's music was turned down to a whisper behind shuffling feet and pouring wine and Theodore's excited acknowledgments to the producer and sound studio and Rhythm Riley's. Emily inched to the back of the room.

"Most of all, of course, we thank Salerno for the music she gave us. The first time I heard her, I was struck by that fluid precision."

Emily saw their Chicago living room strewn with clippings Salerno intended to file. Her bedside table was piled with books, CDs, rice cakes, five-year-old birthday cards.

"She had superb concentration."

Emily thought Salerno sometimes held the sax as if she were a doctor, examining all possibilities.

"There was a tender authority."

At other moments the instrument was a baby in her tentative care.

"Most critics admired the way she enunciated each note."

Emily heard those long, soft, lovemaking sounds, her thick wet mouth enveloping the reed. She saw Salerno creating rhythm on the pads. At their apartment, she'd arouse Emily this way, calling those pads her "tender buttons." Once or twice Emily caught herself feeling jealous of this attractive, polished wooden instrument.

Surveying the room of friends and fans, Emily expanded with appreciation for earnest Theodore. Maybe Eva was right: Salerno would go on and on in her music. This was the ideal place to celebrate Salerno's legacy—in her one true home, surrounded by people who would continue to join her at parties and for late night solo performances.

"As I conclude my remarks, there's another person to acknowledge: Salerno's partner, Emily Adams. Without Emily's copyright permission, we couldn't have produced these CDs."

Applause. Whistles. (Emily noticed Juan had taught Joyce his technique.) Foot stomping. Bravas.

"Many of you may not know that she has donated all royalties to the Valley Forest Guardians."

Again the room erupted.

Emily closed her eyes. She'd ask him not to mention this. It was meant as a quiet gesture, a gift from Salerno.

The volume was raised on one of Emily's favorite fast pieces—"Wild Bird Morning." People began dancing. She looked for the back exit.

"That was generous of you." A familiar voice, one she had been avoiding.

"Oh, hello, Judson, how are you? I haven't seen you since you were carted away in Emil Roberts's shiny new police van."

"Fine. Fine. They only held us a couple of hours. I guess you know the hearing's next week."

"I know."

"Say, really, thanks for donating the royalties. That's a fine gift."

"Not mine to give," she shrugged. "It's Salerno's music. It belongs here."

"That's very Indian of you."

She raised her eyebrows. Emily knew he wouldn't press her on the rattle, understanding that her conscience was already doing that.

Their conversation was interrupted as the rest of the Eucalyptus Road gang found her, kissing, hugging, thanking. She was drawn to the center of the room for a toast.

Eventually people dispersed again to the dance floor. She overheard Virginia introducing the woman in the hat as Monica, a new high school art teacher, to her friends. Michael took particular interest, inquiring about her sculpture, where she'd taught before. They discovered that they had both attended Stanford in the sixties. Emily wondered at the bond that such common experiences brought, even though they had studied in different departments. It was almost as if people believed they were more themselves in younger times.

Theodore inserted the second CD. Emily swallowed back tears at this familiar melody and leaned against the wall, puzzling about the persistence of youthful identities. Maybe she'd drunk too much wine. Were one's twenties the main performance and everything after an encore? Back then, time was so elastic, so endless, so slow. One's mind and body were stuffed with goals, ideas, rather than with hesitations and regrets. Then she believed she could make a difference, would find love. She used to wake up eager in the morning. When she went to bed, she fell asleep. Was the difference that then everything was possible, a world laid out before her? And that now she was too conscious of what hadn't worked, of where she'd lost? The balance of hope and despair had tipped in the opposite direction.

Emily watched Marianne bopping with Lindsey and Malcolm. Ruth asked Jorge for a dance and she curtsied, then took his hand. "Bye, Bye Blackbird," slow and sweet, the melody ruffled and softened and blasted in Salerno's playful way. One of the few pieces she liked to perform on alto sax. Ruth and Jorge moved gracefully. No trace of

Ruth's injuries. Michael and Monica joined in, smiling to others on the dance floor.

Emily pushed aside her wine glass. She'd had enough, if she were going to safely navigate that foggy, windy coast and forest road back to Beulah. Perhaps she had been romanticizing her twenties. After all, she and Salerno didn't meet until each was over thirty. And surely memories from the last sixteen years remained as sharp and poignant as her college recollections. That evening at the pool table. Their first love-making. Salerno's solo performance at Merkin Hall in New York. A quiet dinner in Zermatt after they had climbed all day in that thin, cool Swiss air. And during those years, each of them contained the Salerno and Emily of grade school and high school and college, their first lovers, their lost jobs. So when they came together, they were more (to themselves and to each other) than they had ever been. They were also less— less self-conscious, less insecure, a little less crazy. Maybe they hadn't shared early ripening, but they had known each other intimately in their prime.

Cold air drifted through the room as a man, then a woman, joined the party. She observed Baxter greeting people in what Theodore called the "jazz community," a phrase that always provoked Salerno, who said that what characterized the jazz scene was individualism, friendly dissension, and vigorous rivalry, not community.

The woman wafted to the drinks table and Emily realized she wasn't with Baxter. Not until Virginia greeted her stiffly did Emily recognize Sally, hair stringy, jeans frayed, weighing twenty-five pounds less than when she left the ranch. Over the months people had run into her at the post office or the gas station, returning with the same story. Sally insisted she was fine, taking a leave from UPS, exploring her choices: perhaps a job in Ukiah, at a friend's office; perhaps joining a permaculture collective in Humboldt County; perhaps returning to her mother's house in Chico. Virginia listened carefully to these dispatches, her face alternately washed with longing and relief. She knew, everyone knew, that her life was better without the mercurial Sally. But it was also smaller. Emily took a long breath, fully understanding how Virginia had been enduring her own deep grief after eighteen years of partnership. Perhaps the mourning was worse when your lover's ghost haunted you as a physical presence when you turned into a grocery aisle or danced at a party.

No one had specifically invited Sally, but why shouldn't she come?

Salerno had known her for years. Often enough Salerno sampled some of Sally's primo crop.

Salerno's fusion of blues and jazz and rock dipped and bobbed across the room.

So many people on the floor, dancing everything from the twist to the Mashed Potato to western swing. Jorge was brilliantly partnered with one of Lolo's boys (Emily definitely had to learn their names by the court hearing). Baxter and Judson were mixing it up in a threesome with Joyce, creating an intergenerational, intercultural choreography that would have overjoyed Salerno. Marianne was trying to teach the bop to Michael, who barely remembered it, and to Lindsey, who could barely believe it. Malcolm smiled toothlessly, a wee joey in Lindsey's pouch.

Yes, almost everyone was grooving and she shouldn't have been surprised when Eva appeared before her. She was wearing the brilliant red skirt from the adult school graduation and her hair was braided in a burnished crown around her head.

"We haven't talked all night," Eva said softly. "You've been so busy hosting."

Emily shrugged, blushing deeply. "Sorry, sorry. I meant to come over several times. I noticed you chatting. Dancing with everyone."

Eva cleared her throat. "Not quite everyone." She held out her hand.

Emily remembered holding this hand one recent evening at the pond. She was infused with excitement and fear. All night she had yearned for and resisted this. Someone to lean on, to whisper to. She allowed herself to be led to an unclaimed corner at the back. Cramped. Close. Intimate. They stayed there for an entire set of tracks, first dancing separately, then moving closer and closer to Salerno's improvisations. Emily found herself weeping silently into Eva's neck while the other woman held her securely around the waist, both of them swaying to the sweet saxophone.

Eva spoke first, "Oh, how I've ached to hold you."

"Yes," was all Emily could manage. She closed her eyes, imagined waking up entangled in Eva's smooth limbs, kissing those soft, full lips. Now as her tears abated, she found herself sniffing Eva's skin for the familiar scent of apricots and almonds. Her blood froze. What was she doing? For months she had managed to avoid these feelings. And here at Salerno's CD party, dancing to her music, among all her friends, she had surrendered. The huge hunger was replaced by rapid self-loathing. She had to get out, had to escape this party, had to leave California soon.

Emily whispered to dear Eva that she needed air and solitude. She might return to the party, might not. Carefully, she stepped back.

Eva kissed her forehead.

Emily pursed her lips, holding back tears. She pulled her parka quietly from the rack. The last thing she wanted was a grand exit with more congratulations, condolences, or thank yous. She would slip out the side door, leaving her friends immersed in Salerno's music.

Emily strode toward the headlands, tripping again on the uneven, poorly lit pavement of Main Street. All the stores were shut, the owners now at home in Caspar or Fort Bragg or Little River. Fewer and fewer people actually lived in the village of Mendocino. Property prices were too high and zoning regulations strictly maintained to cultivate Victorian village ambience. If Emily were doing regional planning here, she'd urge something different. Mendocino was pretty but risked being processed into a theme park of shopping and eating, with most beds occupied by wealthy visitors. One company had introduced silly horse-drawn, fringed surreys. She didn't want Mendocino to adopt the designer sprawl of Carmel, so she appreciated the zoning board's attention to building height and design. Yet the town plan was artificial, even stifling, trying to freeze history in the name of authenticity. She knew this from her studies on the ranch: time passed, populations shifted.

Stepping on the grassy headlands trail, she zipped her parka. Out of habit; it wasn't cold. The marine layer had finally blown north toward Eureka, toward Oregon, and now, as she looked up into the clear sky, she saw stars—maybe she'd spot a few shooters before she left for Chicago—and a full moon. She'd have plenty of walking light from that huge yellow globe; all the same, she avoided trails near the cliffs.

The moon shone golden pools in the black ocean and lit up the high waves cresting toward the shore. A world at once quiet and raucous. Eyes closed, she inhaled. What a reprieve from the riot of voices-laughter-music: to be still enough to hear the wings of gulls and cormorants and an occasional squawk, to feel the sea thundering in her chest.

Shapes materialized fifty yards ahead, just at the edge of a cliff. Emily blinked, hoping they were an optical illusion or a hallucination from the wine. With wide, clear eyes, she could identify the tableau now. A cross. A man kneeling beside it. Wind carried the faintest mumble of his prayers.

She supposed they were prayers and not curses, yet with Hayden how did you distinguish? She stood there longer than she should have, wondering. Intruding. Wasn't this a private moment and didn't he have as much right as anyone to solitary acts of witness or supplication or rhapsody? Watching Hayden, Emily felt disloyal to Eva's terrors and Virginia's resentment. But alone here, kneeling by his cross at the precipice, he looked so vulnerable that she could feel nothing more than sadness for his misguided mission. She even had an odd impulse to comfort him.

Snapping back to reality, she tiptoed back the way she came.

On Main Street, approaching the steaming windows of Rhythm Riley's, she felt Salerno's beat in the sidewalk. She stood—out of view— at the window's edge and watched the Beulah women dancing in a circle with Judson and Baxter, waving their arms and laughing. She resolved to release the rattle this week. It was all that kept her here, that and asking Ruth if she'd adopt Phoenix.

Four people entered the dance floor—Eva and Joyce, who were doing a rusty version of swing, and Michael and Monica, who seemed to be talking more than dancing.

Emily would miss her friends terribly. She'd miss her morning view of the hills and her sunset walks with Salerno. She listened now to her partner's "Night Lights," a recent composition, one she had performed only two or three times before she died. They must be getting to the end of the boxed set. Ruth was right, after all. Salerno lived on, and she was surrounded by friends. It was time for Emily to leave her in the Valley.

26

All summer Emily had peered out at the fields for workers but saw no one, no shadows, no ghosts. Maybe she wasn't driving by the vineyards early enough or late enough. Wait for harvest time, Ruth had said. The vines grew tall and leafier then, as the mowed hills receded into the background. Today she looked closely for pickers as she drove to Fairburn to mail file boxes to Chicago.

She watched cars pull up to the tasting rooms. Inside, the vintners and their clerks worked behind minibars, serving communion drops of sauvignon blanc and pinot noir. She varied her patronage at the independent wineries as a way of equitably supporting the local economy and of getting to know people at the same time.

Maybe some recognized Emily as one of the residents of "Gay Ladies' Lane." Ruth first learned the nickname of their road at Emergency Medical Training; paramedics, she discovered, had named all the unmarked streets and roads. Lindsey had been shocked but couldn't say why. The disrespect? Invasion of privacy? Loss of anonymity? But the other ranch women thought it was funny, and when Jorge heard he immediately wanted to rename his road "Fag and Dyke Drive." Laughing, Eva said this would be a novel way of losing her job. Besides, she added, Jaime and Rosa and Mrs. Ruiz might not appreciate the new address.

Through the high brass gates of Blanchard Estates this morning, Emily did spot a dozen people scattered among the row of vines. They were covered in loose, pale clothing, wearing floppy white or straw hats to protect against the sun. Ageless from this distance. Also sexless, raceless. Performers bending and picking in concentrated ballet. She wondered if Rafael were among them, or Juan's mother.

In town, she passed the hotel and recalled last year's Community Fair victory dinner. Bracing herself, she heard again that horrible screech of

the car skidding into Ruth. One moment on the highway had transformed Ruth's year, her year.

Emily hadn't yet told her friends the departure date—month's end—
but they must have guessed her plans as they watched the stack of books
by her desk getting larger and larger. Still, she'd delayed her departure
so often, maybe they decided to postpone thinking about it until her car
was actually rolling out the gate. No matter. She'd promised herself one
detachment at a time. And today she'd call Judson about the rattle.

Once she'd finished errands and summoned courage to phone, it was
two o'clock. Phoenix was cocking her curly head beseechingly. Emily
had promised a long walk.

At four they were back at the cabin. She should start the salad
for Ruth's potluck tonight. She opened all the windows, drew blinds
against the sun. A bad time to call Judson. He was probably clearing
away the day's work, getting ready to head home to his second full-time
job at the rancheria. But if she didn't stop procrastinating, she'd become immobile.

Judson recognized her voice immediately. Just as she said, "Judson
Sands, please," he declared, "Emily! Good to hear from you. I looked
all around at Rhythm Riley's to say goodbye, but you had disappeared."

"I slipped out a little early," she began, "because . . ."

"I saw you at the hearing, appreciated your support, but you sat in
the back row. And poof, when I turned around after the adjournment,
you were gone again. The Lone Ranger?"

Amused, unsettled by his trope, she looked helplessly around her
half-dismantled, half-packed cabin. She was tired, overwhelmed, ready
for a nap, utterly unprepared for friendly ebullience.

"Now I bet you're calling because you're about to vanish again—
to that northern plain city named after the great chief of the Illini
Confederation."

"But first," she forced herself back into the conversation. "There's
something I'd like to bring you." She wanted to explain the length of her
decision, the pressure from the state museum, her own fond attach-
ments to this beautiful instrument, how she had fantasized about placing it on her Chicago mantle to remind her of Mendocino and the
Douglas fir and Salerno. Instead, she said simply. "Something I need to
return."

"Oh, Emily," he choked.

Silence.

To avoid embarrassment—his? hers?—she raced on. "So I could bring the rattle by any evening this week, no, not Tuesday or Thursday, but any of the other days."

"You know, Bax has already made a holder for it, for the display case."

"Wish he'd told me," she laughed, "would've saved a lot of time wrestling with this decision."

"Our Bax is a man of optimism and action."

"And his brother?"

"His brother waits. Sometimes—like now—he's a very grateful guy. Thank you!"

Unnerved, she rushed ahead. "I have dinner with Ruth on Tuesday and tutoring on Thursday. But how about Wednesday or Friday?"

"Friday! Marie's always in a good mood on Friday. Come for dinner and story hour."

"I don't want to impose." Her chest tightened. She wished mailing it were safe. "I mean," she stumbled. "I haven't even returned your hospitality from last time."

"You're returning something more important."

She could almost see his huge grin.

"And I'd like to ask one more favor?"

"Yes?"

"Would you bring your friend Eva with you?"

She flushed. How did he mean "friend"? What made him think she knew Eva that well? She'd resolved not to spend more time alone with her. They'd see each other at tutoring and maybe the ranch women would have a farewell dinner for her. But no one on one. Judson's invitation meant at least an hour's drive each way, alone with Eva.

Judson sliced through her dithering. "That tutoring program she started, the one you're involved with, Bax and I have been talking about setting up something like that here. For Indian youth in the area—Ukiah, Redwood Valley, something that might draw them to the Cultural Center by offering tangible benefits. We do a pretty good job with the young ones, but some of our teenagers, well . . . we're losing them to alcohol and drugs."

"Of course," Emily said. "I'll invite Eva and ask her to call you so you can know how many people are coming to dinner."

"If there's one thing we don't do, it's count people at the dinner table. There's always room for extra friends, so if there's someone else you want to bring . . ."

"No, I think Eva will be enough," Emily answered firmly, wondering if Marie subscribed to Judson's philosophy of the ever-expanding pot.

She hung up, unsettled as always after a chat with Judson, who silently raised questions about every assumption she owned. Emily glanced out the south window to see a kite fluttering over the grasses. Stationary yet moving, like her childhood image of the Holy Ghost. He/ She was called the Holy Spirit now. One of those fashionable changes Mom always resisted. *Ghost* was a perfectly serviceable word. Besides, this divine incarnation *was* a ghost, Mom had insisted, a real presence rather than some theological concept like a spirit. Judson Sands and her mother would have liked each other. Mom would have assured him he was a Pole at heart.

Sometimes Eva reminded Emily of her mother. The practical good will; the unabashed seriousness. These qualities had drawn Emily to her. These and her intense brown eyes, her golden skin, her trim body. But Emily had no room for romance now, maybe ever again. Salerno had offered more than enough grace, joy, and provocation for a lifetime. Emily's Chicago days would be quieter now; she was ready for quiet. Ready to concentrate on her work, to make some contributions. Well past the time for taking. Emily glanced again at the kite before returning to unpacked files.

Poor Ruth. People kept backing out of dinner at the last minute. Lindsey had an emergency at the vineyard. Eva had driven down to San Francisco to help Jorge look for an apartment with his new boyfriend, Stefan, one of Lolo's waiters. Joyce was sulking in the loft with a broken heart.

So Ruth, Virginia, and Emily enjoyed an intimate evening at the round oak table—quiet except for the gurgles of Malcolm, who was nesting in Lindsey's state-of-the art bassinet, and the occasional sob from a young lady in the loft.

"How long has she been like this?" Emily whispered, raising her eyes to the ceiling.

"Oh, a week," Ruth answered, a touch impatiently. "We should be well past the whispering and wallowing stage."

"So what happened?" Virginia leaned forward.

Emily worried about her friend who had lost ten pounds this summer from the lumber protest, the Sally worrying, the strategies for escorting Darwin back into the classroom. Last September had seemed such an innocent time, when major preoccupations were baking and stitching for the Community Fair.

"Well," Ruth said in a natural, audible voice, ignoring the escalating sobs from above. "You've met the Kelloggs, that pleasant, but perhaps conventional family Warren brought up from Hayward to run his new bed and breakfast?"

"Oh, yeah," Virginia said. "The big, bluff guy and the blond woman who wears pumps and skirts to shop in Fairburn."

"Now, now, sisters," Emily laughed. Then more seriously, "Annie Kellogg is a smart woman. She ran some big office in Alameda County and she's volunteered at the tutoring center. And Bob Kellogg asked me about getting involved with the Forest Guardians."

"Yeah, yeah," grinned Ruth. "Slap my New York snideness. Nice liberal folk who moved up here because it seemed a healthier place to rear their kids."

Virginia rolled her eyes. "Guess the Chamber of Commerce hasn't added that page about pesticides in the aquifers and fires engulfing the Valley."

"Shhh," said Emily, knocking on the oak table. "We haven't had a fire in weeks."

"Anyway," Ruth cleared her throat, "young Betsy Kellogg is a very pretty girl."

From above: "Betsy Kellogg is a vamp."

The three women sputtered into their napkins.

"And Juan has a fickle heart," shrugged Ruth.

Virginia called to Joyce, "Oh, baby, I'm sorry. I know this hurts."

Another round of sobbing and bed pounding.

Ruth whispered, "Actually, it's getting better—about an hour less moaning each day."

Emily resolved to do something special with Joyce this weekend. Maybe walk to the waterfall; that would be a perfect time to explain Phoenix was hers now—if she got Ruth's permission.

"So tell us about the meeting with your principal," Ruth said.

"The principal called you in?" asked Emily, alarmed.

"Yeah, Spineless Spencer sat enthroned in his ergonomically perfect chair from the Staples Summer Sale."

Emily would miss Virginia's archness.

"Started out congratulating me on my teaching evaluations, best in the school."

"Just like last year!" exclaimed Ruth. "Brava!"

"Hang on. Then he says, 'I was relieved to hear your charges were dropped, that the judge only issued a strict warning against trespassing.' "

"The jerk," spat Ruth. "It's innocent when proven innocent, yes? Or did this country shift on the global axis while I was napping?"

"Well, you couldn't claim Valley High was ever run on constitutional standards."

"More like ostrich standards."

"You got it," Virginia snapped. "And the Crusade for California has been resurrected."

"Hayden and his sandwich board?" asked Ruth.

"On the sidewalk across from my classroom on Thursday afternoons during summer session biology. Currently we're doing paramecia, so he has a long wait for our primate sisters."

Ruth stared at her seriously, "What will you do?"

"Teach," said Virginia, nibbling the pasta. "Do my job." She folded her napkin into smaller and smaller squares.

"You have all my support," Ruth took her friend's hand.

"Mine, too." Emily felt hollow, knowing how soon she'd be leaving.

"Thanks. What I really could use is a trust fund for when I get fired."

"They wouldn't dare," Ruth flared. She tossed the salad and passed it. "Protestors? Spencer hasn't seen protestors. People would converge from all over the county if they fired you."

"And if it came to money," Emily said. "I know Michael admires you a lot. He'd help out. Look, he got all the bail money back."

"Your brother is a great guy," Virginia grinned, "even if he is a little quick to defend free enterprise."

"Apparently that new art teacher likes him," Ruth raised an eyebrow.

"Oh, really?" Emily asked coolly. "I've only met her once, at the CD party."

Ruth frowned. "Yes, the party. I've been meaning to ask what happened to you that night. You disappeared like some specter. Everyone was worried."

Virginia interrupted, "Lighten up. It must've been a tough night for Em, engulfed by Salerno's music, old friends. Hey, let's get back to the gossip about Monica Kowalski."

"Kowalski?" asked Emily. "A nice Polish girl?"

"Well, Joyce and I saw them at the sheep dog trials, sitting together in the bleachers."

"A real headline!" Virginia's voice lowered in disappointment.

"They were holding hands," Ruth added triumphantly. "And not spending much time looking in the direction of the dogs."

"Okay!" Virginia clapped her hands. "That's pretty cool." She looked nervously at Emily. "I mean, I like your brother and I always thought he was kind of lonely."

Emily finished her salad. Monica did seem okay. A little old. No, she was exactly Michael's age. Her friends waited for a response. Well, now that she was leaving, he would need someone here. Yawning, she said, "She seems nice enough."

Virginia laughed, "Oh, Emily, ambivalence is written all over your face. I felt the same when my sister got married."

Emily's eyes widened.

Ruth mediated. "It's some distance between sheep dog trials and the altar."

"You know what I mean," Virginia said. "And I'm sure you'll love Monica. She can be quite wacky, like Salerno at times. She's also a good political person, a thinker."

"Isn't Michael a bit old for romance?" Emily knew she sounded ridiculous.

Virginia snorted. "What are you talking about—he's four years older than you?"

"Three," Emily admitted. She didn't like this conversation and wondered if there were a tactful way to skip dessert.

"So you're over the hill?" Ruth inquired gently.

"I had rather hoped so."

For some reason this comment sent Virginia and Ruth into hysterics.

After dinner, Virginia suggested they take a walk along Eucalyptus Road to see what the Lumber Corps had done since the demonstration.

Emily agreed, eager to clear her head and to walk off some of Ruth's rich cooking.

Phoenix was out the door as soon as they opened it.

Ruth called upstairs. "Joyce, dear, are you sure you don't want to come with us? It will be a short hike. Sunset is soon."

Silence. Sniffing.

"No, thanks. I've got a math test tomorrow."

"Okay," said her mother. "We'll leave Malcolm then. Will you come downstairs and keep an eye on him? We'll be back in an hour."

Eucalyptus Road was a world away from the scene of last month's protest. At first, in the soft evening light, it felt like one more hidden, beautiful Valley road. The air was cooler than it had been that dramatic morning and drier, too. Each year, Emily thought, the Valley almost disintegrated as it grew hotter and more arid until the November rains. Phoenix dashed ahead. Half a mile up the hill, they spotted the clear cutting. A snag-toothed dragon had gone on drunken binges. Many trees had been trucked out, but branches and stumps were strewn everywhere.

Eyes filling at this mess, Emily struggled, "What about reforestation? Shouldn't they be planting seedlings now?"

Virginia laughed. "Grape seedlings?" She looked at Ruth for confirmation. "They'll take five to eight years to mature."

Emily was baffled.

Ruth explained. "Lots of timberland, once it's been 'harvested,' is converted to vineyards. By large wineries whose sales have expanded beyond their acreage."

"Jesus!" Emily was irritated by her own ignorance. "This place is turning into one huge bacchanal. With wine and dope as the major crops, people will become so oblivious, they'll forget we used to have trees."

Virginia nodded, amused. "You sound like our little Fire and Brimstone prophet."

Ruth checked her watch. "Time to turn back if we're going to make it out by dark."

Emily wondered if motherhood had wired Ruth's internal clock.

She faced her friends. "It's bad enough that they're chopping down old growth and planting redwood seedlings, but now they're redesigning the agricultural economy."

"Glad to know you've changed your stand on ag quotas," Virginia said.

"But they're devastating this landscape."

Virginia inhaled sharply and assumed a teacherly voice. "It's what whites have been doing since we came. Clearing the trees for cattle ranches, which metamorphosed into orchards, which turned into vineyards. Now real estate rustlers have found the Valley. I heard Myra was offered a million dollars for her parcel."

"That flat, ugly acreage across from Fairburn's Intergalactic Air Pad?" laughed Emily.

"Seriously, though," Ruth began.

"I *am* serious," Virginia warned. "A million dollars. You have to track that kind of investment; it could ruin the community."

"Community!" Emily burst out. "Whose community—loggers? Vintners? Migrant pickers? Dopesters? I understand this place less than I did a year ago. Everything keeps changing: the crops, the landscape, the people. Even my friends. I'm glad Jorge and Stefan have found true love, but it's sad to see them move down to the city."

Ruth and Virginia exchanged silent glances. They had almost reached the car. The three women paused to watch an iridescent orange memento of another scorching day sink into the western mountains. Emily always followed the sun in her mind until it reached the roaring Pacific waters, where she imagined it dissolving slowly into a smaller and smaller disk, eventually adding a drop of color to the waters.

"Well," Ruth spoke finally. "Virginia and I are still here."

Virginia blinked her large blue eyes in assent.

"And you, my dear Emily, you're still here and we're grateful for your company, however long it lasts."

Ignoring the hint, Emily slid behind the wheel and turned the ignition key. Phoenix hopped in the back seat. The others joined them.

After dropping Virginia and Ruth at their cabins, she headed up to the ridge, taking the road especially slowly because last week a fawn had leaped into the darkness in front of her car.

By the time she parked, she was shivering from the sharp drop in temperature. Inside her cabin Emily turned on every light, grateful for the solar energy stored during the sizzling day. She'd need these lights to pack her files, label boxes. Why did she go on that walk? She never used to procrastinate like this. Grabbing a sweater, she wished she could light her woodstove, but the grasses were far too dry for this to be a permissive burn day.

27

The wedding invitation shouldn't have been a surprise. She'd learned too much about the vanity of expectation this topsy-turvy year. Yet Emily had a hard time fathoming how much Michael had changed his life, that he only spent half the week at his San Francisco office and then drove north every Wednesday afternoon. And now this.

Emily leaned over her desk, peering across the valley at rows and rows of naked yellow sticks that would soon hold trellised grapevines. Just last fall, that parcel had been Astrid Cumming's horse farm. Now Astrid had moved to Humboldt County, transporting her animals in several new first-class trailers.

"Look at this, Phoenix, my brother is getting married!" Just what was her resistance to the happy event? Over the last year Michael had often talked about his loneliness. She had even tried to hook him up with Eva.

Phoenix cocked her head in several directions, angling for a walk. Unimpressed by the embossed off-white card Emily held, she curled up for a nap on the couch.

"I mean, the woman is pleasant enough." She thought back to their dinner at the hotel last week, when Michael and Monica announced their plans to her. She was grateful they had told her before mailing the invitations. Of course Michael would be sensitive enough for that. "Sure, Monica is pretty—I mean bright brown eyes, great smile. She knows how to style her grey hair so she looks très chic. What do you expect, she's an artist."

Emily stood up and recommenced packing files into a mailing box.

"Monica reached out to me, read up on regional design. And she's careful to let Michael and me have private times together."

Phoenix was snoring.

"Virginia is right, she's got a great sense of humor. She makes Michael happy. She makes everyone happy. She should be making *me* happy. So what's wrong?"

Her attention was deflected by three turkey vultures sailing low over the grass in front of her cabin. Carelessly, she shoved too many files into the cardboard box, then watched impassively as it split, sending papers and folders and maps across the unswept floor.

"Six weeks! That's what's wrong. They've only known each other six weeks! Well, maybe at their age they know what they want, don't see any reason to wait. Okay. Okay."

Composing herself, she cleared the mess. Her mind shifted to a big fire two days before on Eucalyptus Road. The police blamed the blaze on vigilante protestors. Creepy, happening just a day after she and Virginia and Ruth took their sunset tour. Virginia had been so outspoken on the way home that night—well, she was always outspoken. Emily really didn't want to suspect her friend. But then, when Virginia was younger, she'd been involved in some dicey antiwar tactics. Sally had let this slip during one of her higher flights last fall.

Emily wrapped cello tape securely around her mailing box—as if securing it for transport to Kampala—first horizontally, then vertically, then diagonally. Let Vesta laugh when they arrived in the office. At least they would arrive. And she, soon after.

Sally.

Sally, it was so sad. Lindsey had seen her hanging out with those potheads in front of the bakery in Mendocino. She asked if Sally needed help and Sally just waved her on. So Lindsey sadly left behind her neighbor of ten years. Poor Virginia. Poor Sally.

Christ! Emily looked at her watch. Time to pick up Eva if they were going to be on time at Judson and Marie's.

She reached up to the top shelf for the red flannel cloth that swaddled the rattle. Looking out to Salerno's tree, she smiled, nodded. Yes, this was what Salerno would want. For a while she played with the romantic notion of replacing the rattle in the ground to rest with the spirit of her sweet musician. But from the sounds of that CD party, Salerno's spirit was hardly resting and Emily now felt absolutely certain that the rattle belonged at the rancheria.

As she changed clothes, her mind wandered back to the wedding. Six weeks! Emily shook her head. Well, Michael's fifty-four. You could say he's been waiting a quarter century for the right woman. After all that time he should know what he wants. She wouldn't have been surprised if he had eloped with Eva. Maybe she was simply pissed off to be on the sidelines.

Maybe she was jealous.

Phoenix barked at Emily's new outfit.

"Okay, girl."

The dog hopped off the couch.

"Judson said to bring you, said his kids love dogs. You can sit between Eva and me on the ride over."

Both Emily and Eva were astonished by the feast. This was no modest dinner with the Sands family, but rather a banquet for thirty people in the cultural hall.

Wide eyed, Emily turned to Eva.

Eva smiled. "It's a powwow to celebrate the rattle's return and to thank you for honoring their traditions."

"God, if I'd known, I'd have taken it to Judson's office in Ukiah."

"Which is why he didn't tell you." She gripped Emily's hand firmly, as if to keep her from bolting.

Baxter's polished wooden stand was as beautiful as the case of oak and beveled glass. Carefully, he removed the rattle from the flannel and placed it on display.

Everyone applauded.

They sat down to a meal of fry bread and acorn mush and chicken and mashed potatoes and salad. Emily was glad they weren't serving wine because her head was already swirling with the names and handshakes of dozens of new people. Eva and Judson spent dinner discussing the tutoring program, as planned. Emily enjoyed the more low-key company of Marie and her kids. She was beginning to think she might survive the evening until Judson stood and clinked his glass.

"Before we eat dessert and move into the far room for Baxter's stories, I want to make a formal thank you to Emily Adams for returning an important piece of our heritage."

Emily stared at the chicken bones. It had been a perfectly cooked breast. And the fry bread was delicious. She concentrated on digesting her meal, on planning the next day's errands, but she couldn't forestall the rosy embarrassment creeping up her neck, reddening her face.

"The museum people, they're not bad folk," Judson said, holding up his hands to the anticipated hisses of several younger rancheria residents. "But they treat our relics as singular pieces of art. It's almost as if they sterilize them in those temperature-controlled buildings. Here we will keep the rattle in Baxter's case so all of us, especially the children, can witness the craft of our ancestors. But we will also bring it out at ceremonial times and use it with care and honor, listen to what it has to teach us."

Loud clapping. Foot stomping. A shrill whistle. Emily automatically looked around for Juan.

"So let's all give Emily Adams another round of applause. And on your way to the story room, take a moment to thank her personally."

Just as Emily thought she'd suffocate from all this undeserved attention, Eva caught her eye. She was smiling brightly, then carefully mouthing one word over and over.

Emily got it.

"Breathe," Eva advised.

She managed to eat half her rich, juicy berry pie before they adjourned for story hour.

Everyone settled on blankets that had been carefully laid in semicircles on the floor. The children's blankets were near the front. The adults arranged themselves at the back. Eva sat crosslegged next to Emily as if she had attended a dozen story hours, but Emily knew this was her first visit to the rancheria. Graceful Eva was at ease with almost everyone, almost everywhere.

Baxter cleared his throat and began a tale about how the Pomo had learned to dance. His way of speaking, she remembered now, was slow and sonorous, coloring each word. Halfway through the story, Emily began to hear sounds from the next room. Everyone else ignored them, so she returned to Baxter's suspenseful drama.

The door flew open. Judson burst through, holding the rattle. His sons Lee and Sean followed, dancing. Baxter stepped to the side as Judson began to play the ancient elderberry rattle, shaking it rapidly so it opened and shut, clicking, clacking like jaws. Then he brought the rattle down to his palm making a different sound as the top section of the instrument knocked against the bottom.

Emily grinned, remembering Judson dancing at Salerno's CD party. His children had inherited his nimbleness and enthusiasm. Marie watched proudly.

With a hand on Emily's arm, Eva whispered, "This is very special. A big acknowledgment. You must feel honored."

Emily turned to the tears in Eva's eyes and realized they were both crying. Unable to speak, she returned to the performance. Long after her friend scooted back, Emily could feel the warm pressure of Eva's fingers on her upper arm.

It was midnight before they could get away. Driving along 101, they were silent, absorbing the evening's festivities. As they entered the highway toward Fairburn and ascended through mountainous farmland, Emily asked, "Do they have any leads on the Eucalyptus Road fire? It could have been pretty dangerous if it had jumped the firebreak and hit Grumble Vineyard."

"Yes," Eva nodded in the darkness, "the workers' camp is just at the fence line there."

"This fire scared me more than most."

"Did Virginia tell you we saw the trucks and helicopters when we were driving back from Lolo's last night?"

"You and Virginia?"

"Yeah, about 10. Service is slow since Stefan left, and we didn't eat until late."

Emily felt intense relief that Virginia was eating with Eva, not setting fires, and was fully ashamed of her ridiculous suspicion. Then she had to admit that old bad feeling—the stalking fear of not knowing who was setting these fires or why.

"We had to take a detour along Grumble Road to avoid the equipment. It looked like a space launch."

Now a new wild anxiety. Were Eva and Virginia dating? For how long? Sweat surfaced on her palms and she wiped them, one at a time, on the upholstered seat.

"So you and Virginia were having dinner?" She aimed for a noncommittal tone.

Eva paused, as if weighing the question, then said with a teasing lilt, "Yes, Virginia and I and ten other members of the Forest Guardians. Actually, we were expecting you."

"Oh, oh, yes," Emily ducked her head. In her packing frenzy she'd forgotten the dinner.

They drove quietly. Emily noticed the moon for the first time that night. She recalled the delicious meal, Baxter's story, the extraordinary music and dancing, the whole spirited evening. And she sighed again at understanding Virginia had nothing to do with the fire. Her mind wandered back to the timbre of Eva's voice as she described the Guardians'

meeting. She stopped herself. Eva was lovely, but Emily had to surrender any fascination. She was heading to Chicago right after Michael's wedding.

"I hope Jorge and Stefan are coming up for the wedding," Emily
said.

"I forgot," Eva was suddenly flustered. "Jorge wanted me to ask a
favor."

"Yes?" Emily saw Fairburn lights as they took the last highway turns.

"He wondered if he and Stefan could camp on your ridge. I mean, of
course, I told them they were welcome in my house. But he said no
thanks. He loves that ridge of yours. Thinks it has the most beautiful
views in the valley. Says it would be a romantic retreat after a romantic
afternoon." She rolled her eyes.

"Of course," Emily said. "In fact, he can have the cabin. Monica and
Michael are driving up the coast that night to their honeymoon hide-
away, so I'll use his place."

"Are you sure?" Eva asked anxiously. "They don't want to put you
out."

They were turning up Mineshaft Road now.

"No problem." Emily stopped the car.

"Thanks for a very fine evening!" Eva exclaimed.

"A complete surprise to me."

Eva leaned over and kissed Emily on the side of her mouth, then slid
slowly out the door. "See you at the wedding!"

"Yes," nodded Emily, swallowing hard. "A week from Sunday."

She was driving home faster than she should, eager for bed after a
long, unpredictable, emotional day. No danger of a speeding ticket;
everyone knew Sheriff Roberts retired early. His kind of criminal—
Jorge, the Forest Guardians, the pickers—prowled in daylight.

Once she pulled up to her cabin, Emily felt too restless to climb to
the loft. Even though the air was chilly, she wanted to sit outside on the
deck and watch the stars. She poured herself a glass of zinfandel—that
would warm her up—and leaned back, counting planets, visualizing
constellations. Eva's kiss had been more than a friendly peck. Emily's
entire body moved now with a long, full breath. She was a fine woman,
no doubt even more beautiful in bed, long dark curls falling over her
shoulders, her nipples. She imagined Eva's firm breasts and reminded
herself she'd never see them. She was finally returning to real life. Phoenix sighed at her feet and again Emily glanced at the stars, made fainter
by the slice of moon.

She couldn't find busy skies like this in the electrically bright Chicago nights. The moon was waxing, which meant it would be full on Michael and Monica's wedding night. A good omen, according to the bride, who had consulted an astrologer in Caspar. Under this night light, Emily suspected, those Moon Indians must have hidden some flames for themselves. The fire of the wine was working. Warm and sleepy, she let Phoenix into the house, then climbed the ladder to her loft.

28

As Emily drove to the wedding with Ruth and Joyce, she exclaimed over the grape pickers. For months there had been no one in the fields; now they were everywhere.

Ruth shook her head. "Emily, what's the big surprise? It's harvest time."

"But this is Sunday."

Ruth laughed.

"Seriously, don't they get time off?" demanded Emily. "Aren't they Catholic?"

"Well, it works like this—first they're employed, then they're Catholic."

"There's a Saturday evening mass," Joyce contributed from the back seat.

"What about a day of rest?"

"That's why the United Farm Workers is organizing." Ruth explained impatiently.

Emily recalled a recent rally at the fairgrounds, all those black and red flags.

"Haven't you wondered why Rafael hasn't been in class for two weeks?"

"No," she was defensive, "I guessed he was exhausted after long days of picking."

"And long nights."

"They harvest at night?"

"Sure, what do you think those big lights are?"

Again, Emily felt ignorant. She hadn't spotted the night lights. She hadn't noticed a lot this week. Maybe her attention was shutting down as departure loomed.

"Well," she changed the topic. "I guess we're lucky Lindsey's grapes are too young or we couldn't have the wedding at her redwood grove."

They parked on recently mowed grass. The three of them carefully carried culinary offerings to the grove, walking slowly to avoid gopher holes.

Amazed by the transformation of grove into sanctuary, Emily paused, taking everything in. Lindsey and Virginia had set up blue folding chairs on either side of an aisle. At the front, they had transformed an ancient stump into an altar with a lace cloth and a vase of golden poppies and white cosmos. Off to the left, under the shade of grand oaks, were two long tables—one piled with presents, the other crowded with salads and casseroles. In the middle of the food table stood Virginia's spectacular wedding cake: three tiers of vanilla, chocolate, and strawberry. Virginia hovered over the cake, nervous lest it get knocked off by the bearer of a hearty casserole; worried the sunny sky would open with unforecasted showers.

Lindsey tried to reassure her. "Relax, the gods will protect your perfect cake until the ceremony ends, at which point we'll eagerly stand in line to consume it."

"What do you know about gods?" Virginia asked testily.

"I was just coming up with something poetic to distract you."

"Talk about poetic," Emily interrupted to settle both of them, to dismiss her own irrational jitters. "This setting is spectacular, Linz. Michael will be so grateful."

"Well," grinned Virginia, "he's your brother. Your only family—except for us, of course—and we wanted to do right by him."

Lindsey glanced around, distracted. "Has anyone seen Marianne and Malcolm?"

"Yes," Ruth joined them. "Marianne's pushing the pram down by the rose trellis."

Lindsey giggled. "Kid loves roses. Bet we have a little gay boy on our hands."

"So great to watch Marianne bonding with him," said Virginia.

"Now I just wish she'd bond with me," Lindsey sighed.

Puzzled, Emily wondered if they had been arguing.

"Oh, don't get into that again," scolded Virginia.

"Maybe the wedding is making me moody."

Emily noticed how pretty Lindsey was in her long, royal blue cotton dress. Each of them looked stunning. Ruth in her purple silk shirt and pants. Joyce in a lacey green dress. Even unsentimental Virginia was nattily decked out in a dark red pants suit and bolo tie. Emily was glad she had spent so much time selecting her outfit—after all, she was giving away the groom. Yes, the black and white dress seemed just the thing. She wasn't as sure about the crimson straw hat that the clerk had talked her into. She found herself wondering what Eva would wear.

Lindsey persisted despite Virginia's sour expression. "I've been trying to get Marianne to agree to a commitment ceremony," she explained to Emily, "but she's just as intransigient as she was when I wanted to get pregnant."

"Then you're in trouble, sweets," Virginia teased. "You can get pregnant without Marianne, but you can't do a commitment ceremony without her. Anyway, those rituals are just mock heterosexuality. Who needs it?"

Ruth interceded, "What does Marianne say?"

Lindsey smiled reluctantly. "She says, 'Girl, I've been married once, that's how I got those five great kids in the Bay Area. That's also how I got a yearlong headache in the divorce court. You think I'm fool enough to marry again?"

They all laughed, Lindsey the loudest.

A sudden flurry of arrivals. Eight of Michael's friends from San Francisco. Some folks Emily didn't recognize—Monica's relatives? Pals?

Then Eva, in a long, flowery blue Mexican dress, accompanied by Jorge and Stefan, the "blossom boys" in violet and blue tuxedoes. Eva was stunning, Emily thought. She moved—floated—as if the dress were made for her. Long curls framed her glowing face.

Michael and Monica, who drove in together, were perhaps the most simply dressed. Monica wore a long green linen shift. Michael, in slacks, a grey sports jacket, white shirt and blue tie, looked even taller and more handsome than usual.

They had practiced the choreography for days; still, Emily felt nervous. First she would escort Michael to the altar. Then Virginia would escort Monica. The blossom boys would follow the bride, scattering rose petals. Monica's rinpoche, who had traveled from Oakland to perform the informal Buddhist wedding, looked prepared and serene. Everything would be fine. So why was Emily collapsed in the last row of folding chairs, chewing her fingernails?

Eva lit down beside her. "Hey, what are you doing after the wedding?"

"Falling into bed!" groaned Emily.

"No, no, very unhealthy. You need to decompress, relax. I made a big *cazuela* last night and gave half to Jorge and Stefan to eat at your place. By the way, they were so touched by your hospitality. But back to supper—come over for a bite and we can talk about the wedding. We'll unwind together."

"Thanks," Emily persisted. "But I'm going to be exhausted. And how could I eat dinner after that feast on the table?"

"That's just lunch. Then there'll be dancing. Then cleanup. Believe me, you'll want to decompress. I remember my brother Luis's wedding. It's important to have a long talk after something like this."

The first chords of processional music. Emily pulled herself together and went off in search of her big brother's arm.

The opening Bach, played by a harpist friend of Monica's, was lovely.

She felt Michael trembling as they walked toward the rinpoche. Soon Monica arrived. Briefly the couple held hands.

The rinpoche greeted them with a bow, his reddish brown robes glowing in the sun.

They bowed in return.

"Welcome, friends," he spoke with a slight accent, "to this joyful day."

Emily, weeping softly, was missing the ceremony.

Suddenly Michael and Monica were exchanging rings, speaking their homemade vows.

Emily noticed that all the land women, seated to her left, were crying into tissues.

The kiss was so chaste she almost failed to register it.

Then the rinpoche gave a final blessing.

The exit music was a recording of "Mendoline," Michael's choice, and Emily couldn't hold back heavy sobs as the couple walked back down the grass aisle together.

Ruth guided Emily to the drinks table for the champagne that Lindsey had bargained from a colleague. Then to the lasagnas and burritos and raviolis and enchiladas and salads and Virginia's delicious *perfect* cake.

Nibbling on her second slice, Emily marveled how beautifully simple the wedding had been. She wondered what had happened to her brother, the real estate wheeler-dealer with the Venetian glass collection and the Subzero fridge in his model San Francisco condo. But where was the slick wedding photographer? the videographer? the caviar? the canapés? She'd been sure Michael would insist on a caterer, but he gave in readily to Monica's vision of an organized potluck. Could happiness transform a person so? She wondered if she'd ever find happiness again, then told herself to concentrate on the party. This was Michael's day. A long time coming. This was Michael and Monica's celebration, and for them she would throw herself into the festivities.

Soon she was dancing with Jorge, who thanked her for the "honeymoon loft" on her ridge. He promised to take good care of Phoenix while Emily was at Michael's. She looked over Jorge's shoulder to see Michael grinning at his silver-haired bride.

Then Emily was dancing with Virginia and the harpist. Gabrielle, that was the harpist's name, too perfect, but Mendocino was like that.

From the refreshment table, she could hear Lindsey engaging good-natured barbs with Marianne about commitments and ceremonies.

Eva appeared among the dancers to fill champagne glasses. She set down the empty bottle and joined the circle, dancing with Emily and Virginia and Gabrielle.

Emily felt full, happy for Michael and Monica, charmed by Stefan and Jorge, amused by Marianne and Lindsey. And she was beginning to understand about decompressing.

She turned to Eva. "Is it too late to accept your invitation?" she asked quietly.

VI

29

Emily followed Eva's pickup in the softening afternoon light. Late Sunday traffic was always bad. "Pumpkin time," Virginia called it, when tourists queued caravan style, heading home to the Bay Area. Luckily Michael and Monica had gone in the opposite direction—up to a small cabin on the coast. They'd be there now, watching the waves, enjoying quiet after their happy, busy day. Both had relished the frenzy—conga line, limbo dancing, and the pink and purple sequins Jorge and Stefan tossed into the rice shower. They'd laughed as merrily as anyone when Monica threw her bouquet to Joyce, and Marianne, stepping aside to clear the flight path, wound up holding the white and yellow roses. Lindsey had stood back beaming. Yes, Emily hoped Michael and Monica would hang on to their happiness for a very long time. Dear Michael had waited too many years in his bluff solitude. This marriage, this new life, certainly made it easier for her to return to Chicago.

Pickers were still laboring in the fields. She shivered, thinking about those night lights Ruth had described. Surely they worked in shifts—if only for efficiency's sake? A body wore out after so many hours. She was exhausted after attending a wedding! What did they think when they looked up from the vines and watched the parade of Hondas and BMWs and SUVs? Did they resent the visitors giddily sipping the product of their labors? Were they indifferent? Did they aspire to be in the parade? How much time or inclination did they have to look up at all? Emily frowned at her stunningly inadequate understanding. After a year in paradise, she didn't even know the name of the vineyard where Rafael worked.

She caught Eva's blinker and followed her up the dirt and gravel of Mineshaft Road, where she was surprised to see Jaime Rivera had completely finished his house. Eva said all the neighbors had pitched in.

Several kids played on nearby porches, babysitting younger ones while their parents worked the harvest.

The children waved shyly as Emily entered Eva's bungalow. The front room looked completely different than it had when it was occupied by the Rivera kids' Lego pieces and crayon drawings. Yet the place felt full of life. A multicolored rug was thrown carefully over the red tiled floor. A vase of yellow astrumeria adorned the center table. Books were piled next to a lumpy armchair. Eva switched on a CD of gentle Celtic music.

What a mistake! Instantly overwhelmed by embarrassment, Emily knew she should have gone straight to Michael's couch with a good novel.

"So how does it feel to reclaim your space?" Emily hated this dippy California idiom.

Eva stretched her arms wide. "Good! After months of Jorge and the little Riveras. I mean, it was fun hosting everyone, reminded me of home in L.A. Yeah, I appreciate the restored tranquility, but it's also a little strange."

Emily watched Eva fiddling with the silver bangle on her arm.

"Nice to have you here," Eva steadied her voice. "First time you've come to supper."

Eva's nervousness calmed Emily, who laughed. "First time I've been invited."

"But not the last," she said, handing Emily a glass of wine.

"Don't know if I should. It's a long drive back to Michael's."

"Ah, you'll have a filling, delicious dinner first." She clinked Emily's glass. "Salud."

Eva's small kitchen was carefully organized. She slipped the cazuela from the fridge, where it had been stored next to a bowl of colorful salad. The table was set.

"I guess you were expecting someone to dinner," Emily teased.

"Not necessarily expecting," Eva pursed her lips thoughtfully. "Hoping, maybe."

Emily sensed heat rising along her spine.

"Come," Eva took her hand. "The cazuela heats for 30 minutes. Come sit in the garden."

She gave Emily a tour of the double-dug beds, bursting with purple eggplant and green zucchini and tall corn stalks; the stand of fruit trees; the circle of flowers. They sat on the back deck watching the day drift toward evening.

"I had no idea," Emily blurted, "your garden would be so elaborate. What a green thumb!"

"Well, I *am* a forest ranger. In school, we studied all kinds of vegetation." Eva laughed. "Besides, nature does most of the gardening. It's a very sunny spot."

Emily blushed, flummoxed again by her own bumbling.

"Do you garden?" Eva inquired.

"We're not here long enough to enjoy a garden. Salerno and I come out for just a few weeks each summer." She stopped, unnerved by her slip.

Eva's eyes clouded. Then she asked delicately, "But this year?"

"Oh, I planted a few vegetables." Emily stared into the middle distance, wondering how she could gracefully skip dinner and escape to Michael's. She thought back to the months and years after her mother's death and how her only course of survival was to burrow—with memories of Mom—far away from well-meaning people who urged her back to a normal teenaged life. "This wasn't a time for big gardens," she said finally.

"Of course not," Eva agreed. "I'm sorry."

"Don't be," Emily smiled thinly. "Perhaps it would've been better if I had planted more. I used to grow arugula in Berkeley and it shot up in no time."

Eva studied her. "So much has changed for you this year."

"Yes, losing Salerno, that was the most momentous." She paused, surprised by her pouring forth. "But there have been other changes. Regaining Michael in my life."

Eva waited.

"And coming to know the Beulah women, to be a real neighbor and friend. Watching Joyce grow. Hell, being here when Malcolm burst into the world!"

"Then there's all you've done for the community."

Emily frowned.

"Truly. Nursing Ruth. Taking care of Joyce."

"I was simply a chauffeur."

"No, listen. Joyce told me about the movies, the trips out to the coast."

"Well . . ."

"And beyond that, your excellent work with Rafael. If this harvest ever gets in, I think he'll graduate in spring. Then the party for Salerno's music. Allowing it out in the world. You know, some lovers would have kept those recordings for themselves."

Emily reflected on how close she'd come to doing that. She was touched by the detail of Eva's observations.

"And giving the proceeds to the Guardians. That was more than a gesture. It's going to make a practical difference. *And* the rattle. I was so happy with your choice. Admiring the thoughtful way you decided. It was the best outcome, I think, but not a knee-jerk decision. You thought a lot about it until you knew what was right."

Emily shifted uncomfortably on the deck chair.

Eva laughed, "I've been talking too much."

Suddenly—"Oh, oh!" Eva ran into the kitchen.

Relieved to be alone, Emily took a long drink of cool early evening air.

"Delicious!" she pronounced.

"A simple dish," demurred Eva.

Dinner conversation was lighter. Laughter at the campy but loving way Jorge and Stefan participated in the ceremony. At the playful haggling between Marianne and Lindsey. At Virginia's fraught protection of her cake and then at her delight once people had tasted it. They had each been moved by the short, tender ceremony.

"That was one cool rinpoche," grinned Eva. "I mean, a lot of those guys are pretty pious. Too transcendent for words."

"Yeah, he had a grand old time. I couldn't believe it when he joined the conga line in his long robes." Emily shook her head. "Everyone seemed to enjoy the party."

"Almost everyone."

"Yes, Virginia looked mournful at moments. And it wasn't just cake anxiety. I could tell she was thinking of Sally."

Eva leaned in. "What's the latest news? Did she go back to her mother's place?"

"No one knows," Emily sighed. "I hope so. I hope Sally's somewhere safe."

"Somewhere safe," Eva murmured.

Emily shrugged. "Yeah, where on earth is that place called somewhere safe?"

"How about my back deck with a cup of special Mexican coffee?" She glanced out, "The sky's still pink from sunset."

"Sounds good," Emily said. "I'll meet you out there. May I use your bathroom?"

Eva whistled as she cleared the table.

Emily found the small, lightly scented—freesia—bathroom at the front of the house. Eva had decorated the shower wall with shells collected along the coast and Emily now remembered Ruth told her Eva had crocheted the fishnet curtains herself. She washed her hands, splashed water on her face, then stood looking in the mirror. A tall, lean, fiftyish woman with curly blond hair. She would remember this person. She'd wanted one last glance before . . . before whatever was going to happen next.

Emily joined Eva. Sun floated above the horizon. Thin clouds webbed the sky. The air was still warmish, dry. A perfect October evening.

"What a day . . ."

"I bet after your long . . ."

They spoke simultaneously, laughed, then glanced at the reddening sky.

"Sailor's delight," Emily said absently, trying to get comfortable on the padded wicker couch next to Eva. Before them, on a small, blue-tiled table, were a white coffee pot, blue cups, and a pastry.

"Mande?" Eva asked.

"It's something my father used to say, watching a beautiful sunset from his boat." What would Peter Adams, yachtsman, say about his daughter dining with the daughter of a school custodian? What would he think of Michael marrying in his mid-fifties? During graduate school, when she had come out to her father, he'd simply shaken his curly head, saying, "And it's been Michael I've worried about all this time. But he seems normal. Don't you think so?" Mom had been dead a dozen years at that point. Father always looked through Emily, past Emily, to the serious matters of life.

"Qué onda?"

Emily paused and frowned. "Not much on my mind. Except qué comida tan deliciosa!"

Eva beamed. "Now a little Mexican coffee with Mama's special apple postre."

"Coffee sounds great, but I couldn't fit another morsel into my bulging stomach."

Eva rolled her eyes. "You bulging? I could only wish to be half as trim as you."

"You're perfect," Emily began before she recognized what she was saying. Then something released inside her. "As lovely as this sunset."

Eva blinked, poured the steaming chocolatey coffee into Emily's cup.

Emily savored the tart, sweet apples in the pastry. "Scrumptious!"

"The taste comes from above. From this tree beside us. A surprise hybrid."

The entire world was light, fragile. Emily felt the muscles around her mouth lifting and her eyes widening.

Glancing shyly at her garden, Eva fingered the tissuey fabric of her long dress.

Emily watched the small, compact brown hand until she could no longer sit still. Slowly, quickly, with a speed that defied time and space and history, she reached over and took that hand in hers.

Eva studied Emily's face as if she'd never seen her before, as if she'd always known her. With languorous deliberation, she stretched forward, her face closer, until the two of them were kissing.

Emily inched over to put her long arms around Eva's neat shoulders.

Eva caressed Emily's neck.

Emily felt her softness and warmth and desire.

They held on tightly, a lifeboat on a stormy March night, kissing and rocking for minutes. Or hours?

Until Eva said, "Look. Look!"

The moon rose from behind a ridge of oaks. The red clouds had faded to silken threads.

Emily smelled the coffee at the bottom of her cup, the sweet sweat along Eva's hairline, the Valley earth already damp from night all around them.

30

The phone woke them, just before dawn. They'd both been sleeping soundly, Emily wrapped around Eva.

Confused by the noise, Eva surfaced. She let a long sigh swim through her body and kissed Emily lightly on the lips.

Emily held her more tightly, willing the ringing to stop.

With gentle care, Eva disentangled her legs and arms and attention. Still, she was groggy and made several attempts before locating the receiver.

As Emily's eyes adjusted to the light, her mind welcomed the memory of last night—the sweetness of holding Eva's naked body against hers, the tentative, almost courteous caressing and stroking. Although Eva's back was turned now, Emily could see the small, round breasts, perfectly formed, "like apples on your tree," she'd teased. She could taste the reddish brown nipples still. And she recalled Eva's daring tongue, exploring the length of her torso until yes, yes, she was delicately biting her mons, teasing her clitoris and flashing a tongue and entering her deeply, oh, so deeply with thumb and forefinger.

Then the joy of feeling Eva's own pleasure, her moans and sighs and finally the thrilling temblor that moved her whole body and Emily's. Now Emily closed her eyes and inhaled the mingling of their scents, recalling the easy rhythm of Eva's breathing as she fell, first, off to sleep.

The damn phone was still ringing, loudly enough (maybe she was finally awake) to make her wonder what on earth she had done. Betrayed Salerno? She closed her eyes, holding herself very still. No, no betrayal: she suspected the girl was smiling down on them, maybe with a little smirk. Emily had been the jealous one, the frightened one, always wary that Salerno would find somebody livelier, more suitable to her own wild spirit.

What was it, then? Taking advantage of Eva? No, the woman knew, everyone knew, she was leaving for Chicago next week. The fear had nothing to do with betraying or hurting anyone else. It was about herself, about opening up again, about her body hungering, her heart wanting. Just as she was bolting the door for safe hibernation.

"Ruth, Ruth!" Eva spoke sharply. "Calm down, I can, I can hardly hear, can hardly make out what, oh, no, are you okay?"

Emily sat up, leaning close to the receiver to catch Ruth's words.

A fire at the ranch. Emily's stomach turned. She'd been waiting for this; they all had.

Everyone safe. So far.

"So far. What does that mean?" she demanded of Eva.

Eva spoke to Ruth. "Emily and I will be right there. Right there."

She gave Emily a big sweater and some oversized pants that ended at her calves.

As she pulled on her own clothes, Eva spoke cautiously, holding back something. "Ruth and Joyce, Lindsey, the baby, Marianne, Virginia—they're all fine. The fire trucks have arrived. The plane is spraying retardant." She forced calm into the story.

"But Jorge and Stefan?" Emily demanded. "They're okay, right?"

"They haven't been able to reach them on the phone and the trucks haven't made it up to the ridge."

"Damn," cried Emily. Then she caught sight of Eva's drawn face, terrified eyes. "I'm sure they're fine. They're young. Fast on their feet. Probably they got out the back way, climbing up through the apple orchard."

"Let's get in the truck," Eva said solemnly.

In silence they drove through the yawning gate, navigated hills, turned down by the corral and saw the first of the fire vehicles. A red Valley Fire Department truck, then a green one from the California Department of Forestry. Then another battered truck, maybe from Mistral or Comptche. All around the cabins, firefighters in brilliant yellow padded astronaut suits were spraying foam and water, quelling the last licks of flame. Two women and a man were hacking at a tree stump to extinguish lurking embers.

At first Emily was so relieved by the sight of her friends that she didn't hear the helicopter or the airplane. She ran about, throwing her arms around Ruth and Joyce and Virginia and Lindsey and little Malcolm. Marianne was working the hydrant, pumping water from the pond. Ruth headed off to help her.

The fire down here was contained. They'd lost a few trees, but the houses, discolored by blotches of fire retardant, were intact. The real conflagration, it soon became clear, was up on the hill.

Emily lifted her eyes toward the ridge. Flames shot up from tall, high grass as morning ripened into a golden pink in the smoky air. The plane circled in and out, dumping fire retardant.

On the houses down here, the curious orange chemical splotches added to the picture of a burning feast.

In between plane orbits, the helicopter buzzed through and sprayed the area. ("The area," reflected Emily. Jorge and Stefan and Phoenix, the cabin, Salerno's tree, what was left in "the area"?)

She looked around for Eva and caught her just as she was climbing into her truck.

"No, no," she yelled. "Stay here. Don't be crazy. You don't know where the fire has jumped the road."

"What I know is that my brother is up there!"

"Probably not. Probably long gone over the back hills. Through that orchard. Stefan used to teach orienting in Boy Scouts, until he got kicked out for being a fag. Remember? He'd get them out easily. Meanwhile, there's nothing you can do about it." She put her arms around Eva, who stiffened into cold silence.

Ruth came running over. "For God's sake, Eva, all we need is another casualty; don't even think about getting in that truck!"

"*Another* casualty?" Eva wrestled against Emily's strong grip. "What do you know? What's happened to Jorge and Stefan?"

"Nothing," Ruth shouted, then lowered her voice. "I just mean, don't be foolish. You can't do anything that they"—she pointed to the plane and the helicopter—"aren't doing more effectively. If the fire trucks can't make it up the hill, you sure as hell can't, either."

Eva was still pulling away from Emily.

Without a second thought, Emily reached into the truck, grabbed keys from the ignition, and lobbed them into the middle of the pond.

"Puta mierda!" Eva beat on Emily's shoulders. Slowly, Emily drew her closer. The pounding ceased. They rocked together now as Eva wept.

Sun was rising high by the windmill and the air felt moist. As the firefighters hacked and sprayed, the women gathered on Ruth's deck, where she had set out mugs and a thermos. Sipping the hot coffee, they numbly watched the yellow-suited astronauts secure their houses.

Emily's strange wardrobe received several pointed glances from her friends. No one asked.

The women whispered about the fire.

They looked up the hill.

They waited.

31

Joyce was the first to spot the bedraggled figure limping down the dirt road. "Stefan! Stefan!" the girl shouted jubilantly.

An exhausted young man waved, smiled faintly. He was followed by Phoenix, who raced into Emily's arms.

The women coursed toward Stefan in a wave.

Lindsey handed him a bottle of water. He couldn't drink for coughing.

Emily noticed how grey his skin and clothes were. She told him to rest, go sit on the deck, until he caught his breath.

He remained standing, tentatively letting in fresh air until he could say, "Jorge."

"Jorge!" Eva yelled, breaking her paralyzed silence. "Is Jorge all right?"

"Fine," he managed, and feeling better, he sipped Lindsey's water. "Just fine."

"Dios gracias!" Eva declared. "So where is he? Where is my baby brother?"

Stefan began to laugh.

Emily took Eva's hand.

Virginia looked worried, whispering to Lindsey, "Hysterical. Shock. It's finally hit him."

"No, no," Stefan insisted. "I'm cool. So is Jorge. But Hayden, he's not in such great shape."

"Hayden?" Eva and Ruth asked in unison.

"Yeah, Jorge tied the water hose around him. And man, pulling that dude was tough because he was way determined to ascend to heaven in his cleansing flames."

"What? You're going a little fast, here, Stefan," cautioned Virginia. "How about some more water?"

"No, no, I'm okay," he coughed. "This is truth-is-weirder-than-fiction time."

Virginia sniffed. "That's usually the case with Hayden."

"Shhh," Lindsey leaned forward. "I need to hear this."

Eva broke in desperately, "Jorge, where is Jorge?"

They'd all reached the deck and Stefan, relenting to sudden exhaustion, sank into a chair. "I'm coming to Jorge."

Emily whispered to Eva. "He said Jorge's fine. He has to tell the story his way."

"Phoenix was barking," Stefan sat up with new energy and poured himself a coffee. "We woke up to smoke and ran downstairs. There was Hayden, his back against a wall that was just about to explode into flame. Jorge hauled him to safety while I tried to douse the fire. I tried, hard, but it was no use." He apologized to Emily. "It was pretty bad."

Emily nodded, not ready to absorb anything except the miraculous survival of her friends. Phoenix lay exhausted at her feet.

"Hayden kept trying to dive back into that fire, into his 'cleansing flames.' He's strong for an old dude, but we held him secure. I knew this route up the back hills, over the orchard. Hayden wouldn't come. So that's when Jorge tied him up with the only thing we could find, the skinny green garden hose, and together we pulled him along with us, over the hills, and finally down to the highway."

"What did he mean by 'cleansing flames'?" asked Ruth.

"No, no, no!" Eva demanded. "Tell me first, where is he, my brother?"

"Yes, yes, of course," Stefan reached for her free hand. "Well, when we got to the highway, it was dark, obviously. A few cars passed and finally we were able to flag one down. I mean, we must have looked like zombies—one smoky disheveled guy on either side of Hayden, tied up with a green garden hose." He sipped coffee and looked up tentatively, toward the hazy ridge.

Stefan turned back to them. "Anyway, this Samaritan guy stops in a big old green Buick. Says he'll drive Jorge and Hayden to the police station."

"The 'cleansing fire'?" Ruth tried again.

Morning sky slowly turned a patchy blue as smoke dissipated. Emily was waking from a nightmare.

"Well, Hayden just started to talk and talk, once it was clear we were on our way out, alive. We couldn't tell if he was praying or preaching.

Jorge told him to shut up. Myself, I thought it was fascinating. But Jorge just kept asking what the hell he'd been doing."

Emily felt a chill run through her body.

"Crazy man said he'd set the fire because he'd discovered the evil force that was wrestling Eva from his light into a world of darkness and sin."

Eva moved next to Emily.

"Said he was determined to send that force to the fires of hell."

Emily looked at the women, then back to Stefan.

"Beulah Ranch is an evil force?" asked Joyce.

Ruth held her close. "He's a sick man, Joycie, we'll talk about this later."

Lindsey and Marianne had tears in their eyes.

Stefan coughed and took another swig of coffee. "Don't know what he thought when he first saw us: two naked men flapping away at the fire. Maybe he imagined we were the archangels Gabriel and Michael and he'd already ascended to his just reward."

Virginia laughed nervously.

Eva gripped Emily's hand.

"He sure didn't give up fighting until we strapped him in the car. I used the driver's cell phone to call the Fire Department, who said the fire had already been reported by Ruth, so then we figured everyone was safe. He dropped me off so I could check on you all."

"That Jorge!" Eva was crying and laughing. "Why didn't he use Emily's phone to call his big sister and tell her he was okay?"

Stefan held up his palms. "Man, I told him there was no time for anything but grabbing some clothes and getting outta there."

Stefan observed them holding hands and smiled.

"Thank you! Thank god everyone is safe!" proclaimed Lindsey, breaking into sobs. Malcolm began to wail, too. Marianne took the two of them in her arms, shaking her head at the murky sky.

Emily turned to Stefan, calm, steady. "Tell me about the cabin. Is it completely gone?" She waited a moment. "And the tree, the Douglas fir?"

Epilogue

Ruth and Joyce had decorated the table with cedar boughs they had collected after the last storm. Candles shone brilliantly in the center. Food was abundant and the company in good cheer as people caught up on each other's news. So much had happened in the last few months: Marianne's first conference paper, Michael and Monica's delayed honeymoon, Hayden's trial.

Joyce and her new boyfriend Dominic mooned over one another as Ruth answered Michael's questions about the exhibit she had just dismantled.

"Fine, it went fine, thanks," she said shyly, standing to fetch fresh bread for the table.

"You're so modest, Ruthie!" Lindsey admonished. She turned to Michael. "What she's not saying is that her photos got the best reviews in both papers."

"What really matters in a joint exhibit," Ruth shrugged, embarrassed, pleased, "is that the whole event was a success."

"And," Lindsey added in exasperation with her friend, "They've invited her to mount a show next summer."

Malcolm began to cry from his stroller until Lindsey picked him up.

"Not bad. The sitting up, the mobility," Marianne nodded proudly.

"Main thing is," Ruth said, "he's such a happy child."

"Might be happier, though," Lindsey added, "more secure, if his mothers had a commitment ceremony."

"*Who* would be happier if that occurred?" asked Eva.

"Well, now that the meal is over," Marianne said, "I do want to go back to the Hayden stuff. Damn that conference for overlapping with the trial. I'm not sure I got all the details straight."

"Yeah, me neither," said Michael. "It all happened so quickly, during the tiny leave they gave Monica from school."

"I guess the trial was fast," said Virginia. "But he was arrested months ago."

"Maybe after dessert?" suggested Ruth, who had censored the subject earlier in the evening as not conducive to digestion and celebration.

"No, no," Virginia laughed. "We all waited until after supper, Ruthie."

Ruth checked the pies warming in her oven.

Marianne continued, "So he admitted to all the fires? *All* the arson in the Valley this year?"

"Yup," Virginia nodded.

"The fire that Jorge started," Eva grinned at her brother, who winked back.

"The fire that Josh Nyland started," Joyce joined in.

"The fires that the pickers started," Emily declared.

"Why? Why all those places?" Michael was bewildered.

"I don't think," Virginia sighed, "that pyromaniacs need whys."

"But Hayden had them!" explained Lindsey. "He was cleansing the Valley, banishing dope and wine and migrants and . . ."

"I still think the loggers are implicated in that one on Eucalyptus Road."

"Oh, Ginny!" Eva groaned. "It makes sense about Hayden. He would know about setting a blaze and getting out of there on time."

"Remember, Eva said a long time ago that people in the fire department had found evidence of similar techniques after the fires," Emily added. "Apparently the chief always thought it was some kind of inside job."

"Did you really suspect Hayden?" Lindsey rocked Malcolm on her lap.

"I did my best to think as little as possible about Hayden," Eva declared, stretching her arms wide. "Irresponsible, I guess, but I just wanted it all to go away."

"So, Virginia," Michael smirked, "It must be pleasantly quiet around school these days without Hayden's protests."

"I wish. It's almost worse, except that I don't have to look into his ugly face. Really, he always gave me the creeps. His followers still picket. If anything, martyrdom has galvanized the Crusade for California."

Jorge cleared his throat theatrically. "You skipped the most dramatic moments of the trial—the appearances of the star witnesses."

"Yes," Ruth turned to Michael and Monica and Marianne, "Jorge and Stefan performed admirably."

"Once we toned down their costumes," Virginia grinned.

"Still a mistake, I think," said Stefan. "We thought archangel. We thought cape."

Michael's jaw dropped.

Jorge patted his hand reassuringly. "Tasteful capes, in darkish colors."

The whole room broke into laughter.

"Suits," Stefan raised an eyebrow in mock horror, "they made us wear suits."

"How totalitarian," Marianne beamed, then steered the conversation back. "So what's happened with Mr. Martyr?"

"Temporarily in a prison for the criminally insane," Emily explained.

"Temporarily!" declared Marianne.

"It'll be a long temporary," said Eva. "If he gets out, they send him to a regular prison."

"Apparently they're preparing an indictment against him in Yolo County, too," Virginia said.

"Speaking of preparing," Ruth said, "tell them how your construction is going, Em."

"Yes!" agreed Monica. "I still think you're amazing to have the courage and stamina to start rebuilding this soon."

Emily recalled her first sight of the cabin after the fire. The wet, dark carcass of a house. The toppled filing cabinet. The rugs and photos and remnants of furniture washed in water and fire retardant and smoke and flame. Salerno's plane crashing into the sea, into the cabin.

"Emily! Come in, Emily." Michael served his sister a slice of Virginia's open-faced apple pie.

"The construction, yes," she mumbled, then forced herself to speak up. "It's going slowly since you left. We have to work around the rains. But everyone is helping. Jorge and Stefan have come up from San Francisco to hammer nails in the wrong places," she teased. "And I'm grateful to be able to stay at Eva's while the cabin is slowly materializing."

She thought about the morning she woke up next to Eva and knew she would rebuild. Knew she would stay in the Valley and do consulting work. As for their relationship, both she and Eva agreed it was too early for a commitment. If not too early for love.

Michael had grown used to his sister's distractibility. She'd gone in and out like this since the fire. So he turned to Eva. "How's work without Hayden? Does the Park Service miss Mr. Martyr, too?"

"Not a chance," she grinned. "Life is easier for me without him, of course. Harder, too, since I had to pick up his duties, work he ignored for the last three years while he's been praying for the Valley to burn up."

Ruth set down pots of strong coffee and a pot of mint tea.

Finishing dessert, Michael asked, "Say, Em, what about us all having a look at the progress you've made on the cabin?"

Two cars followed Emily's up the puddled dirt road to the ridge. She got out and took a long breath of the cool evening air. Two and a half months of clearing away the carnage, making a new floor, raising the wall beams, nailing the exterior walls, sheetrocking the inside. Two and a half months of help from the Beulah women and Michael and Monica and Jorge and Stefan and, much to her surprise, from Judson and Baxter and Rafael and several neighbors she'd never met before. People had pitched in during the evenings, for a weekend, whenever they could.

"God, Em," Michael followed her into the house with a flashlight, "it's almost finished. You've done so much since we went to Hawaii."

"Just a shell now," she murmured. "But it will keep out the winter rains. I still have all the mudding and taping to do, the internal moldings, and I think I'm going to tile that floor."

Jorge and Stefan were giving Monica and Marianne a tour of their handiwork. The others stood back chatting, making baby faces at Malcolm, playing with Phoenix.

Emily stared at the stump of that stately Douglas fir. All gone now, its ashes mixed with Salerno's. She felt grateful she'd found the rattle in time. In time. She cuddled closer to Michael, extending her hand around his back.

The dog barked. People kept on talking.

Emily lifted her head to an outside noise.

She couldn't make out whether the sound was some kind of siren or a high winter wind.

Acknowledgments

The author is grateful for recent residencies at the MacDowell Colony, the Virginia Center for the Creative Arts, and Yaddo, where I was given space and time in which to work on various stages of *After Eden*. I also acknowledge financial support from the McKnight Foundation and the University of Minnesota.

I am very thankful for the help and advice of many librarians, archivists, local historians, and other people in Mendocino County, where parts of *After Eden* are set. Although Fairburn, other towns, the rancheria, and the Valley are imaginary places, much of the book is informed by my own experiences living part time in Mendocino for over fifteen years.

I want to acknowledge the invaluable assistance of writers and other colleagues who read *After Eden* in one of its many drafts. These people include Maureen Brady, Zoë Fairbairns, Vicki Graham, Elizabeth Horan, Helen E. Longino, Teresa Jordan, Susan Magery, Sue Sheridan, and Janet Spector.

The work would not have been completed without the excellent research assistance of Julie Gard, Elizabeth Noll, Lori Hokyo Misaka, Andria Williams, and Jennine Crucet.

Special thanks go to my fine editor, Matthew Bokovoy, and the rest of the staff at the University of Oklahoma Press. I am indebted to William Kittredge for bringing *After Eden* to the attention of the press.

Finally, let me acknowledge some of the authors who helped me understand the characters, communities, and landscapes of *After Eden*. These include:

Alt, David D., and Donald W. Hyndman. *Roadside Geology of California*. Missoula, Mont.: Mountain Press, 1975.

Baker, Elna. *An Island Called California: An Ecological Introduction to Its*

Natural Communities. Berkeley and Los Angeles: University of California Press, 1971.

Barker, Arthur. *Milton and the Puritan Dilemma.* Toronto: University of Toronto Press, 1942.

Bear, Dorothy, and David Houghton. *The Chinese of the Mendocino Coast.* Mendocino, Calif.: Mendocino Historical Research, 1990.

Cook, Sherburne F. *The Conflict between the California Indian and White Civilization.* Berkeley and Los Angeles: University of California Press, 1976.

Cox, Thomas R. *Mills and Markets: A History of the Pacific Coast Lumber Industry to 1900.* Seattle: University of Washington Press, 1974.

Frazer, James George. *Myths of the Origin of Fire.* New York: Hacker, 1974.

Goudsblom, Johan. *Fire and Civilization.* London: Allen Lane, Penguin Press, 1992.

Halpern, Abraham M. *Southeastern Pomo Ceremonials.* Berkeley and Los Angeles: University of California Press, 1988.

Hazen, Margaret H., and Robert M. Hazen. *Keepers of the Flame.* Princeton: Princeton University Press, 1992.

Heizer, Robert F, ed. *Handbook of North American Indians.* Vol. 8, *California.* Washington, D.C.: Smithsonian Institution, 1978.

Hughes, Merritt Y., ed. *John Milton: Complete Poems and Major Prose.* New York: Odyssey Press, 1957.

Kniffen, Fred B. *Pomo Geography.* Berkeley: University of California Press, 1939.

Kroeber, A. L. *Handbook of the Indians of California.* New York: Dover, 1976.

Landsman, David, ed. *Mendocino County Historic Annals,* vol. 1. Mendocino, Calif.: Pacific Rim Research, 1977.

Levene, Bruce, ed. *Mendocino County Remembered: An Oral History,* Mendocino, Calif.: Mendocino County Historical Association, 1976.

McPhee, John. *Assembling California.* New York: Farrar, Straus Giroux, 1993.

Powers, Stephen. *Tribes of California.* Berkeley and Los Angeles: University of California Press, 1976.

Pyne, Stephen J. *World Fire.* New York: Holt, 1995.

Raphael, Ray. *An Everyday History of Somewhere.* Covelo, Calif.: Island Press, 1974.

Rosotti, Hazel. *Fire.* Oxford: Oxford University Press, 1993.

Sarris, Greg. *Mabel McKay: Weaving the Dream.* Berkeley and Los Angeles: University of California Press, 1994.

Scofield, C. I., ed. *The New Scofield Reference Bible.* New York: Oxford University Press, 1967.

Starr, Kevin. *Americans and the California Dream, 1850–1915.* New York: Oxford University Press, 1973.

Sullenberger, Martha. *Dogholes and Donkey Engines.* Sacramento, Calif.: California Department of Parks and Recreation Press, 1992.

Tucker, Wilma, and Don Tucker. *Mendocino—From the Beginning.* Mendocino, Calif.: Historical Research, 1992.

Weatherford, Jack. *How the Indians Enriched America.* New York: Fawcett Columbine, 1991.